LOVER

LOVER

COURT UNIVERSITY: BOOK FOUR

EDEN O'NEILL

BOOKS BY EDEN O'NEILL

Court High

They The Pretty Stars

Illusions That May

Court Kept

We The Pretty Stars

Court University

Brutal Heir

Kingpin

Beautiful Brute

Lover

Court Legacy

Dirty Wicked Prince

Savage Little Lies

Tiny Dark Deeds

Eat You Alive (forthcoming)

CHAPTER ONE

Ramses

I suppose it'd been around the last two or three top one hundred songs when it all finally hit.

This was almost over.

Like everything, every little moment was done. No more circulating every bridal shop known to man. No more late-night runs to craft stores looking at tulle and other kinds of stuff far beyond the male psyche to even be able to comprehend or understand. No more 3 a.m. phone calls to see how she'd been. To determine if she was stressed or had everything she needed. The bride wasn't stressed anymore. She had it all.

And I finally had to let her go.

I'd stayed away most of the night, keeping to myself. I told myself it was to make sure everything flowed well. I was the go-to guy, the one people came to if the happy couple needed absolutely anything. I was basically the best man without technically being the best man. The actual best *men* I hadn't seen half the night either, but that was because they were either helping themselves to the bride and groom's booze or their own girlfriends. I mean, that's what they should be doing. That's what *normal* people should do. All the planning and shit was over. It was time to have fun now.

My fingers played against glass, the condensation on my beer bottle long gone. Who knew how long I'd been holding it. Even still, I sucked it back, hot yeast traveling down my throat in a lump. I'd managed to make this beer last the whole night, some kind of weird record, I was sure.

Swirling it around, I watched the final dances on the floor, the crowd long thinned out. People started dipping out after the cake cutting and opening dances. Now, it was just the ride-or-dies out there, the bridal party and a few other younger girls and guys like me. I watched friends both old and new have a good time under glistening lights, the winter theme of the event in full swing. It actually appeared to be snowing in the reception hall at one point, mostly a strobe light effect I'd been told.

I just knew it suited the new couple perfectly, hard not to get lost in all the magic and wonder of this place. Windsor House, the wedding and reception's location, had some history, but tonight, it wasn't about any of that or the trials and tribulations of the past. It was about everything but that.

"Can I have this last dance?"

It was about dark hair and brown eyes that twinkled under those snowy lights. It was about *her*, the blushing bride.

Who also just so happened to be my best friend.

Leave it to the woman of the night to find *me* of all people for her final dance. I'd been trying to do everything but stand out.

Grinning, December waved her hands at me, the epitome of the most gorgeous bride in the world. She'd changed into a shimmering gown, making her look like a mermaid the way the precious silk glided along her frame. Elegant as hell, she attempted to convince my loner ass into a dance like she *knew* I'd been trying to lay low all night. Light touched her dark eyes. "Come on. We don't have long."

We didn't have long. Really, this was it.

I think that'd been the only reason I put my beer down, shaking my head before taking *her* hand. I was the damn guy and wouldn't let her have this one.

A spin and I had her out on the dance floor, taking her close but only just. I was well-aware her new husband was around here somewhere, and I wasn't trying to get my ass kicked. Prinze could be a territorial motherfucker, and where I might normally poke at that, I didn't tonight.

Tonight, a lot of things were different.

Tonight, I made myself be at peace with events from the past. That *this* was what December and I were now. We'd been friends for a long time, since high school, but with states between us and our lives on different trajectories, it'd been really easy to pass off old ways. At least, for me. It'd been easy to say this girl was *just* my friend. I hadn't had to see her every day.

I hadn't had to feel *this* every day.

Her in my arms, her *close* and rehashing old shit that didn't need to be rehashed. I almost told her no when she asked me to be her man of honor. I mean, there'd been more than one reason why I'd left town and decided to go to school out of state. A few of those reasons surrounded her in varied ways, but that decision would not only have been selfish but foolish. It'd be admitting to something that I didn't want to admit. That the past was harder to put away than I believed.

That I still hadn't dealt with this.

I held the bride close, being foolish for just a moment. December was all heat, all memories, and God, how I'd wanted her back then. Somewhere along the way, after she'd dropped into my life, she'd been everything. Had I found her first, that might have been our destiny. We were so good as friends.

But you lost.

I had been aware of that. Another man had gotten to her first and actually, was responsible for the reason December and I met in school. Prinze had this thing set up and on lock before I could even step foot in the game. I'd had no chance, my current reality with December already predetermined. She'd always been meant to be his.

"Ramses?"

December placed two fingers to my chin, doing the worst fucking thing by making me look directly at her. Tawny brown eyes sparkled in that snowy white dress of hers. This girl was Snow White from her fair skin to the ruby red tone of her lips. Her dark hair was nearly black, but make no mistake. December Lindquist was no fair maiden, no damsel in distress.

And I guess she was December Prinze now.

I held on to that as much as I had her secure in my arms, forcing myself to smile down at her. I had at least a foot on her up here.

"You've been scarce tonight." Her hand moved to my shoulder, and I breathed. *This* location was okay, easier. Her lips parted. "You all right? I haven't seen you since the bouquet toss."

Oh, and how fun that'd been. I'd actually caught that shit, like she'd been aiming for me, and possibly had. My best friend had been known to meddle more than once in my personal life, and whenever we did see each other, it was like she was always trying to hook me up with someone.

I folded my hand around hers, chuckling. "Yeah, and thanks for that. You pissed off more than one single woman tonight, I'm sure."

I mean, a dude catching the bouquet wasn't ideal, and I

got way more attention than I'd wanted. Like stated, I'd been trying to *avoid* action tonight, not be at the center of it.

December rolled her eyes. "Don't act like you didn't get a million digits." She jostled me with a grin. "You're welcome by the way. Pretty sure you're getting laid tonight, and I'm totally responsible for that."

"I didn't ask to get laid." Spinning her, I brought her back to me, the dance floor a mix of chill sways and swinging hips. I eyed her. "I was perfectly fine hanging out. Being single."

"Hmm. And how's that working for you?"

Not as fine as I would have liked, but I was in a good place now that I was *back home* and out of the fray of all that. I just wanted to chill. Having someone else in my life was not a huge priority.

Truth be told, I'd had my fill of a social life just trying to help her with this wedding. It was unbelievable how women did this shit every day. I considered myself a pretty good multitasker, but having to help her work through the minutiae that was her wedding planning hadn't been easy. Especially since I had to book a lot of her appointments and man her bridal party, the epitome of awkward as fuck since I was a guy and like, her entire party I'd gone to high school with. I'd been given my fair share of handling from the other women, came with the territory since we'd known each other.

It'd been all worth it, though—a good time and I wouldn't have changed a thing. I'd do anything for this girl. Always.

"I'm okay." I attempted to convince the bride now and needed to do a good job at that, too. Tonight wasn't about me and my problems. "You don't need to worry about me."

"But don't I?" Our dance slowed in place. She squeezed my hand. "You still haven't said what happened. Why you came home?"

Because I didn't have to, and I was not talking about that here. And definitely not now. My choice to leave Brown

University and transfer closer to home to finish out my senior year had nothing to do with her.

Even if I had dealt with the issue in the same way.

I'd be lying to myself if I said I didn't have a track record. Running away was how I dealt with things. In this case, I really didn't have a choice. I'd made the ultimate fuck-up, and rather than staring that shit in the face every day, I made a choice. Coming home was the best decision, and I stood by that.

I wet my lips. "Here's not the place. Nor the time."

"Well, where and when is?"

"How about when you're not about to go on your honeymoon." *To another guy.* I shook my head. "We're not doing this. We *won't* do this."

She needed to let me go too, in more than one way. This was our last dance, and we shouldn't do this, ruin it.

Her fingers worked in my hand, her head, ultimately, laying on my chest. The fucker threatened to beat out of his cage she was so close.

This is the last dance.

December gave up the topic of discussion, but that didn't mean she wanted to. I think she too knew this was it. It wasn't the time for fighting. This was her day, a happy day. We let everything go on that dance floor, just drifting into the motions of the dance. We were two friends with a shared past that resulted in two different futures.

"Plan on giving me back my wife any time soon, Mallick?"

She'd obviously found hers, my eyes rolling when I faced her husband. A scowl in a five-thousand-dollar suit.

That was Royal Prinze.

The guy had a face that animators typically reserved for Disney princes. But considering the number of smiles (or lack thereof) the guy allotted over his lifetime, I had a feeling his particular good looks landed him more on the Disney villain spectrum. He was a celebration of a thousand glares and had a healthy amount of those reserved for me over the years.

Truth, we put our beef away long ago, but the guy seriously made it too easy to get a rise out of him. It was almost a game. What could I say to get Royal Prinze to scowl at me?

"Relax, Prinze." I swung December away, sashaying to the beat with a grin. "You've had her all night, and the song's not quite over."

Turned out, it wasn't much.

His scowl deepened, and I even gave myself ten bonus points for the eye tick. It always hit his left, a hard squint before he cuffed December's arm. He eased her over. "Considering she's my wife, that's justified," he growled. His finger shot out. "And don't think I've forgotten about that shit you pulled in Miami."

I may or may not have participated in a coup to keep himself and his groomsmen busy the night of December's bachelorette party. I will say, though, I had nothing to do with the fact that there'd be strippers there… I just happened to know about them. Anyway, that was water under the bridge, and he'd gotten over it—obviously. The fact that I was still alive and standing there now told me that.

Unbuttoning my jacket, I stamped hands on waist. "Don't act like you're still mad about that."

Because he wasn't, not by a long shot. Again, if he was, I wouldn't be standing here tonight, let alone December's man of honor. The two of us just liked to handle each other, and he even secretly liked me.

He'd even told me once.

Really, I should have recorded that shit, because I'd never hear it again. A snarl formed on Prinze's lips before he took his new wife's hand. December, of course, rolled her eyes at both of us. She was used to the caveman shit, and odds were, we'd bicker for the rest of our days. Sometimes, two people were just always meant to be rivals. The common link was that we both passionately cared about the woman between us. He'd won, and the only satisfaction I did have was that he'd love her as fiercely as I knew she deserved to be loved. He'd be there for her.

He'd treat her well.

He will.

My mantra as I allowed my moment to become his. Kissing the back of her hand, he asked if she was ready to go. I guess his three best men had gotten their car ready for them. Knight, LJ, and Jax were his ride-or-dies, still closer than shit. Even after high school. There were some bonds that never broke, some people who stayed close instead of pushing others away. These people grew together. They didn't get lost on the outside even with miles apart for some of them. They had their shit together.

"Arizona?"

December's hypnotic eyes landed on me, letting me in on her world. She didn't forget about me and probably never would. That just made *all* this so much harder. I wanted her to let go, to forget.

To let *me* forget.

She remained my ride-or-die, always in my corner. The issue was, she'd grown where I hadn't. She moved on. She loved.

Prinze was behind her. She told him she'd be just a second, smiling at me. She'd called me the name we both called each other since we met in Arizona.

"'Zona." I shortened the name for her, always my Arizona. Taking her hand, I gave her a hug, and from behind her, Prinze let his entire demeanor slip. Something of a smile touched his eyes before he eyed away and pretended to talk to someone else on the dance floor. I said this guy allotted only so many smiles.

I suppose he spared one for me.

We really didn't hate each other, not anymore. How could

I hate him? He was the sole source of the exuberant happiness that radiated off his new wife. He was her joy, her air.

Her breath.

I couldn't hate that. It was like hating her if I did, and I didn't. I only wanted what was best for her and if that was him, well, that was him.

Taking my attention away from him, I placed it back on December, so much smaller than me. She was like bite-sized to my lanky-ass frame.

"We're going to talk when we get back," she said, smelling like everything wonderful about the world, all flowers and honeysuckle. She pulled away. "You can't escape from me."

She wouldn't let me either, goddamn her. Grinning, I passed what she said off, our fingers laced. "You're going to miss your ride."

"They'll wait. I'm the motherfucking bride."

Fuck yeah, she was. The pair of us chuckled. We just stood there like two goobers, hands together, and I wished for so many things. I wished for do-overs, for do-betters. Maybe if I'd been the one to grow, she'd be on my arm. It'd be our wedding here, now.

A glow hit her eyes as she reached for me, her tiny arms around my waist. She buried her face in my chest, and my insides caved.

"I love you, Arizona," she said, and since I didn't trust my voice, I stayed silent. I merely let her hold onto me, knowing what that love meant to her. It meant this moment, two friends with a shared history. It meant our past.

Whereas mine could have meant our future.

CHAPTER
TWO

Ramses

A sparkle send-off greeted my best friend and her new husband outside, the pair of them rushing through it, and I was at the end of the line. I was the last person December saw, the last smile she got to see before she got into the town car with Prinze. He'd worn a long trench coat while she'd been dawned in a fluffy white wrap, the pair of them like something off a damn Christmas card. It probably would be the shot they chose to send out this year, *Merry Christmas from the Prinzes*.

I'd waved them off like everyone else, my sparkler dead as wet snow and ice crushed under their wheels. They'd chosen one of the coldest days of the year to get married, but odds were, they were the warmest people on the planet in that moment. They'd taken their happiness and shared it in front of all of us, in front of me.

My hand lowered in the chilly air. I'd failed to put on a coat. I'd been in such a hurry to join everyone outside, see the couple off.

Correcting that, I headed in while the rest of the world passed well wishes after their town car. I figured they'd both probably need a way to get their gifts home, and since I was the man of honor, why not.

My steps guided me past ice sculptures and twinkling lights, the entire house decked out tonight for the festivities. At one point, the place actually snowed inside.

I shit you not.

It'd been fake snow, but snow nonetheless and an added touch to Prinze and the extra limb he'd gone out on to make this day the true essence of winter. His bride was named December, so he brought her that, *December*, and it hadn't mattered they'd gotten married after the first of the year. Prinze had pulled out all the stops, totally him.

Laughing a little at it, I eventually found myself back in the ballroom depleted of guests. With most folks outside, nothing but the house band and a few other chatting wedding guests resided inside. As I had a date with the gift table, I ventured there but found a small congregation had already gathered by the time I'd gotten there.

Knight Reed, one of Royal's best men, handed gifts off to another one of Royal's guys, LJ. They had a cart between them, the thing already stacked with large packages wrapped in colorful foils and decorative paper. At the helm of the cart (and waiting rather impatiently I might add) stood Jaxen Ambrose, Prinze's third and final member of his guys-in-waiting. The dude had a joint behind his ear and his girl-friend, Cleo, under his arm, most assuredly the reason for his lack of patience.

I hadn't seen him or the other guys most of the night, but that'd only been half my fault. Windsor House had a lot of nooks and crannies to get lost in, a lot of *bedrooms*, and odds were, these guys were doing their girls as much as the Cha-Cha Slide tonight. Knight and LJ had girlfriends too, both of which

I'd seen outside waving Royal and December off. The guys had probably escaped to handle the gifts, and since Jax basically only left his girlfriend to pee today, he'd most likely dragged her inside with him. I'd heard he actually donated a kidney to her…

Right?

I'd seen some interesting things in my life, but miracles? Well, I could honestly say I'd witnessed four. The first had been Royal Prinze actually deciding to marry someone who wasn't himself, and the second, third, and fourth consisted of these three dudes settling down with something besides their right hands. Don't get me wrong. I'd held my fair share of women over the years, but these guys? These guys had ventured into nothing but fuckboy territory and definitely hadn't looked anywhere close to settling down.

They weren't that now, and Jaxen barely allowed an inch between him and his girl. He lifted a hand when he saw me, relaxed, and when the others jutted their chins in a similar easy-going fashion, I realized how much really had changed. These dudes had *hated* my ass in school, super loyal to Prinze, and though we'd squashed most of our shit back then, they'd never been really excited to pass me their hand. I'd noticed the change first with Prinze after he and December got serious. Back then, the others had followed his example, but I think only mostly due to loyalty. We hadn't been each other's biggest fans, a history there, but with the wedding excitement around us and their girls at their sides, it'd been like I was dealing with different men. They were different. *They'd changed.*

Jax and I snapped after our handshake, and fuck me, if Knight friggin' Reed didn't bring me into a hug after ours. He'd had his pal Heineken in his hand, so I had a feeling it had something to do with that, but when LJ did the same after our hands met, I just laughed and accepted it. These guys really had transformed, wild.

"Bro. We fucking rocked this shit tonight." LJ bumped my fist, then settled back. "I swear, I saw Royal fucking cry."

"Oh, he totally cried," I said, chuckling and again, *wild*. I shook my head. "Never thought I'd see the day."

"Right?" Jax hit my chest. "I thought I was going to have to hand him my pocket square."

"Shit, I did hand him mine." Knight threw his head back in laughter. "It was right after their first look photos. Dude was a fucking mess."

"Don't act like that won't be both you fuckers." LJ crossed a patent leather shoe over the other, smirking. "Especially you, kidney boy. I saw you making goo-goo eyes over at your girl the whole ceremony."

He jerked his chin in the direction of Cleo, the girl instantly flushing to her ears. Out of all the girls, she seemed like the shiest. Apparently unashamed by the comment, Jax knotted his arms around her trim waist.

"Fuck yeah, I'm going to fucking cry." He rested a chin on Cleo's shoulder, staking his claim further when he tugged her into him. He grinned. "Real men aren't afraid to shed tears for their girls. I think my moms will be surprised if I don't cry."

He had been raised by women, his mom and her partner, and he was right. There was nothing wrong with crying. I, too, had been basically raised and supported by a woman, my dad fucking useless. He'd abandoned me in all ways beyond the physical and even worse when I'd gotten older.

In fact, many of these men lacked influential father figures in their lives, Prinze included, and they'd obviously done all right. They didn't let that technicality hold them back. They grew despite that, thrived even.

Not really trying to think about that, I offered to take the wedding gifts myself. That'd been the reason I came inside and had nothing else to do. The rest of my night would consist of Netflix and my own bottle of Heineken, so it was the least I could do to transport the wedding gifts to where they needed to go.

"Oh, let us do that, bro," came from Knight Reed, handing LJ another package. "It's the best men's job, anyway."

"Yeah, we got this," LJ said, placing a rather large gift on the cart between them. "Anyway, you should take it easy. You've been, like, everywhere tonight, brother. Helping and shit."

"Yeah, he has." Jax arranged the gift on the cart, chuckling. "Didn't see you around tonight at all, and when I did, you looked like the maintenance crew."

Had it been that obvious? I shrugged. "Just trying to help out."

"Well, I think you've got that accomplished." That last gift settled, Knight angled his big body back against the gift table. The guy was built like a Marine and I *knew* Marines. Had one or two in my family, and this guy could give any one a run for their money with his size. He was basically popping out of his gray suit. He grinned. "Like LJ said, take it easy. We'll make sure these get to Royal and December's place. Go have fun. Cash in one of those many digits I'm sure you got tonight."

A jostle from more than one of them tonight *for that* and the bouquet toss fiasco. I lifted my eyes to the heavens. "Eh, don't know about that. I was just going to head home. Relax."

Jax's jaw basically hit the floor, like I had the audacity at all to suggest such a thing for myself, and I suppose I wasn't surprised. Odds were, these boys were headed to the club after all this tonight for an after-party and most certainly would get far more action than me since they had girlfriends. Seemingly appalled, Jax tucked his hands under his pits. "Fuck, bro. You serious? All that damn pussy just tossed to the ether? What the fuck?"

No sooner had he said the words, than his girlfriend Cleo looked like she had somewhere way better to be, shoving him with a "Jaxen" before he snagged her arm and inched her back to him.

"I meant for him, babe. *For him,*" he emphasized. Clearly, this girl was the only one in his eyes. Cupping her ass cheeks, he hitched her against him. "You know I ain't about that life anymore. I gave you my damn kidney."

He sure had, again fucking crazy.

And where this girl a second ago looked ready to run for the hills, now seemed hard-pressed to be anywhere but beneath him. He enveloped her in a sea of hands and well-timed kisses, making her giggle, and the rest of us roll our eyes, *hard.* Jaxen Ambrose roped like the rest of these boys.

And so, miracles really did happen.

He got a jostle or four from his friends, but not before I got another push to do something else with my time besides Netflix tonight. They even invited me to the after-party they planned to hit (I'd guessed right, a club), but I turned it down. Today had been a lot. Hell, the last few months had. I'd been December's right-hand guy and that was on top of my own personal shit. I was ready for a cold one and a good night's sleep.

"Fine, brother. Lame ass," Jax goaded, but chuckled when he shook my hand. Our rings clinked, as did mine with Knight's and LJ's when we shook. We were all a part of the prestigious though equally infamous Court, *brothers,* though in the past we hadn't acted like it. Tonight was clearly different, those days of the past gone, and it only helped we shared a common understanding. Our best friends got married today.

I suppose that made us linked for life.

I thought I'd get away with the last of their handling and I had for the most part, but not before Jax could slip the joint he had behind his left ear to my pocket.

"You need this more than me," he said, obviously referencing my night of impending solitude. He patted my pocket. "Don't get too wild tonight."

This received barks of laughter from both Knight and LJ, but a head shake and a pair of flushed cheeks from his girlfriend. I suppose I wasn't the only one who didn't smoke weed. I guess I had in the past, but not since high school.

I flicked it in a wave after them before thinking better of that and pocketing it. Not that kids even a decade younger than me didn't smoke these things in these very halls. Hell, I'd been one of them.

And yes, at fucking twelve.

I used to get up to all kinds of shit, but that was the past for the most part. Even still, I decided to take a walk down memory lane through the halls of Windsor House before heading home for the night. I had properties both here in Maywood Heights and on my new campus, Pembroke University. I thought that'd be best considering my plans to delve more into my father's businesses here in town while at the same time going to school. Having two homes gave me convenience and ample choice about where to stay if I was tired or just didn't feel like trekking the almost two hours to and fro.

The decision to tackle my father's businesses now that I'd arrived back in Maywood Heights seemed like a necessary evil since I didn't have the excuse of states between myself and my family's legacy. Currently, most of my father's businesses had board members running things, but it'd always been the plan for me to take over. After all, he couldn't live forever.

Though, he'd been arrogant enough to play God in the past.

The disdain I had for my currently incarcerated father reached historical levels and wasn't something I planned to touch with a ten-foot pole *at all*, here in Maywood Heights or not. His legacy didn't have to be mine, his sins his own, and as far as I was concerned, I operated through life with a mother—only. One who actually gave a shit about me more than himself. She always had and did try to protect me from him. She'd been hard-pressed. My father had always been a powerful man, something I knew too well. Even from an early age.

That joint sounding real good about now, I got it out as I strode through the brick halls of Windsor House, the thing against my lips before I realized I didn't have a light. I actually had to double back and bum a Zippo off someone from the band, and by then, I got a text from, of all people, December.

December: Hey, goober. You didn't get out of talking to me tonight. This is on when I get back. *wink emoji*

I shook my head.

Me: Aren't you supposed to be, I don't know, doing your husband right about now?

Honestly, the actual thought made me want to barf a lung. Prinze fucking anyone. Let alone my best friend.

And the girl who could have been yours.

The joint twisted in my fingers, basically mangled by the time I got to Windsor House's aquatic area. Back in the day, my friends and I used to get high as hell under the bleachers by the pool, the ambiance a bit different now. Thick with heat, the room painted timid waves from the shallow and deep ends. The lights were off, but the area was bright from the pool's underwater lighting.

My leather shoes squeaked to a stop as December's text message bubble popped up.

December: I'll let you get away with that one because I love you.

I wished she didn't keep saying that, that she loved me, and though I loved her too, I never said it to her. I was scared of what it meant whenever I even had the thought to say it.

That it would come out meaning something else and I'd look like an asshole.

At the end of the day, December and I had a history, a long one. And though it hadn't all been bad, it was filled with more pain and suffering than anyone in their goddamn lifetime should have had to endure.

And that'd been before she chose someone else over me.

She was my friend, yes. I loved her, yes, but we weren't together. We weren't a thing and…

December: I just wanted to let you know you weren't off the hook for our talk. I still want to know what's wrong with you. Why you came back? I'm not stupid.

I knew she wasn't, didn't think she was. But like I'd already told her, tonight and her wedding hadn't been the time. In any case, I was a big boy. Could deal with my own shit.

I wet my lips.

Me: Noted. Will talk in the future. Promise.

Anything to get her to move on.

December: Okay, and I also wanted to thank you. You know, for tonight? You're always there for me.

My hand wavered, and I eyed my phone before taking off my suit jacket. The humidity in the room didn't help, the air heavy and suffocating.

Me: It's no problem. You know that.

I'd do anything for her, still would. Hell, if she got to the airport and said, "*Hey, Arizona, I changed my mind. I don't want to leave. I…*"

And *that* out of everything was what scared me the most. That somewhere deep inside I wouldn't know what to do. If she came back, *said things* that I wouldn't know what to do with it all, if I'd make the right choice.

I didn't know if I'd do the right thing.

The possibility of that sobered the hell out of me, that I could in some deep dark place be just as fucked up as my father. That I could create just as much chaos in someone's life that he had and not just to mine. My father, Ibrahim Mallick, left so many casualties in his wake.

December herself included.

This was my reality, my pain as much as my passion. I would take over my father's businesses, but I'd do it in an honest way. I'd run business in this town as a good man, not one who took advantage of others and lead only by his own selfish gain.

December: You're good people. Rare.

She said this like she knew my thoughts, my body hitching a seat against the pool's handrails. I'd hung my jacket there and leaned against it.

Me: I'll always be there for you. Always.

Famous last words, words that killed me, but I wouldn't let them. I stayed strong. Even when she texted me goodbye. Even when I said goodbye back and knew she was on that next leg of her journey. She was heading into the night of her fairy tale, found her literal prince, and I was in the other kingdom, a place where she hadn't chosen to stay for her reign. That castle would remain dark, dormant.

Angling my phone in my pocket, I flicked the Zippo at the joint in my mouth, attempting to light it.

But then a *plop.*

That shit came out of nowhere, above.

Plop.

Another, the pool expanding in ripples. Peering in, something dark landed in the shallow end, about a foot or so away from something also dark.

What the fuck?

I arched my neck in the direction of the ceiling, finding the high dive. Imagine my surprise to find a woman up there, seated and dangling her legs over the side. She kicked out bare legs from beneath a black dress, a flourish of chiffon and never-ending tulle. I'd seen enough of it inside bridal shops.

Her fingers on the sides, she craned a look over the edge.

My heart rattled.

The woman was easily more than one story up, sitting on the edge of a high dive like she wouldn't mind falling off. Hell, she would fall off.

Tossing the joint at the bleachers, I advanced toward the high dive, scaling the steps in quick time. Even with as much cardio as I did (I ran five miles a day), it still took me a moment to get up there, and I was out of breath by the time I did. I think mostly from adrenaline. The woman sat at the edge, her back to me, but shit really hit the fan at what I saw sitting beside her. A bottle of wine.

And the empty glass beside it.

CHAPTER
THREE

Ramses

I obviously approached this situation with caution, not knowing what else to fucking do. A woman was up here with a bottle of wine, an empty glass, and fully dressed like she wanted to take that evening gown out for a swim. I didn't know if she wanted to just be alone or what, but this felt like a really weird situation.

"Everything okay up here?" I asked, completely bothered when she didn't even move.

Not an inch.

Not a flick of the shoulders, a flinch of the fingers. I made myself known, and she still sat there.

I swallowed. "Miss?"

Say something, goddammit.

I approached her slow, casual with a lifted hand. I didn't know what she'd do honestly, why she was up here. If she wanted to jump, she definitely could. I looked around. "Probably shouldn't be…"

Eyes, dark eyes like onyx glass in an ebony sea. They

pinned me in place, a fan of her hair gracing her shoulder. A tumble of dark waves cascaded down the bare flesh of her back, the woman honeyed like pure caramel and just a shade or two lighter than me. She either held a glorious tan or some kind of distinct ethnicity, my guess Latina. Though I wasn't sure. People often guessed wrong when it came to me, half Syrian on my dad's side. It gave me thick curls and hair only slightly lighter than this woman's. Though just barely.

And woman, she was. Not a miss, or a girl. A straight nose sloped and complemented her cupid's bow, her lips like two full strokes of a paint brush. I didn't paint a lot, more a fan of physical art with hard metals and fortified steel. I was into metalwork when I could, sculpting.

She had hard yet striking angles to some of the more softer elements of her face, her nose buttoned at the tip and her overall face shaped like a heart. She was also intentional and completely deliberate in the way she stared at me. It took me a second to realize her ruby-red lips were actually speaking to me.

And when I did, I questioned verbal assault.

"Can I help you?" she gritted, the stark raven glow of her eyes glaring at me. Her head lowered. "Are you hard of hearing?"

The fuck?

Now, I didn't come at this woman wrong at all. Actually, I came as a concerned citizen.

I was questioning that now, a slow raise of my eyebrow. "I suppose I wondered if you were all right up here."

She had been up here... by herself, alone and with a bottle of wine.

I eyed it. Though, she refused to peel her gaze away from me. If anything, she watched my shoes, as if cautious for an advance. I stayed in my place. "I wanted to know if every-thing was okay."

"Obviously." Another heated jab. This woman was

goddamn beautiful, but her tone certainly didn't match. At least, not at the present. She angled a look over the side. "You can carry on now."

Wow.

I didn't consider myself a glutton for punishment, but this woman didn't seem all right and was up here by herself. I shifted, and that dark mane of hers sliced the air so quick when she turned, I questioned the whiplash of her neck. She kept her eyes trained on me, obviously not wanting me to move.

Yeah, she wasn't okay.

This didn't *feel* okay. At all.

Again, I stayed where I was and to let her know I'd continue doing so, I placed a hand on the high dive's handrails. "What are you doing up here?"

She said nothing. I guess not one for small talk, but she did face forward. Her fingers curled so hard on the edge I questioned if she would push off, go in.

Would I catch her? Go in after her? Chivalry wasn't dead in me so I probably would, but I wondered if she'd hit me or something if I tried. This woman seemed a little unbalanced.

I lowered and found her eyes on me again, calculated and intensely observant. What I wouldn't give to have her in front of a canvas. She actually made me want to paint, funny enough. "Can I have your name?"

A new angle and definitely going out on a limb. She hadn't answered me the first time.

"Brielle." An arctic bite to the word as her gaze appraised me, not completely hopeless tonight in the five-thousand-dollar suit Prinze also made us buy. He'd wanted us to match him and honestly, the cash was a drop in the bucket for most of us. Many of our fathers, uncles, and grandfathers built this town, my dad an immigrant but held so many small businesses and real estate properties under his name, he had enough to buy out many of Maywood Heights' founding members three hundred times over. Shit, this town had even given him the key to the city.

He had been the mayor.

Not for a while now but he had been, that legacy there. It followed me to this day being his only son, and though I got the grades at Brown, I basically only had to make a call to get myself on the Pembroke University campus for the upcoming spring semester—of my senior year. It'd been really rather easy.

My father had funded five resident halls.

That'd been before he'd been incarcerated obviously, but still, the Mallick name held some clout. I used it to my advantage where I could and tossed it to the wayside in any other situation. I had, for all intents and purposes, all but disassociated myself from my father the day he'd decided to do some dirty shit with my uncle Leo. I had no problem using his name, though. I figured it was the least he could do for me.

Brielle eyed the fruits of my father's labor now, but I wasn't quite sure for the price tag. I'd left my suit jacket below. But in its absence, her gaze drifted over my broad shoulders and down sleeves the seamstress may have cut a few corners on, a smidgen tighter across my biceps and forearms than I would like. I hadn't complained, the rest of the suit a perfect fit from the way the trousers allowed what could be considered thick runner's legs to move. I did a lot of cardio, but I worked out my legs probably more than I should. It was awesome for my endurance but sucked for speed. I'd always been a bit of a gym junky, played ball in school and just liked the way my body felt when I kept it in shape. I could eat pizza like the best of them, though.

Brielle's gaze lingered on the area of my squatted thighs before coming up, and though I didn't consider myself shy, I was hella aware of her eyes on me. This woman was beyond a knockout, gorgeous from her soft face shape to the way her full tits hugged and swelled above her dress's bodice. I knew way more than I wanted to about dresses these days thanks to a certain bride, and Brielle filled out the A-line in a way that allowed me to be completely observant of how the sea of black material flared widely over her thick hips and gave peeks of her shapely legs. Something told me she ran too, her calves smooth and defined, and with her tanned skin, glowed like trapped sunshine. Her feet bare and hair raven black, Brielle resembled a temptress in the night, all woman as she sat wrapped softly in the teal hue of the House's aquatic center.

I opened my hands, placing one to my chest. "Ramses. Nice to meet you, Brielle."

Though I wasn't sure the sentiment was shared, her expression more than cautious, observant. That hadn't let up since I'd arrived up here, which I suppose made sense. This woman didn't know me at all.

A nod in her direction as she watched me, and when I lost her gaze again, I questioned my progress. I felt like I should keep her talking.

"You, uh, been drinking, Brielle?" I stated, my next question. I pointed at the bottle. "Seems like it."

She took no notice of that. Like I said, she wouldn't even look at me. But she did face down after I said it, her shoulders lifting.

"Bottle's full," she whispered, again gritted. "And I guess I suck at being alone."

Struck me funny since, apparently, I had attempted to do that tonight too. I put out a hand. "Mind if I sit with you then?"

Shoulders instantly locked, and when her fingers curled white over the edge, I instantly questioned what I'd asked.

She said she wanted to be alone.

But I didn't want her to be. Honestly, I didn't care what she did once she got down from this high dive, but I didn't think she should be up here by herself. It could be dangerous.

It was fucking high up and if she fell and hit the wrong angle, disaster.

"If you must," she said, the dark strobe light of her eyes in my direction. "Ramses."

She'd emphasized my name, and I wasn't sure I didn't like it, enjoying the way it sounded in the smoky tone of her voice.

My lips twitching right, I eased down a seat beside her. Though, far enough away to keep the full bottle of wine between us. Another question. Who didn't drink when they obviously intended to?

Yet another question about this mysterious girl. This mysterious woman. "You, um, weren't planning on jumping off this thing tonight. Were you, Brielle?"

So quick her gaze swung in my direction, lashes of an ebony black fanning over her irises. "Why would you ask me that?"

Because it appeared to be true, and taking my leg, I propped it up on the ledge, my other dangling. Truth be told, I'd dicked around on this thing myself like a million and a half years ago. But that'd been when I was thirteen and hadn't completely fully grasped the finality of death. Sure, I'd jumped off this thing and hadn't died, but thinking back on some of the things I'd done off this ledge and *at this level* had my twenty-two-year-old self wanting to kick my own ass. It was fucking high up. Actual Olympians trained off this shit. We'd had more than one roll through here. Hell, we'd had presidents come through these halls. Being a member of the Court held prestige and typically opened a lot of doors for a guy and now, girls. For years, the Court had been archaic and not allowed women in, but this changed when Royal Prinze became president of the association after high school.

All the Court "honor" had done for me in the past was haunt, but not everyone could say that, I suppose. I laced my fingers together. "Well, are you?"

An honest question and I wondered her answer. If she'd actually tell me the reason as she wet her lips. She wore a red matte to the full width, lipsticks I knew entirely too much about as well. I'd watched enough contouring YouTube videos for a lifetime thanks to December Prinze, and the beauty vloggers who shot them often paired the look with a lipstick that didn't easily rub off, one that could withstand many maneuvers of eating or drinking.

Or bruising.

I couldn't help but imagine Brielle's lips doing that as she moved one over the other, a slight pierce hitting her temple when her jaw worked. She had a dark beauty mark right above the left side of her lip, a soft mole which twitched when her lips moved. "I don't know why you'd ask me that."

And I noticed she hadn't answered, either on purpose or because she didn't know and didn't want to talk to me.

"Well, I guess just let me know if you decide to jump." I shrugged. "You know, before?"

"Why?"

I faced her, fighting the grin tugging at my lips, and her eyes flashed wide.

"I mean," she started, gnawing her lip. A huff and she was tossing her head back. "That's not what I meant. You…" She shook her head. "You tricked me or something."

"No trick." I lifted the hand from my leg. "I was just a concerned citizen, and it can be dangerous up here."

She passed me a sharp look, and when she shifted her full body in my direction, I had a moment where the lungs didn't exactly connect to the brain so to speak. Where I had to remind the guys to do their job, or like, well, die. I'd breathed a million times before this moment. Possibly a million and a half, but who was counting.

Brielle in that stark black dress floored this guy, shocked still where I sat with just a look from her. She had an essence about her, a maturity that demanded me to stop and simply take notice.

I wet my lips. "Anyway, like I said, it can be dangerous. Definitely not a place to be playing around."

I angled my whole body in her direction too, and though she'd been more casual about taking me in, she did notice. Her eyes flashed across the entire width of my shoulders before finding my eyes. Did she find me attractive as well? Hell, if I was hiding looking at her. She was probably one of the most beautiful women I'd ever seen. In fact, top of the charts.

She pushed a lock of hair behind her ear, flashing a single diamond in my direction. It brought a sparkle out in her eyes like nothing else. "I'm not playing around," she gritted, eyes narrow. "And you shouldn't have assumed I'm up here to jump."

"But aren't you?" I opened up my hand. "You're up here. By yourself with a bottle of wine."

"And you're forward," she huffed. "Also, quite possibly a little arrogant."

My eyes flashed. Arrogant was not something I'd been called much. At least, not to my face. I'd had bouts of it back in the day, but today, I was more confident than anything else. When it came to things I wanted, I went for it, you know, only living once and all that. If life taught me one thing, there wasn't time to pussyfoot through it in wait of second chances. There were no second chances for some of us.

This logic had gotten me in trouble in the past, but no, I didn't consider myself arrogant. But I did go after things I wanted, and right now, I wanted this woman off this ledge and to the safety of her own two feet. Fuck, I wanted my feet down there with her. I wasn't trying to play around up here in a five-thousand-dollar suit. I grinned. "If that's what you think."

"Oh, I do." She faced away, blinking. But when she shook her head, I noticed something.

A smile.

It touched her left eye, those smooth lips painted in matte red. A hint of it, a wince even before the expression eased away, and I decided to take a gamble. She'd called me arrogant.

May as well give her what she wanted.

"How about we make a wager?" I asked, getting her attention. "We thumb war for it. You know the game?"

She gave me a look like I was a goddamn idiot, but I'd done that on purpose. Call me a selfish guy, but I wanted another one of those heart-stopping smiles, which I got (a little) when she faced my way. She lifted a naked shoulder. "What are we playing for?"

"For you to go down there," I said, directing a finger once more below. "But via the stairs. You do that, go down there with me if I win."

"And if I win?"

Easy too. "You get to stay up here. All by your lonesome."

"Meaning you'll leave."

Ouch, but I had invaded her clear intent for solitude. Because of that, I refused to take much offense. I nodded. "I'll leave. You'll be here all alone, and really, you can't lose here." One way gave her the peace and solitude she desired.

The other way gave her me.

Maybe I was a little arrogant, but she fascinated me, her grit and so obvious *I don't give a fuck* mentality. This woman, should she be so inclined, would probably set my ass on fire if it suited her, which probably should scare me more than it did. It didn't, though, not really. I wanted to see what she'd do.

I wanted to see what she'd let me do.

If she'd allow me to wrap her into a choice, possibly take away hers personally. She clearly was a fan of control.

Her delicate throat shifted, working as she seemingly considered the decision. Without words, she put out her hand.

"I win, you leave," she said, gifting me with a rare smile. This woman flashed about as many as Prinze. She pointed. "You said."

I did say that.

I gave her my hand, hers smooth and flawless as mine swallowed the digits up. There were few parts of this, quite frankly, string-bean body of mine that didn't come with extended height or thick width. I was just shy of six-foot-eight, had the wingspan of basically an eagle, and it was truly fucking scary how many shoes on this planet came nowhere close to fitting me. I'd actually had to have shoes made coming up, and let's not even get started on how many women I'd literally freaked the fuck out in the sheets. A lot of guys joked about being, erm, um, *big* down there and thought of it like something of a trophy. Not the goddamn curse it'd been for me on more than one occurrence. Besides having to worry about the way certain pants fit, it took a woman with stamina and a high pain threshold to handle the son of a bitch.

That wasn't even me bragging.

In the case of my hands, though, I found I enjoyed the way Brielle's petite digits lost themselves beneath mine, how soft and delicate they were. I decided to fasten our hands only slightly, worried about breaking her, but she hadn't held back with me. She had a firm grip, as hard and rough-edged as she seemed to be.

I counted us down, our thumbs going back and forth. How odd we were doing this. I hadn't played this game since I was a kid.

A flourish of excitement appeared to pass behind her eyes as well, but damn if she let it out. The only indicator had been her eyes, focused, determined. One would think, she was about to compete for the thumb war world cup.

The last number called out, I jabbed my thumb forward, usually pretty good at this. That had been the case way back when, but the tides sure had changed when I, overzealous with my strike, gave way for a second of vulnerability. Brielle stamped down her thumb on top of mine so quick my head spun, her smile coy.

"I win," she said, releasing my hand, and like nothing happened, cuffed her arms. "You can leave now."

Double ouch, and definitely not the outcome I'd gone for. I'd wanted her to come down with me, *stay* with me, but she let me go, and I had nothing to do but take my leave.

"Damn," I murmured, truly unsettled. I hadn't expected this defeat. "No chance for a best two out of three?"

Another ghost of a smile on her lips, her head going back. "Are you a sore loser, Ramses?"

No, I just hadn't wanted to leave. Not yet. It seemed too soon.

But since she accused me of that, I didn't want to be one.

I got up.

It took me a second to regain equilibrium, but once I had, I pocketed my hands. "Nice meeting you, Brielle."

It'd been an experience, that was for sure. I started to walk away, but she shifted, staring at me.

Her head angled up, way up since I was standing. Her lashes flashed. "You don't know any pizza places, do you?"

"Pizza?" My eyes flashed. "You want pizza?"

"Good pizza. Yeah." And then she was getting up, all the glorious angles and inches of her. She was a sea of taffeta and stark black, the back of her dress longer than the front. If I had to guess she stood just north of five-five, more than a foot of height I had on her. She smoothed the bell of her dress. "I'm not from here, but I heard the Midwest has good pizza. Deep dish."

I found myself wanting to smile. Though, I fought it. I didn't want to lose her, whatever this was. I popped a shoulder. "We do all right. This isn't Chicago, but I do know a place. Twenty-four hours, too."

If she was game, I'd take her there, and she seemed to be when she nodded. I'd never seen anyone like her, so poised and polished. Like a diamond-encrusted nut in need of a hard crack. We started to go until she angled a look over the edge of the high dive.

"What do you know about fishing out shoes?" she asked, her shrug subtle. "I seem to have dropped mine."

CHAPTER
FOUR

Bri

As it turned out, he knew surprisingly a lot about fishing out shoes.

The guy pushed up his shirt sleeves.

He exposed long arms corded in lean muscle, ready, but most importantly, *willing* to actually satisfy my request.

How curious.

I watched him behind an observant gaze, this man physically laboring over my error. They hadn't even been my shoes, but I'd lost them, on loan from a friend. Said friend had also left me to fend for myself tonight, busy with a previous engagement surrounding our work. Evie hadn't said what had come up, just that she had to leave town to head into the office but assured me we'd both been placed at the singles table for this wedding tonight so I wouldn't be alone.

I'd been alone, exceedingly so, as I had to watch what was, quite possibly, the most ridiculously lovely wedding I'd ever attended. There'd been magic, *love* everywhere, like a soft slap in the face and a fuck you for ever trying to go out and actually forget your failed marriage.

At least, that was what I'd felt like.

The other singles, not so much. Most of them appeared to know each other, locals.

This *Ramses* seemed to know his way around as well, knowing exactly where to get the pool strainer, and I believed I did recognize him from today. Though, I wasn't quite sure when. I'd made it to the wedding itself late today. I'd actually missed the ceremony, dragging my feet into the reception after Evie finally convinced me over the phone that coming to the wedding without her was okay.

"You'll get to know some people. Everyone will be at this wedding tonight."

She hadn't been lying, the room so full I hadn't even been able to see the bride and she'd been sitting up front with the groom. They'd both been at a sweetheart table, in their own little world. Every time I had seen her, she hadn't been without him, a permanent staple at her side and the groom completely doting over her. It'd been sweet.

Goddamn them.

My manicured nails lodging into my scalp, I dragged my hair around to my front, stepping back on bare feet when Ramses placed sopping wet red-bottom heels in front of me. He'd used that pool strainer to get them out, rising like Mt. Vesuvius when he stood. He was easily over six-foot-five. Six-foot-five *I knew*, and he completely stomped on that number and claimed some inches above. He'd been ready to help me, again, curious.

"One and two," he stated, dashing a grin down at me. He passed them out like penny candy, so ready to give them out. Like he didn't care.

Like he enjoyed being happy.

My brain, as pessimistic as it tended to be as of late,

thought good for him. If it was easy to be happy, people should be happy.

Yes, good.

But with wet shoes, I obviously couldn't wear them, and Ramses made quick work of this as well. He had a towel at the ready, one he'd grabbed after he'd appropriated the strainer, which let me know he was either a very good sleuth or did simply know his way around this place, a local too. A local with a muscular ass who filled out his trousers like David Beckham.

A visual dick print included.

I hadn't been particularly *trying* to check out his package, but it'd been there, and his pants had been tight. They weren't exceedingly tight, but this guy was so well-endowed it was *there* as well as a set of finely chiseled abs that pressed obviously through the thin lining of his dress shirt. He had a tapered body, strong and broad at the shoulders until the hems narrowed and hit tightly at his waist. This Ramses guy was a very big man.

And you so should not be looking at him like that.

I had a few years on him, that much was clear. If I had to guess, he couldn't be any older than twenty-seven or so, twenty-six at the youngest. Anyway, he was young.

But you have eyes.

He had eyes under dark umber waves, thick but controlled curls over his dusky-colored irises. They had a hazel tint to them, like the light couldn't help but come and jazz them up. I noticed it when the underwater pool lights hit them.

"May I?" he requested, asking for my hand. He'd dried off my shoes, the towel off to the side. "You should be good to go."

I seemed to be, taking his hand and angling into my shoes. His lengthy digits wrapped around my entire wrist, his hold strong but steady. I slid bare feet into only *slightly* damp shoes, and as that'd be better than no shoes at all, I'd take it. I wavered slightly, but Ramses had that covered too, the soft heat of his hand orbiting around the space at my shoulder. He'd be there to catch me, if I fell.

I didn't, quickly taking back my hand. "Thank you."

"No problem." Again, handing out those smiles like candy, his jaw clean-shaven, angular and almost boyish. Like he was completely untainted by the world, and with his age, he might not be quite yet. He pocketed those big hands of his, a skinny tie gracing his neck but no suit jacket. A glance and I saw he had it folded over the pool's rails.

"Ready to go then?" he asked, his head tilted. Oh, yes, my moment of temporary insanity. Had to be.

Why the fuck had you invited him out for pizza?

It'd sounded like a good idea at the time, and anything to make the moment less awkward for me.

Sure, keep telling yourself that.

He'd been about to leave. I'd been in the clear, but I'd still invited him out. I suppose I'd only blame that partially on the eyes. He certainly wasn't bad on them, a heritage that straddled the line of two maybe three and left him with the golden complexion of an underwear model. I'd find this guy circulating the beaches of Brazil, his hair dark and that smile of his for days.

It was easy to let him lead me out of the pool area after he grabbed his suit jacket off the pool's handrails, then later to coat check, but I wasn't a complete idiot. I didn't know this guy at all, and even if I had indulged in casual banter with him tonight, I most certainly wouldn't be going anywhere with him.

No, that wasn't happening.

And, like a few things tonight, I'd been once again surprised at how he'd handled that. I let him know I'd prefer to take a ride share, *drive separately* since I didn't know him. I hadn't driven myself tonight since I wasn't sure if I'd be drinking and not only had he *not* gotten offended, he'd pulled the app up himself and got me a ride to our destination.

He even followed us.

His sleek Mercedes Benz crushed ice swiftly behind, a smooth and handsome chrome finish. The ride actually reminded me of my own. I had an SUV that I'd bought with some of the alimony I got from the divorce. A note would have taken me a little bit to pay off otherwise, which was why it surprised me someone of his age drove such a thing. I knew it was him behind the Honda Civic I was in, though. I got a flash of that cool smile of his through the windshield whenever my driver stopped at a light or turned a corner. It was definitely him behind us, and I suppose that type of vehicle could be driven by a young professional. This guy Ramses must have done pretty well for himself.

And he'd picked a pretty packed place.

Several people were coming in and out the pizza house he'd punched in for my driver to head to, and after thanking my driver for his service, I ventured outside.

The elements hit me right away, certainly used to this back home in Jersey. Winters over there could be just as torrential, the snow flurries picking up and making my heels slick in the slush. Evie really would kill me for ruining her shoes, but considering I was out tonight in the first place because of her, I would say the score was settled. I had a night full of awkward shit around people I didn't know.

"Whoa, there. Careful."

A hand folded around my arm, steadying me. Ramses was suddenly out in the snow with me, tossing me just one more of those candy-coated smiles. It lit up his whole face, which, of course, managed to make him just that much more appealing. Something told me this young guy broke a lot of hearts.

Fighting my own smile, I thanked him, allowing him to right me and use his large body to fight the elements. He acted as a human shield, all the way into the pizza shop, a chime at the door sounding as we both brushed snow off our coats and out of our hair. It gathered in thick banks on his. His hair was so thick. He cleared it with the precision of one who'd done it many times once inside, doing the same with the long wool coat he'd acquired at coat check.

"I got just the thing for you," he said, shrugging his coat off his big shoulders. He folded the garment over his arm, and without it, the smooth gray of a tailored suit hugged the stocky width of broad shoulders. He was incredibly lean, generally, but his upper body could easily challenge a linebacker's. I knew a hell of a lot about the way those guys were built, more than I'd liked.

I wet my lips, easing out of the doorway to let a few patrons leave. I brushed my hair off too. "What do you mean?"

"I called the pizza in ahead," he said, surprising me. I struggled a bit with the snow and he helped me by flicking the remainder off my shoulders. He laughed. "Figured you'd want the best. But if you mind, we can order you something else. I just figured it wouldn't hurt for it to be ready before we got here. You know, in case you were really hungry?"

What an unusually considerate thing for him to do. Not that people never did things like that, but still, unusual considering *our* particular circumstances. I'd invited him out tonight but only after I'd been a little rude to him. I was well aware of that, hindsight twenty-twenty.

But I'd wanted to be alone.

He hadn't let me, of course, doing one better and actually trying to get me to come down. It'd been a very unusual situation, which triggered my thoughts about all this now. He'd taken the initiative here. Like he wanted to please me or something. Like this was a date.

Or something.

His lighthearted expression completely faltered at the sight of mine. He raised his hands. "Really, you won't offend me if we switch it up. And actually." He grabbed a menu off the greeter's podium. "I can show you what I ordered. If it doesn't sound appealing, we can get you something new in now."

Fuck me, if he didn't tug a smile out of me. He kept doing that, *tugging* and borderline poking. I'd come in kind of hot at him tonight, but he managed to stand his ground.

And even get a pizza date out of me.

This isn't a date.

No business did I have dating. Especially with a guy so obviously younger than me. I didn't consider myself one of those with an age bias, but I was in my thirties and most recently, a divorcee. Yes, I had no business dating.

I smiled. "It's fine."

"You're sure?" One of those thick eyebrows arched. "Seriously, it's no problem. You don't like what I picked, we can get that shit out of here."

Laughter, like full blown laughter and right in front of him.

"Good laughter?" he questioned, angling into me, and that quieted me down a little. In fact, all but canceled in my throat when he gazed down at me. A soft dance hit his tawny brown eyes. "I'm not joking, Brielle. We can change it. No big."

"Bri," I said, my throat constricting a little. *What the hell?* "Only my mother calls me Brielle when I'm being a jerk."

As well as colleagues and people I didn't know, of course, which was why I'd introduced myself that way.

The dance of Ramses's eyes touched his lips at that point, his head lowering in acknowledgment.

"Bri it is then." He winked. Really, so cocky. Yet, whatever this was he passed off I was apparently completely here for.

Ramses returned the menu to the greeter, a twenty-some-thing college guy, no doubt, with a stain on his apron and what appeared to be flour on his cheek. This place Ramses took us to was a complete and total dive, fully equipped with shoddy lighting and enough decals on the walls to act as a second coat of paint, and looking around the room, there was absolutely no one over the age of thirty.

Well, except for me.

I wondered if Ramses knew, not that he'd probably address such a thing. Despite his confidence, he appeared to be a gentleman, and I noticed he hadn't brought up the whole me up on the high dive thing again. That might be for lack of time.

What have I gotten myself into?

How had I arrived here, in this place with a younger man? I was headed quick toward the wrong side of thirty, and though he may be in his late twenties, that still pushed almost a decade between us.

His hand hovering behind my back to guide me, this didn't seem to matter to him. The greeter told us to sit where we wanted, and Ramses took the full initiative, seating us toward the back and away from the chaos of the foosball and billiard tables. Despite this place being a dive, it smelled good as hell.

My mouth instantly watered due to the yeasty smell of baking dough and hot cheese, and I slid my own wool coat off the moment we were in the booth. The thing was only slightly damp at this point, as I bared my shoulders and folded the garment.

I was tucking it away when I realized I wasn't alone and that the man I'd come with had his eyes well placed in my direction. He hadn't been shy about it either, his coat hovering for the briefest of seconds before he placed it down on the booth's seat. All too quickly, he had his attention back on me, and I was suddenly rather aware of my bare shoulders.

And my flushing breasts.

They warmed to a hot pink across the swell, but I forced

the fact out of my head, making my hands move. I took the measures to place my coat properly, and when I came back, of course, those observant eyes of his hadn't left. If anything, his more than direct stare intensified.

Arrogant indeed.

Again, I must have been here for this as well. Because not only did I allow it, I made no mention of it, my hands folded across the table. The greeter eventually found us again, taking our drink orders, but then, Ramses and I were right back to where we were, him *looking* at me and me, for some reason, letting him do it.

Were we playing a game?

I didn't know, ignoring the currently warm state of my tummy. It seemed the ballet dancer inside couldn't seem to sit her fanny down, and I breathed, passing off what he was doing to study the decals of the various bands on the walls. There was a sign that invited all patrons to place their stickers there, hence all the action on the dive's walls. It gave the place a delightful appeal, I suppose, youthful.

"You going to tell me who you are now then, Bri?" Ramses had his glass to his full lips, no straw. It appeared he wanted to save the sea turtles tonight, my cup empty as well. He swallowed down his Sprite before draping an arm across the back of the booth. "I have to say I'm curious."

Not much to me, I stayed silent, not giving in to his game.

His smile dashed coy. "Were you a wedding guest? I didn't see you tonight, but that doesn't mean you weren't there."

I could say the same about him. Though, how I'd missed him I had no idea. The man was huge, after all, towered over me and actually had to dip his head to make it inside this very restaurant. I touched my chin to the top of my hands, my fingers laced. "What gave it away?"

That observant gaze dragged over my body once more,

but I had to give it to him. He'd glossed completely over my pinked chest to find my eyes. "Just a guess. Were you?"

"Yes. I'm assuming you were as well."

"Also, yes." His fingers danced on the top of the booth. "Bride's side? Groom's?"

"Didn't make it to the ceremony actually." I cuffed my arms. "I was late. Snuck in right as dinner was being served."

He angled his head. "You sure you're not a wedding crasher?"

Definitely didn't have the time to do something like that. Maybe back when I was twenty. Laughter hit my arms, shaking my shoulders. "No. I was invited to the wedding, a plus one actually."

"So, was this plus one a date?" he asked, very obvious what he was doing there with his question. He grinned. "I notice you're not with that invited wedding guest now."

I wasn't. My smile more than wide, I pulled my water glass over. "*She* and I go way back, but she's just my friend. My mentor, actually."

I'd met Evelyn when she'd been an adjunct professor during my time at New York University. She'd been there only briefly, but in that time, she'd offered me so much support as one of her history students. Really, my love for history now had been because of her, and she was the reason why I was here as well. She'd been the first one I'd called when I found myself suddenly seeking work. *I hadn't worked* in a handful of years.

All of this new.

She'd been there for me just like she had back then, a mentor but now a friend. I smiled at the thought of her. "She and I go way back."

"So said friend, who you go way back with." Ramses paused, his fingers waving in the air. He touched his chin. "Who's also a she who you have no romantic interest in whatsoever…"

My God was he obvious. My hand framed my face. "Correct."

Another grin. "Brought you to Windsor House for the Prinze wedding, but now, you've somehow ended up with me."

I suppose I had, nodding. "She had to work unexpectedly today. Told me to go on ahead. She wanted me to meet people. I'm new in town. Came for a job."

"Well, you're definitely meeting people." He tilted his head. "Where are you from?"

"Jersey. Hoboken." I sat back as the greeter topped off my water, then Ramses's soda. I thanked him. "Just moved."

"That's a long way. You said you came for a job?"

"Yes, I'm a teacher. A professor actually. History."

This seemed to intrigue him. He opened his mouth. I assumed to know more, but the biggest pizza I'd probably ever seen was delivered to our table, effectively cutting us both off.

I mean, I'd seen some pretty big pizzas, being from the New York area, but when I mentioned size, I meant the sheer thickness of it. The thing was built like a layered cake, a hefty and girthy stacking of cheese and thick dough and on the top, a layer of marinara and spinach leaves.

"Oh my God."

"Just wait until you taste it," Ramses exclaimed, a wink to his eye before reaching into his wallet and giving a tip to the boy who'd brought it. "Thanks, Ty."

Ty, as he'd called him, unwrapped what was clearly a Benjamin, definitely more than this entire pizza. This seemed awful generous, even for a pizza of this size, but what was really crazy was this guy Ty didn't appear to be surprised by such an exorbitant gift. I mean, he looked grateful. The kid just got a hundred bucks, but he definitely didn't give off any type of surprise, his fist bumping Ramses's before he said he'd see him around. Ramses was clearly a local who may or may not definitely do that all the time.

I wondered what he did for a living.

Many questions about him, but not one of them surrounded how good this pizza probably was.

Borderline orgasmic, I waited anxiously while Ramses picked up the serrated spatula and served it. Thick and cheesy goodness pulled away from the pan when he served me, then himself. He sat back. "Ladies first. I want to see your reaction, Jersey girl."

Jersey girl, huh? I'd let him have that one, picking my fork up in front of this Midwestern boy.

Smirking, I tabled my excitement as I forked the pie hard just to get off a little piece. I had Ramses waiting with anticipation as I blew on the bite before sliding it into my mouth. It was still hot, but once in there, there was no hiding my moan.

"Jesus," I groaned, before taking another bite. There was no playing off how good this thing was and forget being lady-like. My eyes closed at another taste. "You weren't joking. *My God.*"

This obviously pleased him, my delight. He got another wink in before he tasted his himself, and when the *fuck* left his lips, we both laughed.

He raised his hand. "Sorry. I've missed this, and it's been a while."

He had nothing to apologize for, wanting to curse myself. Before I knew it, half my piece was gone and Ramses was already starting in on his second slice. Of course, he asked if I wanted dibs first before going back in, but since I was still tackling my initial slice, I let him have at it. It'd been really nice he'd asked, though, considerate. It seemed I was finding a common trend here about him, my Midwestern knight in shining armor. How ready he'd been to come up on that high dive and talk to me. It'd really annoyed me. I'd wanted to be alone.

And yet here we were.

Him and I, almost hard to fight my smile as I watched him eat and enjoy himself. He ate at his pizza like I indulged in chocolate on a particularly angry month of PMS. I dabbed my lips with a napkin. My lipstick should hold up pretty good since I used a strong matte. "You said it's been a while since you had this?"

If I lived here, I'd eat this all the time, my hips be damned. It'd be well worth an extended run in the morning. I tried to get a few miles in a day.

"Uh, yeah." He'd devoured his third at this point and maybe enough as he sat back. The space between his buttons exposed that glorious chest of his, and I couldn't help but envision what his shirt might look like off. He clearly worked out, that dress shirt leaving nothing to the imagination of his solid arms and thick shoulders.

Easing back, he adjusted in a booth meant for normal-sized humans, not someone such as himself with a wingspan that no doubt put Michael Phelps to shame. He smiled. "And I hope I didn't disgust you. I basically just violated that thing in front of you."

I snorted, like actually snorted in front of him, which I passed off when I took a drink of water. To save myself further, I covered my lips with a napkin, but the fact Ramses noticed wasn't lost on me.

"Cute," he said simply, like it was simple. Simple for him to say.

My face most assuredly hiked up in the same coloring as my chest earlier.

Completely crazy, I passed that off too, *shy* in front of this guy like I was a young girl in front of a boy. My mouth moved a little. "So, you were at the wedding, too. Bride or groom's side?"

Evasion the easiest thing instead of paying attention to my heated cheeks, or other things that tingled and woke up just at a mere flash of that dashing grin or a wink of his brown eyes. This guy was as readily charming as he was handsome, dangerous. I didn't trust myself with handsome. I didn't trust myself with charming. Both made a girl stupid and turn a blind eye to things she probably shouldn't.

At least, when it came to me.

"I was in the bridal party actually," Ramses stated, which explained his suit. It'd been similar to the groom's when I'd seen his. Soft laughter hit his chest as he laced his fingers across it. "I was the man of honor." He opened his hands. "So, I guess I was there for the bride."

Shock silenced me, surprise more than anything else. I suppose that was becoming more and more common, though. A woman choosing a man as her lead attendant. I grinned. "You two must be close. You and the bride?"

His fingers formed around his glass. "I suppose you could say that."

She'd been lovely, the bride. Well, what I'd seen of her. I'd been sitting in the back of a room filled with at least five hundred people, the reception completely luxurious.

It'd even snowed.

Like inside, *snow*. It hadn't been real, of course, more a lighting affect than actual flakes. Those had been there too. I recalled brushing them off in the bathroom. "How long have you two known each other?"

"Since high school." I noticed it took him a moment, his index finger weaving along the condensation of his glass. Eventually, his eyes lifted in my direction. "She was, uh, the first girl I ever really loved if you can believe that."

Choke, like a legitimate choke since I'd taken a drink. Had I heard him, correctly? I patted my chest. "You're serious?"

Yeah, nothing funny about what he'd said there, his finger scratching the side of his neck. "As a heart attack."

Wow.

Super intrigued now, I leaned forward. "Alright."

"I mean, it was a long time ago, but yeah." His chuckle a bit dry on the end there, he sat back, his hands tucked under his arms. "It's there. A history there."

Well, hell. My lips parted. "And that's alright? I mean, the groom was okay with that?"

Obviously, since the pair exchanged nuptials and Ramses had said this was in the past, but still.

Legitimate humor touched his eyes now. He angled his head back and forth. "Prinze, her husband, and I have a history too. And it was *rough* back then when it was all going down. Not going to lie."

"And now?"

"He *tolerates* me." Light returned to his eyes, and I was glad for it. I found I didn't quite like him too serious. If anything, I appreciated how laid-back he was, not so easy for most people, me. His head tilted. "He's definitely softened to me over the years, though. We aren't best bros or anything, but we're far from the days of him wanting to kick my ass."

"My God, had it gotten that bad?"

"We may or may not have thrown down in the hallway in high school."

Jesus, I thought, but he grinned.

"But like I said, that's in the past." He pushed his glass away. "*Obviously.* They got married, and that makes me happy since she is. Prinze is good to her, *there for her*. He loves her, and how could I want anything other than that for her? She deserves that."

How very mature of him. Even still, I could imagine that would be hard. "Are you happy?"

Maybe a too personal question, and definitely one I had no right to ask.

I lifted a hand. "I'm sorry."

"Don't be." But I noticed he wouldn't allow me to go away, pinning me to the creaky booth where I sat with his gaze. That easy grin returned to his lips, his fingers pushing away those brown curls. "But you can't ask me that without giving me some of your dirty laundry."

Well, would you look at him? Thinking, he could go there with me. I tapped my glass with my nail. "You're being cocky again."

"Am I?" And when his fingers eased against mine, my breath stalled, my tummy tight. A flourish of heat ghosted over my knuckles when he touched them, his boyish expression teasing once again. "How about this?"

How about this, his thumb brushing the center of my palm. It was such a subtle touch but drenched my entire core in hot lava. I felt like I flooded my panties.

What the hell?

Absolute panic on my end, and a man of his age definitely shouldn't have this much game. "How old are you?"

It was like I needed to know, that it mattered for some reason. Like this was anything other than just a shared pizza between two strangers.

"How old are you, Bri?" His cockiness showed once again. "Only fair if you tell me too."

Only fair, but since I wasn't going to admit that, I stayed silent.

He got me, goddamn him, his chuckle light when he sat back. I noticed he didn't let go of my hand, his lengthy digits still playing across my knuckles. "I'm in my twenties, if that matters."

"Well, I'm in my thirties." I shrugged. "If *that* matters."

"It doesn't." No lie in his eyes, and when he leaned forward, that entire hard chest of his hit the table. At least, it appeared to be hard.

God, did I want to touch it.

I wanted *him* to touch me. What the hell? "And I'm divorced."

"Doesn't matter." His smile slow on his lips. "You're not married now?"

"No."

His nod touched the air, his hair a perfect wave of ebony dark curls. "Can I ask you something else?"

In that moment, I felt like he could ask me anything short of spreading out on the table for him, completely not me. Again. What. The. Hell? "Depends on what it is."

He played with my fingers as he looped them together, forcing my palm to face the light. He drew soft circles over my flesh, like he was trying to read my palm but simply teasing me instead. "Would you tell me why you were going to jump tonight?"

I froze, and where I might have pulled away, I only breathed harder. "I never said I was going to jump."

He threaded our fingers, completely taking my hand. He tugged me closer, and I tasted his air, tasted *him*, a hot combination of male and confidence. Both of which he exuded in spades. He swallowed. "I never said I wasn't happy."

I hadn't assumed he wasn't. But maybe, he wasn't.

And maybe I was going to jump.

Maybe I wasn't happy either, two not happy people together. Maybe I'd been at the wedding tonight when I didn't want to be, and maybe he was forced to stand idle while another man married his first love. Maybe we were both two freaking losers and who were *being losers* together.

"Want to get out of here?" I asked, my breath heavy. I didn't know what the fuck I was doing. I didn't do this, *anything* like this.

"That depends," he stated, dampening his lips. It was quite possibly the most erotic thing I'd ever seen, and hell, if I could explain that. He looked up at me. "What are the odds that you'll be there too?"

Quite high. "I wanted to jump tonight." Crazy I was admitting this, admitting to a stranger, *this*. I nodded. "I was sad."

And confused, confused why the sheer happiness of the

evening tonight would make me want to do such a thing. That someone else's happiness would physically pain me. It didn't make sense and sounded almost *cruel*. Like I was evil.

Like I was petty.

I expected him to let go, but he didn't. If anything, he held me closer. His fingers wrapped around my wrist again, his throat jumping. "I'm less happy than I am something else," he admitted too, nodding too. "Most days something else."

We were the same, both of us but in different ways. My head bobbed twice in acknowledgment. "It doesn't have to be that way tonight. You could be more happy than something else."

Who was this person? Certainly not me. I mean, I was basically propositioning this complete stranger for sex, his smile soft. Taking my hand, he used my finger to pull down an entire strand of my dark hair.

"And maybe you don't have to jump," he stated, but then a shrug. "Or maybe I could jump. Jump with you? What do you say, Jersey girl?"

I wouldn't make him, of course. But something told me no one could *make* this guy do anything. He had a lot of his own control, his dedication to his friend told me that. He'd stood back once upon a time, allowed someone else to come in who he knew would love her. It told me so much about the control he had over his life as well as something else.

This Midwestern boy's heart.

CHAPTER
FIVE

Ramses

I should ask her last name.

But before I could manage the thought, things were moving too fast and I was taking her home.

Why the fuck was I taking this woman home?

Why had I revealed shit I barely acknowledged myself? Things about my past and who I was? The night started as me trying to save her from... whatever this shit was she was dealing with, and now, she was doing the same for me. This was fucked up.

Right?

My thoughts couldn't help but say yes, and that was opportunist as fuck. I wasn't this guy. I didn't take women home. Well, I took *women home* but not like this and not under certain situations like this. They also definitely weren't anyone remotely close to Brielle. I'd been with a handful of older women before but...

No, they weren't like her. They didn't *feel* like her if that made sense, and I most definitely didn't play out all my shit in front of them like I needed some kind of therapy. I mean, what the hell had I sounded like tonight? I sounded needy, like I needed her.

I hadn't even talked to December about all this.

True, I never aired out all my dirty laundry to my friend, made easier in the past with all the land mass between us. I told her things from time to time but nothing heavy, and I most certainly wasn't a "sharer." I wasn't scared of my feelings or anything, but I wasn't one to sink into them either. I was pretty laid-back. I simply dealt with stuff as it came up.

Or in this case not.

I tried to tell myself this was a different situation with Bri. That I wasn't running once again and not dealing. That I was taking this woman home because we both wanted that. Hell, she'd been eye-fucking me over a deep-dish pizza as bad as I'd been her. I mean, it had to be pathetic the way I was looking at her half the night, her tits perfect and crimson the way the swell flushed above the top of her black dress. She was all woman from the smoky tone of her banter and even to the way she told me off tonight. It'd even turned me the fuck on.

Who was I right now? Really?

Certainly not this guy, but my keys in my hand and the other on her back, we were getting in my car and moving most certainly too fast. It was like I had blinders on when it came to this woman, under her spell, like prey to her. The only one I felt getting played was her since I was allowing this shit to happen. I needed to be the responsible one, *the guy* and analyzing all the cues of the situation.

A ready and willing (but most important of all *sober*) woman?

Check.

A hot-blooded male?

Fucking hell. Check.

Two damage souls with clear avoidance issues?

That was where shit got sticky. That was also where things got a little unethical. True, I was avoiding my own trivial shit, but I was well aware of my own issues. I hadn't even grazed the surface of hers, though. What if she was dealing with something? Truly dealing with something, and here I was letting her use this, us, to not deal with it? This was starting to travel into asshole territory, and I wasn't that guy no matter how much she physically called to me.

Which was a hell of a fucking lot.

This woman was a goddess, point blank, and I had no problem worshipping every inch of her for as long as she'd physically allow me. I wanted her like I wanted my hands and dick to do the very job, but I was straddling a line of uncertainty here.

Bri let me take her home this evening. Different since she hadn't even wanted to get in the car with me when the night began. She didn't know me, so I hadn't been offended. Now, we were both behind the dash with her hand on my leg and mine at her nape, playing with her thick hair that smelled like bottled flowers. It filled up my damn car, and odds were, it would long after she got out.

Think about what you're doing.

I wasn't thinking. Being an asshole who thought more about his cock and avoiding his own feelings. I was getting more than one thing out of this.

Maybe feelings were an issue for me.

Such a stereotype, right? And not the man my mother raised. She'd be looking at me with a major side-eye right now.

Hell, I was side-eyeing myself.

Turned out Bri lived on the north side of Maywood Heights. The drive was silent the majority of the ride outside of the easy listening hip hop beats I played. I was used to sitting with my own thoughts, so I preferred music that didn't drown them out. In tonight's case, the choice had been annoying, but I couldn't change it since it was already playing when she got in. That would have been weird, and in any sense, I found a fair amount of distraction with Brielle's hand simply on my thigh. She drifted rather close to my cock, which made my shit basically unbearable in my tight dress pants.

I squeezed her neck in front of her uptown complex, not the suburbs but upscale none the less. In fact, the city had been developing the subdivision more and more to attract more businessmen and women, as well as young professionals and my father's company, Mallick Enterprises, even had a few properties there. I knew because I'd asked to be sent all his newer projects as well as the ones in progress under my family's real estate and development company. I suppose they weren't my dad's properties *per se* but the ones his company managed and made decisions on while he was away. I guess this was all my cross to bear now, and I got to stare it in the face with this woman's hand near my cock.

A few stories raised high to the night's sky in a snow-encrusted evening. I took to underground parking, but I didn't turn off the car when we arrived, nor did I get out. I was still in debate here, hesitating, but Brielle wasn't. She gazed up at me expectantly, her cheeks incredibly flushed and her lips pouty. She wanted to be kissed, and she wanted me to do the job.

What the hell.

My only asshole thought before I did exactly what she wanted, testing that lipstick when I tugged her head back and devoured her.

Fuck.

Her tongue eased past her matte red lips, dueling with mine as I sought to bruise that very mouth beneath her lip stain. She'd probably look like she was stung by bees after this with the job I was doing on her, but I didn't fucking care. She grabbed for my cock, and I literally growled in her mouth, basically an over-eager teen as I ground into her hand.

She got every inch of me through my pants, reaching for my fly.

"Let's go upstairs," she moaned, my mouth probably looking the same after we were done. Especially since I wasn't quite sure that lipstick would hold up. She was no doubt marking me, and fuck if I didn't want to be marked. "I'm in 518 B."

Out of my fogging haze and back to reality, and I was right when I eased her mouth away. I'd smeared her lipstick but only just.

My thumb outlined the job I did, the soft red of her lower lip painting her sun-kissed skin. It was quite possibly the hottest shit I'd ever seen. This woman was incredibly sexy, and in more than one circle, that probably placed her completely out of my league. I mean, she was older, because of that, more experienced when it came to life and decision-making in general. Most certainly if the shoe had been on the other foot, had she'd been *me*, I was sure the responsible thing would have already been done. She'd be upstairs to 518 B.

I would have let her go.

So much debate in my hands, my chest and maybe even a little in my eyes too. I knew when Bri brushed her thumb across my eyebrow. It felt like fucking heaven, and I wanted to bite her flesh.

I did, goddamn me, teeth sinking into her palm. I sucked her skin, the taste akin to cherries, that juicy, that succulent. We both moaned in my running car and when she probed again, for me to come inside and for me to join her, I forced my mouth to let go of her.

I pulled her hand away, lacing our fingers. "Should we?" Should we do this? Should I *jump* with her? What a time for a conscience, right? I shook my head. "I mean, I don't want to do something you don't want to do."

Weak, I knew. Placing the ball in her court, for her to deny me and not the other way around. I suppose, in a way, it was a bit telling of our age difference. I didn't want to be the reason to shut this shit down, but it was the only way to clear my conscience from the possibility of a heavy guilt. I didn't want to take advantage of the situation. Take advantage of her.

I wet my lips. "There were a lot of emotions tonight."

A lot of *feelings* and I saw each of them play in that moment. They ghosted across her hooded eyes and smoked eyelashes, the soft glow of her highlighted cheeks and flushed skin. This woman was a work of art.

And she was pulling away from me.

She physically tugged free from my hand, grabbing her purse.

"Bri—"

"You know, if you don't want to do this, just say," she said, laying my shit bare when she whipped around. Her dark mane fell in a flourish over her rosy chest, the heat of before returning to her dark eyes. I hated to see it. See her like this. She shook her head. "Not whatever the hell this is."

She waved her hand, but I took it. Definitely not wanting to let her go and most certainly not like this. "Bri, we just... we said a lot tonight." Honest. It had been a lot. "I don't want you to do something you'll regret."

"Well, thanks for looking out for me," she snapped, once again, forcing her hand away. She got out, heeled pumps to the ground. "I hope you think about that while you're jerking yourself off tonight. I'm thirty-five years old, Ramses. I can handle myself."

"That's not what I—"

Door slammed in my face, cutting off my words. I watched her huff as she made her way to the elevator, her head thrown back as she shot inside it like a bullet.

I touched my head to the steering wheel, my car still running before I growled and peeled off to the closest parking space. I was definitely going to regret this. I definitely *shouldn't* give in to this. I'd been impulsive before. I'd been stupid before.

Pocketing my keys, I hit the same elevator punching the five once inside. I was amped the hell up. I didn't fucking care. I was going to chase this woman.

I just hoped she was ready to be goddamn chased.

CHAPTER
SIX

Bri

Man child, my only thought as I gobbled a glass of wine in a swallow. I downed that crap like a frat boy.

I mean, he said *no* to me.

I was embarrassed, on fire. I'd basically thrown myself at the guy when he had no interest in me.

He'd actually been trying to be nice about it.

I didn't want nice. I wanted savage and wanted someone to help me get out of my head. I wanted escape, to feel lack of control but on my terms. I wanted to be able to make the calls, the shots. I wanted the power.

For once.

I poured another glass as a fist hit the door, one then two swift knocks. No way in *hell* should my landlord be knocking at my door at such an hour, even if I had called earlier in the week about a slow-flushing toilet. This condo had been new when I rented it, the first tenant, but they were obviously working out the kinks still. This place was flawless outside of that hiccup, polished marble countertops, sleek hardwood floors, and fresh ivory paint. They'd even added an accent wall in a cool silver, making the place just as masculine as it was feminine, something I hadn't minded since I didn't fall into the stereotype of a woman in need to fill her life with pink and flowers. Nothing wrong with pink and flowers, but that was something I'd never been into.

Thump, thump, thump.

What the *hell*?

I chugged the last bit of my wine, ready to lay into someone's ass and failed to check the peephole before opening the door. I just opened it, ready to unleash the fiery gates of hell, but before I could the back of my neck was grasped and lips crashed down so hard on mine I drew blood.

I tasted *his* blood, Ramses's lips between my teeth and my lower lip clamped tight between his, a fluid exchange.

Oh my hell.

I gasped as he completely grabbed my face and shot into my condo, me in tow. His leather-gloved hands warmed my cheeks, his body hard and solid even through his wool coat. His face chilled from the cold, his lips hot as he tasted mine and I drew from his. He came back. Came after me.

And I flooded in my panties, my leg wrapped around him. He tugged it up, his hand up my thigh as he pressed my body to my ivory walls. He grasped and bit my lips, and I moaned, scratching at his back.

"That invitation still open?" he asked, his grin lazy before kissing me hard again. I growled, a shaking and quivering mess in his hands before he finally let go.

He placed a hand on the side of my face, then the other, standing there like a god in a three-piece suit. His coat open, he displayed all the goods, the entire expanse of his long body donned to the nines in harsh grays and handsome black. He oozed swagger like a seeping wound and was the very reason I never questioned how someone of his age had

managed to pick me up. I didn't consider myself a particularly hard lay, but I'd been hard on him. I pushed him.

He obviously pushed me back.

He tugged a glove off his hand with his teeth, his mouth
stained in red from my lipstick. He didn't have a lot, but he
had some, and regardless, I had a feeling his lips tingled with
natural red just as much as mine beneath the paint. Using that
naked thumb, he brushed a rough pad along my lower lip.

"Well?" he asked, basically rasping, groaning. He panted
like he'd run up here and maybe he had, or he hadn't. The
back of his knuckles ghosted my cheek. "Tell me you
want me."

Oh my God.

The quiver down to my knees, my swallow hard. Technically, I just mourned the loss of him. Well, not mourned per se
but basically. I was forcing myself to get over the fact that a
guy I probably neared a decade on turned me down, and I'd
been trying to handle said denial with a strong bottle of wine
—again. Apparently, I was a borderline alcoholic, wine my
default when I was feeling shitty in any situation.

My lips parted. "You came back."

"You let me." A smile that tipped his lips up, made him
boyish. Guiding my mouth up to his, he fused our lips
together again before ensnaring my hips and pressing a knee
between them. He'd had to deal with the gathering of my
dress, but I easily rubbed hard friction against his muscular
thigh. He groaned. "Fuck, I need you naked."

I needed *to be* naked. I needed to be out of this dress.

And the door was still open.

I wasn't quite at the point of voyeurism yet, even post-
divorce, and wanting the freedom of whatever this was. I
gripped the lapels of his coat, a stark black that hugged every
inch of his big body. "Give me a minute?"

He let go, but I didn't think by choice. He wavered a bit
before his forehead dropped to my bare shoulder. I'd taken

off my coat and shoes but nothing else. He warmed my neck with his mouth, borderline tonguing me. "How long?"

Good God.

My throat constricted as he peppered kisses dangerously close to the swell of my breasts. But with the strength of a thousand readied females, I forced distance between us when I grappled his shoulders. I held up two fingers. "Just two seconds."

I needed to get my shit together, my first legitimate one night stand.

And with a younger man.

Something about that excited me, that he desired me. I wasn't what one would be considered *busted,* but I was more modest and didn't do things like this. When I'd met my ex-husband, we'd been in college and he'd done all the work. I hadn't been easy, made him prove himself to me. In fact, looking back, I think I focused on all the wrong things, how good he'd been on paper and how motivated he'd been. He'd been hungry for his goals as much as I had to become a professor and hit every one of them.

Yes, yes, he'd done that.

That was the past, *behind* me. That wasn't now. That wasn't Ramses.

Ramses.

He kissed my fingers midair, looking like a hungry tiger when he licked, then sucked a polished digit completely into his mouth.

Holy shit.

The vision of him between my legs charged my bud (also between said thighs) on overdrive. I could probably charge a light bulb with it at the present, fuck.

"Two just," I laughed, *giggled* like a little girl. Oh God. I forced him back. "Just two. That's all I need."

This made him smile, laugh with the timber that hummed deep from within his chest. He pressed his hands to the wall again, staring down at me. "I think I've only two within me, Bri."

I had even less, my hair flicked when he slid a digit down it. He followed all the way down to the tip of the follicles, and my panties were basically drenched, but I managed to ease from beneath him.

I closed the front door.

"Just make yourself at home," I said, hearing him chuckle from the entryway. Along the way, I picked up my shoes and coat. I hadn't even bothered to put them away when I'd come in. I'd literally gone straight for the bottle but tucked them both in my closest when I made my way in.

Holy fuck.

I stared at the image in my vanity, hair mussed and lipstick smeared. I decided to rub the matte tone off, which took nothing short of a power sander considering it was virtually smear proof.

We'd been kissing rather hard.

Oh God, was this actually happening?

It was, and I was about to let this guy dick me down until I couldn't feel my legs anymore. I wanted him to. God, did I want him. I wrestled in my closest for something easier to get out of when I heard him chuckle again from somewhere in the condo.

"Uh, Bri?" he questioned, another deep laugh. "You don't have any furniture."

Shit.

I faced palmed myself, all my living room furniture still waiting on delivery. I'd bought it all from the furniture store, but it wasn't supposed to be delivered until next week. I basically only had what I'd come down from Jersey with, my car, my bedroom furniture, and a fraction of my personal items. I'd wanted to start over here, *start fresh.* I angled my head. "Sorry. I ordered it, but it hasn't come in yet."

Silence from the living room, another laugh. "Well, do you, uh… at least have a bed?"

I did have one of those, and when I reappeared, I noticed he'd dimmed the lights, the electric fireplace on. He'd obviously managed that and made do with my lack of furniture by lounging his big body on the floor. He'd been staring toward the hearth, his coat and dark shoes off. He had the shoes arranged neatly at the edge of the coat, which he spread out like a picnic blanket beneath him, his suit jacket off and folded beside that. The sleeves of his shirt rolled up and tie loose, he angled up on his knees to adjust the flame. Looking like a complete erotic vision.

Looking completely beautiful.

His hair waved in a tousle of angry curls over his eyes, the state he'd been in when he rushed to my door and made himself known to me again. When he'd taken what he wanted, when he'd given himself to me but only after I pushed him. Something told me this Ramses was a very good boy, and I never thought I'd be the one to turn him savage, *raw*, as that was completely not me.

"Brielle…"

His eyes on my *teddy*, a raven black as it fluttered over what he considered imperfections. My hips wide and tummy soft. I worked out, but there we just some things the Stairmaster, constant sit ups, and daily runs couldn't hide. There were things that held history, thighs that subtly weaved with not one, but several tiger stripes. I had stretch marks, most women did, and I was front of Ramses, literal perfection and probably would be well into his days. Guys, in general, were just built differently, age or not.

He angled up, as if in awe of me by the way he stared, but something told me, since I flashed him tits beneath this teddy, his focused attention had something to do with that. I pebbled tight, *diamond hard* especially in front of his more than observant gaze. His mouth parted. "Damn."

Good damn or bad damn? I'd ask him if I was bold enough, and really, did people *do* lingerie if they were causally sleeping together? The last time I'd dated and flirted, I was pretty sure Twitter didn't even exist.

I scratched bare toes behind my ankle, a nervous tick and something I couldn't hide. I shrugged. "Too much?"

Please don't say too much. Please don't make me feel embarrassed or judged. I already feel completely inferior in front of you.

It took a second for his response, and all the while I felt the pull of a slow retreat back to my bedroom. But then he shook his head, so slow.

"No," he said, *no* before waving his hand. "Come here. Come to me."

Come to him.

Okay.

I couldn't help but smile, some of that shyness fading away, he brought me down to my knees with him, and on just his hip, he still outdid me in height by like a foot. He was a really big boy, a big *man*.

He cradled my face as I came down, pushing my hair away. He eased me down to my back, a full hand between my breasts.

I sucked in a breath as he eased the teddy off one of my tits, warming my breast beneath a fisted hand. So Ramses was a breast man, noted.

"You're fucking perfect," he growled, my throat jumping. My thighs held a tremble but mostly due to surprise as his hand disappeared between them. I didn't consider myself particularly body conscious, but this was new, and he was, well, a stranger.

A stranger with beautiful eyes and a hungry mouth, his tongue gliding down my thigh as his finger hooked the lingerie over my sex. He teased me beneath the sheer lace, his eyes peeking up and his grin wicked. He blew hot breath over my pussy lips, his digit playing at the seam. "How do you taste, Brielle?"

He continued to play and tease, and I was up on the balls of my feet. I wanted to grab him. I wanted him to *do something* but all he did was allow his knuckle to graze my flesh. Eventually, he worked his way through, knuckling my clit with soft pressure but not long before he tugged away.

"Will you rock my shit?" he asked, pinching my nipple. He tongued my lower lips. "I have a feeling you will."

A guttural moan when he sucked my folds completely into his mouth, tonguing his way between them with reckless abandon. He latched onto my sex, disappearing completely between my thighs, and the comment I'd made about him being a breast man I completely tossed away.

Ramses seemed to have a taste for nothing but my buzzing flesh, devouring every gush and burst of my heat. I ached over his wool coat, my nails digging into his scalp, which only made him feast harder.

"Fuck," he growled, his hands completely on my thighs as he spread me wide. He brought both thighs over his shoulders, knotting my ankles behind his head. "I knew you'd taste fucking good."

I groaned, my ass up as he tore my panties. Like literally ripped them off and tossed them away. This gave him better access to my tiny curls, his teeth biting my mound before retreating back to my hot juices. I buzzed like an angry hive, a bee queen on a throne, and he made me feel that way, not allowing me to escape as he drew from my heat and his fingers bit into my flesh. I was going to come and *fast*. I wouldn't last.

"I'm going to come," I admitted, biting my lip. I tugged on my nipple, expediting the process, and noticing, Ramses pushed my hand away.

He pinned it underneath my butt, holding it with no escape.

"You only get to come from my mouth," he said, taking my other hand and doing the same. He lifted me up. "Only from me."

Oh. My. Hell.

Ramses was definitely a pussy guy, laving and working my charged sex. A hard suck, then a bite to my clit, and I flooded like a broken dam over his tongue, and the instant I had, he'd been readily aware.

His eyes hazed to a lazy hood, complete euphoria in his eyes as he groaned and his ministrations between my legs picked up. He drank from my body like a man dying of thirst, licking and sucking with great care. He didn't want to lose a drop, his mouth seeking mine before my bottom could even return to the coat.

He worked the teddy off my shoulders, guiding me to my front.

"On your knees," he coached, my body spent and my limbs lazy. I honestly didn't know if I had the strength, but he clearly had. He grabbed my hips, getting *me* in position. He removed the straps of my lingerie completely off my arms before pulling the whole thing over my ass.

The sheer lace pooled at the back of my knees, but he made quick work of that, guiding each leg out before I was completely naked with him behind me. I couldn't see him this way, completely vulnerable.

But he could definitely see me.

My sex buzzing again and *so soon* after he made me come, his thumbs spreading me apart before his hands squeezed and worked my ass cheeks. He breathed heat over those too, a feral husk to his breathing.

"You got a gorgeous ass, Bri," he said, actually biting it. He pulled the flesh deep into his mouth, and my sex charged again.

Oh my hell.

A deep chuckle sounded behind me, and I realized I said it

out loud this time, Ramses drawing back to his haunches. I knew because I peeked behind me, my legs shaking and weak, and especially, due to the position he had me in.

"Hell is right," he said, completely undoing his tie. It slid like a dark serpent beneath his collar, flipping it up and basically making him the poster boy for PornHub. Especially when he tossed it and began unfastening his shirt buttons. He revealed inch by glowing inch of golden skin, a dark trail dusting down to his abs before disappearing beneath his belt buckle. He worked the shirt off, exposing a muscled torso assaulted with fine definition, his pecs thick and immaculate, his shoulders big without being bulky. This definitely had something to do with his height, more narrow than anything else, but he was still firm and large.

Large… everything.

The outline of his cock lined his pants, something I'd already felt up in the car. My mouth watered as he hovered over me, leaving his pants on and grinding against my naked bottom. He gave me a tease of that massive force between his thighs, really *big*.

Oh my—

He guided me to touch him, *feel him* as he eased my hand back and rubbed himself over my palm. He undid his pants, let me inside and…

Oh my God.

I couldn't see him, but I could definitely feel him, fucking curious now, and what the fuck?

He really is big.

"This okay?" he asked, like he knew, like he maybe even dealt with this kind of reaction toward, um, himself. "I'll go slow."

"Okay." I swallowed, closing my eyes. "Can I see you?"

I wanted to, his hand slowing mine down on top of him. I'd considered my ex-husband moderately sized, and I'd only been with a couple of others but that'd been a while ago, back in college.

Ramses slowed his hand. He basically froze upon my request, both hands easing onto my naked hips. "You sure?"

The uncertainty in his voice made laugh, that was until I glanced back and saw him. More than one wrinkle worried his brow, like he was actually worried.

Oh, wow. Is he?

I had to say, his confidence definitely had slipped a little, his eyes on me as he guided himself out and pushed his trousers down his golden thighs. Dusted in dark hairs, the same tone dusted around his extended length.

"Oh, fuck."

I'd said it out loud. Though I hadn't meant to, and the worry that twisted his brow pinched his lips tight. He fisted a dick well longer than the size of his hand, which said something because Ramses had some pretty big hands. He was thick at the top, veiny at the sides and his balls hung heavy, weighted beneath it all. This man had the most glorious cock I'd possibly ever seen. But that had nothing to do with the size. He was just, in a word, perfect.

I hadn't spoken again soon enough.

I knew because he started to reach for his pants, like maybe I'd changed my mind and *again*, he'd expected it. I mean, I wouldn't lie and say I wasn't intimidated by all that, but I sure as fuck was game.

"Come over here," I told him, like he had me before. I pulled him to my lips, kissing him from behind. This appeared to be enough to charge him on because he guided me to my back and let me see him full on, him on top of me, large and solid as he hung over me. I felt like a mortal to his god, an unyielding force above me.

I drew my fingers down solid muscles, Ramses biting my lip again. My mouth filled with his metallic taste, and he hovered that big body over me, his cock hard as it pulsed my inner thigh.

"I'll go slow," he explained again, like he had to. He'd been about to take me from behind but obviously felt comfortable enough to let me see him full on.

And how crazy was that?

I'd felt inferior to him before, this beautiful man who appeared to have his own insecurities. Honestly, the realization floored me that he could feel in any way similar to the way I'd felt when we first began. That only proved to make me even hotter for him.

"Don't hold back," I urged, not wanting him to. "I told you I'm a big girl."

Apparently, a match for him, his laugh throaty when he worked his pants off those thick thighs. He had a condom in his dress pants, which he took and sheathed himself with.

"You've been warned." He smiled, kissing me deep into his coat. "It might hurt. It might hurt *a lot*."

Well, I must have been a masochist because not only did the prospect thrill me, but I pooled so hotly between my legs I questioned if I'd come before. He made me crazy, made me *feral*. I kissed him deep as he guided himself inside, and at just the tip, I borderline felt half full. He wasn't joking, my core stretching and laboring to adjust to his size. The pressure tugged hard at my walls, but even still, I didn't want him to go slow.

"Go."

He did, a hard thrust that ripped a cry through me, sharp pain that shot fire between my legs and made Ramses stop completely. He really stopped, right inside me, more than unease etched across his brow, but I tugged his hips.

"Fuck me," I ground out, jerking my hips forward to make him move his. As extra incentive, I locked my legs around him, pressing the balls of my feet into his muscular ass. "Come on. It's okay."

It was okay even though it did hurt. God, did it hurt, the muscles more than tight, but I wanted him to keep going, to know he didn't have to be gentle with me. *To listen* to me and trust what I had to say. I'd let him know if it was too much, and he needed to trust that I'd do that.

How curious, trust. This man didn't know me at all, but I was asking him for that. A chance I was taking here, too.

His stare intensified as he cradled my face and thrust into me so hard and so fast we both called out. Sweat beaded Ramses's brow as he dipped his head and sucked hard on my tits. He laved, suckling before tugging hard on my nipples, and it proved to be just the distraction to curl my toes.

I *burned* beneath him, my head falling back as he fucked me hard from above. I was along for this ride, and he was taking me with him, his ab muscles tightening with every thrust. His hard chest glistened with sweat, my core burning and aching from every thick slam and rock of his solid hips. He didn't take it easy on me, that was for sure. Kissing me hotly, he dueled our tongues together.

"Fucking fuck," he gritted, slamming his hands to the hardwood above his coat. This proved to be the stability he needed, his thighs slamming against the apex of mine, and each heated burn charged my flesh to my simmering blood. He rocked me to my bones, my hands gripping his forearms just to hold on. "Fuck, Bri. Fuck."

More expletives, from *both of us*, my eyes rolling back and my fingers digging into his back. Between that and my nails embedded into his tough flesh, he roared above me, jerking my head back before taking my lip between his teeth. I instantly tasted blood again, the pair of us losing our minds.

"What are you fucking doing to me?" he grunted, looking right at me as he fucked me into his coat. "Goddamn."

He pushed my hair out of my face, really looking at me while he did this. Like he was trying to see something in me, find me before closing his eyes and covering my mouth with his. It was the most intimate thing he could have ever done and possibly the most intimate thing *I'd* ever done. I'd never made love with my eyes completely open like that nor had a guy done that with me.

This Ramses didn't seem like any other guy, my eyes closing as I lost myself beneath him. His labored thrusts ached forcefully between my legs, so good, so *perfect*, and the minute he came, I felt it.

I'd been right there with him, my walls expanding and contracting as his dick twitched and filled the condom between us. He spasmed hard between my legs, my heated juices flooding around him. I was covered in sweat myself and reeked of charged sex. Both of us did, Ramses's scent a thick combination of male, aftershave, and whatever ocean breeze notes he used in his hair.

His dark waves hung in a curled veil over his eyes, sticking to his brow and mine. He lay me down and kissed me while still inside me, the pair of us burrowing into his coat.

"So, *do you* have a bed?" he laughed, making me laugh. I suppose I hadn't answered him, coming right out and all that. Caging my face, he kissed me over to my ear, and I nodded, letting him know I did. I felt him smile against my ear, and more laughter touched the shell before he buried his face in my neck.

"Good," he said, his teeth pinching my radiating flesh. He grinned. "I'm not quite sure we'll leave it. At least, not tonight."

His hand slid between my legs, a promise as he guided himself out only to pinch me there, pinch me hot. Apparently, something else I needed to know about Ramses surrounded his stamina, his finger entering me to the knuckle. His used his right hand, the finger he wore a ring on. I'd noticed it when we had pizza, a dark silver with an animal on the front.

He used it now to pleasure me, angry like the animal had

been on the ring. I think it'd been a gorilla, its presence in my body tight within my already spasming walls. He used that ring to get me there again, and I wasn't sure I'd survive this night with him…

But I had a feeling the sex may be only partly the reason.

CHAPTER
SEVEN

Ramses

Disorientation occurred first. Realization of my feet hanging off the end of a bed only a fraction of my size? Hard second. My third thought surrounded the recollection of sex.

Lots and *lots* of sex.

Oh, yeah. Right. That.

The smile pulled lazily at my lips, my fingertips grazing the hardwood floor. My face lodged in a pillow, my nostrils filled with the most glorious scent, bottled fucking flowers.

My smile attempted to widen, but I frowned—hard—at finding the bed consisting of nothing but me, my hand empty of hips and/or Bri's ridiculously beautiful ass. The woman had a great ass, and I'd brought us in here around 4 AM. I planned to drive back to campus today, an almost two-hour drive. Classes hadn't started yet, but I'd been finding I stayed there more often than not as the date crept closer. In any sense, I hadn't been trying to make that drive stiff as a board. I had a feeling Bri might have thanked me too for taking us in here this morning. A crick in the neck was a son of a bitch.

Fuck, had you really slept with her?

Lots and lots of times, yes, and shit, had she been a trooper. Ramses, erm, um, 2.0 *below* hadn't even freaked her out last night. I'd hurt her. Well aware of that, but she'd been game and most importantly, there for it. I hadn't been able to shy her away. Go figure.

Fuuuck, what are you doing?

Emotions obviously filled the evening last night. I caught the woman trying to attempt to jump off the high dive with a bottle of wine. Then she *got me* to admit some fucking feelings I hadn't wanted to admit. Add that to the fact that I'd turned her down, came right back to her, and the two of us fucked each other's brains out until we both forgot about the reasons we'd entered into whatever this was together?

Yeah, completely and epically fucked, and don't even get me started on the fact that *this scenario*, i.e. her and me, hinted at shit I really wasn't trying to deal with.

Don't even go there. Don't.

One of the first things I'd asked Brielle, one of the first things I needed to know, she'd cleared up over a pizza, and that right there put my mind at ease in regards to that latter bit at least. She had no reason to lie to me, a stranger.

This isn't like what happened before.

It wasn't, in so many ways. For starters, last night had just been easy. It'd been hella tense too. Don't get me wrong there, but it'd been casual and when we did get together, come back to her place, even more casual. We were just in sync or something.

Like I said, easy.

I angled my face toward the door at the sound of a clatter but smirked at the sight hanging on said door. She had my entire suit hung, and it appeared to be crisp and pressed next to her vanity mirror. I wouldn't put it past her if she'd ironed it.

Getting up, her comforter cinched at my waist in a fist, I ran a thumb across the skinny tie.

Yup, she'd pressed it.

This woman and her control, this woman and her *clanking*. Creaking open the door, the metallic tune of pots and pans reverberated from somewhere in her condo and gave me a little indicator as to what she was doing.

As well as the bacon.

Fucking heaven, this woman was actually making me breakfast. I couldn't remember the last time a girl had done that for me. I was usually the one in the kitchen, lots of practice helping my mom out. Especially after her divorce from my father. She'd served him papers right before he went into the clink, but that didn't mean it'd been easy for her.

I felt like I was coming home from college every other month to help her out, making her breakfast. I stopped coming when it started to be the other way around, her making me breakfast, and probably the last time a woman ever did that for me. Actually, that was probably also the last time I had a woman press and handle my laundry for me.

And my boxers.

Jesus, Bri.

She had them right there, folded and perfect on her vanity table. My wallet and wrist watch also beside it, she had all the shit I'd taken off before bed perfectly aligned.

Laughing, I slid the watch over my Court ring and to my wrist, clasping it before picking up my phone—also there. That was arranged on top of my boxers. This Bri was something else, and I had to say, getting her out of what was clearly her anal comfort zone would be fun. Had been fun. I liked to push her, make her laugh and smile when that seemed difficult for her. It'd only made it better for me since it had been hard to get her to break down a little.

I slipped my boxers on, and my next move had been to go out to her until my phone buzzed.

A text from December flashed on the screen, completely killing my vibe. Of course, the fact it did completely radiated the guilt. I obviously cared about my friend, but I'd just gotten out of my head and hadn't really been trying to go back to that place. Not when I'd just gotten out.

You're fine. You're good.

And I was still her right-hand man, technically. I didn't know if the official man of honor duties stopped just because the wedding was over, so it'd look really bad if I just ignored her now.

Only that made me swipe, look at my device. I started to read the screen until my phone buzzed again and her entire face flashed on the front.

Shit, is she really calling me right now?

She was. She was calling me here and now when she was supposed to be doing only God knew what with her husband. God definitely knew and I did too.

Chriiist.

I answered. Like ripping off a Band-Aid, I answered because I always did. I was always there for her.

The wedding had just given me an excuse.

Scrubbing into my hair, I let my head fall against the wall. "What's up?"

A laugh on her end. A laugh because she didn't know. I mean, I was her friend. Always answered for her so why should this morning be any different?

"What's up?" A curious tone to her voice before a light chuckle. "Who pissed in your Cheerios? No good morning? What the fuck?"

"Good morning." I tried to keep the growl out of my voice, the frustration not warranted. Because she didn't know. Because I wouldn't let her know.

Just call me Sergeant Pushover.

I opened my eyes. "Sorry. What's going on? Just surprised to hear from you."

She did just get married last night, and her husband in the background growling let me know that. How was it possible to hear a scowl over a line? Well, Royal Prinze managed it.

"It's Ramses, babe," I heard her say, and before I knew it, her protest rang and his stick-in-the-mud voice drummed into the phone.

"Mallick," he said, his chuckle dark but there. "These calls going to keep up when I'm on my honeymoon with my *wife.*"

My eyes lifted toward the heavens, my foot propped against the wall when I tucked a hand under my pit. "She called me, bro."

"Did she?" A pause. "Did you?"

She obviously hadn't told him, and when another, "*Babe,*" sounded into the line, I rolled my eyes again. Royal Prinze could be a possessive motherfucker. Warranted or not.

Another barked laugh. "Well, would you look at that."

"Yeah." And I really didn't have time for this. Not now. "What's going on? Why did she call?"

"Don't know. Let me ask."

He started to when another voice sounded behind me effectively causing me to push off the wall. It was like a knee jerk reaction and surprised the hell out of me, how incredibly aware I already was to her.

Her voice.

"Ramses, you up?"

And then Bri's fingers, petite when they curled around the door. She pushed her face and shoulders through as well, and I almost damn near dropped the phone where I stood at the sight of bare shoulders.

Smooth, buttery, the tops peeked above her silk robe, completely exposing her neck and a place I spent a fair amount of time on last night. I'd tasted every inch of this woman in the past few hours. Pussy was like my favorite fucking thing, but I'd spent more time buried in this woman's neck than anything else. In her hair and that sea of raven black I was pretty sure existed just to completely tease my shit. She had it all up and wild-like this morning, a face fresh and clear and clean of any make up. She was, in a word, gorgeous, and that beauty mark above her lip only put my focus more on her mouth. She held a perfect pout to that cupid's bow, incredibly sexy and knowing just a tug of her belt graced me more than a flash of her mouthwatering tits...

Phone hanging from my fingers at this point, voices I knew were either Prinze's or December's chattering in the air. I had no idea if he was still asking her about what she wanted or what, but rather than find out, I turned off the phone, placing it on the vanity table.

I hadn't even thought about it.

Instead, I tugged Brielle in the room, summoning her smokey laugh and basically triggering the urge to blow my load in my boxers.

"What are you doing in here, Midwestern boy?" she crooned, clearly missing the fact I'd been on a call seconds ago when she dropped her arms across my shoulders. And also, we both had nicknames now? Cute. "I'm trying to make you breakfast."

So fucking hot, my hands undoing her robe. I didn't stop until I placed my hands on her bare hips. She was completely naked under this thing. Goddamn.

"I heard," I said, dropping to my knees. I smelled her sex before my kneecaps even hit the floor, her perfect pussy untamed besides a slight shaping to her tiny curls. I wasn't really big on women doing too much work down there. I liked it all, liked it natural.

I placed a hand between her legs, touching a kiss to her mound which effectively got me a quiver to her honey-toned thighs. This woman did taste like honey *everywhere*. "God, if I can't stop tasting you."

And God, if she didn't want me anywhere else. Her legs easily parting for my fingers and lips. Her fingers buried into my scalp and the mess of curls I had lazily dragging over my brows. I'd let them get too long over the summer. A nightmare to tame even on the days I had patience for it. I was about ninety percent sure I had a halo of them over my head, but Bri didn't seem to mind them, and really, I did nearly blow my load when she tugged me back by them to look up at her.

"You're being bad," she said, and without warning, threw a thigh over my shoulder. Her clit glistened in front of me, completely drenched, but when I growled in for a taste, she held me away from her. She was teasing me, being bad herself. "I told you. I'm trying to cook for you."

Yeah, she definitely liked control. But as I was a fan of that too, I eased her leg off my shoulder, spreading her wide. I had all I needed to eat right here.

I fucking showed her, latching onto her like a man deprived. She cursed above me, still fighting me when she added a hand to my scalp. She yanked—hard—at my curls, but my only response was to roar, pining her thighs down and sucking her lower lips into my mouth.

"Fuck, Ramses."

The sound of her giving in, *giving in to me*, and what a glorious one it was.

Her nails dug deep into my scalp now, guiding me on to the task as she rocked her hips in the direction of my tongue. This was still her trying to take control, and I gathered the back of her thighs, slowing down her ministrations.

"Slow down, Jersey girl." She was going to enjoy this, and she was going to let me give it to her. I blew heat over her sex. "*Slow*, let me have this."

I didn't know if she'd listen. So stubborn, so imagine my surprise when the tension left her legs and her back eased against the wall. I stared up, and she had a tit out, perfectly beaded and hanging heavy above me.

I fisted it, guiding her clit into my mouth as I made her

ride my face. I grabbed her ass, flesh hot and pinched between the spaces of my fingers.

"Oh, hell," she gasped. "I'm going to come."

Hell indeed, and I was going to get her there, Bri on the tips of her perfect little toes. There wasn't much about this woman that wasn't.

She gushed into my mouth like a river, crushing through brick walls as she came. I hoovered in every drop, and she let me, to her mouth in the next second when I trapped her against the wall and made her taste herself.

Her moan between my biceps jerked my cock, the girth probing above her tummy. The fact I completely dwarfed this girl turned me the hell on like nothing else, but even cradling her face, I couldn't deny a buzz sounding from within the room. My phone was ringing.

It probably hadn't stopped.

I didn't think Bri noticed since I'd been distracting her. Not on purpose, and honestly, she'd distracted me too. It hadn't been until I made her come and had her juices in my mouth I'd been pulled back into reality.

Out of the corner of my eye, my phone dimmed, silent, but I clearly knew who it'd been. I also knew I was still technically December's man of honor and she obviously needed me for something.

"Mmm. Breakfast now?" Bri asked, knotting her arms around my waist. "Or are you still hungry?"

I definitely was, but when the phone buzzed once more, I realized I had to handle some business first.

My knuckles grazed Bri's cheek. The phone fell into silence for the third or fourth time, who knew, and when she hadn't noticed, I felt like an ass. She was completely in this moment where I'd allowed my thoughts to run off. But the sooner I handled whatever this call was, I could come right back to her. I could be here *with her* completely.

I kissed her knuckles. "Mind if I, uh, head to the bathroom first?" I smiled. "That is, if you have one of those."

I was joking because of the lack of furniture she had in her living room, and she obviously had a bathroom, so what I said didn't make any sense at all. But I liked that she played along when she shoved me. I liked her playful side completely.

"You really are naughty." Her head shook, and all those delicious waves of jet black cut across her clean face. Before she left, she captured a hand behind my ass. She was an ass woman, noted. A gentle squeeze before she slapped it. "It's down the hall. Kitchen the same. Follow the sounds."

Before I let her leave, I got her mouth, planning to make quick work of whatever this was with Prinze and December so I could get back to her.

Back to this.

Bri

Ramses took a long time. In fact, so long I went down the hall just to check on him. He was obviously fine, but typically men didn't take as long as women when it came to getting themselves together in the morning. I heard the shower running when I arrived at the door and almost knocked to ask if he needed anything. I'd actually left towels in there for him. Being proactive and all that. I assumed he might want a shower later, and I guess I was being a little bit anal retentive.

I stopped at the sound of voices.

Just his, but he was talking to someone. I heard one name, *December*, but it'd been enough for me to step back since I recognized it. I read it on menus when I arrived at the reception last night.

His friend.

His friend who'd just gotten married. His friend who *he'd admitted* being in love with back in high school. His friend who (again, just got married) he secretly spoke to behind my bathroom walls...

With shower on.

All right then.

I didn't consider myself one of those women who jumped to conclusions. I was reasonable, but that most certainly didn't make me blind. Especially when it came to some of the conversations we'd had last night. The reason we came together in the first place and fucked basically like animals last night. I'd been hurting, yes.

But he had been too.

He said he was less happy than something else, i.e. *hurting*.

Gliding away from the door, I left Ramses to it, that conversation and whatever that was not my business. That was his friend, not mine, and I didn't know the dynamics of their relationship. Him talking to her the day after her wedding might have been perfectly okay. And possibly was on her end.

She wasn't in love with him.

He said he had loved her. Had.

Easing a breath, I tabled all unreasonable thoughts and returned to the gravy. I had it set to slow burn, the biscuits I'd made to go with it off to the side. I'd had to make do with what I had in the condo today. I didn't go to the store a lot, usually had someone deliver.

I turned the burner off in thought, then placed my hands on granite counters tops, trying really freaking hard to convince myself the guy who'd gone down on me just this morning (and hell, had he been good at that) wasn't still in love with his high school crush—a married woman.

Ramses...

Like a summon through the air, extended limbs hung

heavily around my waist, hitching me back toward a solid chest. My feet actually escaped the floor a little.

"I could get used to you standing around in an empty kitchen saying my name." His teeth pinched my earlobe into his mouth, his body moist and thick with heat. He didn't have a shirt on.

Christ in heaven.

He also smelled like my body wash and rather harshly of male, his limbs so long he'd not only been able to pull his arms completely around me but lock his hands on his biceps above my hips. He backed me up, completely hard in his boxers, trousers, or whatever he wore behind me. He chuckled. "You summoned?"

I hadn't meant to say his name out loud, but now that he was here, I found myself hard-pressed not to want his arms around me, not to want him. He made me feel so good, something he knew as his hands slid down my thighs.

"Bri?"

Wake up, be present. Be in the now and unfortunately, I wasn't so good at listening to myself.

Getting a firm hold, I unlocked his arms from around me, then went stupid a little at the sight of him, a well over six-foot-five male in nothing but his trousers and feet bare on my kitchen tiles. His abs pulled solid and ridged under his tanned skin, his curls wet and sweeping above his dark eyebrows. He wasn't one of those guys who had curly hair and didn't know what to do with it. No, he made it work for him, his quirky waves clipped a little shorter on the sides and with the natural sweep, glided out in a perfectly barbered sway across his brow. This guy was incredibly handsome, his body immaculate, but I think what appealed the most about him was he didn't take every opportunity he could to flaunt the way he looked. I mean, obviously he knew he was good-looking, took pride in his appearance, and though he flashed me that cockiness from time to time, I noticed he leaned harder into his sense of humor and charm. He had charisma, liked to smile.

Liked to make me smile.

He reached for my hands, making me dance in my kitchen. He made it easy to forget what I stumbled upon finding him doing, making a call and clearly keeping it from me.

"You said food?" He locked his junk against me, freaking hell, and how I really shouldn't be considering tossing breakfast off to the side and allowing him to give me a morning fuck on my granite countertops. I was ridiculously sore, and considering I hadn't had sex since my divorce a year ago, I needed to give the space between my legs a rest.

Try telling her that, my inner walls actually vibrating at the prospect. I let him kiss me once before the rumble I audibly heard emanating from beneath his tight abs got us both to come to our senses and laugh a little. I was hungry too and decided to serve him first.

Getting things together around the kitchen, I found myself hard-pressed to do the job, Ramses pinching at my robe whenever I placed something to eat or drink in front of him. Eventually, I managed to fill his plate and his teasing definitely lightened the mood on my end.

"You sleep okay?" he asked me, funneling biscuits and gravy into his mouth like a vacuum. Really, to be young and able to do that.

Oh, don't do that.

Okay, so he was young, *his twenties* but being twenty-six or whatever he probably was really wasn't that big of a deal. It wasn't like I was forty, fifty, or more, and even if I was, so what? My prerogative, and in any sense, I was getting ahead of myself. We'd only slept together, all this casual.

I gave him his second helping before reaching for a plate to make mine. "Good, you?"

"Have you slept in your bed?" A wink before he devoured more food. "Slept *with you* in your bed?"

"Only every night." I winked now, being cheeky, which was something I never did. Clearly, this Midwestern boy was doing something for me, but I noticed the fact he didn't mention his secret call from before, nor address the sound of his phone buzzing right next to him via his seat at my kitchen island. He'd apparently taken his phone with him into the kitchen when he came in, glancing at it before going back to his food. He didn't answer the text or call, but he didn't address it either.

"I could be about that visual," he said, his leg extending out, his naked toes getting me. I started to laugh, but then the phone buzzed and he looked at it *again* before waving a hand and pocketing it.

"Everything okay?" My way to see if he'd bring it up, not my business but I didn't know how I felt that he was being all secretive. I mean, he had taken a call in my bathroom.

He lifted fingers. "It's fine. December, the bride, just lost her house key. I was trying to tell her how to get into my condo to get her spare."

My mouth parted. Like a serious drop, which he didn't notice because the phone came out and he raised it to the air.

He smiled. "Looks like she got it okay so the texts should stop. I guess she stopped by the house to drop the wedding gifts off before boarding a plane today for the honeymoon."

Back into his pocket, back into his food like what he said was normal and maybe, it was. But… "You have a key to her place?"

He nodded, completely casual about it. "Yeah, she's my neighbor. I bought a condo and didn't need both spaces, so I rented the other side out to her. It's basically a duplex set up so, yeah. Tried to help her out. The place she was in—"

"With her husband." I tried to sound casual about it, but

noticed I placed my back to him when I turned around. I put the gravy back on the burner.

"Yeah, with Prinze." I turned, and he was sitting there, staring at me with a wrinkled brow. He frowned. "Plumbing went out in their old place. They're renting from me."

And so, she was effectively and intricately weaved within his life.

Wow.

I, well, had more than enough of my own drama, more than enough of my own shit but *this*.

"Brielle?"

My head shot up to find his fingers pinching at my robe again, his reach that long. He cleared me from the burner, hugging my hips. "You okay?"

"Yeah, yeah." I passed that off, way off but wow. Wow. I shook my head. "Yeah."

"I'm not sure I believe you." His look curious before his eyes danced at me. "You lying to me?"

"No."

Curious again before he chuckled and pinched my chin, tipping it down. "Okay, play your games, Jersey girl," he paused, but then, smoothed his hands over my hips, cupping my ass. "But after you're done doing all that, how about we play some together? Finish breakfast and get back to where we were."

Back to all *this* he meant, his hands massaging my hips and making me feel good. His hands distracting me and clearly avoiding literally everything else. His business was his and maybe it wasn't drama. Maybe he was okay with being so close to someone who had such a firm hold over his life in the past. I really didn't know his dynamic, but I did know what last night was for both of us.

It'd been avoidance.

It'd been giving in to pleasure and passion, so we didn't

have to address other things clearly in the room here. It'd been fun for a night true, but long term?

I unknotted his arms from around me once more but this time he stood and cradled my elbows when I placed my back to him.

"What's up?" His chin touched down on the top of my head. Like I was his bite-sized kid when really, our age difference favored in my direction. It wasn't a big deal he was in his twenties but being older did give me a perspective he didn't have. It let me see things he didn't see, even easier when it wasn't your own life. I couldn't handle my own crap for anything, a big reason why last night even happened.

I palmed my face. "I'm not looking for anything serious," I said, making myself. His fingers paused on my elbows and I turned within his hands. "I just moved here, got a new job I'm starting soon, then getting this place together?" I shook my head. "I've got my plate full."

All of these things were very true—in fact, so true I forced myself to believe they weren't complete and utter bullshit. That they were the reason I didn't want to see him again and ignore the fact that all I actually wanted were his hands all over me and to be completely surrounded by him. We were in different places, him and me.

And I really couldn't add to my own drama.

Ramses's fingers grazed a jawline on the cusp of shadow, like he had a lot of thoughts but wasn't quite sure how to voice them. He opted, in the end, to hitch himself back against my kitchen island, his big hands handling his biceps. "Was it something I did?"

Oh, fuck.

Yes. "No." Both answers really, both of us and our shit. I touched my face before my fingers settled at my neck. "I'm just busy. Don't have time for anything serious."

He should be used to this, right? Young and turning women down himself. Ramses was a very handsome man, and I was quite sure he'd been through his own fair share of letdowns.

Though maybe not so much on his end with his response, taking a seat before facing me. He opened his hands. "I get it. I actually just moved back here. Busy too."

I hated that my heart squeezed, like someone kicked me in the gut and sucked all the air out of my chest at the same time. That he was denying me.

He took a seat, his fist dropping between his long legs. "Well, can I at least have your number?" he chuckled, but I noticed the smile didn't quite reach his eyes. Not like last night anyway. "I'd like to keep talking to you. We can just be friends."

Yeah, I couldn't be this guy's friend without something more, impossible.

How did he have so much of my heart already?

It must have been infatuation only and a hell of a lot of good sex. Ramses was great at sex, great at oral sex. I lifted my hand off my neck, saying nothing, and this did get a full laugh on his end this time. Though, a clear hint of frustration weaved within it the way he smoothed his hand over his curls before setting back at his neck. I wasn't going to give him anything. I couldn't.

It would make all this easier. Cutting off ties was easier. Bracing his arms, he stared at me.

"Jersey girl…" He sighed before reaching and dipping two fingers in my robe's belt loops. He hooked me over and though I didn't want to, I did. His arms came to fall around my waist and though he sat, he still had to look down at me with his size. "I can't change your mind?"

Since he couldn't, I shook my head. "We had fun. Let's not complicate it."

The way I'd simplified last night, everything that went down clearly didn't sit well with him, and he showed me that when he let go of me and picked up his fork. He started eating food that'd long gone cold, but that didn't stop him from distracting himself from me.

"Yeah, fun," he said, his tone dry, and I hated that *I* did that. He'd thank me for this later. He didn't want any more drama in his life either, and he'd get a lot of that with me. It was like it always seemed to follow me.

Even if it hadn't always been this way.

CHAPTER
EIGHT

Bri

I ended up running late for my first seminar of the term, go figure. Apparently, testing my daily commute nearly two weeks before the start of classes meant nothing. The city of Maywood Heights had been gridlocked the entire way out of it, then my almost two-hour commute to campus the same. Queenstown Village, where Pembroke University and my new teaching job happened to be, had been just as much of a cluster fuck coming in so I'd been screwed either way.

The past two weeks had been me trying to get my life together as much as trying to forget about how it had basically started. I hadn't heard from Ramses. Obviously. I hadn't given him my number, nor had we exchanged full names. We hadn't even been intimate before he left. We'd just left things.

And that was that.

Easier, I think for both of us, in the end. I could focus on my new life in Maywood Heights, and he could do whatever he was doing. He clearly did pretty well for himself if his choice of ride and the fact that he rented a condo out to his friend was any indicator. I rented myself at thirty-five and on a professor's salary. He didn't need the distraction of me in his life any more than I needed him in mine, and as I felt before, we saved each other from that with a clean cut-off.

We'd also given each other a night not to think about our own shit, and I'd had a lot of it. I'd chosen to move to Maywood Heights via a direction from my friend and support system, Evie. She also happened to be the dean of the history department at the university, so when it came to deciding being close to her in town versus my new job, I'd decided to rent in Maywood Heights. This was apparently pretty common for both students and faculty to commute. Pembroke was the closest university to the city, esteemed, and lots of money came out of Maywood Heights just to go into the university's programs. At least, according to Evie. I guess even her family funded several programs in the campus's rigorous curriculum.

"*You'll love working there,*" she'd said to me, the pair of us getting coffee over the weekend before my first day. She'd apologized for basically ditching me at that wedding, and since I was hard-pressed for friendships as of late, of course I'd forgiven her. I also owed her a lot. She'd taken more than one phone call through the panic of my failed marriage and understanding of my quick need to get away from both the place and the person I'd been with. She'd gotten me this job at the university and heard all about my ex-husband, Alec.

At least, all the stuff I could verbally say out loud.

I'd had to sign an NDA in the end, customary since my ex-husband used to play sports for a very popular team. He was still a fan favorite, despite being retired for more than a few years. Had an image to protect.

I just wished he'd cared about protecting me more.

My ex-husband was an asshole, a pathetic, uninspired has-been who spent more time indulging himself in vices instead of trying to rise above the problems in this life. I suppose we were the same in that aspect.

No, you're nothing like him.

No, I would *never* have done the things he did to me pre-divorce and definitely not after what had transpired to basically cause the divorce. We'd both been a mess, but at least I'd tried to handle things, keep my chin up.

Refusing to think about all that now on my first day, I peeled my Benz into the faculty parking lot of Pembroke University. The weather had cleared a little since that wedding a couple of weeks ago, but still, the evidence of slush and dirty snow remained. It packed onto my heels good upon sliding out of my SUV and nearly sucked me beneath my car like Alice into Wonderland.

On concrete, I scraped and slid around in my woman's cigarette pants, a taupe-colored crop-style to go with my blazer. I didn't want to be matchy-matchy today, so I went with a warm brown to complement my black top beneath. Honestly, the juxtaposition of tones reminded me of what I used to wear back in the days when I frequented dig sites in Egypt and other more remote areas of Africa. Of course, that'd been before I'd decided to become a sports star's wife.

I grumbled in the wool coat I wore atop it all, trying to balance my coffee, bag, and purse. I managed to lock my car with a chirp, then glided through campus without killing myself. Faculty parking got me right at the entrance of the history department. My first class was early western civilizations. Definitely fitting since that was my background. I'd actually met Evie during my first early western civ class during my time at NYU.

I passed her office on the way to mine. Her light was on. Odds were, she was in there doing her own work, but I didn't have time to say hi since I had maybe thirty minutes before my class started. This may seem like a lot of time for the students, but since I was a professor, I needed to prepare a bit.

I dropped my personal items inside my office, still packed with boxes and other personal items I'd moved over here. I still had a lot to do regarding getting the place together, but obviously didn't have time this morning.

A sip from my coffee and my coat hung, I dashed out the door with my messenger bag, thankful I didn't have any overly eager students already in there. I appreciated that, but not today, embarrassed enough since I was already what I considered late.

I turned on the overhead projector, then logged on, hitting the lights while the computer booted up. I also got my syllabus out as well, stacking them at the front, and by the time the computer came on and I had my presentation on screen, I sorta kinda looked like I had it together. I always found it funny how I believed my professors in school and teachers in high school always had things together. I was definitely not a great example of that.

"Morning, professor."

"Morning."

A few students chirped as they filtered inside, and I passed a wave in greeting to them as I finished setting up. This was an undergraduate class, a general elective for most, so odds were, it'd be mostly freshman in here today. Sometimes an occasional junior or senior would make their way in as well, waiting until the last minute to get their gen-eds in and all that. I smiled at the small group. "Go ahead and grab syllabuses before you sit. I'll be with you in a moment."

Today should be a rather easy day. Usually, the first week or so was pretty easy. I'd let the class read the syllabus today, then as the weeks progressed, we'd get to the more detailed stuff regarding class work. By week three, the class had usually thinned out pretty good and long gone were the days that I took offense to that. Especially when it came to undergraduate classes. Early western civ wasn't for everyone, and it wasn't a course I let my students sleep through. They had to do the readings and the work, and some found they could get by with an easy art or media class instead.

The students took my direction while I worked my jacket off, already hot from rushing around. I fanned myself out behind the podium, leaving my arms bare in my black dress tank. I probably wouldn't stay the whole period that way, but it worked for now.

I drew my hands down my face, before lacing my fingers together and greeting each new student in with a smile. I gave them all the same direction, take a syllabus before sitting and they did, the room filling up quickly. Before I knew it, the whole classroom was filled aside for a few seats.

I closed the door promptly at the top of the hour. Literally the most annoying thing to me in the world was to start late, and the second, late students.

In the center of the room, I stood. "Good morning, class. My name is Brielle Whitman-Quintero. Doctor. But you can just call me professor." I put my hands together. "And this is History 275, Early Western Civilizations."

Making my way to the podium, I flicked to a slide about myself and my credentials before coming around and hitching a seat against the table up front.

"First thing's first," I said. "I'm pretty laid-back, but I abhor lateness. In all forms. I don't start late. I don't like late. I promise I'll show up for you guys, *on time*, and I expect the same in return. I respect you guys enough to not waste your time, so I just ask that I get that from you too."

A general consensus with their nods, so it seemed like we were clear, but then, the door creaked open and the gates of chaos and trickery unfurled its wicked mischief directly into my classroom, a man in sharp black gliding in with a brown leather cross bag strapped to his broad chest. He wore all black down to his suede shoes, laced and immaculate beneath the cuff of his twill pants, his dress shirt left a button or two open and hugging his tapered frame. The entire room directed their eyes to him, just like me, but *unlike them*, they got zero of his attention.

That, well, was reserved for me.

He stopped on me, almost like he'd been looking for me, but clearly, he hadn't, his steps slowed, his mouth parted. He even looked around to make sure he was in the right place.

I had the feeling he was.

I had a feeling someone *hated me,* had to because no way was he in there right now.

No way was he in my class.

But sure enough, even from the back of the room, those thick curls swayed in their awesome way, those eyes danced and that smile ticked right as the seconds passed. Out of the periphery, someone tapped him with a syllabus, making room when he took his attention off me long enough to take the handout, then the seat they offered. He sat right in the back, fingers laced and popping his focus in my direction. That smile never left.

And I was dead.

Ramses

Dude.

What the fuck?

But there she was, right there at the head of the class like some slow-reeling fantasy, a wet dream in her tight pants, ankle strap heels, and a black top that glided easy silk over her glorious rack. She nearly peeped side boob out of the side of it, fucking hot and had me seriously about to adjust my shit right under this damn desk. I almost hadn't even made it into class today, a scheduled board meeting with my name on it. It was my first one, and I hated to move it, but I had class and the board had been accommodating. There'd been more than one moving piece to make that happen though and I literally had to wait until confirmation this morning before hopping in my ride and huffing it to class. The board agreed to get me in tomorrow, so I made it here today.

In front of Brielle, apparently.

Brielle, *my professor,* with her gorgeously matte lips and firecracker personality. I was about ninety percent sure she'd been chewing out the class before I walked the hell in here. I caught the tail end of it as I opened the door and the class had been silent. I questioned turning around at the sound of a spiel about being late but figured I could take the handling. I wouldn't let it happen again and would apologize to my professor for the error.

My professor.

Fucking gorgeous and in awe of the situation just as much as me. She hadn't said anything when I'd come in, and since I'd been surprised to see her myself, I merely took my seat before letting her continue. She did, albeit, after a beat. She flicked a lock of that silky black hair of hers, taking the time to pull it around like she could ever, *in her life,* cover up how awesome her chest was. In the end, she opted to return her jacket on, flipping out her hair over its boxy shoulders. She looked like a real professor up there, a doctor apparently. She had her presentation all up on the projection screen and with a hurried urgency dove right into it without addressing me or our situation at all. At the present, she was going to act like it never happened, *like we never happened,* and since we were in a room full of her students and my, well, classmates, I didn't blame her.

How had I found you again?

She'd been slippery, slithered right away out of my life, and I'd allowed that to be divine intervention. We'd gotten together in a weird way, a given, and I was going to let the universe do whatever the fuck it wanted. I'd tested Mother Earth enough to know better than to fuck with her again. If

Bri didn't want to see me, cut this shit off, I was going to let it happen and be at peace with how the cards ended up falling. I really was busy and didn't have time either and honestly, really had no business getting involved with a woman. Not right now, not at all and here one continued to fall into my lap.

I pretended to follow along with the syllabus, listen to her with the rest of my classmates, but there wasn't a moment where I didn't follow her mouth to the rest of her, to that banging body, thighs all thick and supple beneath her tight pants like they were made for squeezing hands, my hands. In fact, the moment I knew I started to drift into creeper territory was when my focus did go back to what she was saying, and the fact she was doing everything in her power *not* to look at me. Typically, in these first classes the professors either had us read the syllabus ourselves or take turns reading out loud while the professor followed along. But this allowed room for silence and wandering eyes, clearly, on Brielle's part. Reading herself kept her busy, kept her eyes *off me*, because the moment she slipped up, whether from fleeting attention or stumbling across a word, our eyes immediately clashed. We were back in her home.

We were back in her bedroom.

She was *back with me* while I made her moan beneath her sheets or in the middle of her empty living room. I idly wondered if she had furniture now, envisioning licking her clean on her sofa, coffee table…

"All right. I'll see you all later in the week."

My gaze flicked up to see her packing, quickly, while students squeaked their chairs out and exited swiftly in manner. A second flick gave me the wall clock and the fact we'd wrapped after only twenty minutes of lecture wasn't lost on me. That was a new record for a first day's class, leaving ten maybe fifteen minutes early not unusual for the first day.

Yeah, she was trying to get out of here.

But seeing as she had a lot more stuff to put away and shut off than the rest of us, not right this minute. I scooped up my syllabus, shoved it in my bag, then helped her, grabbing extra syllabuses left behind.

I sauntered up to the front of the room after that, no one surprised more than me to find my heart racing as the seconds before our impromptu reunion disappeared along with the space between us.

What is she doing to me?

Something, my grin easy as I came to a stop in front of her. She had herself tucked away behind the podium but had to step around to get the extra syllabuses left behind. Seeing I already had them, her heels squeaked back on the tiles, nearly stumbling, but I had her covered there too.

My hand shot out with precision, those reflexes from playing ball in the past good for something.

I grabbed her, had her, and she returned to me with an easy accuracy, her body warm and that close when her lapels grazed my chest and her flowers touched my nose. My whole suit had smelled like her after we'd parted, and I'd left it out, still hanging there on the other side of my walk-in's door. I told myself because I needed to get it dry-cleaned.

Unsure now as my blood heated, hovering above her as my body instinctually wanted to glide over her. I was painfully aware of how suddenly uncomfortable my pleated pants were, needing to go into the office today after my classes. I planned to work Monday through Friday, or more. Classes be damned. I was still my father's son, more than one thing instilled in me unfortunately. Just because the firm had my name on it didn't make it mine. It was still his, his until I took it.

That was something he'd reminded me every day before he went away, that I wasn't entitled, *nothing* could be mine until I'd earned it. Took it. My father was a fan of tough love as much as making bad decisions, but even if he wasn't, I was going to show up. I wouldn't give him the satisfaction of anything else, the first to think me weak if he ever got the chance. He'd never say it, of course, too proud to put *weak* and his son in the same sentence, but that fact wouldn't stop him from thinking it.

Honestly, I didn't know why I cared and didn't in this moment now, roses and wild flowers misted in a spring rain surrounding me. Hell, a monsoon assaulted me, as equally torrential as this woman was soft. That was Brielle Whitman-Quintero, as tough as she was pliable. She didn't take shit, and now, I knew she was a doctor too.

My professor.

I saw that completely in her eyes, what I was to her, what she was to me. Whatever the case, I probably wasn't supposed to have my hands on her, her body stiff, *her hands* stiff. She had them curled and embedded in my shirt. I believed to keep from falling.

I righted her, and she let go, backing away. She straightened her top before tugging the jacket. "Thank you."

My response was handing her extra syllabuses, for which she thanked me too, before I pocketed my hands. "No problem."

I was happy to help her out, see her again.

I'd really wanted to see her again.

And here she was, right in front of me. A vision to dream, a memory to a ghost. She'd been in and out of my life so quick my head spun, and I was still recovering from the whiplash. I shrugged. "So, you teach at Pembroke."

I hadn't asked her—obviously. In fact, we hadn't done a whole lot of talking at all that night.

Restless fingers had Bri tucking some of that raven black behind her ear, her shrug a subtle one before giving me her back and sliding the syllabuses into her messenger bag.

"Appears so." Laughter awkward, nervous. She shook her head. "And you're my student."

"Appears so." Definitely awkward, but I didn't laugh. I didn't want to make her more uncomfortable than she clearly was. I made an attempt to see her eyes, but she denied me. "Though I guess I should have figured when you said you were a professor."

Pembroke was the closest campus to Maywood Heights. I suppose she could have taught at the local community college, actually in town, but I hadn't questioned a lot of things that night. We hadn't talked at all, things so fast.

Did you really fuck this shit up? Again.

It seemed like it, but I wouldn't go there. Not yet. More nervous laughter on Bri's end before she whipped around, hands cuffing her jacket sleeves.

"But you are at least in your twenties, right? Didn't lie to me to make yourself look cool or something?" Frantic, she flicked and weaved her fingers through her hair. "Because if you're like eighteen or something I'm seriously about to lose my shit right now."

She looked on the cusp of an expedited breakdown between us, my eyebrow arching slow. "I'm twenty-two."

Though it makes sense why she asked. One of my gen-eds hadn't transferred coming out of Brown, this typically a freshman class.

The announcement of my age didn't seem to comfort her *at all*, and if anything, her laughter grew more frantic, more manic.

"Brilliant." She rose and dropped her hands. "Anything else I shouldn't assume about you?"

"What did you assume?"

"I don't know. That you weren't over a decade younger than me *and my student*." She growled. "Ramses, do you realize how bad this is?"

Not really. At least, not to the degree she was taking it. I cuffed my arms too. "I wasn't your student when we got together, Brielle."

"Oh, yeah. You were. I just didn't know it. That was two weeks ago, Ramses." She held up two fingers. "Two weeks. You were obviously enrolled in my class."

"And?"

She groaned. "And I can't do this. I *can't*. I…"

She was panicking, needing to stop before her mind ran off with shit and she got crazy. She'd given me a teaser of it before, and I think that was why I did what I decided to do next.

I grabbed her, just her wrists, but it was enough to make her look at me, to get out of her fucking head for just two seconds.

To *feel* me, my hands on her and that she was innocent in all this. That we did nothing wrong and there wasn't any reason to think we had. I knew the school had an ethics policy, that she could get in trouble depending on the context, but that most certainly wasn't our situation. We'd gotten together before we even knew our roles in regard to each other.

"What are you doing, Ramses?" Her breath shallow as she looked at me, but I noticed she placed no distance between us. Didn't push me away.

So, *I* pushed.

I angled against her, hitching her up to me, and her throat jumped.

Mine tightened. "I want you to listen to me. You're not in trouble. We didn't do anything wrong, and you acting this way is just messing with your head."

And messing with mine, but clearly in an entirely different way. Her flowers hit my nose, hard, and I wet my lips.

She noticed, followed it down my neck and completely across my chest. In fact, her gaze took complete inventory over my shoulders, my arms, *my hands* before settling on their place at her wrists. Her body knocked fluid, all but languid in front of me.

Shit. Is she still…

Into this, into me, her student who was twenty-two to her thirty-five? I didn't fucking care about that, but she sure seemed to.

"Ramses…" The warning in her voice contradicted the dilation of her pupils, her irises darkening, her eyes hooded. "Please."

Please what? Kiss her?

Just give me the go.

I had no problem taking this woman, right here, right fucking *now*, the growl on my lips as my chest met hers. Her ass hit the table, my hands too, when I caged her between my arms.

"I can drop the class," I rasped, gliding my breath along her ear. It took every ounce of strength within me not to fucking touch her. "Just tell me, Jersey girl."

At the sound of my nickname for her, what I said in general, or whatever the fuck, she sucked a breath through her teeth.

Okay, it's on.

Unable to fucking fight it, my hand slid between her legs, pinching her sex through her tight little pants. The moan escaped her lips in an instant and I buried my face in her neck, a single kiss before she forced me off her and headed me straight toward the valley of fucking blue balls.

"I told you. I'm not…" She worked her way through her hair again. "Just no. *No*."

"Why?" I growled, tired of this shit. Tired *of this*. She was clearly attracted to me, and me to her. I cleared hair from my brow. "I'll get out of the class. It won't be a big deal."

"It's not about the class," she shot, my eyes twitching open. Seeing that, she pressed palms to her eyes. "I mean, it's about the class *now*, but this can't happen. It won't happen."

"Why not?" I repeated. Was there something else? She had been acting weird that day, right before I'd left. I'd passed it off.

Shit, was there something?

I witnessed that all over her face, something when she cleared her hands from it. She fisted her knuckles. "Ramses, I don't know if you noticed, but we're both a hot mess and you're completely unavailable."

"How so?" Intrigued now. "What are you talking about?"

She put out a hand like it was obvious. "I heard you in the bathroom with your friend. Your friend who's *married* and you were talking to the day after said marriage, who also just so happens to live next to you, and oh, yeah, you were in love with back in high school."

I frowned. What the fuck? "Where are you even going with this?" And wait, she heard me? Fuck. "I didn't mean to sneak around with the call. But she's my friend and I couldn't leave her hanging."

Her brow jumped. "That's all you got out of what I just said?"

Was there something else? Confusion, clearly on my end, and her response to that was grabbing her bag. She instantly fled toward the door, but I got her by the arm.

"Bri."

"It's Professor Whitman-Quintero."

Like a chill immediately into the goddamn room. Polar ice, a wintry glaze.

And just like that, I pocketed my hands, my shoulders shrugging. "Professor then."

Her expression fell instantaneously, but she'd drawn the line here. She pressed a hand to her head. "You won't drop the class because this won't work. I'm your professor. You're my student. I'm thirty-five. You're twenty-two and even outside of that," she paused, adjusting the bag on her shoulder. "We both used each other that night—clearly, and I'm pretty sure you know that."

I stayed silent but not for long. It took me a second, but I think I got what she'd been getting at before, and she was a wrong, completely wrong. My jaw shifted. "That may all be true, but what you may or may not be insinuating about me and as you said, *my friend* is not. That is all December and I are. Good friends, and it is not like that with her. She's married, and I'm not unavailable."

At least, when it came to the situation with my friend, again, not like that. I maybe would have argued against that in the past when what happened between us was fresh, but not now. Now, I was just prone to getting into stupid shit.

And Brielle didn't believe me.

I saw *that* all over her face too. She chewed her lip. "I wish that we both could have come at each other differently that night. That there weren't so many variables. That maybe if I hadn't been so sad and you yourself weren't…" A shallow breath, an eye pinch before she thought better about what she'd been about to say.

Instead, she chose to leave, block herself and whatever she was going through from me. It felt very familiar, chillingly so.

"I need to go," she said, backing toward the door. She touched it. "And don't drop the class. It's not necessary. I'll deal if you can."

"Bri—"

She didn't correct me because she let the door slam in my face again. I pinched the bridge of my nose but, this time, didn't go after her.

I wasn't confident she'd actually let me this time.

CHAPTER
NINE

Ramses

"Ramses?"

My sight lifted to find more than one board member's eyes on me, but the only one who appeared to be in right form today was Duncan Salsbury, the one who'd spoken.

His lips pinched tight and his back ramrod straight, he lifted his chin. "Are we boring you, son?"

I wasn't this man's son, but it was cute he'd decided to put that out there. I did have to call him mister, uncle, or other various forms of male superiority when it came to myself growing up, so it really must chap his lily-white ass how things were now. How he had to answer to me. Call me boss.

My lips tipped slow, actually doing very important research on my end surrounding a certain professor. I'd decided to stalk Brielle's social media profiles, a dead end since the one she had was locked and her pictures the same. I'd just wanted to find out more about her, figure her out and give me some indicator into why she was so closed off. The venture had turned up empty for the most part, and after a flick of my fingers to minimize her page, I swiveled the laptop around to show Duncan and the rest of the board.

"I'd like your opinion on something actually." *Nosy bastard.* I directed a finger to what I now had on the screen, a catering menu. "Yellow or brown."

"Yellow or... brown?" His eyebrow lifted slow, and he angled a look in the direction of my Mac. Pretty much everyone did, which was fucking funny as hell. About a dozen suited professionals, men and women completely disrupted since this man decided to call me out on the carpet. Duncan shook his head. "I don't under—"

"Yellow or brown, Duncan. Mustard?" Chuckling, I lounged back in my executive chair. "It's getting close to lunch, and I find myself simply plagued by this decision. Yellow or brown mustard on my pastrami on rye. I'd really love your opinion since you appear to be so concerned about me, what I do?"

There was more than one chuckle in my direction and a rose-colored tint to Duncan's aged cheeks. He'd attempted to put me out there, but only ended up embarrassing himself for causing a completely unnecessary disruption to today's meeting. I may have been bored as hell, but I hadn't needed him to call me out on that.

He pressed a hand down a chunky tie his grandkids probably got him for Christmas. It was boring and humdrum just as himself, but his grandchildren couldn't be faulted for that. They were probably just giving the old coot what he wanted. His throat cleared. "I'd advise brown myself. Typically, can't go wrong there."

I had to fight my smile now as he managed to make that actually sound serious, like it really fucking mattered and was a huge decision. I placed out a hand, and he took that as direction to continue, good man.

I fell back into the discussions of figures and projections, nothing over my head but dull, nonetheless. The board typically met once a month to discuss all this shit, and since I was the new guy around here, the new boss, I unfortunately had to be here for all of it. I tried to be since they had gone out of their way to reschedule things for me. They gave me their respect with that, knowing my frantic schedule with school and its combination with work, so I did give them the rest of my attention before the clock summoned its end, and I got to finally leave and go through things in the privacy of my own office. I really didn't need these guys telling me every little thing, the hand-holding like I couldn't read an email or open a file folder. I was a class or two away from getting my BBA, and even without my education, I already knew how my father's company worked. I'd been born and bred for this shit since I came out the womb, always known this was what I'd be doing and where I was going to be. There were pictures of me in this very downtown office in diapers, sitting on my dad's desk while he made phone calls and made powerful decisions.

I made that office my own now, on the top floor of a glass-enclosed fortress known as Mallick Enterprises. This was the man hub of my father's real estate and development company, its location in downtown Maywood Heights, and I hoped, now that I was here and running things, to bleed some of the negativity and arrogance out of it. My father had been a piss-poor human being, which just so happened to make for an excellent businessman. He'd brought quite a few people lots of money through the years, but I was a firm believer that money could still be made without being a dick and making people feel inferior. That may be foreign to this office and the company he used to keep, but that's what I was bringing around here. All I needed to do now was get familiar with things since I had been gone for the last few years. I'd had my father's people keep me abreast of things, sending me those same figures and projections in the form of spreadsheets while I'd been in business school at Brown. They thought it funny I actually wanted it all since I was in school, but I didn't want these people to forget about me, who I was. I was coming back, and they shouldn't get too comfortable.

And they especially shouldn't expect my father.

In the comfort of what was now my office, I opened my laptop and got right back to work, only occasionally trying to stalk Bri between emails and phone calls. That final conversation we'd had didn't sit well, and I had a feeling this woman and I shared more in common than she'd readily admit. I may be twenty-two and she may be thirty-five, but she was right, we both had shit going on and we both obviously opted to deal with it in a certain way that night we met—together. She may have been completely off base with some of the things she'd said, things surrounding December and me. We were just friends, and though some of those old wounds from the past were still there, I'd accepted that long ago *and* the relationship we had now—just friends. Bri hadn't been entirely wrong about maybe a few walls I had up, but I wasn't unavailable and had a feeling we both may deal with sudden conflicts that arose in our lives in similar ways. Brielle seemed like a runner, just like me, and conversations definitely should probably be had between us.

I probably should address these things with her in person, not stalk her on the internet like well, a stalker, but at this point, I felt like a man obsessed. It was like I needed to know about her, everything I could find out, but as I clicked around on the net behind the close doors of my office, I, again, came up empty.

Who wasn't on social media?

She had that one profile freaking under lock and key, and I wasn't bold enough to try to friend or follower her, not with me being her student now and all that. Frustrated, I slammed my laptop shut right as I got a call from up front.

"Mr. Salsbury wants to speak to you, Ramses," my secretary, Leann, said on the other line.

Fucking perfect.

"Send him in," I told her, noticing he made all staff call him Mr. Salsbury when he had known all these people for years. I didn't even do that shit, and I was *his* boss, and what would I look like doing that anyway? These people had known me since I was in diapers.

My eyes were on my laptop when Duncan came in.

I admit I pretended to be at work, but fuck me, if I didn't still have Brielle's Facebook page up. She had a profile picture of her in a football jersey, a New York team with black grease paint under her eyes and a sexy as all hell grin on her lips. I'd basically been pathetically salivating over the thing for the better part of an hour but I forced my gaze up to the world's most well-dressed stick in the mud. Good ole Duncan loved to spend his money and had pretty much been me for all intents and purposes while I'd been away at school and my father had been in prison. Mallick Enterprises wasn't just a family company, others had shares such as himself, but I held the majority. This effectively made me this man's boss, but he was still basically family since I'd known him all my life.

"Ramses," he said, his smile a firm but respectful one. He pocketed his hands. "How are you holding up, my boy? Adjusting well?"

Had been, but could do a little less with the *my boy* and *sons*. I smiled. "Can I help you with something, Duncan?"

I admit I was still a little annoyed over him calling me out before and wondered if I needed to make him call me sir or mister just to take me a bit more seriously. I just worried it might be a slippery slope, and I did want to do things differently around here. People may have respected my father, but they had also feared him. He was the law and I'd feared him, too, in the end.

I guess he'd given us all a reason to.

My jaw working in thought, Duncan decided to take it upon himself to appropriate a seat in front of my father's desk. I had no serious problems with the guy, that annoying uncle type, but he did *hover*. He was supposed to be showing me the ropes because he did used to be me, and unfortunately, I did have to put up with it at the present. He knew more than me about all this, my dad's company, so I did have to listen to him. I wasn't arrogant enough to think that I knew everything, but I could do without the training wheels and what seemed to be constant check-ins. That first week the man had been in my office every hour on the hour, a buzzing bee and me without my goddamn repellent.

He crossed his leg at the knee. "I suppose I just wanted to chat with you about the boardroom incident. I really meant no offense. I merely noticed your attention had drifted off and wanted to make sure everything was clear for you that we were discussing. Make sure you were comfortable and still with us."

Subtlety had never been this man's strong suit in all the years I'd known him. Even still, how he'd gone about it had been inappropriate and definitely hadn't been necessary. I followed along just fine. I leaned forward. "Your only job when it comes to me, Duncan, is to advise—as needed. I don't need you calling me out, and I don't need you babysitting."

Both of which he'd done since I'd gotten here. I was about to change the locks on the goddamn door, this office his after my father's, and I'd allowed him to keep a key as a courtesy.

A nod in understanding on Duncan's end. "I apologize, truly. I didn't mean to overstep."

"So don't."

He frowned, sighing. "But I do want to make sure you're comfortable."

He kept saying that, *comfortable*, and lounging back, I laced my fingers across my chest. "Are you getting at something, Duncan? Because if you are, you're going to have to break it down for me."

He was going to have to say what was obviously on his mind, his fingers pulling through snow white hair. He placed a hand on his knee. "We're so very happy to have you here, Ramses. Been waiting for you, to have a Mallick at the helm again."

"But?"

His head tilted. "But we understand if you're not quite ready. If you need time to finish school or even take a break if that's what you want. We'd completely understand that, expect it."

Expect it.

And so my age was an issue again, my hands opened. "I wouldn't be here if I didn't feel I was ready. And I assure you, neither my age nor my commitments to my education will affect my ability to run this company. So if that's your, and I'm assuming the rest of the board's, issue as well—"

"We know you're brilliant, Ramses." His sigh was incredibly heavy this time. "We've seen how you've come up and grown. We know you've got what it takes, but you are young, and after that incident at Brown…"

Which had nothing to do with this or this conversation. I put a finger down. "Careful, Duncan. You might be crossing a line."

He'd fucking leaped the hell over it. I was aware of how he felt about the issue. The company's lawyers, my lawyers, had to get involved. So yeah, I was aware of how he felt regarding my personal life. He thought I was reckless.

He thought I was young, like he said.

He, along with anyone else on the outside looking in, saw a snapshot of a situation, and since I'd been forced to save face, yes, the "incident at Brown" definitely had looked a certain way. But that was the outside perception, not the truth, and he should know that since he had known me for so long.

"We just don't want you overwhelmed." He passed a look to me. "There's a concern about that, that all this is too much."

"Well, it's not." I wet my lips. "So, if we're done, I'd like to get back to work."

Maybe actually do some work this time and though he did get up, his shoulders sagged.

"*Please* let me know if you need anything," he urged. "No one will fault you for waiting one, two, or even five years if you're not ready for all this yet. Don't make me or any of the rest of the board the enemy. We are here to advise, to help you."

I said nothing, and he took that as the sign it was. He left the office, and I would be changing the locks. Too many people had a say in this office besides me.

———

"So, I had a rather interesting call with Duncan Salsbury this afternoon."

I bet she had.

Snitch.

My mom's voice had drifted from her place across the kitchen, cutting away at bell peppers and onions with the precision of a sous chef in Gordon Ramsay's kitchen. No sooner had she sliced and diced than she grabbed for the mushrooms, doing the same for our weekly taco night. I tried to come over weekly to have dinner with my mother now that I was back in town, and we both made time for it.

To my dismay, considering I was currently being probed.

Obviously, good ole Duncan had been running his mouth after our little tiff this morning. I grumbled.

"And how is everyone over at the country club?" I asked, knowing that was where she'd run into him, talked to him. They were still very much friends, and I was sure the entire town knew about my struggles at the office, thanks to a certain board member. These people spouted gossip like a TMZ Kardashian spotting at a club. I growled. "Still being complete busybodies?"

My mom's serrated knife paused on a portobello. My mother was a blond woman, tall and who'd been about half the reason I ended up reaching six-foot-eight. My mom was just shy of six-foot-one, which was basically fucking awesome when I'd been a kid and needed to find her in the store. I passed her in height around seventh grade, and the woman looked like Daryl Hannah walking off the set of *Splash*. This basically made my life hell my entire middle school career. The whole MILF thing and all that, but seeing as how I attended boarding school on the other side of the country for most of high school, I hadn't had to deal with the ridicule there. For my boarding school days, I could thank, once again, my father. He'd shipped me off back then, easier to do that than actually deal with me.

My father had a tendency of sweeping things under the rug when he didn't want to deal with them, and how ironic as he had gone off to prison. There wasn't sweeping away anything there, and *this family* had to deal with it, the busybodies over at the country club completely in our business.

Mom grumbled now. "How is it that I raised such a complete and ridiculously smart aleck of a son?"

"Just lucky, I guess," I stated, being extra bold when I winked at her.

She tossed a piece of mushroom at me, as she should for being smart, but that was our dynamic. In fact, I got most of my sense of humor from her. Hell, if I could ever crack a smile across Ibrahim Mallick's lips, former mayor and who had more scowls to his name than Royal Prinze. He'd cashed in quite a few in my direction as well, for being smart-mouthed and all that.

Mom frowned. "Ramses, don't be mean. Those 'busybodies' as you put them were there for me. There for *this family* when we were going through the most difficult time period. They would have been there for you too had you let them, had you *stayed*."

My gaze lifted from the romaine I was cutting, hesitating but only for a second. I angled the knife into leaves. "Are we talking about that now, too?"

She'd shared her opinion about Brown as well. Everyone basically had, so why not just give this thing another go?

A sigh fell from my mother's lips. "I just worry about you. Duncan said you're being resistant to his help, and I think we all were surprised to see you so ready to just jump in and get started working after you came back."

"Why?" I'd been born into this, bred for it. This was my legacy, the plan, and she knew that.

Mom eyed me like it was obvious. "I don't know, because you expressed zero interest every time your father actually tried to get you involved with the business. You basically went kicking and screaming every time he tried, and eventually, he just gave up. Gave up on you."

"He was really good at that, wasn't he?"

Another frown in my direction, and had she'd been close to me, she probably would have shoved that entire cutting board of pre-cut vegetables into my face. She lay the knife down. "I'm just saying you never wanted to get involved before, but that's the first thing you did when you came back."

"So, I'm trying to get my shit together," I said. "Obviously."

"Or you're trying to prove a point," she countered. "Prove a point to yourself, or him for that matter. Your dad?"

I smirked. "Ma, no offense. But I don't give a fuck about that man."

"Ramses," she gritted.

"What? I don't." And why would I care about proving a goddamn point to him? I hated him. I growled. "I don't care about trying to please Dad."

"All right then," she said, like she didn't believe me at all, which frustrated me. She placed her hands on the counter. "You're obviously struggling with something, and it's been known that your father has loomed over your life for a very long time. So long and in so many ways."

Since she was right about that, I said nothing, my knife rocking back into romaine. I cut a little while more before I had a healthy stack, which I deposited quickly into a bowl. I looked up to find my mother's gaze on me, her hands cuffing her blouse and her wristwatch blinging. Mom was successful in her own right, a hotel heiress actually, before she met and married my father. Her passions mostly surrounded her love for history, though, which was why she'd become a professor and later a dean at Pembroke-U.

"It's made you irritable with the world—clearly," she ventured on, raising her hand. "Cop a continued attitude with me over the years and is probably responsible for some of your—I'm sorry, Ramses—piss-poor decisions you've been making as of late."

Piss-poor decisions. I couldn't help but smirk again. "So we're back to the Brown thing again. If I knew this was going to be such an issue, I would have just stayed."

I could have. The school hadn't been involved with what happened or anything. Hell, they hadn't even known about what went down.

Our family's people had taken care of that.

In the end, I'd chosen to leave, easier and apparently my MO. I was an all-star at avoidance, and our family's attorneys had advised me to cut all ties anyway. Mom had also secured me a place back at Pembroke, so there was no reason to stare my "piss-poor" decisions in the face anyway.

I never would have come back knowing I'd be poked and prodded, though. I'd gotten quite a few texts from December as well. She and Prinze had come back from their shortened honeymoon in Aruba to be back for the start of senior year, and the first thing she'd done was text me to meetup. To *talk* and I'd been avoiding her like this talk with my mom.

"You know that what happened at Brown wasn't the real issue. You're channeling, son." She squeezed her arm. "Acting out? This is how you're dealing with your crap with your dad. You've never talked about anything. Never dealt with anything. Brown is the end result, not the issue."

"The issue being Dad?"

"I think so."

"So, what do you advise, doctor?" I asked, my mom not that kind of a doctor. She had her doctorate, but definitely not anything medically related.

Her brows narrowed. "To start, how about someone to help with the attitude?"

"Therapy?" I'd seen enough therapists for a lifetime. Especially after Dad had gotten his ass locked up. "I'm not seeing a therapist."

"I'm just saying you should talk to someone. You know, maybe give you closure? Help you deal with some of these changes in your life."

Someone who could bill me hundreds of dollars an hour just to nod their head and pacify me. I'd done the song and dance before and no thanks.

Mom dropped her shoulders. "Or maybe you should just talk to the source. You know your father asks about you. He asks about you all the time."

Because she was what? Talking to him? My gaze jerked in her direction. "You're talking to him?"

She nodded like that was normal, like that was *okay*. She shrugged. "It's how I'm getting my own closure."

"I don't believe this." Enraged now, livid. I shoved the food away. "So, what does that mean? You talking to him?"

"It means just as I said." She lifted her chin. "I've been seeing him. It was advised by *my* therapist, and it's been helping."

Well, then maybe she should get a new goddamn therapist because no one in their right mind would ever advise her to see that man. He was cold, *poison*, and I didn't want her anywhere near him. "I don't want you going to see him."

Her laughter touched the air as she pushed the veggies into their separate containers for the tacos. "You don't have a say in that."

"Well, I should." I growled. "What the hell, Mom?"

"You won't talk to me like that," she stated and shot me such a hard eye I thought she'd send me to my old bedroom, simply one room of many in this mansion she'd kept after the divorce. Located in central Maywood Heights, the place was my childhood home, and I used to resent the place, so big and expansive. My friends loved it, of course. It had a game room and a movie theater, but all the toys had been nothing but virtual babysitters, a place to get lost in and a way to keep me quiet and out of my dad's things. He'd never dealt with me, leaving Mom to that but she'd had her life too. She couldn't be with me every hour of the day. She had her own goals, her own passions, and I never resented her for that.

I just resented this place, him. I came around to her. "Nothing good can come out of talking to him."

The doorbell rang, and both our gazes flashed up.

"Christ in heaven," Mom said, rarely cursing which let me know the tone of the conversation had been heated. She looked at me. "I invited a colleague over for dinner with us, an old friend. She's new to town and doesn't know anyone yet."

And what a perfect time for a stranger to come in.

"Please set an extra place setting on the table," she said, completely avoiding the rest of our conversation and going into Mom mode. She pressed down her blouse. "You're going to act like the son I raised and not make us look entirely and completely dysfunctional."

I smiled. "So only partially or…"

She shoved me, like actually shoved me like a linebacker, and she would have gotten me under her arm if I didn't have her on the height. Instead, she slapped at my head, and I dodged.

"Just get the table together," she said, rolling her eyes before scurrying away. She pointed at me from the door. "And put on a different shirt. Something nice since we have company?"

I gazed down to my band tee, my eyes lifting. I didn't mind walking around in suits and dress pants all day for the office, but when I came over for weekly dinner, I thought I was safe to, I don't know, be myself.

I still did have a few things here to wear, so after getting the table set up in the dining room, I took the grand staircase two by two up to my old bedroom. I heard voices drifting from somewhere in the house as I did, and I assumed Mom was showing whoever her friend was around the house. She'd be doing that for a while since the place was so big, so I took my time to find a decent shirt before coming back downstairs.

I had cuffed my teal dress shirt at my forearms, but I didn't tuck it into my jeans like a nerdy asshole. Mom just wanted me to look presentable, so I did that coming back downstairs. Since Mom was entertaining tonight, I was surprised she'd asked the staff to leave for the evening. She'd cut down on people since the divorce but usually asked them to be around if she was having people over to help serve and everything. I suppose, with our weekly more intimate dinners, she never did that, though.

I followed my mom's voice and another female's into the dining room to find them both already sitting there. Her friend had her back turned, facing in my mother's direction, but the long flow of inky silk waves struck me as familiar.

And that raspy voice.

No. Fucking. Way.

But then, I circulated the room to find the woman's face. Brielle's head tossed back with smoky laughter. She had her hands pressed together, lightly chuckling at something my mother had said to her, her dress equally black and exposing her honeyed arms. She hugged them with her perfect manicured hands, her lips always that hard shade of red. If I didn't know any better, this woman was an assassin in another life, a femme fatale who never failed to slay and lasso me.

Jersey girl, what the hell?

But then thoughts of my mother being the dean of the history department surfaced, and I totally got it. I *got it*, but that didn't mean this all made sense.

"Oh, there's my son."

Oh, fuck.

"Ramses, honey." A wave in my direction, my mom clearly not aware of the colossal shit show she was about to display in high definition right in the middle of her dining room.

But I did. I watched those curtains draw back and the screen illuminate as a goddess in raven black tossed those chocolate brown eyes in my direction. Watched them twitch *wide* as her mouth parted and her friend, i.e. my mother, introduced me back into her life. All of which Brielle was forced to sit back and endure.

Brielle's lashes fanned in quick succession, my mother waving me in like a plane coming in for a goddamn landing. I came, of course. What the fuck else could I do?

"Sweetheart, this is Bri," Mom said, smiling through this shit. I mean, she had no idea, so why not smile, right? "She's teaching at the university. Just moved here."

She sure had, hadn't she? The pair of us well acquainted.

I swallowed with a dry mouth. Shit was about to hit the fan. I had no idea how my mother would react to the news that I'd screwed one of her colleagues, but considering she said Brielle was her friend, probably not great.

Oh, shit was Ma *the* friend? The one who'd gotten Brielle the job at Pembroke?

The stars friggin' aligned right in front of me, all this shit really making sense now. Mom had been the reason she'd been at Royal and December's wedding, *Ma* had been the reason Bri was in town and now had the job at my university. Mom had, of course, been invited to the Prinze wedding—everyone who's who in town had—but Mom also was head of the history department and worked *a lot.* Especially surrounding the weeks getting closer to a new semester. I was lucky to get her on the phone at all right before term started.

Fucking fuck.

This really did all make sense now and maybe for Bri as well, the way she looked at me. Her lips pursed, and I thought maybe she'd be the one to come clean first.

"Nice to meet you, Ramses." But then she said that, put out her hand, and once again, pretended nothing had gone down between us. She swallowed a little. "I'm Brielle, Bri."

So this is the game we're going to play?

Not surprising, considering this was her and had been her MO since I'd met her. Mom thought I was good at avoiding shit, but something told me my professor here could teach me more than a few things.

I simply stared at her, the hand between us. Bri urged me with her eyes to take it, and lucky for her, I had no desire to bring any more disappointment to my mother. I'd given her a boat load in the past few months.

I clasped Brielle's hand. "Nice to meet you. Ramses."

We shook on it, a slow shake with a bucketful of crap in it and unsaid words. What I wouldn't give to high dive head first into Jersey girl's mind right now.

At the present, I was forced to ease away from those thoughts, the shake over and both our hands returned. Between us, Mom sat like the friendly hostess she was, all this unbeknownst to her and lucky for it. Mom laced her fingers. "Bri teaches history at the university, honey."

"Does she now," I stated, gripping the back of my mom's chair. "What do you teach, Brielle?"

Obviously, I was poking her, seeing what I could get out of her when she choked on the contents of her water glass. She just so happened to be taking a drink then, one that clearly came back up in her throat with the slight cough she allowed to escape.

She pressed a napkin to her lips, passing the whole thing off with her sultry smile. Or maybe, it was only sultry to me, this woman's wiles not lost on me. She straightened. "Early western civilizations and ancient European," she stated, manicured finger easing the neck of her dress away from her throat a little. "To name a couple."

"Nice."

"Aren't you in a history class this semester, Ramses?" Mom worked around in her chair. She faced Brielle. "Ramses is a senior at Pembroke. His final semester."

Brielle took that with another shot of water, but something told me we'd both need something a little stronger by the night's end.

I smiled. "Uh, yeah, but I haven't seen Bri." I passed a glance her way. "Maybe that will change. It is a big school, but it's possible."

Bri touched a hand to her dress again. "Yes, maybe."

A small smile before I pushed off mom's chair. I jerked a

thumb back. "I'll run to the wine cellar. Get us something for dinner?"

Something told me Bri wouldn't protest and didn't as I left the room. Mom actually yelled at me to get a couple of bottles.

Here we go.

CHAPTER
TEN

Ramses

The evening was filled with Bri and me, my mother between us as Bri pretended not to know me and I, once again, let her. I understood the game she was playing, that she hadn't wanted to create tension between her and my mom, her friend. Since the woman who gave birth to me and I obviously got up to a little tension of our own only nanoseconds before, I readily endured the casual banter about work, school, and the like. Mom told Bri all about me, a proud mama, which wouldn't have been so bad had I not, uh, well, fucked her friend. I guess she and Brielle had history from when Mom used to work at NYU. My mother had done a stint there for a few years while Dad had been extending his business out there. Mallick Enterprises was global, properties all over. Maywood Heights may have been home, where he'd gotten his start, but once he'd gotten a handle over the area he'd ventured out to some more lucrative areas. This put the Mallick name all over the globe and apparently, in New York during a time where my mother had been the professor of the woman I'd slept with.

Weird or fucking what?

That was thick between us, but I had to give it to Bri, she rolled with the punches. Like in class, she didn't allow for a break in the conversation, a social butterfly with her laughter, her essence. I spent most of the time just looking at her over a dish of tamales she'd brought. She said her mom's recipe.

My lovely Latina.

Damn had this woman gotten in my head, but with my mom between us, I wasn't going to get to talk to her anytime soon. Not that Brielle allowed for absolutely any of that. She kept the party going, the conversation and wine flowing. I actually had to get a third bottle and figured, once dinner was over and dishes cleared, I might be able to sneak away and get a second to talk to her.

This appeared to come when dinner wrapped up, but once Mom made the call to get the dishes, Bri, of course, insisted on helping her with them.

Of course.

I started to help too, but that was when Bri suddenly needed to use the bathroom.

"Oh, down the hall, honey," Mom said to her, grinning. "And Ramses and I have got all these. You're the guest."

I helped Mom with the dishes. Even doing one better by offering to load the dishwasher for her. This got me extra special brownie points and basically forgiveness from words earlier exchanged. My mom was nothing if not a sucker for helpful gestures from her kid.

"Thanks, darling," she said, taking the dish towel. "Can you check on, Bri? I'm going to wipe down the table."

This saved me from making up an excuse to go do that very thing. I made my exit quick.

I found my professor down the very hallway she'd escaped

down. I caught her looking at the pictures lining the walls, pictures of my family and me. She was stopped in front of a particularly obnoxious one of all three of the Mallick brood, my dad standing behind a chair while my mom sat in it with me to her right at age like ten or eleven. What made it obnoxious was that it was a painted portrait and we all literally looked like the royal family. We'd had to stand for hours for it, and I hated that day. Dad and I had been completely at each other, and Mom had to play Switzerland between us all day.

That was us though, the Mallicks. My hands in my pockets, I sidled up next to Bri, the wine glass in her hands a permanent staple tonight. She might have to take an Uber out of this bitch once she was done.

"Enjoying our legacy?" I asked her, and when she didn't jump, angling her head back, I assumed she knew I was there. It seemed every time I spoke tonight, she launched out of her seat, like the two of us were seconds away from being caught knowing each other… intimately.

She wore that like a weighted badge, incredibly stiff when I came up on her. In fact, she eased back to the other side of the hall.

"I suppose you think this is funny," she said, looking at me. "That your mom is…"

"Your friend," I countered, not letting her have all that space. It was too much. I stamped down steps right to her, solid when I looked down at her. "Your mentor?"

Because I'd figured that out too, but what I hadn't was why she'd think I found all this funny.

"And something's funny about all this?" I asked her, placing a hand on the wall. I got right into her space, and she backed away.

"Ramses."

"Bri?" I braced my arms. "Or is it professor here?"

She shook her head, laughing. Her glass to the air, she

indulged in a healthy gulp before she rubbed her neck. "No, it's not funny, but for some reason it keeps happening."

It did keep happening.

Which was why I was confused she continued to fight it.

I steered into her space again, but once more, she angled away, and this time, I did laugh. All this was completely exhausting.

And I was so over this.

She was right, none of this was funny. But it was reality, and we had slept together.

Even if she didn't want to address it.

Regardless of how she felt, it had happened and there was no point in pretending.

We both backed away when another's steps graced the hall and we weren't alone, my mom's rag in her hands. She must have finished wiping down the table.

"How about a game of cards, you two?" Mom asked, really so unaware of the situation, the tension in my shoulders and how Brielle seemed to look at anything but me in that hallway. Mom exchanged a look between us. "Everything okay?"

Or maybe she wasn't so unaware. But like a champ, Bri passed that off quickly. She rubbed her neck, starting to say what was most assuredly a denial. Heaven forbid she spend another second with me.

"Actually, Ma, I think I'm going to head out," I said, Brielle's eyes flashing wide. No, she hadn't expected that. I directed a look at my mother. "I planned to drive back to campus tonight, classes in the morning."

This was true, but I would have stayed.

I guess I didn't see the point now.

Brielle clearly didn't want me here, but Mom did, all but frowning at my announcement, and I truly felt bad. We really didn't get to see each other a lot with our busy schedules, but this felt like it was all for the best.

"You can't stay, love?" she asked me, and when I shook my head, she did frown. "Okay."

Okay.

Taking her face, I kissed the top of her head before hugging her completely around it. Something I always did since I got taller than her, and it annoyed her.

"Oh, Ramses." She shoved at me, but knew she loved it, laughing before tapping her cheek and making me kiss her there. "Be safe."

"I will."

"And look into what I mentioned," she said, eyeing me. "You know about talking to…"

"Got it." A nod as I backed down the hallway and refused to make eye contact with a certain professor. Mom was right. I probably should talk to someone and maybe I would once I got the time.

Yeah, maybe.

For now, a drive sounded just like the trick to get my head right while at the same time giving Brielle just what she wanted.

A night so obviously away from me.

CHAPTER
ELEVEN

Bri

"My son's nice, isn't he?"

My feet caught on a chunk of ice, and I went flying, sliding across the sidewalk like a figure skater. Evie basically had to grab hold of my jacket just to keep me from falling on my ass.

"Oh my God, Bri."

Embarrassed *to hell* as she stabilized me back on my running shoes. For the most part, the sidewalks of Maywood Heights were cleared and sprinkled with salt for our early morning runs, but one still had to stay vigilant, i.e. pay attention.

Hard to do when your friend mentions the son you slept with.

A reality between both Evie and me, but definitely not mentioned to said friend who currently had a hand on me. We'd jogged downtown this morning before work, the air crisp and our Lycra tight. I typically liked jogging through varied seasonal elements, gave me a challenge, but Evie couldn't always make it and did prefer the gym. Sometimes we met after work at the Maywood Heights community center, something I preferred due to my schedule, but mornings worked out best due to hers. We tried to sync up as much as we could, but there were many days I was off on my own and she herself the same. I also preferred outdoor runs, so today we compromised. I got up early to run with her downtown, and she agreed to a sprint outside.

This felt like a mistake now as my friend had to stabilize me. Her cheeks red from the chill, her eyes twitching wide in her North Face jacket. "You okay?"

"Fine. Fine." Though not playing that off very well. I'd done just as well at dinner the other night.

And how hadn't I realized that was her son?

Mallick… freaking Mallick. God.

Evie had been married when I met her but had gone by Mallick-Pierce back then. Pierce was her maiden name, and now that she was divorced just like me, she went by simply Pierce. I honestly hadn't put two and two together and definitely not that her twenty-two-year-old kid had been the one making me moan for hours on end and well into the morning.

God, had I kept that on the down low, necessary. Though, clearly Ramses himself had felt different. I thought he might say something during taco night, and it'd only been my quick thinking to keep that from Evelyn.

I didn't know how she'd react, but she obviously wouldn't be, well, happy. Why would she? Her son was younger than me.

And you're his professor.

I wasn't touching that one with a ten-foot pole, catching my breath as Evie urged us to sit on a bench by the street. This allowed me to get things together a little, take a breath. Standing, she placed her sneaker on the bench. "You okay, hun?"

No. "Yes." I suppose I had to be, watching as she took a

seat. She started to give me some of the water she carried, but I turned it away. "Sorry. Feet just slipped from under me."

She nodded like she knew, like she cared, and I knew she did. I mean, she was the reason I was here in the first place and not back in Jersey. She did care, listened to me, which made me feel completely shitty. I was keeping a secret from her, a big one.

God, you're a terrible person.

It wasn't often I felt evil. That wedding and all my sadness during had been an example and right now in this moment another, my friend smiling down at me. Evelyn Pierce was nearly over six feet in height, well above my five foot six.

She definitely was his mother.

The woman was built like an Amazon and gorgeous to boot, a debutante in her previous life from what I understood. She came from money, married into money, and so now I knew even more why Ramses was on the level as much as he was. He came from legacy, wealth on both sides.

I mean, his daddy's name is on half these buildings.

Well, not the buildings per se, but the development signage. There wasn't a construction site in visible sight without the name Mallick on it. The only one I saw more than that was Reed, whoever that family was.

Yes, there was a lot of money in Maywood Heights, and many of the buildings themselves were graced with the name Prinze. Apparently, Ramses's friend December was linked to money as well. I was assuming so since that was her new husband's name.

Okay, so why are you thinking about her now?

Because I was obsessed, obsessed with him, and getting up, I passed off that I needed a continued break. Evie, of course, looked at me like I was crazy. I just fell, nearly splitting open my leggings, but I was ready.

Laughing, she jogged alongside me again, and this time when she brought up her son, I wasn't completely blindsided, agreeing with her about how nice he was. Ramses was nice, charismatic, charming…

Handsome.

Had he not been in his twenties and my student, I may have been all over that. Oh, and of course, the fact he was the son of like the only friend I had in the world right now.

I didn't have a lot of those at the present, lost a lot in the divorce. Everyone loved Alec Norrington, star lineman for the New York Giants. He was a big freaking deal, even now post-retirement.

The asshole.

I still had to see his face on Sports Center, grinning like an asshole just to spite me. It seemed he'd edged away from the booze enough to start making money again, like our divorce freed him up and made him actually want to do something with himself. Perhaps, losing it all made him stare his own life in the face.

I jogged to a stop. Evie did too beside me. She was easily twenty years my senior, but she was in better shape than me. That said something since I ran every day. She propped hands on her hips, getting her own few breaths in before taking a chug of her water bottle. She offered again, but I denied her.

"I suppose I just worry about him," she said, *still* talking about Ramses. It hadn't stopped, and I felt really shitty listening to that, too. She said he'd been acting off and wondered if I noticed anything at dinner the other night.

I'd answered honestly, of course. I mean, how would I know?

You don't know him, right?

I didn't technically. Anyway, this conversation was far too personal. I shouldn't be talking to his Mom about him.

"I can't help it, I suppose." She laughed it off. "You know, being his mother."

God.

"He just..." She shook her head. "He's dealing with a lot right now. Did I mention he used to go to Brown?"

She had during our run but hadn't said why he left. He went to Brown, but he was here now, working and taking over their family's businesses. The businesses thing was mentioned at dinner, in passing, but yeah, he was getting acclimated working for his family, whilst in school. Quite busy like he mentioned to me the day I cut things off initially.

Really all his priorities and his ability to juggle them made him just that much more appealing. Something else I needed to fight. Ramses may have his youth, but he was determined and appeared to have his life more together than me.

This stuff, his involvement with his family's business endeavors, was all things mentioned in front of him, though. Not this Brown issue. Whatever it may be. Even still, talking about any of this stuff without him around felt weird. It was far too personal and didn't seem to be my place to hear any of it.

Then again, this was my friend. She should be able to tell me things, right?

"What happened at Brown?" God, why had I asked? I really was obsessed. "Sorry."

"No, you're fine. He'd kill me for talking about it, but he got himself into some trouble." She propped hands on her hips. "Anyway, our lawyers had to get involved. Now he's here, working like a dog, and trying to get through school at the same time. It's a freaking mess, and he doesn't have to do it. I think he's just working to try and prove he can do it all, that he's okay, which he's not."

I wanted to ask what kind of trouble, goddamn me. Thank God Evie prattled on; otherwise, I would have asked.

"Anyway, I'm throwing all my business on you instead of asking how you've been." She cuffed my arm, smiling and how I didn't know Ramses was her kid floored me. He obviously held an ethnicity that differed from her own, maybe more than one but that smile couldn't be denied. Evie liked to smile just as much as Ramses.

What kind of trouble had he gotten into?

"Brielle?"

Evelyn's green eyes settled my way, her hands rubbing my shoulders. "You okay?"

"Yes." No. I shook my head. "I suppose I'm just still adjusting."

Still *trying to deal.* Every day was a damn struggle and only got worse as the days slogged on. I had classes to trudge through, ones involving her son and when I wasn't dealing with that issue, I had to come to terms with what had become my life. I had to come home every night and sit at an empty dining room table (yes, my furniture had finally arrived) and be by myself. I had to eat alone.

I had to think about my life.

I had to engulf myself in the reality of my situation, and like Evie knew my thoughts, she squeezed my shoulders.

"You know, there's classes you can go to, right?" she asked me, angling a look down to my level. "You're not the only one going through divorce, life changes, and other things."

Life changes.

She'd put that nicely, few things I could tell my friend about my divorce. I'd signed an NDA surrounding all marital issues involving my celebrity husband, but one I could speak of had been what she referenced. She knew about my life change.

She knew about my entire world upheaving.

She had, hence why she'd been trying to get me to go out that night of the wedding. She wanted me to be a part of the world, make friends, and now, apparently wanted me to go to therapy.

"I'll send you some information for a group I know about," she said. "You can meet with others. *Talk about it* and, of course, talk to me."

I did know I could, but how would I? I didn't have the audacity. I mean, I'd slept with her son.

I was lying to her like I lied to myself on any given day, that I was okay, that I had moved on from things in my past.

It seemed she had two liars in her life apparently.

CHAPTER
TWELVE

Bri

I'd been surprised to see Ramses had decided to not finish out the rest of the week's classes. There were only two, but he didn't show for the last one like the rest of the class. I assumed he'd been the smart one and decided to put us both out of our misery by dropping the seminar, but the following week, he'd been there in the back row.

I knew because he texted through most of it.

He was casual about it, but as I was also completely aware of him, I knew exactly what he was getting up to in that back row. He had his phone out on the table, his gaze jerking over it as much as he took notes on the laptop in front of him. He took notes like the rest of the class in that way, but his cell got just as much of his attention as his notes, and that'd surprised me.

I wouldn't say I expected to have his eyes and attention on me the entire time in class...

Actually, I did. I very much expected it because I was his teacher and he should have his attention on me. The fact we'd hooked up even more a given, as arrogant as that sounded. He'd been a frequent flier in my mind, so yes. I expected the same. Especially after that awkward-as-hell dinner and him cornering me in the hallway, him *leaving me* in the hallway. He'd dashed out rather quickly that day and I figured to save me, to save us from more awkwardness.

Well, in class today it seemed he'd forgotten about me. I was apparently his professor and only that when he came in and immediately started taking notes with the rest of the class. He did so at the top of the hour, his focus on only that. Of course, I did catch those dusky brown eyes on occasion, but never longer than it took for him to get the point before he was back to taking his notes or on his cell phone. He was either really into today's lecture or doing other work, or something else out of class. That annoyed me, yes, but it made me equally sick to not have as much of his attention.

What the hell, Bri?

These feelings were completely unreasonable, of course. Completely inappropriate, I knew, but we did have a history and, yeah, he was on my mind. He was naturally since I did have runs with his mother either before or after work. When I wasn't with him, I got to hear about him, naturally since that was Evie's kid. None of our topics were as deep as the other day, but he made it into the conversation more than once since then.

"Can I see you in my office after class, Ramses?"

His gaze jerked up at the end of the hour, his classmates putting their note taking devices away. He'd been doing the same as well and at the sound of his name, actually looked around like he wasn't the only one in class with his name.

Well, after he realized I was speaking to him, actually speaking and not avoiding eye contact, he nodded at me. I'd been bad about that, trying not to look directly at him, which made it even worse. It annoyed me he'd been attempting to do the same. We didn't clash a lot, not on either of our ends.

God, I was a hypocrite.

Amongst other things, a cradle robber… well, not really. But I was a liar to a friend who'd been nothing but gracious and helpful towards me.

Evie had been so kind to me since I'd come to Maywood Heights, and here I was lying to her on the daily. The only relief I got from that was the fact that she was very busy and didn't always have time to visit with me in my office or go for our runs. We hadn't gotten to run together at all this week yet due to her tight schedule.

Ramses stood up in his suit, not surprising considering how formal he'd dressed last week. I assumed that had something to do with his job and today, he'd come in a full suit. In fact, the gray tapered blazer and tight trousers reminded me very much of the outfit I'd met him in, the wedding where we'd had so much fire. He'd basically blown me out of Evie's Louboutin heels, and I had offered to give them back to her on a few occasions. She'd insisted I keep them, though, claiming she had a closest full of them and those were her gift to me. My friend was very generous.

I didn't allow Ramses's gaze to stay on me long before I was gathering my things and dashing out of the classroom. I needed time to get to my office and get myself together. He knew where my office was like the rest of the class since I put the room number on my emails and syllabus. I emailed the class quite a few times so, yeah, he should know where he was going.

It wasn't far, down the hall, and after unlocking it, I tossed in my bag, then fluffed my hair like an idiot. I even swiped on a fresh layer of red across my lips, like that mattered.

What are you doing? This isn't a hookup.

Tell my body that, completely buzzing at the fact my student was going to be here in nanoseconds. My hot student with the height of a demigod and a smile of an actual god. I'd missed seeing it in the class he'd missed, and today, he'd avoided my eye contact.

Yes, I was a complete mess, but I did stare in the mirror a second before smoothing out my cigarette pants and easing myself into my desk chair. I had my laptop out and ready. I did have office hours after this so I could pass off trying to look like I was working.

Tap. Tap. Tap.

Like he was trying to be timid, or maybe just hesitant. I had pushed him away on more than one occasion. I blew out a breath. "Come in."

He did behind my laptop, again lowering his head for basically every door frame he had to walk through. Outside of that, he filled the thing nearly shoulder to broad shoulder, that blazer he wore sans the tie. Perhaps, whatever work function he was doing today didn't require it.

"You wanted to see me, Professor?" he asked, grinning when he took off his leather bag. He adjusted it to his shoulder. "Am I in trouble?"

He would be if he kept call me *professor* in that way, an edge to it I most likely put there because I wanted to hear it.

Cool your jets. This ends here.

Hence why I asked to see him, waving him in. He closed the door, then stamped those big thighs of his directly in front of me. I swallowed. "Probably don't call me that."

"What?"

My lips pinched together. "Professor. It's just…" Weird. Ridiculous? I pushed my hair out of my face. "Just not professor."

His grin easy now, he eyed me. "What do you want me to call you then? Professor is what you wanted. What you said, right?"

He hadn't been smart about it, but direct, and I didn't miss how his throat tightened and worked a little. He may be aware I requested he call me that, but that didn't mean it sat well.

It just showed me even more that this particular arrangement, what we were, wouldn't work out any more than anything else had before.

I opened my hands, inviting him to a seat, and though he took it, he was hesitant about it. Like most things, he caused the seat to completely dwarf beneath him, his long limbs squeezing in just to adjust. He was like Goldilocks in a little chair but made do when he crossed his leg at the knee. He frowned. "*Am* I in trouble?"

I closed my laptop. "I just noticed I missed your attention today," I said, nodding. "You were texting and possibly doing other work. At least, that's what I'm assuming."

I was speaking to him like I would any other student, but the issue was Ramses wasn't every other student. He'd been mine.

At least, for a night.

He'd been a heavy cross, a sin in an evening charged rife with emotion and no matter how hard I tried, I just couldn't seem to wash all that away.

His lips parted, a lengthy digit scratching his bare cheek. He flashed that chunky ring he wore, the one he'd fucked me and tightened my walls with.

I crossed my legs beneath the desk.

Like he noticed my reaction, either to the ring or him, he dropped his hands between his legs and leaned forward. "Sorry. I didn't mean to be rude. And you're right. I was working. Doing other projects but not school. I've been working really long hours. My father's business, but that's no excuse. You're right. I shouldn't have been doing that."

I nodded, sitting back. "I remember your mom mentioning that the other night. You working for your family's business?" I messed with my wristwatch. "I get it. You have a lot of responsibility."

This seemed untold, and I wondered why he took on so much. If it was really like Evie said, him trying to prove something...

Not my business, I shook my head. "I do want to talk to you about something else, though."

"What?"

I breathed a shallow breath. Could I really let him go? I needed to. I was well aware of that. My fingers danced on my desk. "I don't like that I know so much about you. That I know how busy you are outside of the teacher-student relationship. That your mom and I are friends and that I have to lie to her—"

"But you don't." His lips tightened. "I wanted to tell her the truth that night. You never gave me the chance."

I did know that, but that was only part of the problem. "I don't think this is working out."

"What isn't?"

"You being in my class." I couldn't see him in my class every week, just too hard.

Weak, I knew.

I was just too emotionally invested in him, and it didn't feel good. It was a distraction, and it had to be for him too. He, too, had been trying to avoid my eyesight, and he shouldn't have to do that. He couldn't do that. I was his professor, and that was obvious.

I pressed my hands together. "I know what I said. That I could deal, but I don't think either of us should have to. I should be able to teach without thinking about... what happened. And you should be able to come to me, or any other professor you have, as a professor and nothing else. You should be able to *look at me* without—"

"I can look at you." His chest hovered over the desk. "I do."

Okay, so that was the problem. *That.*

He did look at me. He did see me, and I did as well.

I laced my fingers. "Don't make this hard." *Don't make this inappropriate.* "You already have it hard enough, don't you think? You're working. You're also in the last semester of your senior year, and you should be able to focus. I am a distraction, and I don't want to be that for you."

He said nothing, his lips closing. "So, you want me to drop the class."

"I'll sign off on any class you want to get into. I'll even speak to anyone whose period you want to join in the department. Doesn't have to be early western civ."

Just as long as it wasn't with me.

This was so very selfish what I was making him do, to completely adjust his life to mine, but I couldn't do this. This was week two, and I already couldn't do this. I couldn't see him weekly.

I couldn't lie to Evie.

At least with him not in my class, I wouldn't have to keep in that lie, and he wouldn't have to either. He was lying to her too.

Because you made him.

I waited, just waited. I needed to give him time and it was completely warranted.

Ramses jaw shifted, tightening before lacing his fingers across his chest. I thought he'd fight me on this. He had before, so it definitely surprised me when he reached down and picked up his bag.

"If that's what you want then," he said, and my stomach immediately turned sour. I really had expected him to fight me on this. To give it to me good like he always did. That was just who he was. Ramses pushed. "It'll probably be for the best anyway."

I guess not today.

That sickness stirred deep. Especially as I watched him walk toward the door.

"I'll sign whatever transfer slip you give me then." I swallowed hard. "Just let me know whenever."

He leveled me with his brown eyes, giving nothing more
than a nod before letting the door close behind him. He left
me to my thoughts without another word, and I suppose I'd
gotten exactly what I wanted.

I guess just remember that.

CHAPTER
THIRTEEN

Bri

I was late for the meeting Evie had suggested I go to that evening.

A bereavement group.

Actually, I'd gotten there on time but simply hadn't been brave enough to go inside.

Instead, I watched from outside the class doors, waiting until the next group, Coping with Change.

This one seemed better suited. So after that wrapped, I made my way inside, tugging off my coat and taking a seat. They had a podium up front, and I very much intended to make myself blend in. I most assuredly wouldn't be talking and definitely didn't want to be there. I figured I'd sit back, relax, and see what these people had to say.

Evie: Did you go? How was it?

I decided to pocket my phone and respond after this class. That way, when I gave my friend a response, it wouldn't technically be a lie.

God, I was still lying to her. In a different way, but lying, nonetheless. She wanted to help me, and I had actually come to the building.

Even if I hadn't gone inside.

I sat within the seating arrangement with a shaking leg, my wool coat on top as I circulated my gaze around. I found myself rather happy that I opted not to eat dinner before coming. I'd thought about it since I was fresh out of work and after that long drive, but when I'd stopped home, I'd simply showered before putting on a pair of jeans and a casual top. I'd had just enough time to get downtown, then park in front of the building in Maywood Heights's capitol district. Of course, everyone working had already gone home, the evening settling into a quiet chill, and I had managed not to trip outside on the ice this time.

I should leave. I should definitely leave.

My confidence was quickly leaving me the longer I sat, and even though this was only a group meeting about trying to deal with change, I wasn't quite sure I was ready to deal with my changes. I could win the award for avoidance these days.

To fill the time before starting, I pulled out my phone, playing a game with jewels. I exploded a few before tossing my head back and shoving my phone into my purse. I shot up out of my chair.

"Sorry."

My head jerked up, nearly colliding into someone with my coat in my arms and my purse on my shoulder. I'd wimped out, trying to leave.

But then him.

Ramses picked up the program I'd dropped. *Ramses* was standing in front of the aisle with his coat on and his cheeks flushed like he himself had just rushed over here. He had snow in his hair, a white mist on those ebony brown locks. He handed out my program. "You dropped this... looks like."

What the fuck?

But there he stood. Again in my life after I, once more, tossed him out of it just today. I idly wondered if this would keep happening, since we both obviously frequented the same towns. But really, this shouldn't be happening. There were more than two people who lived in Maywood Heights and even more who frequented Pembroke's campus.

And yet, here we were.

I swallowed, taking it. "Thank you?"

A question to it, because well, what the fuck?

His hand now free, Ramses brushed the snow out of his hair before eyeing the empty seat I hovered over. He pointed toward it. "This, uh, taken or are you leaving?"

I was leaving. I should leave.

Instead, I opted to stand there like a loon. I think mostly due to shock and Ramses took my silence for, well, I didn't know what for, but he crossed in front of me.

He completely bypassed the seat he'd eyed and without a word, sat himself down in the one next to it. He immediately took the next steps to make himself comfortable, taking off his scarf and coat, then placing it there on the seat beside his chair without a word. He literally didn't speak to me, fisting his hands before resting them on the chair ahead. Eventually, he passed a look over to me who was still standing there.

"You going to sit?" He eyed me, actually curious. His eyebrows furrowed in—tight. "Though, I am quite curious why you're continuing to stalk me."

Me stalk *him*?

I chortled, barking a laugh before righting with my stuff. "I'm not stalking you."

"Sure." His eyes twinkled now; his fingers laced. He glanced at the seat beside him. "Well, are you going to sit?"

No, and I showed him that when I exited out of the aisle. By then, the room had basically completely filled, but I made it only about halfway to the door before a woman in jeans and a beanie hat closed it. She was middle-aged, gray and brown curls under her hat, and pulling off her gloves, she looked at me. "Oh, you're a new face. You joining us today, sweetie?"

Well, fuck.

But before I could fight her, she was guiding me back toward the chairs, telling me her life story and how nice this group was. She also said she hoped I'd participate and after literally walking me toward the front of the room, deposited me maybe a row or two behind Ramses.

I plopped down with basically a plop as the woman smiled at me.

"We're about to begin," she said. "Happy to have you."

I forced my own smile through gritted teeth. I was here now, so I obviously couldn't leave.

I placed my coat down as I watched the woman waddle her way up toward the front of the room, about to curse then growl when I noticed shaking shoulders ahead.

I caught Ramses mid-glance as he faced forward, the jerk *laughing* and clearly at me. Call it a freaking feeling, his head going back as he crossed his legs then placed his hands on his knee.

"Welcome to Coping with Change," the woman who seated me said, grinning at the crowd. "This is a very easy going group, and I hope we can all help each other. We have a lot of new faces today, so let's start by saying our names. How about you first over there? We spoke before. Would love to know a bit about who you are. Happy to have you."

All gazes navigated in my direction and Ramses, well, completely turned around. He'd also gone casual today, his band t-shirt cuffing hard over his shoulders as he rested a thick arm on the back of his chair. He actually looked his age today, a typical college guy in his well-worn jeans.

He passed me that Ramses's grin, dashing his eyebrows in my direction to tell these strangers all about myself.

Shaking my head, I faced the room, making my name and occupation known but quickly. After that, they moved on and

I didn't miss those large shoulders shaking with silent laughter. Ramses got great satisfaction out of my discomfort.

I shrunk in my chair.

I tried not to the whole meeting, but all this was terribly awkward even if I hadn't run into the guy I'd slept with, who was also my student and my friend's son.

I wrestled with my coat above a rocking knee, only partially listening to everyone going around and sharing. I found myself distracted by the guy not two rows in front of me, the one paying complete attention like he was in class.

Ramses listened to everyone's stories. He mentioned nothing about himself but did participate with the other's in the group. In fact, he'd engaged a lot with them, in that social way and that gift of the gab he had. He was still doing the appeasing thing he did, clearly. I'd seen it on more than one occasion with myself. The last time he'd made me look at him. Just look at him to calm down.

"Listen to me and get out of your head."

I heard his voice in a paraphrase circulating my brain, how I had come down from panic. He was really good at that, keeping others from panicking.

"We'll take a short break, everyone, and maybe those who haven't shared yet can. Though, of course, you're by no means obligated, as always."

I faced forward to find a woman's eyes on me, the one who'd worn the beanie hat. She winked at me, acknowledging me before I rushed out of my chair and immediately went to get coffee at the group's coffeemaker.

Of course, I wasn't the only one with thoughts to head there, and the guy at the brewer stood ready as if waiting for me.

Apparently, he was. Ramses literally had two cups of coffee in his hands, one he gave to me the moment I got up there. At this point, he seemed to have his life together more than myself.

"Thank you," I said, taking it but not drinking. Something told me it'd go down in nothing but a lump.

"No problem." He eased out of the way for the crowd, both of us did. He tipped the cup in my direction. "So, Coping with Change."

"Coping with Change," I mumbled. "Your mom suggested it." Kind of a lie, kind of the truth. She'd actually suggested bereavement for me. My jaw moved. "I have a lot of changes. You know, being new here. I also just got divorced, so…"

"Right." He lifted his coffee again. I hadn't told him I'd *just* gotten divorced, but he knew about it. He nodded. "So, I guess you're not stalking me then?"

"Not."

He appeared to be let down, feigning it before chuckling. "Mom suggested this to me. Texted me with the details about a week ago, but I'm finally getting off my ass to do it. Apparently, group therapy will help me with 'my attitude.'"

I frowned.

"I've got my own changes I'm going through." He shrugged. "Most recently, coming back home. I used to go to Brown University before Pembroke."

"Yeah, she told me," I informed him, and when he blinked, I thought to say more as well. "Not the details, but that you used to go there. That you don't now and that you maybe got into some trouble."

"Ah. Seems my life is an open book." His brow lifted, not much humor there. Not like he usually had anyway. He took a sip of his coffee, but when he cringed, I laughed.

That was until I tasted mine.

It was freaking terrible, the epitome of, and seeing my face, Ramses took my cup.

"Let's, uh," he started, making quick work of them both by tossing the paper cups in the trash. After that, he ventured over to his stuff. He slid those long arms into his coat, and when he popped his collar, I asked him what was up. He laughed. "I think I've had enough coping. I'm going to go get a real cup of coffee."

"You're playing hooky?" I eyed him, being coy, something I never did. Well, before him.

"Maybe. You game? I don't see you trying to cope with a lot of change either." He leaned in. "You know, since you basically almost ran me down trying to leave."

I shoved him and immediately noticed when my hand lingered. How it burned at even just a touch of him. He made it so easy to be in his presence, and though I definitely shouldn't be ditching anything to go and be with him, I did notice my way of coping, feeling better, only seemed to happen as of late with him around.

Bringing my hand back, I studied the room. "Promise not to tell Evie?"

But he was already grabbing my stuff. He handed me my coat. "As long as you promise not to tell my mom."

———

Ramses chose a donut place, one easy to walk to downtown. We hadn't had to drive and made quick work of dodging the intensifying snow. We eased inside the shop like we had that night for pizza, but this time, he let me order for myself. Not that I didn't want him to order for me. It just didn't seem appropriate today.

Things were different at this moment in time, the two of us acquaintances, and acquaintances ordered for themselves.

Yes, that.

Anyway, I got my favorite donut, a chocolate-covered long John. He'd chosen about half a dozen donut holes and black coffee. My bottle of water was good with my food after that terrible coffee at the meeting.

We joked about that again as we sat down and after taking

off our coats, found ourselves once again in easy conversation. I didn't know what it was about this guy who was over a decade my junior. He was just freaking easy to talk to. He told me about his day of work after class, and I told him about my day teaching. It hadn't been hard for either of us, and though I think we both had a few questions about how the evening began, we didn't talk about it.

At least, not at first.

I saw the topic shift into something different quickly. How the easy stuff started to lull and the harder stuff poked toward that awkward silence. How the urge to find out something about each other besides the physical or the trivial stuff on paper was there, and really, that was when we had left together last time. We'd didn't want to talk once we hit that point at the pizza place. We'd wanted to avoid.

Because if we had, we would've had to look in each other's eyes.

We had to *see* each other, flaws and all. We had to reveal truths and the struggles of our pasts, and that night at the wedding, I didn't think either one of us wanted to do that.

We'd shown that in spades.

"So, your mom thinks you have an attitude," I chose to say, still easy and way more painless to endure than his eyes on me, searching me. I found myself avoiding their probe behind my bottle of water, the perfect way to avoid the seemingly endless press of his gaze.

Perhaps, he noticed what I did there, turning the tables and topic in his direction. If he did, he didn't call attention to it, wiping his hands on his napkin before leaning back. He once again filled the entire booth, a mighty titan and the world his tiny abyss. His smile lifted right. "I do have an attitude. Honestly, I find it hard to believe she hasn't disowned me at this point."

Well, I found *that* hard to believe, this guy a perfect

gentleman to the point I thought I should search for his robotic wires. I crossed my arms. "You're messing with me."

"Not messing." A chuckle as he tapped his cup. "I'm a smart ass and you yourself said I was arrogant."

He was, sometimes. I eyed him. "Why on God's green Earth would Evie," I stopped when I realized I was talking about his mother. Dumb, I knew. "Why would she think you have an attitude?"

"Because I push. I push her. She doesn't get me some-times, and when she pushes, I push right back. I'm stubborn that way."

He stole a drink of his coffee, cold at this point, but then the guy behind the counter came over and filled him up.

Ramses grinned. "Thanks, Charlie."

He passed a bill Charlie's way. Not quite a hundred but way more than the dollar and a half that brew had cost him.

"I have no idea how I didn't know you were Evelyn's son." I uncapped my water, taking a drink. "She's very generous too."

Not to mention, he looked quite a bit like her. They had the same smile and same eyes, despite the color. There was that other part, though.

I tilted my head. "Where is your dad from? Well, I guess I mean his heritage."

I, too, had a few in there: Mexican, Puerto Rican, and a myriad of others that made me tick quite a few checks on the European spectrum in addition. I sort of knew the breakdown since I did one of those cheek swab things about a year ago. I didn't do much with it after that, since I started getting notifi-cations about distant family members wanting to connect with me. One of them had been one of my high school teachers and that had just been friggin' weird.

Ramses hadn't said anything after my question, adjusting himself in his seat. He angled his neck back and forth before popping his fingers and I wondered if I said something.

"He's Syrian." Gruff, rigid before he took another sip of coffee. He put his cup out. "You? You said at dinner those tamales were your mom's recipe so…"

"Mexican. She is and some Puerto Rican. Dad is Caucasian. A bunch of stuff there. Though the breakdown is a little unclear."

He seemed to stop listening to me at this point and that so didn't seem like him.

I tilted my head. "Ramses?"

"Yep?" He jerked his attention in my direction, and I laughed.

"You okay?"

"Why wouldn't I be?" Another stiff drink of his coffee. He pulled it down. "I'm fine."

"You're not." I spun my half empty water bottle on the table, catching it with my fingers. "So how about some truth? What? You don't talk with your dad?"

I knew his parents were divorced from Evie. Not much more than that, though. I didn't know if he lived in town or whatever. I assumed he did since their family's businesses were here.

"I do not." He said this with a smile, but it was false and didn't reach his brown eyes at all. "Not in over four years, and as far as I'm concerned, not long enough time has passed."

Ouch, and definitely, not like him. "Ram—"

"He's in prison, Brielle," he said, and my eyes twitched wide. He frowned. "You didn't know that? Mom didn't tell you… that?"

She hadn't, just that she was divorced. I shook my head.

"Damn." A shake to his head before he looked at me. He lifted his hand from his cup. "Sorry."

"No. I didn't know."

"Even still, I shouldn't have bit your head off." He drew fingers down his face, and I finally noticed how tired he looked. He had a darkness under his eyes I definitely hadn't noticed in my office.

I guess I hadn't been looking for it.

I'd been too busy trying to shove him out of my life once again. I eased forward. "Want to talk about it?"

"Not really." His laugh was dry before he gazed down at me. "But I guess that's why I probably should have been at Coping with Change tonight."

And here I thought it was whatever his issue was at Brown.

Or maybe they were one and the same.

Wow.

I'd pegged this guy completely wrong, thinking all his issues had to do with his friend, feelings for her. Maybe those were there, but there were clearly other things going on too.

His throat worked. "I told you I have an attitude problem."

"But you don't." He was just hurting, clearly hurting.

I started to reach for his hand across the table, but I hesitated.

Don't do that. Don't comfort him, console him.

It was so easy to want to, indulge in his pain if only so I didn't have to feel mine. We really were the ultimate distraction for each other.

I slid my hands into my lap. "I'm sorry you're going through things."

He tipped up a large shoulder. "Poor little rich boy, right?" he stated off a chuckle. "Tale as old as time. The world is my oyster, and I still manage to find shit."

"I think you're simplifying things."

"I don't." His lips turned down. "It's reality, but I guess it's a good thing that at least I'm aware of it."

I guess.

I played with my bottle again. "So that had to do with your issue at Brown?"

"Mom seems to think so, yeah." He nodded. "She may be right. I hold a lot of resentment for my dad. He did some bad things. Hurt our family pretty bad."

I wanted him to talk to me about it, share with me but it wasn't my place. I cuffed my arms. "And here I just had a divorce."

Now, *I* was simplifying things, readily aware of that.

As if calling me on the carpet, Ramses shot daggers at me. At least, they felt like daggers. He gave me a look that said nothing but "Yeah, try again" and I laughed.

I opened my hands. "It maybe was more complicated than that."

Ramses landed his big fists on the table, eyeing me, and I knew I had to give him more than that. I did, but...

I worked my jaw. "I can only say so much, but things got intense." *Physical.* I forced out a breath. "He put hands on me."

I think it was the first time I'd said it out loud. Though I wasn't allowed to technically say it out loud. I'd signed a long paper that said I couldn't. Not that my husband had beaten me within an inch of my life or anything. But he had hurt me, enough to put bruises on me, and made it so I couldn't show my face in public for weeks. My ex-husband was a pretty powerful man, popular in his sphere, even post-retirement, and that couldn't get out.

And here I simplified things again.

The beating had been the end result of something else and actually only happened once but was enough to make me see things were done. That we couldn't heal, and it was actually easier to talk about than prior traumas.

In fact, a lot easier.

Ramses's expression shifted at that point, a darkness hitting his eyes I'd never seen before. His fingers worked on the table, and I wondered if he'd actually flip it over.

And he hadn't said anything.

Not a word.

But that didn't mean none of them flashed across his eyes, that there were so many things he wanted to say but just didn't know how to say them. He simply kept them to himself.

"Coping with Change and Emotional Stressors," he growled, saying the full title of the class. That was one of the reasons I'd decided on it.

I'd had a lot of emotional stress.

Ramses dragged his fingers down his face, his mouth pinched tight and his brow furrowed. "How long ago was this?"

I shook my head. "Doesn't matter."

"How long ago?" It was like he needed to know, like it did matter. "Brielle?"

"Not long." I wished it had been longer. "I moved for a fresh start. He's a public figure, and technically, I'm not supposed to talk about this. I signed an NDA."

"An NDA?" His laughter was thick and throaty before he forced down more coffee. "How much of a fucking coward could this guy be? What's his name?"

"I told you. I'm not supposed to talk about it. This is a breech, me even talking about it now."

Why the fuck had I talked about it?

Goddamn it.

I started to get up, but he grabbed my wrist. I shook it off. "*No*, Ramses. I have to go."

"Why?" He got up too. "Bri—"

"I tell you too many things," I shot out, definitely getting others' attention if they'd been there. Fortunately for us, there was just the donut shop owner, and he must have been in the back somewhere since I didn't see him. I faced him. "I talk to you about things, and I'm not myself. I don't trust who I am with you."

"You don't think I feel the same way?" he asked, angling

himself in front of me. It wasn't hard to do. He towered over me, an unyielding force of male and body. His lips pinched tight. "You don't think I tell you shit I don't want to say? That it's not driving me freaking crazy?" He forced his hand through his thick curls. "If anything, that's why we should be friends."

"Friends?" I frowned, shaking my head. "Ramses, I *cannot* be friends with you." Like I said, I didn't trust myself around him, not at all. I was like a walking drunk with him in the air surrounding me. I squeezed my arms. "We'd be horrible friends."

Besides wanting to fuck each other every moment of the day, we did tell each other a lot of personal shit. I broke an NDA because of him.

I started to walk off, but he grabbed my arm again.

"Just hear me out," he said, quick and in front of me. "We talk to each other. *Vent* to each other instead of letting that shit bottle up."

"And what? We just pretend we didn't screw?"

I was suddenly incredibly aware of how quiet the donut shop was, and that old man behind the counter did make himself known.

He wiped it down with a small smile before lifting his finger and heading to the back, and Ramses and I surprisingly both busted out laughing. Like full-blown laughter to the point where I grabbed my knees and Ramses shook his head.

He rolled his eyes. "Don't worry about Charlie. He's known me since I was a kid, but he's old reliable. He won't say anything to my mom."

I hadn't even thought about that, but trusted Charlie if he did.

The laughter dying down, Ramses braced his arms.

"My own mother said I need to talk to someone," he

admitted. "She obviously said the same thing to you, and I can't see why we can't be that for each other."

I could, the first starting with said sex mentioned before. "And the screwing?"

"Well, I'm not your student anymore. Won't be soon once I get the transfer."

"Ramses—"

He grabbed my hand, cutting me off, and I let him hold it because I was selfish. Because I wanted him to so desperately I could taste it.

I think he did too, his long digits playing with the back of my hand. Eventually, he let go, and when he did, he took a step back.

"I'm joking obviously," he said when it wasn't obvious, not at all. He forced a heavy breath. "It's also obvious that's not what you want our relationship to be, and I respect that, but I am selfish enough to ask for your friendship. I think it would be good. *For both of us.* And like I said, I'm not going be your student once I transfer out. It won't be weird."

It would still be weird.

But I was selfish too.

My hand still burned despite being absent of his. I looked up. "And Evie?"

"I don't like lying to my mom, but I will if you don't feel comfortable mentioning *we are friends* and only that." He stepped forward. "Please. I'm begging you. This is me begging."

He started to get on his knees before I grabbed him and forced him up.

He chuckled. "I'm joking."

Clearly, his need for friendship was desperate—clearly.

But wasn't mine as well?

I'd been so lonely.

"Only friends?" I asked him, needing to be sure. "I really can't have anything else right now."

I wasn't ready for anything else. I think I could take being Ramses's friend.

But his lover?

God, I hadn't known him long, but I felt he literally had the capability to destroy my entire heart. It'd be a blazing fire with him, so good and hot all the way in.

But on the way down?

Even worse, if I let him go there.

He approached me again, his smile down on me. He lifted a hand. "Thumb war you for it? I win, you stay and be my friend. You win, I walk away."

He'd sucked at this game before but offered anyway.

I raised my hand. "You promise?"

He didn't have to say, our hands touching. He counted us down, and I didn't think it mattered who won. We both knew I'd call him back like I had that night.

Because I sucked at this game too.

CHAPTER
FOURTEEN

Bri

The foray into Ramses's and my friendship started with texts.
Just texting. He'd send me these meme things he found funny
throughout his day. Completely ridiculous, but I went along
with them because they were funny in how often hilariously
outlandish they were. They made sense with, well, his age
and his laid-back personality.

Don't do the age thing.

I didn't for the most part, not really a thing. In any sense,
we were friends now, and only that. I'd been hesitant when,
during one of those ridiculous text messages, he sent me one
about running. Apparently, he liked to run, just like me. He
tended to go in the evenings since that was the best time for
him after work and school.

And so that was how *that* happened.

Ramses and I running.

Ramses and I exercising together like actual friends.

Go figure, right?

I'd been hesitant at first. Texting had been one thing but

meeting up entirely another. He assured me there'd be no funny business, and since his running schedule matched my preference, I decided to try it out. Doing so also let Evie off the hook. She hated running outside during winter anyway and did prefer mornings.

"Oh, I don't mind, dear. Have fun!"

I'd literally gotten her blessing. I left out the detail I was running with her son, and at this point, I wasn't sure there really was a lie. I was running with a friend, a platonic friend at that. I could run with a guy and it not be a thing.

So that was what I did.

Ramses and I started jogging that first day after my last class. He was getting off of work too and actually offered to pick me up. That felt kind of weird. I mean, for me. I knew we were just friends now, but I thought it'd be best we meet up at a park or something. Of course, he understood, so that was what we did. We'd both shown up with winter running gear on.

And he'd basically looked like a Nike ad.

He was the epitome of in his stretchy black Under Armour, long and lean as it smoothed over his biceps and thick legs. He wore a dark hoodie and shorts over the bottoms and long-sleeved shirt, basically the hottest friend I'd ever had in my entire life. He had dark gloves on and a hat beneath his hood as well, completely ready for the run.

"Ready, buddy?" He grinned that first day, and I suppose I had to be. I still couldn't believe I'd told him about Alec, but he was right. There was something about us just dishing our secrets together. I told him things I didn't mean to tell him, and he seemed to do the same.

Hiking up my legs in my stretchy Lycra I allowed him to lead the run into the park, my "hot friend" beside me the whole way. It wasn't lost on me Ramses had long basically everything, and though I did have to pump extra hard to keep up with him, I liked the challenge. He rarely had to adjust to me, which I caught him doing more than a time or two. For the most part, he wasn't obnoxious about it.

Though he did run backward a couple of times.

He liked to taunt me, push me, and as it never failed to crack a smile out of me, I let him.

I let him every time.

Before I knew it, a couple weeks flew by like this. Weeks of me rushing through classes just to see my text messages, to see his silly memes or pictures of him bored at the office. He texted me whenever he had time, and I didn't complain, basically high off the anticipated moments before. I was very aware of how this may have looked from the outside.

I just didn't care.

I let him send the text messages. I ran with him almost every day and even ignored the fact that he still hadn't opted out of my class yet. He mentioned looking into a minimester during our runs, one of those classes with a reduced length that had longer class periods. He planned to sign up for one once he figured out how it would coincide with his current work and class schedule. In the meantime, he was still with me, my student.

My student who I ran with and listened to his silly jokes. My friend who talked to me about everything that wasn't my divorce or his own issues. We probably should talk about these things. I mean, there was a reason we'd decided to dive into the valley of friendship, and it wasn't just to be around each other.

Or maybe it was.

I liked being around Ramses, the heat of his hard body when we rounded a corner and his Under Armour brushed my white fleece. I liked the air of Ramses, how he consumed it with his male essence and heady flavor. I tasted him every brisk step during our runs and probably the same on his end as well. I often caught him staring down at me, his cheekbones haloed and chilled with red tint, his curls shifting and swaying beneath his hat. Our gazes collided a lot while we ran together, talked and enjoyed each other, but never once did we acknowledge the awareness between us. It went unsaid, like our various dramas, and there was nothing wrong with being attracted to each other.

Not when it felt like this, easy with our laughter and banter. I found myself longing to be with him just because he made it easy, and today's run was no exception. We'd decided to stick to some of the neighborhoods on campus, sprinting through suburbs and uphill. We'd started to venture back when I made the mistake of telling him about my internship during my undergraduate studies. Mistake because Ramses couldn't take anything and not make a joke about it.

"Wait, so let me get this straight," he said, basically a visual feast in his sweatpants and breaker jacket. I was starting to get used to how ridiculously hot my friend was, his sweatpants low but fitted tight to his muscular ass, his jacket bulky and thick across his broad shoulders. I may be used to it, but that didn't mean I failed to notice it. Ramses was hot, but there was no rule that said a girl couldn't have hot friends.

Yeah, that.

Currently, said hot friend pressed an elbow into my side, an indicator a jostling was coming. Ramses couldn't help but jostle, and I'd care more if I actually hated it.

Which I didn't.

Again, it was so easy to be with him it was scary, and I think I needed more fear in my life. If fear was this, I needed more of it. More of Ramses Mallick and his carefree attitude. He grinned at me. "You used to do digs? Like actual digs like some shit out of *Jurassic Park*?"

Nothing quite so *Jurassic Park*-esque, but he did get the gist of it. I shrugged. "Not nearly as exciting but yeah. We mostly dug up pottery and stuff."

It'd actually been the time of my life and the reason I'd

gotten into early western civilizations as much as I had. I liked stumbling across and waking up old life. It was like a rebirth and completely exhilarating. Most of my work had been in Africa as well as some parts of Europe. I'd only come back because I had to graduate and had gotten married shortly after that time as well.

It'd been early and exciting days, days before drama, trauma. It'd been days before Ramses, and I forgot about them as quickly as they surfaced with just a flash of his smile. He still handed those things out like penny candy, his jog backwards as he picked up.

"You totally saw a T-rex," he stated, eyebrows bouncing. "But if you wanna be modest and all tight-lipped about it, whatev."

"I didn't." I shoved him and he grabbed my hands. Trying to get this guy to move at all was hilarious. One, because he was bigger than me, and two, well, because he was bigger than me. He didn't move an inch, and all shoving him did was get him to cradle me.

He literally brought his entire big body around me, grappling me in a bear hug, which made me laugh my head off and nearly pee my pants. There were days I swear to God I lost a few pounds from sheer laughter due to this guy, but that didn't mean I refused to fight back. I pinched at his wrists, digging my fingernails in until he cursed and released me.

"Okay, claws are so not fair!" He chuckled, grabbing for me, but I was fast. I bolted off, but since his legs were long, I think I got maybe five feet before one of those Michael Phelps arms of his shot out. He got me completely around the waist, my feet off the ground, and I kicked.

"Ramses! Oh my God. *No.* Don't you dare!"

Oh, he dared all right, laughing the whole time as he hugged me to his chest and spun me around like he was a carny and I was the Tilt-A-Whirl.

He directed this ride while I laugh-screamed my lungs out, cursing all kinds of things at him, but that didn't make him stop. Truth be told, I didn't want him to stop, and I think he picked up on that. He spun me until I was thoroughly dizzy. I think he was too because the moment he put me down, we both fell to the ground.

We both tumbled into the street like a couple of idiots, the cold, dirty street, but for some reason I didn't care. For some reason, *he* didn't care. We just laughed, me crying at this point, and it took me a second to realize I fell on top of him. That he still had his arms around me.

That he hugged me.

That he had me there, right against his chest as the laughter disappeared and our breaths clouded the air. We hadn't seen a car our entire run, one of those residential areas with little traffic.

"You saw a T-rex," he said, his lips full and flush just like his cheeks. His hat had fallen off, his curls rogue and tousled. "Tell the truth, Jersey girl."

He shouldn't call me that. I wasn't his Jersey girl. Really, I was still his professor. He hadn't gotten out of my class yet.

I shouldn't be on top of him. I shouldn't be running with him. This whole exchange was completely inappropriate and had been for a while.

Try telling my body that, my heart racing on top of his. His chest, mighty and solid, labored rapidly with heavy breath beneath me. His hand cradled my hip, his fingers moving to hover over my ass, but it didn't stay there long before I shifted.

Cold pavement touched my knees, my gloved hands on the ground, and Ramses lay there a second before shifting his head in my direction. He started to say something before his Apple watch pinged, and he raised his wrist.

"Damn," he cursed, and I frowned.

"What?"

LOVER   183

"One of my colleagues needs a client file for a meeting in the morning. I forgot to send it before I left the office. The whole thing's on my hard drive."

"Should we head back then?" We were going to anyway.

We probably should anyway.

Our gazes collided again and I saw that there. We should probably wrap things up today. It'd gotten weird and I think we both let it. Honestly, this was the first time something like this had happened. Ramses had never been any other way than completely respectful with me. He'd made good on his promise of friendship.

What had happened just now had been natural. Him grabbing me, him touching me, and me letting him. I suppose it wouldn't be weird if we had been just friends.

He really needs to get out of your class.

He said he had his reasons. I was just waiting for him to give me the transfer slip, but it was on me for not pushing him about it.

"I don't want to," he said, making me find his eyes. He still lay there, but then shook his head. "I mean, we don't have to rush. I have another copy of it on my laptop at home. If you don't mind jogging over... I can send it off real quick, and we can get back to where we were."

Should we? Get back to where we were?

I faced the pavement, and he did too. Getting up, he lounged next to me on his hip. His place wasn't far. I mean, I hadn't been to his home here in Queenstown Village, but we often jogged through this neighborhood, and he always mentioned he lived a block or two away. We'd just never jogged that route.

I didn't know why really, but maybe I did. Maybe that was just a little too much, and he knew that, us being friends or not. It didn't matter if we were actually going inside.

Just too much.

Just like this moment, and I should tell him no, say no.

"It won't take but a moment," he husked beside me, and my lips instantly closed.

"Okay."

Okay, famous last words as he got up, then helped me up. He grabbed his hat, and with little movement, I realized how cold I was. Usually, I stayed pretty warm during our runs because we were constantly moving.

Maybe it's a good idea to go inside for a moment.

That, in the end, was what I used as justification. How I justified the decision to go to my student's house. I said going inside and getting warmed up wouldn't be a bad idea, all the while something screamed in my head that this was a bad idea.

Something tugged at me as I followed Ramses on and we took the route in the direction of his house, but whatever it was didn't seem strong enough to keep me from following him. We jogged the one or two blocks it took to get to his house here near campus, and I wasn't surprised to see a property so modern and handsome.

Ramses had mentioned a duplex set up, and though the condo had been that, there was nothing traditional about it with its upscale design. Multi-level, the property stacked on top of a three-car garage, all gray brick and dark wood paneling. It was one of many in a luxurious neighborhood donned with sculpted trees and driveways lined with soft lighting. Evening was starting to set in, and we should probably wrap up this jog quickly anyway.

The words continued to scream at me, a bad feeling I really couldn't place. I thought maybe because I knew this was wrong. What we were doing, what *I* was doing, but I still followed him up the driveway and through the garage. His sleek Mercedes was inside when he opened the garage door and the space immediately hummed with heat. My sneakers the same when they touched down. He either had heated floors or the garage was just that warm.

"In and out," Ramses assured, like he knew too. He unlocked the door and let me into his space.

And what a space it was.

A foundry type feel to the place and an underground look with the high brick walls and open space. He had large glass windows, which gave views of the entire neighborhood, a fireplace he summoned on with a click. It gave the room a soft glow, so he didn't have to turn on the lights, and when he slipped off his shoes, I did too.

"Laptop's upstairs," he said, backing inside. He didn't bother to take off his coat, and why should he? We were supposed to be leaving soon. He palmed his keys. "Make yourself at home. If you need a drink, kitchen's down the hall, bathroom near that if you need that."

I nodded, not going to make myself at home. We were supposed to leave soon.

That unsaid, Ramses directed a thumb back in the direction he planned to head. An uncertainty lined his features that hadn't before, and I wondered if he too realized this was a bad idea. That we hadn't really gotten to this point in our friendship. *That it felt weird*, but I guess now that we were here, we both had to deal with the decision.

"Be right back." He disappeared up a set of spiral stairs, but rather than make this weirder than it already felt, I did decide to look around.

I started with the living room, taking off my gloves and shoving them into my fleece. The place was completely decked out, very masculine and mature. I wondered if he had a designer come in because even I had used the advice of a catalog when designing mine.

One thing I noticed were his sculptures, like so many and all weaved and wrapped in hard metals. He had some near the fireplace and his leather couch, more down the hall and passed the kitchen. It seemed I'd found his vice when I observed even more in an open space toward the back of the condo. He had quite a few back there. Though, not displayed like the others. It was almost like they were ready to go, some still in tarps, but the foundations told me they were the same metal pieces like the ones displayed around the property. Ramses might be some kind of collector.

Or an artist.

An easel stood by one of the back glass windows, oil paints stacked and arranged on a stepladder beside it. He had the easel covered, but a drop cloth and paints beneath and around told he was working on something. There were also shop tools around like maybe he did make some or all of these sculptures.

Are you keeping something from me, Midwestern boy?

The secret life of an artist, a passion he'd maybe not shared with everyone. I felt like I was getting a sneak peek into a secret world.

I approached the canvas and though completely not my business, I tugged at the cloth he had over it. I just saw the edge of gold paint before the floorboards creaked, and I whipped around.

"Ramses, you're—"

A girl I'd seen before. A beautiful girl with dark hair and porcelain skin. She'd been a lovely girl in a luxurious white gown.

Not in a towel in the middle of Ramses's condo.

Which she was, *in a towel* and standing there, feet bare and fair skin flushed. She had it tucked and secured above her rather abundant rack, lips a natural red like Snow White. She did look like Snow White, hair so dark almost raven black like mine. What I didn't quite understand was why she was standing in the middle of Ramses's condo—basically naked.

"Oh. Hello," she said, like actual Snow White. Seriously, the girl was just missing the birds to pick up her cape. I actually snuck a peek around her to make sure they weren't flanking her like an enchanted entourage. She grinned. "Are you a friend of Ramses—"

"December?"

Not alone now, this party suddenly three.

Ramses stood with his laptop, the Mac secured under his arm. His gaze volleyed from December to me.

December.

I obviously knew this was her. I'd seen her, but she'd been getting married back then. Not half naked in Ramses's condo.

And so the sick feeling I'd felt upon going with him, coming here with him, was confirmed. Something had tugged at me that this was a bad idea, and here I was with foreseen bad idea. It flashed at me like a feature presentation. But before I could act, or react, to any of it, Ramses cut between the naked girl and me.

After placing the laptop down on a table, he got a hand behind me but faced her. "Hey, uh. Did you find everything okay?"

I jerked my gaze in his direction. So he wasn't surprised to see her here? Like this…

Brilliant.

Why I was surprised I didn't know and at this point, I think the only thing keeping me from fleeing was the fact he'd stood between this girl and me. He literally blocked my way with his huge frame.

"Yeah and the hot water worked great." She placed a thumb up, casual about it, and I had to say, for someone caught in… whatever this was this girl and him had going on, she didn't seem panicked. Like she'd been caught or whatever. If anything, she stood casually as if this were normal when it certainly wasn't. She placed her hands out to me. "And I hope I didn't interrupt anything…"

She hadn't, a wake-up call for me but again, Ramses was blocking my way from getting the hell out of dodge.

"Bri and I were running." He placed his big body in front

of me like he knew my plans to leave, angling completely around me. He shoved a thumb back. "Bri, you know December. From the wedding?" Yeah, I knew of her. She'd been getting married at the time, and I'd shake her hand if she wasn't wet, in a towel, and this wasn't completely weird. He dampened his lips. "She's using my shower. Hot water is on the fritz in her place. I told you she's renting from me. I've called someone to fix it."

Each word came out more rushed than the last, and at this point, I knew he was attempting to save face. That he knew that I knew this was weird, and why he felt the need, I had no idea. This, whatever he was doing, was his business.

And we were just friends.

Instead of shaking the girl's hand because she was in a towel and this was just too freaking much, I lifted my hand. "Hi. Brielle. I was at the wedding. I'm a friend of Ramses's mom. I was her plus one."

Since Ramses faced in my direction, I completely saw what he did after what I said. How his body went rigid, how his eyes closed. I'd said *his mom* was my friend.

And it'd been deliberate.

The two of us had had a good time, a great time in fact, and so good, I'd let a few things slip. I got too settled in his friendship and completely dismissed my instincts or the ability to make good decisions. I'd allowed him to carry me along into this friendship, to completely forget that he hadn't actually gotten out of my seminar and indulging in our back and forth exchange whether it be via his texts or simply seeing his face a couple times a week in class. I did that because I wanted to be around him. I wanted it so desperately that I allowed a few things to slide.

December smiled at how I'd introduced myself, her expression sweet as if it was nice. *Nice* what I told her about Ramses and me. Her smile widened. "Oh, that's great. I'm sorry I didn't see you that night. Did you have a good time at least?"

"Great." I nodded, keeping my sight on her. But in my periphery a waiting Ramses cuffed his arms, his head hanging. He probably had a few things to say here but at the present couldn't. I smiled at December. "The whole event was simply lovely and congratulations."

"Thank you."

That was my cue.

I didn't know what game these two were playing. Maybe there wasn't a game. Maybe she was just using his shower. Either way, it was my time to leave. I braced my arms. "I should be going. I have to head back to Maywood Heights tonight. I teach over at the university but live there. Long drive, so better get at it."

"Of course. And good to meet you."

She'd said it at my back because I'd used her distraction to cut around Ramses. I'd gotten to the door as he hit his living room.

"Brielle."

He said it to me as if I were scolded, as if I were a child when the only childish person seemed to be him in this moment. Really, I didn't know what was going on here. Frankly, I didn't care. I left the situation, hit the exit, because I was hurt.

And that scared me.

I was hurt by something I didn't understand. I was invested, and I hated that. I opened the door, but Ramses put his hand on it. "Let me leave."

"I will." And then he lifted his hand, freeing me up to leave but not before angling me around by the shoulder. "But not until you talk to me."

He made me face him full on, standing solid in front of me. I toed into my shoes, but when he started to do the same, I held him back. "Don't."

"Don't what?" He jerked a head toward the door. "I'm going with you so we can finish our run."

"You're not."

"I am because you're not leaving this situation thinking whatever you're thinking."

"Which is what exactly, Ramses?"

He gave me a look like it was obvious. "You thinking whatever you're thinking about December and me."

"I'm not thinking about anything."

"Right. Sorry, Bri, but I'm calling bullshit on that. You're thinking things when you don't need to be thinking things. December is using my shower. She warned me she might be using it because her hot water isn't working. I told you. I've called someone for it—"

"But that's the thing. You don't need to tell me."

"I do." He cut in front of me, the door closed via his back. Pushing off it, he simmered above me. I'd yet to see Ramses truly panicked. Frustrated, yes. I'd seemed to have done that countless times to him in a span of merely a few weeks. Even still, he always regained his cool rather quickly.

He wasn't now, like he had actual fear in his eyes. Fear of me leaving or... whatever, and that told me something really strong.

He was way too invested too.

He was way too into this too. We were friends, yes, but we were both way too emotionally invested.

"I do because it matters to you," he continued, his lips parted. "It means something. December is my friend."

"Like we're friends?" I directed my gaze up to him, his eyes flashing.

He shook his head, slow. "Bri—"

"Why haven't you dropped my class, Ramses?" I wet my lips. "Why are we playing this game?"

"No game." He came forward. He pushed a hand into his

curls. "And you are my friend. December's my friend too, but there's a difference."

"What?" My throat thickened, my swallow tight. "What's the difference?"

"She's my friend by choice," he admitted, eyes scanning mine. "And though that may not have always been the case, back then with our history, it is now. She's my friend *by choice*. A choice *I* made."

"And me?" My nostrils flared, but when he shifted, I turned away. I couldn't look at him.

And definitely didn't want to hear what he had to say.

I didn't think I was strong enough for it. Because if she was his friend by choice, and regardless of her lack of availability, that only meant one thing.

That it truly wasn't like that with her. Because he wanted it to be that way. He was friends with her because that was what he desired, but with me, he didn't have that choice.

Because I'd made it for him.

No, I couldn't hear that. I couldn't let him *admit* that. It was too much, and I needed to leave. I eased around him.

"Brielle. *Please.*"

"I'm leaving." I didn't face him. "And you're going to let me."

Because he wouldn't trap me. He wouldn't hurt me. He wouldn't do anything I wouldn't want him to do.

Of that, I knew.

I'd gotten to know this guy, this man. He played all his cards in front of me.

Always honest.

"Text me when you get to your car."

He stated the words at my back, so easy to read him.

You have to go.

I did go into the cold air and didn't look back.

I suppose I was weak again.

CHAPTER
FIFTEEN

Ramses

I knew December was behind me even before I turned.

I think that was why I'd done it.

I think that was why I'd put it all out there and said what I had to say. *I* needed to hear it.

And she had as well.

I turned to find her still in her towel, completely blind-sided by whatever had just happened. I'd been too good about keeping previous things away from her. They'd been my own crosses to bear, and I'd sat in silent torture with them. They'd been my burden, my plague, and something I had to come to terms with. They'd had nothing to do with her.

But that didn't mean she shouldn't know.

It'd taken fear to actually admit it. To see that things had really changed. I wanted them to change, and I needed them to. They were a roadblock to getting to where I needed to go, which, surprisingly, wasn't in December's direction.

I glanced toward the door, December's near-silent steps padding toward me.

"We need to talk," she said, and I sighed.

It'd been a long time coming.

We did talk after she came back, *got some clothes on*. God, the clusterfuck that had become my life had been my own doing. Still, it was goddamn shitty.

December and I did have that talk, in front of my fireplace, where she sat on my coffee table and I lounged on the couch. We had a few talks this way, casual.

But never so serious.

By the end, her hands had dropped between her legs, her swallow hard. I'd hit her with a lot of shit.

"First off," she started. A veil of her hair had hung over her face, and she drew it back, tossed her head back. She frowned. "Your mentor is a complete piece of shit."

Oh, yeah. So, I'd told her about that too, the Brown thing. It had all just kind of come out.

I figured if I was admitting shit, coming to terms with shit, she needed to know that too, and her reaction had been one that hadn't surprised me. She'd been pissed, gone all female cavewoman. For some reason, she felt the need to protect my honor like I wasn't a goddamn dude.

Even still, her reaction made me smirk, but her frown only deepened.

"Second." She ticked off a finger, then moved close. "You know what happened over there, back at Brown. You know that wasn't your fault, right?"

I did. Not many people were in my corner besides my mom. Our lawyers had just seen it as a PR mess, the Mallick playboy. They'd thought I was just trying to get my dick wet with some taken pussy since I fit the profile, and why should they see it as any different?

I dropped my fists between my knees. "I know."

A nod on December's end like we'd come to a consensus,

and when her lips worked, I knew the ball was about to drop. That she was about to talk about the real shit. I'd talked to her about her and me, everything about her and me. I'd basically said it without actually *saying it*.

She was about to say it.

Sighing, she tucked a leg beneath her, the dance of the flames from my fireplace playing on her fair skin. Not so long ago, I would have drowned in her beauty. Hell, I'd have suffered in it. Now, I just fought everything I could to sit in front of her and not be someplace else.

With someone else.

My gaze dragged back to my cell phone beside me. She'd text me. When she made it to her car. She would. She hadn't confirmed it, but she knew I was serious.

You shouldn't have let her leave.

Like I had a choice. She'd taken it from me. Like a couple of things and that drove me crazy. Even still, I continued to chase her.

I swallowed, December's lips parting.

"Three is," she started, her other leg coming up and crossing on my table. She cradled them. "Why didn't you talk to me?"

Her statement clearly wasn't about the things she'd ticked off. A big reason why I could keep her eyes at the moment.

I scrubbed a hand down my face before working them both. "And say what?" I faced her, shrugging. "'Zona, I ran out of this town like a bat out of hell because I couldn't deal."

"Well, that would have been a start."

"And how would I have looked?" I tilted my head. "It's because of me *you* suffered. Because of my family."

Because of my father. My father and my uncle Leo. Together, they'd stolen so much from her. When it'd come to my uncle, it was *her family* he'd stolen from. And my father's theft?

Well, her closure.

She'd been so close to not knowing the truth about what happened to her sister Paige back in high school, and that'd been due to me and mine. I was a product of my father.

How could I not take responsibility for what had happened to her?

I couldn't look her in the face every day. Fuck, back then, I couldn't look at my own self in the mirror. All I did see was my father, what he did to land his ass in prison, so no. Woe is me wasn't coming out of my goddamn mouth to the person who'd been the victim.

What I said appeared to pain my friend, her expression tensing, her lips pinched tight. Her head lowered, and a visible sigh racked her shoulders.

"The people who are responsible for that, what happened to my sister, are behind bars," she said, the words from her sobering. We hadn't talked about this in so long, not really much at all after it had happened. I'd left so quickly that summer, taken a summer class and moved to college early. I'd run. Her mouth parted. "And you know, that had nothing to do with you."

Obviously, I hadn't been the one to move the pieces. But it was because of my family that she and hers suffered. The Mallick name branded me.

"But I wasn't adding to any more of the colossal shit you were going through. There wouldn't have been a point." It all would have been redundant, pointless. My jaw shifted. "I'm a grown man and can handle my shit."

"But you weren't back then." More pain backed her eyes, her gaze drenched with it. She shook her head. "You were a boy, and I was a girl. And the only difference between us was that that girl had someone. She did and you didn't."

She did have Prinze, but her problems far outweighed mine back then. I'd just been a lovestruck kid.

And she'd lost a sister.

In our silence, her feet touched the floor. "You didn't have me when you should have during those days, and I let you go, leave Maywood Heights, knowing the truth. I did, but I let you go anyway."

I smirked. "Let me?" I hadn't been silent about my feelings for her during that time. Of course, she'd known, but they weren't her responsibility. "I left a flame trail I ran out of that town so fast. No one was stopping me."

"I could have stopped you."

And maybe she could have. In fact, I was so caught up in her she might have.

But that hadn't been how the cards had fallen and wasn't how things should have been. Like she said, she found her person.

She leaned forward. "I've been a shit friend to you. All these years, I've drawn on about all kinds of shit knowing…"

"What?" I asked her. "That your best friend from high school was completely in love with you?"

It'd been the first time I'd said the words out loud.

And how freeing they'd been.

To be able to say them, to feel them.

And all in the past tense.

I had been in love with her, *was* in love with her.

Was.

It was like air fully came through my lungs, like I could breath for the first time. It made me sit straighter, see clearer.

Was.

"That," she said, her eyes meeting mine. She chewed her lip. "Like I said, I've been a shit friend. I knew that but I wanted to be your friend so bad. You're addictive, Arizona."

I was addictive?

I'd been obsessed with her for years, locking away shit inside myself for years because of her. Because I had been in love with her.

Was.

The thought made me smile now, but December obviously

didn't know why. She just continued to chew her lip, studying me.

"What do you need from me?" she asked, her breath hitched. It was like she anticipated my next words, like they worried her. Her lips worked. "How do I not be a shit friend?"

She could never be a shit friend, not truly. A shit friend completely abandoned you, but in this case, I'd abandoned her. I'd done it through both physical and metaphorical distance. I'd kept her at arm's length when she'd always, always been there as a resource for me. She always reminded me how she was there, never forgot about me.

But I had her, and though I'd always made myself available to her in the technical sense, I had kept a part of myself away.

Perhaps, the most important part.

I worked my palms. "First off, you could never really be a shit friend." I dashed my eyebrows. "You check on me all the time and bug the shit out of me until I tell you what's up. Always fucking do."

The woman was the first in my DMs during finals week, making sure I wasn't stressed or needed anything. She was as attentive as I'd been for her at the wedding, and I did tell her most things.

Ironically enough, it was the stuff that didn't matter that she always got. My life was an open book to her besides anything that actually counted, and thinking back, she probably had poked so much over the years because she'd known the truth. During those final days in high school, I'd admitted my feelings to her, but I think we both thought I'd get over them after she chose someone else.

As the years passed, it must have been apparent I hadn't, and she had done all the poking. She never let up, always wanting me to be open with her I just never did.

Completely on me and something I was correcting at the

present. I was finally past all those old feelings. I was and it felt good.

I eyed her. "And second, I don't need anything from you. But there is something I need to start doing."

"What?"

I studied her. "Saying no to you," I said, laughing. "I've never been good at it."

Brielle was right. Things may not have been a certain way with December. I may not have been "unavailable," but I certainly acted like it. I allowed myself to become a yes man and probably due to nothing but fear. Maybe I'd been afraid of losing my friend. Maybe I'd just been afraid. Either way, I couldn't do it anymore and had a feeling I didn't need to. She'd always be in my life whether I said yes to her or not.

She was annoying in that way.

I couldn't get rid of her any more than she could get rid of me and she knew that.

Laughter as she threw her head back and brought her legs up. She tossed her dark waves around. "Royal said this was coming."

"What?"

"You," she said, grinning, "*cutting me off*. He seems to think I take advantage of you."

Okay, my jaw dropped seriously to the damn floor. Royal Prinze coming to bat for me? I must have heard her wrong.

But then a twinkle flashed in her eyes as she leaned forward. "I think he secretly likes you."

"Of course, he does," I played off, like it didn't shock me to hell every time I saw elements of that. That we were no longer rivals.

That we may even be friends.

It was still a bit much and nothing I'd ever voice in an open forum. I felt he'd share the same sentiment. As stubborn as myself in that way.

I popped a shoulder, grinning. "What's not to love?"

With that, she grabbed one of my pillows off the couch, slamming me with it. I swear to God, this girl could put Mike Tyson to shame, and with that arm she'd had at her wedding when she'd flung her bouquet clear across the room at me, she seriously should consider a career as a professional athlete.

"Arrogant ass," she chided, dodging when I tossed the pillow at her. "Always so smug."

My laughter dissolved at what she said, how it sounded so similar to someone else. And like that someone knew, my phone pinged, Brielle's name on the front.

Bri: Just wanted to let you know I'm on the road. Since you wanted to know?

I had, immediately texting her back.

Me: Thank you. Drive safe.

Bri: I will.

Me: I wish you hadn't left.

No other texts came in, but since she was driving, she shouldn't be texting anyway.

Try telling my gut that.

It clenched like someone clocked the son of a bitch, and I gazed up to find another's eyes on me. December, of course, had been watching me. Always in my business.

Always caring about me.

She smiled in my direction, but it was a sad smile and one I didn't want to see. It was like she knew what was plaguing me, conflicted me. I didn't want to push Brielle, but she'd been more than adamant about a friendship and only that.

"That woman that was here before," December said, and Bri was definitely that. She held a maturity far beyond mine and I believed before was out of my league. For a few reasons, but one being what happened here tonight. She called me on the shit with December, but it'd taken me time to see the truth. That I had let that relationship, as well as quite a few other things in my past, distract me. December leaned forward. "Is she just your mom's friend?"

I really wasn't ready for this conversation, still trying to figure all this out with Bri myself.

"She started as a stranger," I admitted. "Ended up being my professor."

"Your professor?" Her eyes widened.

I nodded. "But in between that she was something else. I met her at your wedding. Met her before I knew she was my professor."

I couldn't tell her what that something else was because, truth be told, I didn't know. I just knew it felt like I'd fucked this up.

December tapped her fist on the coffee table, and before I knew it, she was dipping below it and sliding out a wood chest I kept an old chess set in.

"What are you doing?" I watched her dump the pieces out, getting them arranged on the board. After, she pulled up my leather ottoman and took a seat on it.

"I feel like this talk requires chess." She laced her fingers, then grinned. "You have until checkmate."

CHAPTER
SIXTEEN

To: brielle.whitmanquintero@pembroke.edu

From: ramses.mallick@mallickenterprises.com

Subject: Class Transfer

Hey. I just wanted to let you know I took care of that class transfer. Had my mom sign off on it since she's the department dean.

Before you ask (because I know you will), she had no idea it was your class I was trying to get out of. She didn't ask. Just signed it, but I don't think she would have cared anyway. I know you care so that's why I'm telling you. It's taken care of and I'm sorry for dragging my feet on it. I could blame work and being busy, but it'd be just an excuse. It was simply two more days of you.

'Nuff said.

Anyway, the changes are effective immediately. I'm no longer your student, but I'm emailing because this is technically school related. And well, because you're not texting me back, and I don't really have a choice.

Hope you're well and thanks,

- R

To: ramses.mallick@mallickenterprises.com

From: brielle.whitmanquintero@pembroke.edu

Subject: Re: Class Transfer

Ramses -

Thank you for letting me know. Sorry, I haven't been texting you back.

I think you understand why.

I hope you're well too, and I wish you nothing but the best. I really enjoyed your friendship. It was really special to me.

- Bri

To: brielle.whitmanquintero@pembroke.edu

From: ramses.mallick@mallickenterprises.com

Subject: Re: Re: Class Transfer

Well, since I both have and don't have you—since I know you're watching and reading—there's this too.

I had a talk with December after you left, a long one, and I'd like to tell you about it. It won't be over an email, though.

I value your friendship too so let's *be friends.*

The ball's in your court, Professor.

- R

To: ramses.mallick@mallickenterprises.com

From: brielle.whitmanquintero@pembroke.edu

Subject: Re: Re: Re: Class Transfer

I wish I could.

I wish I was strong enough.

- Bri

(Recalled)

CHAPTER
SEVENTEEN

Bri

I'd agreed to go on a date.

Because I was an idiot.

Like I didn't completely have enough drama in my life, I agreed to go on a date with a man from the history department. Okay, so it wasn't a date per se. It was a charity event, and he needed a date.

It was a date.

I'd put it out there I wasn't looking for anything, though, and Guy had been understanding.

Yes, that was his name: Guy Donahue and Evie had completely vouched for him. I'd met the man during a staff meeting. The three of us had casually chatted after, and Evie had just so happened to mention her son. She'd asked Guy how Ramses was doing in his class. Apparently, Ramses had signed up for Guy's shortened seminar and mentioned doing so at their last weekly dinner.

Guy had said fine, of course, moving on, and Evie did too. People often chatted and socialized after staff meetings, all of us getting together rare, but after she parted off from Guy, I eased him into conversation.

Now, I was well aware how this looked. That I'd gotten to know Guy just because I'd been checking up on Ramses. I'd mentioned that day at the staff meeting—casually—that Ramses had happened to transfer out of my course and I just wanted to know how he was fairing. I had been ignoring Ramses's texts at the time (which had stopped eventually). My student was persistent, but not a stalker. Yes, his texts had eventually stopped, and also yes, I'd wanted to know what happened to him. I had just wanted to make sure he was okay.

And so, a friendship with Guy began.

Of course, that was just how it had started. Casual lunches. Guy taught American history, and that was the class Ramses had gotten into since it had started later in the semester. I'd told Guy I didn't hold that against him, a jab at him teaching American history instead of something as "exciting" as early western civ. I'd been joking, of course, and it had lightened the guilt a little. A friendship with Guy had been intentional. I'd been nosy and wanted to hear any and everything he had to say about Ramses. The casual exchanges hadn't been much but gave me enough to let me know my previous student was okay and had settled into his new environment nicely. And duh, Ramses did well.

It was Ramses.

Something told me he could adjust in the most turbulent situation, but I needed to know and after I had, I planned to stop the lunches with Guy. The meetups shifted into something less intimate after that, others from the department eating with us, but during those socializations, the charity event came up. Faculty members tended to go since the funds did go back to the school. It was a small event, in Chicago, and that was when Guy had made his move. He needed a date.

And I needed my head checked.

I was not interested in anything romantically, at all, but I'd already committed. I also felt bad about my hidden agenda inquiring about Ramses. Going as Guy's date would get me off the hook with that. At least, in my mind, so we met up at the event after a three-hour drive. One we'd made *separately*. I needed those clear boundaries with Guy, and he'd been cool about it.

"Brielle, I want you to meet Blake and Daniel."

Other staff he'd introduced me to once we'd gotten there, the event, in all places, a VIP box at a basketball game. I hadn't made the connection that the gathering would be there. Not even with the Chicago address (United Center). I hadn't been there before, so I'd assumed other events besides sports could be had. Like banquets or whatever. It wasn't until Guy handed me my VIP badge, I realized we'd be at a damn Bulls game during all this.

Of course, that was where we'd be.

I couldn't seem to get away from sports, sports people, and the like. It was like it followed me like an angry storm.

Even still, I was civil, introducing myself to Guy's friends. Outside of the chaos and uproar from the game and its viewers, one would never know we were actually at a basketball game. The VIP box sat well away from the fray, private, and the game itself like wall decor. It played out behind a glass wall, and inside, another world of opulence, riches, and shimmering walls of silk and flashy lighting. The room resembled the VIP lounge at an exclusive club, formal attire required.

I shook Blake and Daniel's hands above my handbag, tucking it under my arm after the greeting. Guy, Daniel, and Blake fell into cozy conversation, and after I became room furniture, I slid a glass of champagne off a passing server's tray. The bubbly might help me settle my nerves and forget the fact I was here and didn't want to be. I just had to get through the night.

"Oh, Brielle. There's Ramses."

My gaze darted in the direction of Guy's point, and sure enough, there was his current student.

And with an entirely different look.

For starters, he'd buzzed his hair, wispy dark curls gone and replaced with an equally dark fade. Their absence did nothing to take away from how classically handsome he was. If anything, his chiseled features stood out more without the distraction of them. He appeared striking without his hair, even older. He had a blond on his arm who he introduced as people swarmed him like a celebrity socialite.

The girl by his side was Penthouse Barbie, fully equipped with a buxom chest and cocktail dress that rested well above her knees. She paired perfectly with him, a young CEO in his fitted suit with the open collar. Tailored, the smooth gray ran down his lean body like butter, his jacket tight and coursing thickly with his muscles. He placed a hand over hers on his arm, grinning when others shook his shoulder or acknowledged him. Was he with her?

Do you care?

Of course, I didn't. He wasn't mine, but I couldn't help but stare. I also had no idea why he was here.

Guy's friends Blake and Daniel immediately went over to Ramses with, surprisingly, many people from the room. The event was maybe fifty or so, but Guy stayed with me.

"I suppose I'm not surprised," Guy continued on, finishing his other statement surrounding Ramses's arrival. He faced me. "This is his box."

Wait. *His* box. As in this was *his* charity event, his party?

"Come on. Let's go say hi."

I didn't want to say hi at all, but Guy had a hand behind my back and nudged my heels in the direction. I just about stumbled in my stilettos, adjusting myself and the slit of my dress so I at least appeared presentable. The amount of skin I displayed was nowhere near centerfold celebutante's, but the slit in my dress did hit above my thigh and the dark gown was strapless, my shoulders bare. It was something I'd dug out and had worn to countless events I used to frequent over the years with my ex-husband. He often went to things like this, and the black silk evening gown got the job done. I'd paired it with a red lip and my hair down. Completely functional.

"Ramses," Guy greeted. "Good seeing you."

But one would have thought I'd been scandalously clad, naked the way Ramses's sight followed down the length of me. It stopped on my slit, a flash of my thigh parting through black silk, before Ramses smiled and found my eyes. He was that arrogant about it.

And I forgot where I was.

I forgot how to breathe and with whom I'd come. I forgot myself, being stupid when Ramses's hand eased out for Guy's and Ramses completely forgot about his date. Well, he hadn't forgotten about her. She was there and he introduced her. Her name was Meredith, one of his classmates.

But with all that out of the way, he came right back to me, that arrogant confidence of his returned. He was too bold to stare at me in such away, acknowledge me in *that way* after our history, and Guy knew he'd been my student. I'd told him that so I could be nosy.

"You know Professor Whitman-Quintero," Guy reintroduced, grinning at Ramses. "She was just asking about you."

Okay, I hadn't been just asking. I'd asked about him. In the past, past tense.

I certainly hadn't in a while, and Guy made me sound completely thirsty.

"I hadn't just asked," I cut off, attempting to save face. "But I have. In the past. How are you? Doing well in Professor Donahue's class, I assume?"

I hid behind my champagne flute, a long and full drink.

Even then, I didn't escape the stretch of Ramses's grin nor his hand seeking mine.

"Quite fine, Professor," he said, and I almost believed he'd kiss my hand. He certainly held it for long enough. He cradled the back in undying heat before letting go, and I passed that off with another drink. He shook his head. "And it's nice to know you've been asking about me."

So goddamn arrogant, so cool.

He stood in front of me in a way that blatantly teased. Though, no other parties outside of us would know. We just had an underlying thing between us, something we both could read. Right about now, I'd be shoving him while he made me smile.

Another stiff drink as Ramses went on about how well he was doing. His marks were already at the top of the class in the shortened seminar, something Guy quickly let our small group in on. Ramses seemed to be shining without me and doing so beautifully. His lovely guest stood rather silently beside him and seemed more fascinated studying the way the lights flickered across the walls than actually engaging in conversation. This pretty, young thing was eye candy, nothing more, but that didn't mean she and Ramses weren't a thing.

Why does it matter?

It didn't, another solid drink on my part. I needed to take it easy since I was driving after this. I wasn't going home. Too late for that, but I did need to head over to the hotel I'd booked before getting on the road. I was staying downtown.

"Well, we don't want to keep you," Guy stated, being polite. He was polite, seemed like a good man, but he wasn't my man. I really wasn't interested, but he wasn't bad to socialize with. He shook Ramses's hand. "We'll let you get back to it. Great event as always."

So this *was* his party, interesting.

This surprised me. Especially since Ramses only started going to Pembroke this term, and the money tonight went to the school. I suppose the Mallicks did donate money to the university. Perhaps, Ramses was merely here as a representative. I knew Evie wouldn't be here tonight, another event she had going on back in Maywood Heights. It wasn't charity, something about a country club event, but she had invited me since there was a dinner and she had another plus one.

I kind of wished I'd taken her up on that now, Guy passing his final greeting off to both Ramses and his date. I gave the same, but not before catching Ramses's eye. I found almost a promise in them, something I didn't realize until, well, he did corner me later that night.

He found me actually cutting a check in donation, not much but I could do something. I still was getting alimony from the divorce, so I had a little to spare. I tried to conserve since I was on my own with not quite a six-figure salary. I'd been out of the teaching game for a long time, and Pembroke had offered a place to start over with room for growth. I'd taken the contract very quickly. Especially since Evie had done me a favor by putting a good word in for the job.

Her son had wiggled his way into my life not long after that, the same way he continued to do so now. Catching me after my donation, Ramses offered me a glass of champagne.

He had two.

I probably shouldn't—for a couple of reasons—but I took it. One of those reasons was I didn't want to be piss-ass drunk, and reason two seemed obvious.

The gesture had been a gift from him, the pair of us stealing a sip together. I hadn't seen him in many weeks, the term more than half over now. He appeared to be thriving, a beautiful lady on his arm. Said arm candy wasn't with him now, but perhaps, she needed a potty break.

"Where's your date?" I asked, and he shrugged.

"Somewhere." A buck's dark coat in my direction, those eyes a hazel rosin. "Yours?"

"Somewhere."

This game we played. Enough for me to shake my head. It made him smile, a hand coming over his buzz cut. I directed a finger at it. "New do?"

"It's functional. Easier." He chuckled. "Mom nearly killed me. She loves snatching me by it when I'm being an asshole."

"And why did she decide not to be here tonight?" I knew she was somewhere else, just didn't know why if he was hosting an event. "I heard this is your family's box. Your event?"

"Ma never comes to this thing. Me either. Obviously, since I didn't go to Pembroke until recently." He cuffed his jacket sleeve. "This is one of Dad's old events. I'm here out of formality."

"I see."

With that between us, he took advantage of another sip of his champagne, his father I knew to be a sore topic. It was one of many things I hadn't gotten to break down with him. Not that I'd given him a chance.

I hadn't given either of us that, but it was probably for the best.

"You look good, Bri," he said, smiling. "Or should I still call you professor?"

"You *don't* have to call me that." And he didn't. I wasn't his professor. I shrugged. "And you do, too."

He looked more than good, heaven actually. He looked like a man, but I'd never seen him as a boy. He took on too much responsibility, had too much passion, to be anything else.

His incessant joy and love for life had been the only thing that made him slip a little. He was so hopeful for things, his optimism undying. Even though I'd pushed him away, he still came over here with me now as if not missing a beat. He didn't let the world or *me* taint him, his spirit.

"You didn't answer my last email." He appeared to come out of nowhere with this, as if in my head. I'd pretty much just been thinking about that, how I'd pushed him away. His head tilted. "I know I said the ball is in your court, but how long are you going to make me wait, Brielle?"

He was still waiting? Really?

Really.

I saw that in his eyes, that intention, that confidence. I hadn't responded to his email. Well, I had but chickened out and recalled it. I hadn't been able to send my response that day. I couldn't be weak to him. I knew what would happen.

"What did you want to say?" I asked, stupid that I asked. I couldn't help it. "The conversation with your friend. How did it go?"

I had wondered about it, naturally curious.

His smile dashing right, Ramses indulged in another sip of champagne.

"You don't get it that easy," he said, lowering his flute. His eyes danced. "You made me wait after all. You want to know, you get the info with a caveat."

I didn't want to know what happened that bad.

But I did want to know.

Playing his game, I deposited another empty flute on the tray of a passing waiter. "What are the terms?"

And if he said another game of thumb war, I'd laugh him out of this place. We *weren't* doing that, ridiculous, but I was curious what he wanted from me.

Finishing his champagne, Ramses dropped off his flute as well before taking my hand. I started to protest until he pressed his hard body into my side.

"Come with me," he said, his voice playful, excited. "I got a place to show you. You agree to check it out, I'll tell you there. It's in the city. Won't take long."

He was in no place to bargain with me. Especially if it allowed him to whisk me off someplace.

Even still, I found myself hard pressed to move, or to push him away.

This gave him access to me in a way that allowed him to angle his big body around me.

"Come on, Professor," he said. "Take a chance? The ball's in your court again."

My lashes flashed. "I came with Professor Donahue. I can't just leave."

What was I saying?

But the words already came out, a smile to Ramses's voice.

"We can be back soon." His hand escaped mine to find my wrist. "As soon as you want. Meredith won't mind. She had no intention of leaving with me tonight, not with all the other money and status in here. I needed a date, and she wanted the ticket. We're doing each other a favor."

Eye candy indeed.

I guess we were in the same situation. I wasn't with my date either. Not really.

But this was just a field trip, what he said.

I faced him, way too close for my liking, but I was curious.

"Quick trip?" I asked, studying his eyes, and his danced again.

"Quick trip."

CHAPTER
EIGHTEEN

Bri

I told Ramses we didn't have to rush. Why I told him that, I didn't know, and when I also told him Guy and I drove up to Chicago separately (with also no intention of leaving together), he'd merely shook his head.

"Of course, you drove separately," he said, being a smart ass and I was tempted to shove him, flirt with him. It was like automatic when it came to him, which was another solid reason why we shouldn't be going anywhere together at all.

Yet, here we were, downtown after I followed behind his Mercedes with my SUV. He'd had us park in alley parking, behind an old brick building that wrapped around the corner. At this point, I wondered what was up with the locale, but I was game. My interest was piqued more than anything. Especially when he said to close my eyes.

"Just play along," he said, those ebony dark eyes playful once more. I asked him how I could walk if I couldn't see.

That was when his hands pressed over my eyes.

"What are you doing, Ramses?" I spent more time asking

him that, questioning myself and everything I was when we were together. I questioned him all the time yet traveled into the dark with him anyway.

His hard heat came in behind me, his voice low.

"You can see with me," he said. "Trust *me*."

It wasn't him I didn't trust. It was myself, and though he wasn't my student anymore…

I still let him lead me into the dark, whatever this was. The indicator was creaking floorboards under my heels, an aged smell, earthy and maybe the brick around me. Once inside and out of the chill, he stole my coat away from me, the room warm. He still urged me to keep my eyes closed, and I laughed while he did something with my coat. I stayed in the middle of wherever we were.

His hand came to my eyes again, a gentle press as he loomed near. "I'm going to stay behind you."

"Why?"

Laughter in his voice. "It's the only way I'm brave enough to show you this."

So, he had his weak points, too? I knew that. He'd shown me on multiple occasions.

We kept showing each other parts of ourselves we didn't necessarily want to expose. That was the big reason why we'd become friends, as short as that'd been.

My throat jumped.

"I'd never laugh at you." And I wouldn't. "Whatever this is. I wouldn't laugh."

His soft chuckle hit the air. Even still, he stayed behind while he lifted his hand from my eyes. I kept them closed until he told me it was okay to open.

"What do you think?" he gruffed, still behind me. "I want your opinion."

Honestly, I was still focused on his presence behind me. How he smelled so familiar, all heat and solid man. He remained that close, but I did open my eyes, and well, I was surprised.

My eyes adjusted to dim light, low-hanging light fixtures above. On that aged brick hung works of art, paintings.

And so many.

Countless pieces decorated the room, many spotlighted, which was why the actual room's lights shined so dimly. Too much light would distract from the main pieces, and there were sculptures as well.

Mostly metal, they were displayed about the room and reminded me of pieces I'd seen before.

I cuffed my elbows. "It's an art gallery," I said, obvious. He was still behind me, and I faced him. "You're showing me an art gallery?"

Curious indeed, Ramses with few words. In fact, his hands in his pockets, he rocked on his heels.

As if he was nervous.

Ramses wasn't a nervous person. At least, never in front of me. He bumped his big shoulders. "What do you think of it? The place and the setup of everything, I mean."

Well, it was nice, I suppose. I'd been in quite a few art galleries. I'd actually lived in Manhattan for a time with my ex. In fact, most of our marriage.

I wondered why Ramses wanted my opinion on this place now, but since I was curious, I played along. The place was stunning really, very modern and classy.

"It's lovely," I said, and he visibly sighed. I almost chuckled, but I'd promised him I wouldn't laugh. "Why?"

"Well, I bought it," he stated—*he bought it*, like that was obvious. He shrugged. "You're the first to see it."

I was?

And he'd bought an… art gallery?

I didn't know why or, well, any of this, but Ramses broke the tension when he laughed. He scratched a finger behind his neck. "But you like it?"

"I do." I shook my head with a smile. "But I thought you were working for your family."

"I am. I do." He put his hands out, stressing the fact. He pocketed them. "I suppose this is a passion project. I hope the first of many."

I thought he'd expand on this, but before I knew it, he was taking my hands.

"Come on." He backed up, guiding me in front of him. "I wanna show you the best part."

The best part turned out to be in the back, a studio of sorts when Ramses flicked on the lights. In fact, it was a studio. Both what appeared to be finished and unfinished pieces were situated across the room. Many he had under tarps, but the ones he didn't were all done in metal. He had power tools around and the materials used to create the works. Quite a few of them sat in various stages, and I realized how quiet it'd gotten since we came into this room.

"You're making these." He wasn't just making them. He *made* them. I studied him. "Did you make everything out there…"

"Oh, no." He chuckled. "I acquired most of the pieces on the main floor. I'm completely amateur, but yes, I made all this stuff in here. I dabble. Art's my minor. Business, my major."

This was more than dabbling. This was passion, and just like he'd stated out on the showroom.

I ventured toward one of his pieces, his style abstract. I knew a lot of people who'd buy work such as this. Hell, I'd bought work like this to decorate our brownstone in Manhattan. Of course, the purchases had been frivolous and the first to go in the divorce. I had money like that, so I spent it.

If I had these, though, what Ramses had made, I wouldn't have sold any of it. "This isn't amateur."

"Go on."

"I'm serious."

"No, seriously go on. It's all I can do not to freak that I'm actually showing you this." His laughter was light as it hit the air, and I realized his cheeks were red. I'd never seen shy or vulnerable Ramses like this. It was completely flooring him that he was showing himself in this way.

And I liked it.

I didn't know why, but I did. I guess I liked that he was showing me this part about himself. That I was the first he showed.

I studied the room a bit before he joined me at my side. "So, you're going to sell your art here?"

"I'm going to feature it. The point of this place was to get into the game, though, and the only way my financial advisors didn't completely look at me like I was crazy. My family does real estate and development. We have a few small businesses too, but nothing quite like this. This isn't even in the same ball park."

"So why did you do it?" Why did he show me he was doing it? Something like this seemed very special to him and basically confirmed what I'd seen at his place on campus. Ramses lived the secret life of an artist, and people like that, it wasn't always easy to show that part of themselves.

"I suppose to prove that I could." He faced me. "I have a tendency of not going toward the things that speak to me. I'm trying to not default to that. To take chances. At least more of them."

"And the reason for the change of heart?" I asked the question upon a glance of the room, so bouncing back, my gaze collided with his. It stopped me in my tracks as it always had.

Even from day one.

The first day he'd stood in front of me in a suit, brave enough to challenge me to a dare. I won, and he'd leave me. He'd actually said that like the odds weren't stacked in his favor. I think he'd known the probability of his chances to win.

He directed his gaze down on me from above, his jacket tight with his thick shoulders. He hadn't come in with his coat on at all, bearing the cold and this man physically stunned in front of me. Without his hair, I could see his eyes, his soul, too, probably if I looked hard enough. He took a step forward, but before he could speak, I asked for the rest of the tour. He hadn't shown it all.

We should see it all.

"Of course," he said. I noticed he was slow to retreat. He struck off the lights behind me, leaving the room dark, then I followed his big frame through the rest of the place. I guess the studio was someplace he could work since he came to the city a lot. He explained his family also had properties out here too.

Ramses proved to be a man of the world, and this little slice he had of it ended up in his office.

His display was very simple in there: a Mac, large granite desk, and a couch. The couch actually had blankets on it.

"Sorry," he apologized immediately upon getting inside. He grabbed and quickly balled up the blanket. "I slept here last night. I was in the city to prepare for the charity event. Decided to do some work here in the studio. Never left as you can see."

He had nothing to apologize for. I liked his dedication. This, what he was doing here, seemed like it should be his full-time job, but I understood his obligations to his family. Sometimes our calling didn't always match with what was predetermined for us. But kudos to him for trying to find a balance between both.

"You promised me a story," I said once we got inside. "I come with you here, check all this out, and I get a story."

I wasn't sure I was quite prepared for this story, but I did still care about him even if we weren't friends. I cared about him as a person, and that seemed obvious. I shouldn't, but I did.

I also shouldn't be here with him and I knew that, but that didn't stop me. I truly did care about this guy.

Stupid, I knew.

I had a feeling he cared about me too. I mean, he showed me all this first, and he did have friends. It was *the friend* I'd been curious about, but I'd been neither bold enough nor brave enough to push him on what had happened after I'd left. I just wanted to make sure he was okay regarding that situation.

Then you leave.

The only reason I stayed now. I gave myself a mental out. He'd tell me what happened with her. I'd find out he was okay, and then I could leave.

A messy fold and Ramses tossed that blanket on the couch, and in a quick, but also surprising action, he picked up a remote on his granite desk.

Soft tunes drifted into the room, easy listening hip hop beats. If I didn't know any better, I'd think he was trying to seduce me.

He opened his hands, waving them for me to come to him, and I thought he was. He frowned. "Come to me."

"Why?"

"Just come." He sighed, but still kept his hands out. "This is some awkward shit I'm about to tell you about, and I need the distraction." His head lowered. "Dance with me and distract me. *Please?*"

Dance with him.

I suppose it was the *please* that did it.

And maybe the big brown puppy dog eyes.

He'd even placed his lip out, making me laugh, so of course, I came. I stopped just before. "No funny business."

He appeared offended. "Funny business? Me? I'd never."

My eyes lifted, but I did give him my hands. His form was

fine, so he'd obviously done this before. He spun me out, and when I came back, we slowed into something a bit closer. I quickly realized it was because he didn't want me to look at him.

How had he gotten so shy?

How had we gotten like this? Together again?

I fingered his lapel, my head rested on his chest, and I closed my eyes. The beauty of this was he couldn't see my eyes either.

He had me vulnerable, too, in this moment, enjoying him, *this* with his arm around me. He folded our fingers together, and his jaw touched my hair.

"I told her," he whispered. "I put everything out there."

The sway threatened to stop, but I refused to allow it. I swallowed. "You told her your feelings?"

He told her he was in love with her?

Because that was what I really meant. He had been in love with her.

Was he still?

Why did it matter?

I stayed in heated silence, my entire body buzzing but only with nerves. I wasn't sure I could handle what he'd tell me next.

Because if he said he was in love with her…

It did matter. It mattered to me, and though I wasn't woman enough to say it out loud, I did think it. I cared if he was still in love with his first love.

Even if I didn't want to.

He spun me again, but this time, he didn't hide his eyes. This time, he made me face him, a beautiful god in a man's body. A young man straddling the same line, but I was the only one who felt sophomoric in this moment, young.

Ramses's hand formed around mine. "I did tell her my feelings. I told her a lot of things."

"Like?"

He angled me around again, and when I returned, he pressed his lips close to my ear. "My feelings for you."

My head jerked up, eyes narrow. "What?"

He… what?

"My feelings for you," he emphasized, as if it didn't mean anything.

As if it didn't mean everything.

He kept me in a gentle sway, studied the effect of those words. His lips parted. "I told her about *those* feelings, and yeah, I told her other things. How there were feelings directed toward her, too. In the past."

In the past.

"She basically already knew, but those didn't seem so significant," he said, shaking his head. "Not, well, after the other thing. They were the main things, so the others weren't significant."

Why was he saying this? *Voicing this* to me. I swallowed. "Ramses—"

"You asked me about the change of heart." He studied my eyes. "Why I changed."

I had but hadn't known what I asked. It wasn't until after I'd voiced it, when it was too late, and it became this.

Ramses blinked so slow, and pulling me close, he eased my hair away from my eyes. "I'm tired of being the one who gets in my own way," he said, his throat constricting. "I've done it for years. I avoid and don't deal with shit."

I did too, how we met and connected. It wasn't unknown to either of us. "I—"

His mouth dropped down in a breath, a charged pulse as he forced my lips apart. I hadn't tasted him since his friend's wedding night.

And God.

God, how he tasted, how he felt and smelled. He gathered my face and tugged my lip between his teeth, no chance of escape. There was no place to run. There was only him and me.

My mouth burned with a bruising kiss, and though he took what he wanted, he didn't stay long.

He retreated with another breath, husky as he dragged his thumb across my mouth. His digit came away red, his lips the same. My lipstick hadn't held up.

"Now, I can say I did everything I could when it came to this, you and me." He nodded. "That I acted with no regrets." He looked up. "Just like I did when I bought this place."

His words made me emotional. Like I actually wanted to cry. He wouldn't let me be a regret.

"I want you to be my girl. My girlfriend." He smiled a little. "Whatever you want to call it, I want it. And I know what you said—"

I hooked an arm around his neck, stealing his lips before he both said and did more things that scared me. I didn't want him to be a regret. And though, he may be one in the morning…

He wouldn't be one now.

I kissed him, hungry, angry. I was angry.

Why did he have to ruin things? Break me down.

I was so damn vulnerable with him, but clearly, I wasn't at the same place he was. It was enough to be here and in this moment.

And at the present, it seemed like enough.

His hand slid down my leg and beneath my dress slit. I toed out of my heels and weaved my legs around his waist.

He growled, pressing his lips to mine, his hands hugging my ass. I tongued his lips apart, grinding my hips against him, and he eased me away.

"What?"

He grinned, sliding me down his hard body. My feet returned to the floor, and he hooked a finger beneath my chin. He tipped it up. "Brielle, look at me."

I did, and how beautiful he was, features defined and angular. Lips bruised from my mouth and smeared red from our kiss. I wanted to kiss the fuck out of this man, taste him everywhere.

But for some reason he was keeping that from me. He peeled my hands off his chest, kissing the back of them.

"For once, don't use this." He touched a lengthy digit to my temple before pressing my hands back to his desk. He angled in. "I got it from here. Trust me to. Okay?"

"Okay." I stayed put, watching as he worked his jacket off his big shoulders. He tossed it back on the couch, then proceeded to unbutton his shirt starting at the wrists.

And holy fuck.

Lean, sinewy muscles defined solid forearms dusted with dark hair. He wore a wristwatch, which he took off, depositing it in his pocket before removing his shirt.

Tanned skin exposed readily to my sight, his body golden and perfect. He folded his shirt in front of a flat stomach. Like that mattered.

I think he just wanted to tease me, nothing but those playful eyes as he smirked. He set the shirt to the desk in a fist before hooking my waist and picking me up with one arm.

My bottom touched his desk, and though I wanted to touch him, take control, I didn't.

"This is driving you mad," he mouthed over my lips, my entire body buzzing. He eased my legs apart. "Good."

He fingered the zipper located at the back of my dress, his voice heated and gruff. He tugged, then worked my dress bodice down, bunching the material at my hips. I sat there in a strapless bra made out of lace, and Ramses groaned, gathering my waist in his hands.

"Your tits are fucking gorgeous." He arched them toward his face, immediately peppering the swell with kisses. He tugged at the lace with his teeth but didn't expose me.

Frustrated, I pressed his mouth between my breasts, his close-cropped hair rough beneath my palm. I spread my legs to hug his hips, but he yanked me away from him by *my* hair.

He arched my neck, studying me.

"I told you I got you," he said, almost growling. I frustrated him, too. Good. He smirked. "I can make you wait longer. Do you want that?"

"No."

He pulled my lips apart with his thumb. "Will you trust me, then?" He honed in. "To take care of you?"

I did.

"I do."

His entire hand covered my neck, but not in a threatening way. It was more possessive, stating *mine*. He was staking a claim.

He was taking care of me.

He dropped to his knees, and I quivered. Even from the floor, this man was within clear access of my pussy. His desk wasn't a short desk. He was freaking tall, so it had to be big to accommodate him.

"Give me my favorite thing," he growled, forcing my legs apart. He got them as far as they could go, hooking my panties over. He used his digit, that ring he always wore playing at my sex. "Is it your favorite thing, too?"

Oh, it was definitely my favorite thing, and he was frickin' good at it.

Chuckling, Ramses worked my panties off, using his ring again to tempt and tease my pulsating bud. I wondered if he'd fuck me with it again, but when he pressed a hand to my tummy, urging me to lay back, he simply buried himself between my legs.

He merely kissed me first, hot sensual kisses. He was so gentle with it, like he was kissing my mouth instead of down there.

I arched off his desk.

I stared at the ceiling while he made my toes curl, his fingers circling and preparing my entry while he tongued my lower lips apart.

He latched onto me once he had, gathering my breast in a single palm while he licked and sucked, and I cried out.

I elbowed up to see him, his head lost in the material of my dress. It was the most erotic sight I'd ever seen, my legs shaking to hook around him, but I worried he'd stop.

"Can I touch you?" I asked. Maybe if I did, he wouldn't stop. This wasn't me taking control. He took my hand, growling into my sex, and guided my fingers down there.

He made me touch myself while he tasted me, his smile forming against my heat.

"Touch yourself," he urged, making me. He had me finger myself while he tongued my buzzing clit. "Feel how good you feel."

I closed my eyes, so close to coming at this point it wasn't even funny. Ramses was taking me to the edge, but at the brink, he rose.

Fingers behind my back, he flicked my bra off, exposing my chest. He picked me up without acknowledging that, my nipples diamond-hard while he returned my feet to the floor. With his height, it was like looking up at a mountain. The sun.

And once there, I didn't want to leave.

Popping up on my toes, I tasted him, kissing him deep and full, and didn't care about his game.

Yes, I had issues with control. I liked to make myself feel good, safe, because that was what control gave me.

That safety had been taken away too many times. With my ex-husband… other things, and I liked feeling like I had the power.

But Ramses definitely liked when I took control.

He liked fighting me for it, something I'd totally picked up on him during our time together. In fact, that give and take was probably one of the main reasons we couldn't keep our hands off each other. We both enjoyed playing this game of power.

"Bri…"

I dropped to my knees in front of him, undoing his pants. I hadn't seen his cock in way too long, and I was gifted the moment I had his pants and boxers worked down his thick thighs.

He angled long, erect and oh so thick. Seriously, the man hit the second section of his abs at full attention, and my mouth watered.

He growled. "Bri."

I ignored him, driving my hands up his hips. He gritted my name again, and I gazed up at him.

A strong warning flashed in his amber eyes, making them narrow, hard. I was ignoring him, and he didn't like that. I was *testing him*, and he might not even want me to do this for him. He'd been more than vocal about his hesitance when it came to his size. I mean, he was big, so I got that. He might have even scared a girl or two, and with how attentive Ramses was, he probably didn't want to hurt me.

Well, what he failed to realize was he didn't need to worry about me. Anything he had, I could take. He also did like it when I challenged him.

I flicked my tongue across the head.

"Shit," he ground out, his fingers burying into my hair. His thigh muscles pulsed, his body stiff and tight. "You don't know what you're about to do. I could destroy your fucking throat."

The tail end of that came out on a chuckled rasp, rough and aroused, but he gave in when I pushed the head past my lips.

Holy shit.

Inch by glorious inch, my swallow long and full as I opened my throat to let him inside. He touched the back, and

I still had a ways to go, but I teased him out and in. Sometimes I got there. Sometimes I didn't, but regardless, I didn't stop.

"Shit. Goddamn. Shit." Awe in his voice, like serious awe as he took my face between his hands. He rocked slow, in and out. He pushed back my hair. "Fucking hell, who are you right now?"

I was the woman who had him shaking, at his knees if I wanted him. He had the same affect over me, and moaning over his length, I worked his balls in my hands.

His powerful body immediately stiffened, his thighs clenched tight. I thought he'd come in seconds, and he may have been at the brink because he guided me off him.

"Not so fast, professor," he said, angling me around. He gathered my dress above my hips, hugging my back to him. "You only get to see me come between your legs."

A promise in his voice as he pressed hot kisses across my neck. He pinched and worked my nipples, kicking his pants and boxers off. He removed my dress and we were naked in the middle of his office, his length tucked between my ass cheeks.

Whipping me around, he took my face again, backing us up toward the couch. He guided me down toward it as he loomed on top of me, his mouth touching mine.

I thought I'd come with the way he kissed me, and I wasn't even joking. So gentle, hot and heavy before hungry and intense. He kept me on my toes, ready for anything.

It felt like this was Ramses in the complete sense, as exciting as he was equally passionate. He made me feel nothing but safe within his arms.

"Don't let me think," I rasped, hooking my legs around him. I tugged at his lips with my teeth. "I just want this."

I just wanted him and to not think so damn much. Thinking made me make logical decisions, and I didn't want that. Not in this moment.

A smile as he turned me around, then pressed his body on mine. He mouthed heated kisses across my back beneath him, and this had to have taken so much effort, to control himself without crushing me. He was so much bigger than me.

"I promise," he said, his hand between my legs. He fingered me, my body tense. "Just stay here with me."

My eyes closed as he tunneled deep within me, tight strokes with his long fingers. He got me so close toward the cliff before he reached for his pants and put a condom on. By the time he did, I was on my back, and he was on top of me again.

I knotted my arms behind his neck, my chin tilting up as he entered me, and my eyes rolled back.

God.

So full, so *tight*. He had the capability of ripping me apart, which he knew because he always started slow.

"Open up," he urged, sucking my earlobe into his mouth. He rocked his hips. "Let me in."

His hips dropped hard the moment I gave him the sign, my legs spreading apart the instant the discomfort subsided, and the pleasure took over.

I called out, my chest arching for his hands. Ramses took full advantage of that, his hands kneading my breasts.

"Stay with me," he panted, his hips rolling in quick succession. "I got you."

His fingers pinched my aching peaks. He fucked me deep into his sofa while he pleasured my breasts.

"Ramses, fuck me." I buried my cries into his neck, tasting his sweat. I licked his pulse. "Hard. Please. I don't need gentle."

He trusted me on that, fucking me hard and fast. Raising my arms, he stretched me, and he swelled hot inside me.

He came before I did, his eyes rolling back. Even still, he didn't stop his hips until the fire exploded in my tummy.

I spasmed around him, completely lost as he pulsed hard

inside me. He finished well before, but even still, continued to kiss me.

"That's it. Come back with me," he coached, so tender. Gathering my breasts, he squeezed before cradling and massaging my back. He kissed my neck. "Don't disappear on me."

It was like he knew to say these things, that I would if I thought too much. I still might, sighing when he kissed me deep into the couch.

Ramses pulled out, but then there were his hands, his body. He tucked me tight into his mighty conclave. His unyielding wall of safety and security. He gave that to me. No questions asked.

I wasn't surprised as he tucked me back into his arms, but the thing about us was, we were always a distraction for the other. We never allowed ourselves to be real enough with the other to be any other way. It would take effort to be with each other, an effort he seemed to want to make.

I want you to be my girl.

Too much thought, too many words. I'd create a new reality if I listened, so I closed my eyes.

I went to sleep within his heat and his soft hip hop beats.

CHAPTER
NINETEEN

Bri

Ramses and I didn't go back to the charity event. We went to my hotel room, where we didn't leave.

We'd done the civil thing, of course. He'd texted his date, and I'd called mine. Meredith, as he'd said, hadn't expected to go home with him so her quick response of "Catch ya later" hadn't been surprising on his end. He hadn't told me the excuse he'd given her for leaving, but they seemed amicable about how both their nights ended. She'd probably, like he'd also said, gone home with someone else, and though Guy hadn't expected him and me to leave together either, he had been surprised by the call.

Initially, I'd given him some lame excuse for leaving. I had to stop at my hotel room to get something. He hadn't protested, but when I called to say I wouldn't be returning, his concern rang through the line. I gave yet another lame excuse, this time feigning illness, and I felt a little guilty about that. I didn't like lying to people, and I had been clear things weren't going anywhere between the pair of us.

Ramses had me doing things I didn't normally do, this man, this... *young* man making me live and breathe life in a different way. When I was with him, I didn't think. I didn't *want to think* so it was easy for me to give in to a night of passion.

And passion we had, basically *everywhere*. There wasn't a surface in that hotel suite where he didn't taste me, make me come. By the end, we'd collapsed in a tumble of spread limbs and moist flesh on the chaise lounge in the suite's sitting area. We'd both fallen asleep there, but when I woke up, I was in a bed by myself.

That didn't mean Ramses wasn't around me, on my flesh or in the sheets. We'd made love here too, several times.

Love. Was that what this was? It was infatuation, definitely, and obsession, most assuredly. I was obsessed with Ramses, had been for a while. He was like a forbidden candy I couldn't help but taste, the urge to be naughty and sample his flavor ridiculous. We didn't hold back sexually, and we'd only spent a couple of nights together. Something told me more wild days were sure to come, but I wasn't sure I was prepared for them.

I want you to be my girl.

But what did that mean to him? Did he understand what that meant? Did I understand what that meant? Sex was one thing. Perhaps, the easiest thing. It was society and pressures to be a certain something that was the problem. We did have a decent age gap, and we'd also have to stare his mom in the face and tell her the truth.

After I'd already lied to her.

I lay with so many thoughts in that bed I basically drowned in them and Ramses had been gone for so long, I turned to find him. I grabbed my phone first, a text message on the screen.

Ramses: Come get breakfast when you're ready. I'm getting it ready for you.

Oh my God, he made me breakfast.

Like a legitimate boyfriend, he doted on me, but then again, I'd done the same for him that first night.

Mostly, because I was a control freak.

The game from last night was over without the sex-induced haze, and the urge to grip hold of that control tugged me out of bed.

I showered quickly, the bedroom connected to the bathroom. It hadn't been until after I toweled dry and threw some clothes on that I smelled, well, food. It wafted in like he'd started to ready it after I woke up. He might have even been listening for me to wake up so he could start.

I wouldn't put it past him, shaking my head when I cracked the door open and a myriad of smells hit me. I was talking eggs, baked goods, *bacon.*

I'd even smelled steak.

I got a suite with a kitchen, but he'd have to have gone out to get food. Or called a delivery service. I padded down the hall with my bare feet in a pair of jeans and a tank top. My hair still wet, I towel-dried it on my search to find Ramses and that food. I found them both in the sitting area.

And he'd completely outdone himself.

He hadn't cooked, silver domes indicating room service lining the counter between the kitchen and the sitting room. But it appeared he'd ordered everything on the menu.

Platters with stacks of danishes, three-tiered stands arranged with muffins and scones. He'd order pancakes, as well, and he did have steak and eggs. It all sat arranged on their various plates near the bacon, a feast with at least two types of cold beverages and coffee. Ramses was coming out of the kitchen with silverware for it all. Two place settings had been arranged next to each other. The table sat at least twelve, but he only put silverware in front of the two chairs. It reminded me of the sweetheart table at his friend's wedding.

And God, was he delicious too.

He hadn't spotted me at first, in only his lounge pants, gray sweats that cuffed at his ankles. He must have planned to stay overnight in the city as well, a complete and ab-lickable god with his shaven head and magnificent body. The sweats helped his *Men's Health Magazine* aesthetic, the outline of his package on full display. Whoever invented gray sweatpants needed to be knighted for their service to womenkind.

I cleared my throat, and Ramses jerked that buzz cut in my direction, his grin wide. Eyeing me, he placed a hand toward a chair, and I took it.

"What's all this?" I asked, letting him push me in, and he joined me.

"This is a do over." He snapped out a napkin, placing it on my lap before draping an arm across my chair. He folded a hand behind my neck. "And you're sexy as hell."

I didn't understand the whole do over thing, but I definitely computed his mouth on mine.

He captured my lips in his hungry kiss, smelling all fresh like he'd showered. He must have snuck one in while I'd been sleeping. The fact only made me want to get in his lap and bury my face in his neck, but I resisted.

He didn't.

He mouthed his way down to my rapid pulse, hooking my waist and actually tugging me on top of him. A heavy hand kept my ass on firm thighs, his thick cock probing me right through his sweats.

He groaned, tasting the other side of my neck, and if we kept this up, we wouldn't be eating. I smiled. "Ramses?"

"Yep?"

"Do over?" I fisted his biceps, physically easing him away from me. This was no easy feat.

He was definitely hungry.

Though I had a feeling that hunger ebbed more towards me. Even still, he picked up a fork and speared a piece of melon for me.

He summoned me to open my mouth, which I did, the taste explosion absolute heaven and even better since he fed me.

He allowed me to enjoy myself, sampling what he'd clearly had brought up for me. Everything in front of me was cooked to perfection. He'd even ordered poached eggs for me, which I loved.

His arms ensnared my hips while I ate, what I deciphered as pleasure across his face as he watched me feed myself. I offered him a bit, but he refused. He just liked watching me.

"The do over seems to be going well," he said, and I noticed he hadn't answered me the first time. I'd been too busy eating and enjoying his presence to poke him about it. He rested a chin on my shoulder. "Are you happy?"

I faced him, actual worry knitting his brow, and he smoothed a hand over his shaven head.

He sat back. "The last time we did this, you left. Though, obviously not physically. You had me do that part."

I had, guilt and something else sagging heavy like a sopping blanket on top of me.

He wanted me happy?

At least, he was worried that I wasn't. That I'd leave. I placed down my fork. "Ramses..."

"No."

I faced him again, his expression serious. He cuffed his wrist on the other side of my hips, his lips pinched tight in thought. Or maybe hesitance. I'd given him more than one reason to do the latter.

I had run.

I planned to possibly do more of that today, but I said nothing at the present.

He lifted a hand. "Before you say anything, give me a list of reasons why this won't work..."

Wow. He knew me so well, didn't he? At least, thought he did.

I adjusted in his lap, my jaw shifting. He may have thought I was uncomfortable, so he returned me to my chair.

He hung an arm on the back. "Tell me I'm too young for you again or how much it bothers you that I'm your friend's son…"

He was both those things, our reality. I wasn't very comfortable with the age gap, but I may be able to get over it, had we not had the other issue.

I'd lied to his mom. I'd lied to my friend, and though he had as well, he was her son. Kids lied to their parents. But friends?

I followed the hard curve of his bicep with my hand, solid and unyielding beneath my flesh. I wished it was different. I wished we were different, our circumstances, and I'd said that before.

Ramses wouldn't allow me to say it again, cuffing the back of my neck. Bracing me, he caused our foreheads to touch and breathed me in.

I sighed.

"Just," he started, my skin warming beneath his hand. He squeezed. "Tell me what I need to say. Tell me what I need to do for you to give this a chance."

He brought my head up, scanning my eyes.

"To be my girl," he said, basically my entire insides fluttering. "To be with me, as *mine* and not just for sex. To be out of the dark with all this. To be a real thing."

My throat thickened, my mouth dry. "Can I speak now?"

"Depends on what you have to say." He sat back. He lifted a hand. "Do I even have a chance? A chance with you?"

I hated that he felt that way, that I gave him such a run around, that that was the relationship we had.

I fucked with this guy's heart something crazy, and I hated that.

I cuffed his other arm, so powerful beneath me. He was

mighty Ramses, all-powerful pharaoh of the world. At least, mine. "It's not so simple."

"What's not so simple about it?"

"People who are different ages, our kind of age difference is fine on paper. But with that difference comes life experiences. *Different* life experiences, and relationships are already difficult enough."

"Well, I'm willing to try." A frustrated hand came over his head again. "And it's not that different. Our ages?"

"It is enough of one, yeah, and then there is your mom."

"Yeah, and she'd be cool with it."

"You don't know that."

"You don't either, but you're quick to say it. Shut this down."

This all seemed moot, the back and forth. We were arguing about things that hadn't happened. "I've barely been divorced for a year."

"And I'm not asking to get married." He shook his head. "I just want to give this a chance. Are you saying there isn't one?"

"No."

This surprised him, clearly. His eyes flashing. He leaned forward. "Okay."

Oh my God, what are you doing?

I was being selfish. Willing to entertain this was completely selfish. Because what other words defined this?

He was a young man and had many more experiences that awaited him. Many young women like Meredith last night, ones who hadn't been married and didn't have all this baggage.

And I had a lot.

They went beyond my ex and how cruel he'd ended up treating me. They were buried, deeply rooted.

I needed them to stay there.

Placing them there was all I could do to function every

day, and in all my thoughts, Ramses made me look at him once more.

"You're doing it again."

"What?"

He tilted my chin. "Using too much of this," he said, touching my temple. "You're so in your head right now when you don't have to be. It doesn't have to be so hard. In fact, it's so simple."

"Explain it to me then." I worked my hair around. "Make it as simple for me as it is for you."

Dampening his lips, he faced away. His fingers dragged across his mouth before he returned. "How about we put a deadline on it."

"What?"

He nodded. "One of your biggest issues is my mom, right?"

"Yes."

"And the fact I'm only a few years younger than you. Which I can't help, by the way."

"I know."

Smirking, he hugged his arms around my entire waist. He'd actually been able to grip his biceps this time. "We figured out the whole me being your student thing. I'm not anymore, but maybe you'd feel better if we *officially* came out with everything if I wasn't a student anymore."

"Meaning…"

"Graduation hits, and we are a couple," he stated, smiling. "We acknowledge it. We tell my mom. We skip over a few details. Say we started talking shortly before but didn't actually start dating until after graduation. We still will be dating *before* graduation, but this way, in the eyes of my mother, it looks a little more innocent."

"I don't see what difference that would make." It was still lying. I shook my head. "And what? We sneak around? Behind her back?"

We obviously couldn't go anywhere together.

His big shoulders lifted. "I don't want to, but I'm willing to do that for you. It also puts a hard deadline on the secrecy, and who knows…" His brows waggled. "You may be tired of my ass before then and we won't have to worry about telling her at all."

I'd be hard-pressed to imagine that. He drove me crazy, yes.

But I liked his crazy.

I liked our crazy, and I wanted to scream about how ludicrous this entire thing was.

This won't work. This won't work. This won't work.

"This will work."

Crap. I'd said that out loud.

He took my hands, grinning. Using our fingers, he tugged some of my hair out of my face. "Or maybe it won't. But at least, we're giving it a chance. I told you. No regrets."

I released a heavy breath, and I knew what I was going to say before I even said it. There was just something about this guy. He always got his way with me.

I wrapped my arms around his neck, and he covered the back of my head.

Bending my head forward, he warmed the top of my crown.

"Ball's in your court, professor," he said, the smile in his voice evident. He pulled his big arms around me. "My Jersey girl."

I closed my eyes in wild wonder that his friend could ever not love him back. Ramses was so easy to love.

God.

I hugged him tighter, nearly wishing she had. It'd be a lot easier for him. It wouldn't be easy with me.

I was too damaged for it to be.

CHAPTER
TWENTY

Ramses

I almost regretted the commitment I'd made with Brielle, the urge to keep what we had a secret.

But then I had her.

I had her every day in my DMs, messages between lectures and board meetings. She'd given me her personal email too, so at least I wasn't hitting her up at school when I did that.

She'd been concerned about that too, if one could imagine.

Like my mother was literally monitoring her emails, her need for secrecy apparent. I didn't like it. Not at all, but that made her comfortable. She also didn't run, so I didn't argue.

I had her.

I didn't have to chase her anymore, which I liked. I seemed to always have my running shoes on with this woman, but over the next few weeks, I didn't have to do that with her.

I couldn't take her out or anything, and between her schedule and mine being tight, that did make a relationship difficult. That'd happen even without the whole keeping us a secret thing, but we made it work. When we could arrange it, she did come over to my place, stay the night. We recommended our runs after school and work often, so that made getting together easy. Her staying at my place on occasion also made it easier for her to go to work in the morning.

And hell, if I didn't take full advantage.

I liked waking up to her, kissing her awake until she let me inside her. The best shit was the shower sex. I couldn't fucking get enough, and it was lucky if either of us made it on time to classes the next day.

We always did, though, and she made sure of that. My responsible ex-history professor. She stayed at my condo a few nights a week, and when she didn't, we were texting the shit out of each other. I didn't push for anything more outside of that since I did get to see or hear from her most days.

I was also busy, so pushing for more wasn't really an option at the present. I was still bound by obligations with school and work, and her life was the same. Our current arrangement made it easy.

But I was still looking at the calendar.

I'd even circled the event on the date: graduation. Like her getting my ass out of the shower for class after morning sex, I planned to hold her to that date. I refused to let us lie to my mother forever.

Me: So, once I'm considered an educated adult by the prestigious standards of Pembroke University (i.e. have grad-uated), you know I'm going to take you out, right? Treat you?

I damn well planned on showing her off and sent her many text messages just as this. She needed a reminder. We had a deadline and all this secrecy shit would be over eventually.

She texted me back while I waited for a client, a surprise on my roster today. In fact, I'd been a little confused by the name, but more curious than anything. I had a few minutes before it yet, so took full advantage of texting my girlfriend.

My girlfriend.

We didn't use such words, girlfriend and boyfriend. Not because I didn't want to use them, of course. I'd shout it from the rafters that I was seeing her.

Brielle Whitman-Quintero proved to be a special case. AKA skittish as fuck. It didn't take much for her to run. So, no, I didn't use labels.

Bri: You're so silly.

Me: Rude and completely disrespectful to your fellow educated adult.

Bri: You haven't graduated yet.

Me: Burn.

Bri: LOL!

Smirking, I eased my feet off my desk and pulled up my executive chair.

Me: Anyway, you're avoiding the initial topic of discussion. I'm treating you so I'm going to need to know your favorite places to go. We'll go anywhere. Any place you want.

I wanted to know these things about her, and though I had learned a lot, I could stand to know more. I knew her favorite color was blue now. Her favorite food was poached eggs. Like the woman could eat eggs for days, but there were so many more things I wanted to know.

Bri: You don't have to treat me. I can treat myself. Thank you very much.

A typical Brielle answer, and I loved that I knew that. I was getting a lot of information, understanding her. We still had a ways to go, but I felt we were getting somewhere.

Me: Make the list. And if you want, I'll make one too. You can treat me. Show me off.

I waited for the telltale eye roll emoji or comment about me being arrogant. I was really starting to know this girl.

"Ramses, you have Mr. Johnson here to see you."

My secretary left after I lifted a hand to her. Time to get back to business.

Me: Gotta go make that money, but I'll get at you later.

She'd been in the midst of a text (probably with one of those eye roll emojis).

Bri: Okay. See you later. Miss you. *heart emoji*

And did I love seeing that.

I pocketed the phone after telling her the same, and by then, my door was opening again. I hadn't seen Lance "LJ" Johnson since Royal and December's wedding. He'd been one of Royal's best men, of course, and even though I hadn't seen him, that didn't mean I didn't constantly hear his name in the wind.

For starters, he'd been buying up all kinds of properties across town, real estate and small businesses. Actually, I figured him being here was only a matter of time, considering that was the game Mallick Enterprises played.

Why I'd been surprised to hear he wanted to meet with me today was because I knew the guy's background. He'd come from poor, despite his rich friends Knight Reed, Royal Prinze, and Jaxen Ambrose. I'd heard LJ had gotten into the drug game for a while. (What can I say, people talked in this town). But I also heard, he'd put all that aside as of late and ventured into the stock market. He was apparently doing well for himself and that showed the moment he waltzed into my office covered head to toe in Armani.

The guy had always had one of those surfer-dude looks, even back in high school. I was talking bleach blond hair twenty different shades and a tan that damn near challenged mine. The dude was pretty, I'd give him that, and he had that long blond hair cinched back today. The moment he saw me, he thrust out a hand but did one better once he took it.

"Mallick, brother," he greeted, slapping my back when he tugged me into a hug. "How's the high life in the sky?"

I had to say, treating me well, and I grinned, pulling back

and looking at him. He looked so different from high school, but not far off from the wedding. Fly as fuck, he rocked a diamond-encrusted Rolex and a gold chain in his gray suit.

My father's voice in my head screamed "new money" at me, but I admired the guy. He wore whatever the fuck he wanted, self-expression as bold as the statement it made. People should be able to do and be whatever the hell they wanted to be.

"No complaints here," I returned, and not many today. Things were starting to look up, and really, I had no complaints.

Our Court rings clanked when he slapped my hand a couple times again, and what a moment to be had. He and the other guys really were brothers to me. We shared a commonality, and like me, the others seemed to be rising above.

We talked about that for a moment, our days in the Court and high school a bit before sitting down, and I put my hands out to him behind the desk.

"How the hell you been?" I asked, smiling. "Seems like things are going well."

Well, indeed. Like stated, he'd been buying up all kinds of shit.

It'd been enough to make a few people around here nervous, but mostly because they didn't know his agenda. LJ was a new player, no ties to anyone in the inner circle. That naturally made people nervous. People doing rogue shit was nerve-racking. I'd never held concerns. I figured LJ would surface eventually with his objective, and even if he hadn't, whatever. There was a piece of the real estate pie out there for everyone, and I knew something about this guy's character. We'd gotten pretty acquainted during the wedding days, and he seemed like a stand-up dude, classy.

He folded his fingers. "I feel like you've expected me to come through."

A shrug as I passed that off, which had him grinning. I did

the same. "What you been up to? You planning on making your own city?"

He chuckled. "It's been that obvious?"

Obvious enough, a flash of LJ's smile when he tucked his hands under his arms. "I'm trying to get into the game. More specifically in Maywood Heights. This is home, and I want to start cementing some stuff here. Especially since we are graduating soon."

I nodded, understanding. "I thought you were going into architecture?"

December had mentioned something during the wedding plans, and LJ also went to an Ivy League. He'd really been doing well.

"I am. Have a few internship offers. I'll need that knowledge for what I'm going to do once I finish whatever program I choose."

He had a guy bring in some documents then, like an actual guy holding his briefcase and stuff. He looked like nothing more than a college kid like us, and I smiled.

This guy had a legit entourage, only missing the women. Though, I knew him to be settled down romantically. I'd met his girlfriend Billie at the wedding too, of course.

With his stuff, LJ laid it all out on my desk. He had a business plan, one he slid over to me.

"I plan on looking out for the little guy," he said, taking his seat while I thumbed through what he gave me. "I'm talking affordable housing, nice but without the markup. And also, businesses that are affordable and cater to regular people. It's so hard to get a damn come-up in this town. The plans I have for the properties I'm buying will help with that and also provide safe neighborhoods for people to live."

I saw that, *all that*, and surprisingly, his plans weren't just altruistic.

The guy could stand to make an actual profit on the endeavor. He simply looked out for the little guy first, which was the exact opposite from how things were done traditionally.

"Some of these are Mallick properties," I mentioned, which had LJ grinning wider.

He nodded. "Hence, why I'm here in front of your lovely face, brother."

His manservant came back in, this time with an offer for said Mallick properties listed in great detail in a binder.

LJ had the figures listed under each property, and as I turned the pages, I actually chuckled at the sight of them.

But not because they were low.

"Shit, you're not playing," I said. At another exorbitant figure, my brow dashed up. "This is like triple what these properties are worth." Anyone would have thought he'd lost his mind, mostly my board. "Does Knight know you're doing this?"

Knight Reed, his buddy and another of Royal's best men, headed Reed Corp. Had since his grandfather, Gerald, died our junior year. This was well known in our circles, and like me, Knight had a board running things until he graduated from school. I'd just decided to get involved with my family business early, and his was technically number one in the real estate and development game. At least, when it came to Maywood Heights.

The Reeds and Prinzes built this town, partners in its creation. The Prinzes had their names on everything, and the Reeds help them build the empire. The Mallicks, my father and the other members of our family who later emigrated over, came in late, but our income was more diverse. Mallick Enterprises was global, but my father always had full backing from the Reeds and Prinzes.

I mean, they made him mayor.

Funded his campaigns and everything.

At the mention of his friend, LJ lifted his eyes to the heavens.

"Oh, he knows." He sat back, opening his hands. "I went to the fucker first. Wanted to buy some of his properties."

"And?"

"Completely shut my shit down." He chuckled. "Knight may be my boy, but he's also a competitive prick. I think it actually got him off I was trying to get into the game."

Not surprising, knowing him. The dude was scary, but in this case, had both LJ and me laughing.

He braced his arms. "Ain't getting any help from him. I'm on my own with this. A one-man show."

Something told me he wouldn't be for long. He wasn't just trying to get ahead but build something, help people. I opened my hands. "I'll deep-dive more into this, but I'm going to be real, man. I do answer to people."

Even with as big as the offers were that didn't mean my people would say yes. Some of them thought the same way as Knight. Though, obviously not for the same reasons. What LJ and Knight had was a friendly rivalry, but in business, people could be money-grubbing douchebags.

Some of the board might want to white knuckle the properties just maintain their current status in the game. Stupid, I knew.

I did make the final, final decisions around here, but going all rogue after just arriving probably wouldn't be a good idea. I had to pick my battles, and people already thought I was crazy for buying *one* art gallery. They didn't trust me, thought me young and naive, and with all the drama I came in with, the Brown shit…

"I get it." LJ shook my hand, the pair of us standing. "Just let me know."

I certainly would. I actually really admired the guy, coming in here and putting it all out there when he was new. It also took a lot to do what you wanted to do. It took bravery.

And that was something I'd forever respect.

CHAPTER
TWENTY-ONE

Ramses

Honestly, taco night with Mom nearly got canceled that night. One, because it was yet another night Bri's and my schedules clashed and I couldn't see her. She didn't feel comfortable schmoozing up to my mother while the pair of us secretly fucked behind the scenes. And two, I found myself so wrapped up in LJ's business plan I hadn't wanted to leave the office. I'd actually brought all that shit home with me, pretty engulfed. By the time I looked at the clock to meet my mom for dinner, the hour had gotten away from me. I called her to cancel, but she wasn't having that.

Before I knew it, she'd driven over to my house. My actual home in Maywood Heights. My condo on campus was just a place to keep my stuff while I went to school, but I saw it more than the old colonial-style I'd purchased my freshman year of college. My inheritance had opened up around then, and naturally, I'd needed a place near my mom.

These days, it was merely a place to rest my head on days

I worked too late, and Brielle had never come here. I hadn't asked since I barely stayed here myself.

I had people to keep up on it, dust and what have you, while I was away, and Mom made herself right at home the moment she arrived with her arms filled with bags upon bags of food. She knew how I ate so she brought a lot.

"Don't you worry. I'll get everything all set," she said, making me spend time with her. I told her I was bringing work home with me, but she insisted. She eyed me. "I see you basically once a week, and you won't deny me my fix."

She made me kiss her on the cheek after that before she filled both my kitchen and home with amazing smells. I felt bad. I didn't see her a lot, but LJ's plan intrigued me and I wanted to know more about the properties he sought to acquire.

Oddly enough, the files for said properties had been readily available when I'd asked for them. As it turned out, Mallick had just finalized a deal surrounding them. They were scheduled for demolition actually.

For a mini mall.

And so, the powers that be in my company had planned for what they obviously considered their own progress and had actually paid people out of their homes to do it. It'd been a fine deal—on paper. But definitely not with people in mind. According to what LJ had given me, he wanted to fix up the neighborhood.

"Are you going to work the entire night or actually interact with your mother?"

On the floor with me, Mom toed my leg in her pantsuit from the office. It'd been a long time since we'd done things like this, ate on the floor like when I'd been a kid. She had been a housewife during the days of her marriage to my father, putting away her dreams. He'd gotten locked up and she'd gotten to take them back, her love for history and academia.

Pembroke had welcomed her back with open arms. Of course, they had. She was fucking awesome.

I smirked at her above my Mac but did steal a taco off a plate she'd put together. She'd laid everything out for me to work.

"I told you I was bringing work home with me," I said, after basically shoving the whole thing in my mouth. Again, my mom knew how I ate. I winked. "But give me two seconds. Won't take long."

Of course, I'd probably been saying that for like an hour now. I couldn't help it, and I had told my mom about what I was looking at. I think because I found it sad how terribly inhuman the whole process of business, progress was. I knew it was that way—obviously. I mean, I was in the thick of it and knew no other way. I'd also been trying to mind my Ps and Qs at the office, so I'd gone out of my way not to make waves.

I felt I should make more after reading over everything LJ gave me, though. He seemed to have big plans for the city, and changes didn't have to be bad. In fact, there were many things in Maywood Heights that could use an overhaul.

Clicking away, I went back to work but noticed my mother's eyes still on me. She had my flat screen on while she ate, keeping herself busy with HGTV, which was basically her drug of choice.

Because it was, I definitely shouldn't get her eye as much. Of course, she wanted to spend time with me, but when it came to work, she didn't bug. She got it. I eyed her. "Something else?"

I knew my mom. *Something else* was definitely in her eyes. She started to pass it off, but then brushed taco bits off her hands. She picked up the remote, shutting the TV off.

"Uh-oh."

"What uh-oh?" She frowned. "I can't just talk to you?"

"You can." But lately, she'd been delicate about it. Like

there was always something she wanted to say while we ate tacos and scarfed guacamole together. I figured that had to do with our talk about therapy at the beginning of term. It hadn't gone well, and when she found out I'd only gone to the one group session, she hadn't been pleased. My mother never wore her worry well, and she was definitely worried, worried about me.

She crossed her legs, her arms rested between them. "There actually is something I want to talk to you about."

"Really?" I feigned shock. "Totally didn't pick that up."

At this point, I really didn't know how I wasn't disowned, and my mother toed at me so hard I nearly dropped my computer.

Chuckling, I righted it, then tugged her over.

She sat next to me, but that worry never left her eyes. "I've spoken to your father recently."

My fingers hesitated for only a second, starting an email. I was aware she was talking to him, part of her therapy, she'd said.

I said nothing, *nothing to say* about that. She knew I disagreed with their meetings, so no point in creating any tension.

"Aren't you going to ask what we spoke about?"

My mom was a pusher too, the place I'd completely gotten it from. I typed on, and she sighed.

"Ramses…"

"Ma." I gauged my time with emails between work and school. Once I finished the office stuff, I moved on to those in my inbox from professors. Those were nothing important, updates here and there and questions they'd answered from other students. Certainly nothing that needed my attention now, but I felt it was better placed there in that moment.

Mom angled close, her arms threading around mine. She took one of my hands off my Mac, lacing it. "He wants to see you, Ramses."

He wants to see me.

"He wants to talk."

He wants to talk.

Politely, but most importantly, calmly, I slid my hand away from my mom's. I returned to my computer without a beat.

"Did you hear me?"

Of course, I'd heard her. I was sitting next to her, but she knew that. That wasn't really her question. Not really, and I think we both knew that.

Shifting away, my mom blew into her hands. She opened them. "What do I have to do to get you to seek closure with your father?"

That was the thing. My closure, my pain had nothing to do with her. It was my own and she couldn't rush it.

Let alone dictate it.

I hit keys in rapid strokes, worried about what I'd say next. Words bubbled tight at the cork, pinched tight between my lips.

"It's really helping me, Ramses," Mom nearly whispered, and she didn't whisper. She had no problems making a point, telling me off if she thought I was being stubborn. "It's making it so it doesn't hurt as much. It's allowing me to move on…"

"Move on?" I faced her, surprised by what she said. "And what makes you think any of us have a right to move on? Like we were the victims in what he did."

Because we weren't, not by a long shot. The true victims weren't here and one of them couldn't move on. Dad and Uncle Leo had made sure of that.

Mom pressed her hands together, touching them to her lips. "You know that's not what I meant."

"Well, you're going to have to break it down for me."

"Don't be mean, Ramses."

"Mean?" I sat back. "Mean. You know what's mean,

Mom? Mean is stealing a daughter, *a sister* away from a family. Mean is how I see that sister every time I'm around my best friend and knowing my family is the reason she'll never see her again."

The words sobered between us, and at this point, Mom refused to look at me. She held her arms. "I know how December's family has suffered." She faced me. "And they are not the only ones. You can't even talk about what happened. That is the problem, Ramses."

"Okay. You wanna talk?" I directed a look her way. "Let's talk about that closure, Ma. Let's talk about *poison*. Let's talk about how your ex-husband—my father—is such a visceral piece of fucking shit that there are places *in your own house* you can't even stomach to walk into because they remind you of him."

She'd gotten the house in the divorce, and she hadn't stayed in their bedroom for years, his shit still in the closet like he had a right.

She couldn't even bring herself to throw it out.

It pained her, still obviously. She closed her eyes. "Ramses…"

"You say he's still such a part of my life? That I can't talk about it. Talk about him?" I shook my head. "When will you move on, Mom? When will you start *dating*, Mom? Because you haven't. Not in all these years."

Her lashes opened, her head raised. "I'm not ready yet, son."

"And maybe I'm not ready." I lifted a hand. "For that closure you think I'm ready for."

I was aware of how I was being, an asshole. Especially for talking to my mom in such a way. I didn't do that.

Why did she always have to push?

The pair of us sat in silence as she cuffed her legs and I worried. I worried about what she'd say. That she'd push again, and I'd say something I really couldn't take back. I only saw red in that moment, blinded by a haze of internal bullshit. It was because I hadn't talked to anyone.

Of this, I knew.

Of this, I was completely aware. But I was so stubborn, I couldn't get out of my own way. Mom was never like that.

I really was my father's son.

The thought sobered me, kept me silent and clicking on keys again. I didn't even see the emails I was drafting, but that didn't matter. It kept me distracted.

"I was just trying to help, baby."

And like a son of a bitch, I let my mother kiss the top of my head before getting up. I let her leave, and it wasn't until my phone buzzed beside me, I actually moved.

Bri: Just wanted to say goodnight. Hope everything was fun at taco night. *taco emoji* *dancing girl emoji*

I fucking laughed, actually laughed. What the fuck?

Wetting my lips, I texted her back.

Me: Where are you?

Bri: Home, of course. Why? Everything okay?

Everything wasn't okay. Not by a long shot. I started to text her the details.

But ended up doing this.

Me: I want you to come over. To my house in Maywood Heights.

I'd never asked her. We usually just stayed on campus. It was convenient. But we obviously both weren't there.

Bri: I'm not sure. You know, meetings in town…

Couldn't be controlled and something we never did. Mom lived here so naturally we avoided in-town meetings. But she wasn't here now.

Me: Mom left. Please. I need you.

Bri: What's going on? Did something happen?

Rather than try to convince her, I tossed my phone down. I probably could have pleaded with her.

I just chose not to.

Honestly, I didn't know why. Why I had such a goddamn hard time reaching out. Instead, I sat with my thoughts, but it wasn't long before my phone buzzed again.

Bri: Text me your address.

Bri: I'm coming.

CHAPTER
TWENTY-TWO

Bri

Ramses had a big house. Gray shutters. Pale brick. A true home from the white columns out front to the quaint decor inside.

The choice surprised me. Nothing screamed bachelor about the place. Like one day, he'd planned for a family to be here with him. The fact that Evie lived maybe five blocks away only emphasized it. Grandma only a hop, skip, and a jump down the street.

The size of the tub matched the house.

It had to be to accommodate him and made it easy to wrap my legs around him.

It made it even easier to hold him.

Ramses angled his big body back into my arms as I scooped cups of water over his broad chest, his large shoulders. I followed the muscled surface down to his biceps, lacing our fingers once I got there. There was something incredibly intimate about this besides the obvious, and we'd been in the bath so long the water wasn't even warm anymore.

He'd said that was what he wanted to do.

He'd wanted to bathe together, be together, and we hadn't even had sex. We just *were*, and I'd be lying to say I wasn't worried. His text messages had been so off, and we never met up in Maywood Heights. I had my reservations about it. Small town, people talked. True, people around here didn't know me from Adam, but they knew him. A mere description and Evie would know exactly who had strolled down the sidewalk with him.

Went to his house.

I held him, hugging his chest. He'd been silent so long, smelled like heaven. I mouthed kisses across his neck, and something deep and carnal radiated from his chest. He held my hand, his forehead grazing my chin.

"I got in an argument with my mom today," he said. His Adam's apple bobbed. "A pretty bad one."

My throat constricted and almost immediately. An argument?

With Evie?

Basically instantly, I thought the argument surrounded us. That maybe she found out about us somehow. We'd been careful. We didn't even meet on campus. Just at his duplex and for our jogs, of course.

Had it been that?

All kinds of scenarios traveled in my head, and in my silence, Ramses tilted his head back. He cupped a hand to the entire right side of my face, his smile faint as he pushed it up into my hair. He was a complete god, skin moist from our bath and muscled frame oozing of sex. I was even getting used to his hair, which he still kept short. He shifted in the bath. "It wasn't about us if that's what you're thinking." He laughed light. "She doesn't even know about us, Bri."

He kissed me as if to assure me, and as my guard loosened

and anxiety faded, I felt like a complete ass for even thinking that. For defaulting to that. He'd said he and his mom got into an argument, and freaking immediately, I'd made whatever that regarded about me.

I was an ass.

I was selfish and definitely when it came to him. I had him all to myself, in my own little world with him like I had that right.

"I'm sorry." I nudged his cheek with my nose, because I was sorry. So damn sorry for being selfish. I gripped my wrist around his front. "What happened? I mean…"

I had no right to that information either, to butt in, especially when it came to the private relationship he had with his mom. Neither was me knowing appropriate, either. She was my friend, and I had to draw the line somewhere.

I lifted my hand. "You don't have to tell me. That's private."

He sat with that, the candles he'd lit flickering waves across his golden skin. He'd lined the tub with them, this whole thing romantic, soothing. I wasn't quite sure he'd been aiming for the former. The ambiance brought this whole room peace and maybe that'd been something he needed. We could only see each other through the warm light with the lights off.

Like stated, all this was incredibly intimate.

The conversation somehow embed that way as well. Ramses's hand circled my arm. He ran it up and down, sliding along my damp flesh.

"Ask me about it." He angled a look up at me again. "Ask and I'll tell you. I want to tell you."

He did?

We definitely didn't operate that way. In fact, when we told each other stuff, it simply spilled out like word vomit. It'd never been by choice. Like the need to tell each other our innermost thoughts and secrets just pulled from each other. Like our bodies knew to trust the other.

Even when our brains didn't.

This was a new level, actually initiating that trust without frenzy or panic. I touched my chin to his shoulder. "I only want to know if you want to tell me."

He extended his neck, staring up at the ceiling. He shifted and the water sloshed, looking at me. "I want to tell you. So, ask me."

Something scared me about his statement. I didn't know why, but it did.

It reminded me of that day I'd caught December at his house, this feeling of impending doom I couldn't identify.

In this case, fight or flight surrounding something more internal. That something was happening here, and I wasn't sure if I should stop it.

Or if I wanted to.

He laced our fingers, and I swallowed.

"Please tell me?" I asked, because I did want to know. I wanted to know everything. Everything about him he could give. I hugged him. "I want to know."

And so, he did.

He told me details about him and his mother, the argument, of course, but something else too. He told me about his father, and something Evie had never shared. I'd never pressed her about it. I mean, people got divorced every day.

But this?

"My father is in prison for covering up a murder," he said, tugging my arms in like he was holding me and not the other way around. Like it wasn't *him* who needed the security, the warmth and love. He wet his lips. "The murder of my best friend's sister. *December's* sister."

My God.

"It happened in high school," he said, nodding. "And I left this town. Haven't seen my father in years."

He went on to say it'd been his uncle to commit the

murder, Ramses's old headmaster from his school, and the story surrounding was like something off of *Dateline*.

As well as the stuff of nightmares.

It was Ramses's nightmare in real life, December's nightmare. They'd come into each other's lives because of all that had happened.

They'd somehow become best friends.

They had such a deep history, and one I hadn't understood. They really were here for the other.

And God, Ramses.

His mom was pushing him to see his dad, get closure. His dad wanted to see him, and the retelling made his chuckle dry.

"He actually said he did it for family back then," Ramses said now, smirking. Though, he found nothing funny. In fact, most of his story he'd been in a far-off place, eyes vacant, voice hollow. He encircled my wrist. "Before the trial and all that, *family*. He said he had to protect us. My uncle Leo, my mom and me and the family's image." He shook his head. "He said he'd do anything."

My chest hurt, physically pained but only for him. I squeezed him. "How is December?"

"She's fine. Well, as fine as she can be." His chest rose with weighted breath. "Time has passed. That helped."

But still.

I closed my eyes before facing him. "Will you see him?" My knuckles ghosted his cropped hair. "You don't have to, you know."

"Maybe I should." His smile was faint. "Get that closure. My mom's probably right. It's plaguing me. Makes me do stupid things."

He didn't go into that, but really, he didn't have to. In all honesty, I had no idea why he was telling me any of this at all. He most certainly didn't have to.

I touched a forehead to his shoulder. "I'm glad you told me."

The smile tugging his lips widened. He angled his head back. "I'm glad I did too. Made me feel better. Go figure. Talking."

That same smile pulled at my lips as well, his hair rough against my fingertips. "But you know you didn't have to, right? You never have to tell me anything you don't want to."

I'd never make him, nor expect it. Our problems were our own, and we didn't have to share them.

The water shifted as he rose from the bath, inch after inch of hard body. He captured me in between his solid arms, his wet fingers gliding through my hair. The first thing I'd done was tug my hair down, the tips wet.

Ramses followed them down, looping around a lock before tipping my chin. He framed my face, guiding me to face him.

"I will tell you anything you want to know about me," he said, eyes scanning mine. "I'm an open book when it comes to you. I told you I want to try."

And so that fear returned, that hesitance. His reason for telling me this and being open. We'd never had that relationship before, not without frenzy or backed by fear. He told me things when he was scared. Not when he had control.

It told me something about him, where he was and where I was. It told me he was open. That *he was* willing to try like he said.

He tilted my head forward to touch his mouth. "I want you to know me. Everything, Brielle." He lifted my head. "I told you, no regrets."

No regrets. No fear.

If only it were that easy.

CHAPTER
TWENTY-THREE

Bri

When Ramses texted about drinks tonight with his friends, I almost dropped my phone.

Which was why he immediately followed up that said drinks would be at a friend's house—in private.

Ramses: It was December's idea. She wants to meet you without being in a towel *grin emoji*

Which meant he'd talked about us... fine. She already knew, but now, it sounded like more than one friend would too.

So, then he sent another text.

Ramses: Stop freaking out because I know you're freaking out. This is an intimate gathering. You and me, December and Royal, and their friends, Knight and Greer. Yes, they are all students at the university. No, they won't say anything. You know, I told December because I can trust her. Well, she told her friends because she can trust them. None of them talk to my mom. We're good.

Ramses: Anything else? *smile emoji*

This had all been sent without a response from me and told me epically how much he got me. It told me severely how much he knew me...

Without really knowing me.

I still guarded a lot of my heart from him, even when he had opened up that night in the bath. I was aware of this and planned to work at it. I did want him to know everything about me too.

It was just hard for me.

Spilling my secrets didn't just tell him but made me face them when I didn't want to. I did a good job of burying them deeply.

Ramses reminded me on the daily, no pressure. He wouldn't pressure me but wanted me to know he was open.

He made it so easy to be with him, trust him, so I did agree to go have drinks with his friends. As it turned out, they'd be held on campus at December's place. We'd be near his, right next door.

The event was BYOB, and in addition, we'd been assigned sweets duty. The others were bringing finger foods as well.

I had no problem with that, and Ramses took us both by the grocery store after I got out of work and he finished his classes.

I'd been better about us being in the same vicinity as the other when we were just out and about. Places like grocery stores were fine. Everyone shopped for food, and if we did run into someone we knew, a colleague or even his mom, we could pass off we'd run into each other.

I knew this probably sounded silly. We'd been seeing each other for over a month at this point, but with graduation (and our deadline) around the corner, I didn't see the need to change anything. Our arrangement had been working fine, so I didn't see the point in changing things up.

Ramses and I split up once we got to the store, assigning me to the liquor while he got the sweets. The liquor department was on the other side of the store, so we covered more ground that way. Of course, he offered to go with me, but I didn't mind. Anyways, we could get in and out quicker.

He merely shook his head at me, knowing that was why I wanted to split up but didn't say anything. He never did. He simply kissed me on the top of my head before parting off, and I ventured to get one half of our supplies.

The grocery store had an entire liquor wing, so actually finding what I wanted was a chore, but I found the wines I liked. I figured a dessert wine would be good with whatever Ramses got.

I'd been scanning the shelf when a girl in a short jacket and shorts sidled up beside me. It'd warmed up outside since spring had hit, but it wasn't that warm. Her arms were full of wine coolers, and I thought she'd just grab something off the shelf next to me, but she didn't.

"Oh my gosh, it's totally you!" she chanted, actually giddy in her flip-flops. Again, it wasn't that warm, but what could I say about young people. I'd caught Ramses wearing flip-flops in the snow one time to get the mail. She grinned. "Brielle Norrington?"

I stiffened immediately.

And for obvious reasons.

I'd changed my name back to my maiden name following the divorce.

But hell, if this girl knew. Why did she know?

She bounced on her thongs. "It's totally you. Oh my *god.* How are you even here right now?"

I shook my head, not really knowing what to say and she giggled.

She cuffed my arm. "My dad, hell, my whole family *loves* your husband. He was our favorite player back in the day."

"Ex-husband," I squeaked, and her face immediately fell.

"Yeah, I know," she tsked, actually tsked, like it was a shame and not the relief it'd been to leave him. I guess that part of my life had been secret. She shook me. "We were all so sorry to hear about that. Still can't believe that. You guys were married what?"

"Over ten years." How was I even having this conversation right now?

You have to leave.

Fight or flight back in full blown action, and perhaps she knew, her face falling.

"You guys have been through so much," she said. "It's a shame you both didn't stick together. Paparazzi suck. You'd think they'd learn after Princess Di."

I swallowed.

"Anyway, can I get a picture? My family would just…" She made a motion like her head exploded, and I felt so outside of my body I allowed this girl to tug me over and snap a selfie with me.

Like I was a circus performer.

She placed a filter on us and everything, tapping a caption before popping it on social media in front of me. She giggled. "I'm low-key freaking out right now. Just… Ah! Thank you. This is great!"

"No problem."

She pumped her little fist before asking for a hug. One I gave her.

Because I didn't feel anything anymore.

My life literally flashed before my eyes.

After, she hugged her wine coolers again, her smile suddenly sad. "Hope you're doing okay. I can't imagine. Losing a baby…." She shook her head. "Alec must have been crushed."

He sure had. Enough to wallow in his grief.

Enough to hurt me.

Enough to blame me for things that weren't my fault, and I said nothing.

Just forced a smile.

It gave this girl, *his fan*, exactly what she needed. It made her go, and I was left with nothing but staring at a wine shelf. Eventually, I grabbed a bottle.

"There you are."

An arm folded around me, a long arm and a snug embrace.

Ramses smiled when he hugged me back into him. He kissed me on the top of the head, holding me close before seeing what I grabbed.

He lifted it up, a frown on his lips. "Honey, we're basically about to go to a bro event and everyone in attendance, December included, will drink like it is." Chuckling, he put the wine back. "Come on. We can do better than that."

He laced our hands together, a platter of cheesecake bites in his hand. My first thought was if he could see what had just happened all over my face, but the second was what he'd said. He called me honey.

He must have seen the second thought.

Because he smiled, so big when he guided me away. He wrapped his long wingspan around me, and I almost forgot what had just happened. Ramses Mallick was a hell of a drug.

But that didn't mean he could numb me.

———

Forever the optimist, Ramses chalked up my abrupt change in comfort as nerves on the way to December's. He said everything would be okay.

He had no reason to think otherwise.

How exactly did one tell their twenty-two-year-old... youthful, *vibrant* boyfriend they'd lost a child? How did she break something down he'd never had to deal with?

How could she explain?

How could she describe that feeling to him? Something he'd never experienced. Ramses was perfect, untouched in so many ways. He'd had his own traumas, but he'd been fortunate not to bear the weight of this.

And hopefully, never would.

He stole my hand in his car, more assurances on his lips. He told me it'd be okay again.

I hoped it would.

"Arizona!"

Okay started with meeting his friends, December when she opened the door. She had a perfect flush to her cheeks, a video game controller in her hand. Apparently, she'd been playing.

Completely youthful.

She greeted Ramses and me at the door, enough beer in Ramses's hands to provide for a frat house kegger. In fact, I'd believed it overkill. But I suppose younger people liked to drink.

Ramses held up one of the six packs to her, a smile gracing his lips. His other hand fisted the rest of the booze, but that didn't stop him from hooking an arm around me. "'Zona!"

I didn't understand the reference, or why she'd called him Arizona. I assumed it was something between friends, and when she shifted to hug him, the same.

"Took you long enough," she teased, squeezing his shoulder.

The gorgeous level of this girl exceeded the charts, her wispy dark strands cinched high in a messy bun. It complemented her pale skin, flushed with rose tint. She still looked like Snow White, still stunning. She propped the controller on her hip. "I was about to send out a squad car. You get lost coming all the way over from next door?"

But she wasn't afraid to stick it to Ramses, the man jokes and sarcasm for days. I could definitely see why the two were friends.

"Nice," he gritted, his eyes lifted, but he hugged me close with a warm grin. He hadn't let me go, but he didn't need to do that. I understood where these two were in regard to their friendship.

I trusted him.

Even still, there was hesitance there that hadn't been, a nervousness at least on December's end. Her smile slipped a bit in my direction, her hand working over that control, and perhaps, Ramses noticed that as well.

"December," he said before placing a kiss down on the crown of my head. He was so tall, always did that. He smiled at me. "You know my Bri. My girlfriend."

His Bri.

Like him calling me honey before, the sentiment warmed inside me, but a dull ache was there, too.

It hadn't left.

I think it'd been seeing him with his young friend, her, too, in flip-flops and shorts. Though, she was at home. There was just such a simplicity about her too, a vibrancy in her youth.

Never in my life had I been envious of someone younger than me, but in that moment, I was. I didn't know why.

"Yes." She took my hand, formally shaking it. Then did one better when she hooked an arm around me too. I had the cheesecake bites, so it was a maneuver.

It made us both laugh, smile when she came away.

She pushed hair out of her face. "And gratefully, this time I'm wearing clothes."

Laughter again from all of us, this meeting between us all so different and when the door widened, even more of that difference.

December's husband came in, a ridiculously beautiful man with the features of a prince and the jawline to match. Blond, he squeezed December's shoulders from behind before reaching out to help Ramses with some of the beers.

He shook his hand.

"Mallick." He squeezed, a polish about him that differed

from his casual wife. He stood taller, stance straighter despite wearing a Pembroke hoodie. This guy was basically huge. But not nearly as tall as Ramses. He smirked. "Good. We can get things going, and you can shut Knight the fuck up. He keeps going on about LJ and some deal. I'm about to goddamn kill him."

Whatever this reference was made Ramses bark a laugh. He waved a hand over his head. "I'm sure," he said before introducing me. "This is my girlfriend, Brielle. Brielle, Royal. I'm sure you saw him at the wedding. Royal, Brielle was a guest."

I was shaking his hand, too, when he offered it. "Nice to meet you."

"Same here." Royal shot a thumb back. "We taking this inside? Seriously, I'm about to fucking kill Knight. What the hell is he going on about?"

"Business, which I don't do in my free time." Ramses chuckled, shaking his head. "I'll talk to him, though. His boxers are probably just in a twist because his boy, LJ, is about to make a name in Maywood Heights."

Royal grinned. "I heard and can't fucking wait. These two are hilarious and so damn competitive."

"There ain't nothing to compete with!" came from inside. Then the guy I assumed was Knight appeared at the door. If Royal was big, this guy was a building. All big shoulders and thick arms.

He had a blond under his arm, a little thing that barely came up to his chest. I assumed this was their friend, Greer, his girl apparently.

"Mallick, brother." Knight shook Ramses's hand. "Glad you're here. We can talk shop and why there ain't no competing when it comes to Reed Corp."

Royal dropped an arm around Knight, patting his chest. "Keep telling yourself that, brother."

The two jostled each other like a couple of actual brothers, making their girls scoff and Ramses laugh. Ramses once again emphasized he didn't discuss business outside of the office, and I assumed these other boys were just as affluent. I mean, I knew Royal was. I'd seen his last name Prinze all over the town, and I'd definitely heard the name Reed Corp.

Between these young men, there was a nice little empire going, a building or two named after the Mallicks on campus, and I'd seen the name Reed, as well.

Something told me there was probably a connection, and after meeting Knight and his girlfriend, Greer, who turned out to be super sweet, we all did take the party inside. The others headed immediately in with the things Ramses and I had brought, and when they got ahead of Ramses and me, Ramses hooked my elbow.

He held me back at the door, an inquisitive look to his brown eyes. He was searching for something in my direction. Not surprising considering the car ride.

"We can leave when you want," he said. He pinched my chin. "If you're uncomfortable."

Once again, he had no reason to assume anything else.

And I hoped it'd stay that way.

As the night kicked off, Ramses may have called Knight and Greer, December and Royal's friends, but the way he fit in with them, the way they all fit together in a snug little community of kinship, read nothing but friendship. He was friends with these people.

He fit with them.

From their jokes, to their laughter and exuberant delight. Knight did try to talk shop with Ramses. Ramses did fight him, and Royal fought laughter in the center like the poorest referee. There were finger foods tossed in mocked rivalry. There were smiles exchanged over conversation and video game controllers. There were young people having a good time and living life. There was no drama. There was just fun.

I sat in the middle watching it all, under Ramses's arm on

a couch and in a room that held a similar layout to his own. His duplex basically mirrored December and Royal's, neighbors from the high brick walls to the wide windows. They all sat around on various couches, constant glee and laughter in the air. It felt so overwhelming.

I engaged when I could, of course. Ramses made sure I felt included and apart of him and this group. And though it should feel good to be around people, be out with him and not hiding what we were, it wasn't as free of a feeling as it should have been. I was thinking about other things.

When was I not thinking about other things?

At one point, December decided to help clear all the dishes from the living area. To keep myself busy, I decided to help her, and Greer, the little one, joined us as well. The girl was too cute and looked like a doll.

I'd found out she was the youngest, a sophomore at the university where the others were in their final semester. They'd all be moving on soon, to the real world like Ramses after this semester.

"Thanks, Bri," December said, taking the empty cheesecake bite platter from me. The boys had done well to quickly annihilate that and were currently arguing over business *again* from Royal and December's couch.

Their friend Knight was standing up at this point, pleading his case about their friend LJ, who was apparently trying to get into whatever business endeavors the boys had going. It was falling on deaf ears as Ramses really wasn't trying to talk about any of that. This only proved to frustrate Knight, who was going red in the face. Royal, who'd been trying not to laugh half the night, was laughing, and that just frustrated Knight more. His voice boomed at this point, and even Ramses was laughing now.

I liked his laughter, watching him. It was always so easy for him.

I noticed the other girls looking at me and I slid my smile

away to help with putting away the food. "Everything was great tonight, December. Thanks for inviting me over."

It had been nice, to be with people. I did so well about keeping to myself.

December grinned, Greer helping her refrigerate the rest of the food. After, both girls sat at the kitchen island, the view from there well without view of the boys handling each other. Eventually, when Knight was looking on the cusp of tackling both Royal *and* Ramses for laughing, Greer slid off her bar stool.

She said she needed to go play referee as she rolled her eyes, and I smiled. She had done that a lot tonight, calm Knight down. She appeared to be his kryptonite.

"She's the only one who can handle *that*," December stated, referencing Knight when she cupped her glass of juice. I noticed she hadn't been drinking tonight, which surprised me. A lot of the reason the boys were so riled was because they had a few or *ten* drinks in them. Ramses hadn't drank as much, but he might have just been holding back for me. He always wanted to make me comfortable. That was just who he was, and he had mentioned December drank like the rest of them.

She wasn't now, smiling, and I thought it funny about her comment toward Knight and Greer. Royal had been the same way with her. He'd been super attentive, never far away from her. It was like he was an extension of her, which reminded me of someone else tonight.

Someone who currently had his gaze directed back at me from the couch. Funny, in the midst of a fight brewing literally in front of him, Ramses did nothing but look for me in the sea of it.

He found me, of course, always found me. He placed a wink in my direction before facing the guys, and that caused December to tilt her head.

"God, I've never seen him like this," she said, and when

my eyes narrowed, she eyed me. "He really likes you. Like *completely* likes you."

Completely...

I fingered the wooden grains on the island, looking at Ramses. He faced away now, but his laughter radiated decibels above the others. It never failed to not make me smile.

Completely.

"He certainly seems invested," I said, nodding. "Intense."

Ramses was so intense, *serious* about this because he was. I could feel him falling, all in more and more every day.

"That's Arizona," she stated, and when I faced her, she grinned. She shrugged. "We met in Arizona. Just something we call each other. He calls me 'Zona. Short for that."

I nodded, their friendship so deep. I got it now with the story he'd told me.

December leaned in. "And I'm so sorry for how we met, Brielle. I can't help but think what you might think of me. I mean, I looked like a cheating ass ho."

I couldn't help it, laughing at that. December, as I quickly found out, didn't hide how crass she could be. She was fun in that way, fit right in with the rest of them.

Her smile was apologetic. "Sorry."

"Don't be." And she shouldn't. People should never apologize for being who they are, and that was her. She should never lose that, a tragedy to lose it. I lifted a shoulder. "And it's fine. Ramses explained everything."

"Oh, I'm sure he did." She chuckled. "But you need to hear it from me. I'm sorry. Sorry, if lines ever looked blurred and I apologized to him, too."

I frowned, and she opened her hands.

"One thing you'll quickly find out about Ramses is that he loves to please," she said. "Because he's good. Such a good person, and it's easy to forget that. Easy to run away with that. He's got a good heart. A good soul." She swung a glance his way. "And in the wrong hands, a person could take advantage. I've seen that. Hell, I've done it, too. That's why I apologized to him. I have overstepped my boundaries when it's come to him, more than once."

My lips wet, definitely hearing her, and I saw what she said too. Ramses did like to please, to the point where I'd seen life make him unhappy. That was something he'd told me firsthand he'd been trying to correct.

"Can I ask you something, Bri?"

I looked at December, and for the first time, she wasn't smiling. She'd gotten intense, too, serious.

"Are you invested?" she asked, then lifted her hand. "What I mean to say is, are you completely about him, too? I wouldn't be a good friend unless I asked." She swung a glance his way again. "I just worry about him. He's had some crap in his life. Some crappy people. At least, recently."

Recently?

She wet her lips. "He deserves all in. And like I said, he really likes you."

I really liked him too.

That was what scared me.

"I like him too," I almost whispered the words, haunted by them. "So much."

The words instantly brought a smile on December's face, but it couldn't completely form on mine. How much I cared about Ramses wasn't the problem. That'd never been the problem. My heart had been invested before I'd even really known it. It'd been my brain and everything else that'd been the problem.

December hugged her arms. "I'm happy for you two," she said. "Arizona deserves happy."

He did, so much.

I just worried if he'd ever be able to find that happiness with me.

CHAPTER
TWENTY-FOUR

Ramses

I watched my dick disappear in and out of Brielle's mouth, my girlfriend on her knees in my shower.

And what a fucking vision.

She'd asked to do this, God love her. I never made women give me head. Though, I loved it as much as tasting pussy. I never wanted to overwhelm them and had a time or two. They'd get all embarrassed about not being able to fit me all in, which made me feel like fucking shit because I used to ask. That was a big part of the reason I'd taken up eating pussy, no pressure there, and I'd gotten fucking great at it.

Little did I know how addicted it'd get me, and I'd forgotten about that sexual pleasure when it came to me. Well, I hadn't forgotten. I was a fucking dude, but yeah, I'd learned to live without.

Brielle was making me a very greedy man, her head bobbing, her mouth filled with cock. The sight was enough to make me bust a nut right there, but I resisted.

Her tits soaked to the nipples under the shower, dark

peaks angling down, flesh heavy. Her hair a dark veil behind her, she stared up at me with curled lashes framing her eyes, and I grunted, physically rejecting the urge to come. It struck a burn into my legs, which had them shaking, muscles locked and tense.

But then her throat opened up.

I hit the back with ease, her lips touching the base of my cock. The fact she could even do that blew my fucking mind, and it hadn't been the first time. Brielle took whatever I gave her, accepted whatever I had for her, and as she fisted my balls, I drilled into her in return. She didn't like me holding back.

So, I didn't.

I growled as I jutted my hips, making her gag at every thrust. I tugged her head back, making her look at me while I fucked her mouth, and that only made her moan.

She blinked beneath the shower's current, running her hands down my thighs until she found and squeezed my ass. She still liked ass, in and out over me. It was enough to make me spill down her throat.

But as stated, she'd created a very greedy man.

I needed inside her, and I eased her off me until she stood. Flushed, ready, she panted with her wet hair coiled tight in my fist.

I forced her mouth on me, fused and tasted her lips under warm jets. The multiple shower heads had her drenched, both of us.

"Ramses..." Her taste and mine exploded in my mouth, my arm hooking around her as I fisted her breast. Growling, I arched her body before dropping my mouth to her tits.

A sigh as her nails scraped the back of my head, scratching raw, aggressive in her agony as I tongued my way between her breasts.

I showed no mercy, her tight little body quivering in my

arms. I hungered for her, ached for her. A roar and my hips thrust for her to let me in.

"Condom," she cried, and I got one, ready for that. We kept a fucking box in the shower, and we already had it down to half in less than a week.

"Let me in," I gritted, the condom ripped open with my teeth. I rolled it on and encircled her thighs.

Golden and honeyed flesh spilled between the spaces of my fingers as I parted her legs to hit the walls.

I gave no follow-up.

No warning before I angled in and drove my hips forward. Her ass slammed to hit wet granite, her eyes wide and body trembling in pleasure. I used to think I'd rip her apart, and the first few times, I had noticed moisture in her eyes. It was a lot, *painful*, but now, second nature.

For us both.

I lost myself in that heaven, the ease and warmth of the abyss. It'd been scary in the beginning. How easy it was to get lost in her.

How easy it was to succumb to her.

Somewhere along the way our fucking wasn't just fucking anymore. It wasn't sex. It was passion and filled with so much intense shit I think it'd surprised us both.

I'd even caught her crying once, the last time. There'd been actual tears in her eyes, but not because I was hurting her. I just had a feeling.

Like these same tears now.

Her eyes shined as she looked at me, her chin tilted up, her skin moist and flushed with red. I saw her crying through heated jets, and I framed her face to keep her here, keep her with me. She gazed away the last time.

She wouldn't now.

I picked up, making her feel it. This thing we had… it was fucking awesome, and she should feel it. *Feel what I felt* every time I was with her, how deep it was. Some days, I thought it'd bring me down to my damn knees.

"Look at me," I coached, and she did. I caught a tear. "Stay with me."

My hips slapped her inner thighs, so deep inside her. I almost couldn't keep focused on her, the urge to get lost in the influx of this definitely there.

But if I wasn't leaving, she wouldn't either, her hands cuffing my wrists. She used her thighs to stay here with me, rock with me.

I kissed her, bleeding into her like an open wound. I didn't know where she ended or I began, the torrential impulse to come physically ripping me apart.

I roared as I picked up, my balls tightening, my thighs and body charged like a fucking freight train. I exploded into her without warning, railed tight inside her, and nails bit into my wrists so hard she easily drew blood.

That was when I caught her arms, knotted and locking around my neck. Whimpers soft and muted panted in my ear, and I cupped the back of her head.

"Baby…" I peppered kisses into her neck, soothing her. I angled my mouth into hers, allowing the shower to go luke-warm on us.

Something told me that didn't matter. Something told me she didn't care and that she needed this, to come down from the high with me.

She really was crying.

Like actual tears when I guided her to look at me. I ghosted a knuckle down the trail. "Hey."

I slid those tears away from red eyes, all this some really emotional shit. She'd cried before, but she'd tried to hide it from me the first time. I never actually made her look at me, okay with that.

Now, I kissed the trail, making her stay with me. The tears let me see she was breaking down her walls, and I loved that.

I loved.

My smile was faint as I held her face back. The tears away now. I turned off the shower, then tugged our towels in. The first I wrapped round her, the second to her eyes.

I dabbed under one and two before she took the towel away, doing the job herself.

"Thanks," she said, then moved that towel to dry her hair. The third towel I had I cinched around my waist, then followed her out.

I looped arms around her, her skin heated and perfect. She dried her hair in the mirror with a smile but didn't stay with me long before she maneuvered out of my arms.

"Everything all right?" I asked, the second time in one evening. She'd seemed a little down before we'd gotten into the shower. I figured that may have been just because she'd been out of her element tonight with December and the others. I believed the night had gone well, though. She'd even been talking to Greer and December at one point.

"Fine." Shifting on her bare feet, she pecked a kiss to my lips. "Just tired. Bed?"

Bed.

I nodded, following behind her. Normally, I'd pinch at her, tease her but her body language felt off.

Maybe she is just tired.

We got under my sheets after we both toweled off and got dressed. My bedroom was a loft style on my duplex's second level. I preferred my bed in Maywood Heights, but the duplex on campus made do.

It helped having my girl in my bed with me, and no sooner had the lights flicked off than I pulled my arms around her, easing her perfect ass back into me.

I settled my cock between the curve from behind, completely ready to take her from the back. This was the song and dance with us. Shower. Sex, then more sex and some-times even before the shower. It really just depended how we're both feeling that day, but ten times to one, that was our routine.

"Not tonight, Ramses."

Not tonight, Ramses.

I suppose there was that one.

I turned her over in the dark, her cheek beneath my fingers. My eyes adjusted enough to see her frown.

"I'm just tired," she said, answering a question before I even asked. She was good. She sparred with me before I could even press her. Before I could possibly ask her a question she didn't want to answer. I really was starting to get to know this girl.

At this point, something felt real damn off, besides the obvious. Of course, she didn't have to have sex with me. I wasn't a prick.

Her cheek left before more words could be exchanged, and when she took my hand, wrapping it around my front she eased back into me. She nestled herself away from me in the dark.

Like I said, she was real good.

CHAPTER
TWENTY-FIVE

Ramses

I didn't know what time I woke up that night. I just knew I was alone.

My bed empty.

I angled up to find my phone and maybe the time, but I found Bri before I could. She sat at the edge of the bed, back hunched and head lowered.

"Bri?" I eased over until I sat beside her. She had her arms cuffed, and I reached behind her for the lamp light. My loft illuminated, and I braced her hip. "What's up?"

She wet her lips, her fingers embedded into her flesh.

It sent my back up like nothing else.

"Do you want children?" she asked, seemly haunted as she stared down. She swallowed. "*Will you* want kids?"

The ache in her voice immediately made my heart race.

As well as the need for the question.

"Why are you asking me this?" I squeezed her shoulder, and she sat up.

Eyes red rimmed, nose flushed and sniffling. She brushed fingers beneath it. "That's not what I asked you."

I'd heard what she'd asked me. That shit radiated me down to my toes, but not because I didn't want kids.

Why is she asking me this?

My tongue drew across my lips before my answer, my hand folding over her arm. "Yes. Eventually, yes."

This was the wrong answer.

Her body locked, and she eased out of my hands, standing from the bed.

I followed her across the room with my gaze before joining. "Do you not want kids?"

If she didn't, that was okay. Having children wasn't some grandiose dream of mine. I figured it'd just be part of the plan *eventually*.

Mom would fucking kill me for even considering the possibility of something else, of course. She was a mother and always wanted her baby to have babies. Naturally.

Bri said nothing, and I hugged my arms around her. "What's going on? Kids aren't your thing?"

Her lips pinched tight. Like she was doing everything she could not to cry, and I made her look at me.

"I don't want kids." That first tear blinked down, and it was like someone took a dagger to my insides. Her crying in the shower had been different.

Or had it been?

I framed her face. "Okay—"

"It's not okay, Ramses." She backed out of my hands. "That's not okay, so quit pacifying me. Quit being so goddamn good all the time."

My brow twitched, eyes wide.

She pressed palms to her face before folding her arms. "If you want kids, you should be able to have them. That's not in the cards for me, and I don't want you to get your hopes up about something that'll never be there. Not with me."

Not with her.

Not in the cards for me...

I wasn't an idiot. I could read between the lines.

Shit.

In an attempt to put her back to me, she braced my bed frame. But when I snagged hands around her waist, she drew back to me.

She hit my chest, so warm, soft. She had all these hard edges. Played them up to hell.

But she forgot how delicate she was, how fragile.

I breathed her in, folding her arms in until we were locked. Until she couldn't get out.

Until she couldn't run.

"I don't want to have kids with you, Ramses," she said, a tortured ache in her voice. It twisted my gut, what she'd said only making the sick sensation worse.

Even still, I didn't let her go. I wouldn't. I closed my eyes. "Why?"

Was I not enough? Was all this too much? Our relationship too unconventional for her? I really hadn't considered the age thing that big of a deal, but she always had and suddenly insecurities ran as rampant as my theories. I'd always considered myself a pretty secure guy.

But in her silence...

It radiated through the room.

Her sob accompanied it.

She physically broke down, tears gunning down her cheeks. It threw me for such a loop.

"What's going on? Why don't you want to have kids with me? Are we not..." My throat constricted. "Is this not working for you? Us?"

My worst fear, but that shouldn't have her like this. Crying.

Her body shaking, she gripped her arms. "I don't want to

have kids with anyone." She gasped, faced drenched. "I can't. I can't go through that again."

What?

"It hurts too much." She blinked tears down to my arms. "It destroyed me the first time."

Whoa.

The unease of before transformed into something different, and when she keeled forward, body racked with emotion, I turned her around.

I buried her into me, swaying with her.

"Talk to me." This wasn't a request, not this time.

It was a goddamn need.

She needed to talk to someone for once, to get things off her chest and not bottle this shit up. She needed to vent, and I wanted her to do that with me. I wanted her to trust me.

I wanted her to let me in.

Bending, I scooped her up, bringing her with me onto the bed. I sat with her in my lap for a long time, as long as we needed to work this shit out.

She sobbed into my chest so long it felt like it'd been hours, hell days.

"There was an accident," she whispered, face wet, cheeks red. "I told you my ex-husband was an athlete."

I didn't move, not a goddamn inch, and I wouldn't. Couldn't risk it.

Come on, Jersey girl.

I needed her to keep talking, didn't want to move so I didn't.

She winced. "He was pretty popular. Even being retired. Still had a following and fans. They even still followed him everywhere. Us everywhere."

Fire shook my limbs, no world in which I wanted to envision her with someone else, period. Let alone the man who'd struck her. She hadn't gone into details, but she had said he'd placed hands on her.

"There were always paparazzi," she continued. "Always noise. Always chaos. That was that life."

Haunted again, her voice completely hollow.

In her silence, I curled a hand over her shoulder. "What happened, Jersey girl?"

I felt the words before she said them, physically felt them in her quivering limbs. I drew her chin up, and she looked at me.

"It was an accident. I was driving, an accident." Her swallow hit her throat. "I was three months pregnant. They just wanted a picture…"

What. The. Fuck.

I shifted her, framing her face, and she blinked down more tears. I forced my breaths even. "They hurt you."

"Not on purpose." Her head dropped. "I saw them following me, and I tried to get away. I was by myself, and they were aggressive. They always were. They just wanted a photo."

Lungs in an ice bath, stomach in a vise.

Her shoulders quaked. "It was a head-on collision. I lost the baby."

I closed my eyes, folding back her hair.

"And it changed things, Ramses," she retched. "Changed my ex-husband. Changed me. He dealt in his own ways. Drinking. Gambling."

"Hurting you." I tipped her chin in my direction. "He hurt you. Hurt you because of this, didn't he?"

In the silence she forced me to wait for the answer, I could have shot my fist through a wall. It actually had me to the point where I was physically shaking.

She nodded without words, acknowledging my fear. I'd thought this guy was a coward before, but that hadn't been the word.

To physically put your hands on someone, a woman, after something so tragic had happened to her? There weren't any fucking words for that. None in the goddamn dictionary. The man belonged in a cell right next to my father, two assholes with too much power.

This guy had a faux power. Because what did it take to hit a woman? Someone, no doubt, a fraction of his size.

A grieving woman.

I braced Bri, rocking instead of doing something else.

"It was only the one time," she said, like that meant something. "He turned into someone completely different. His grief made him a monster, a shell of himself."

I folded a hand on her cheek. "Don't justify anything he did. He doesn't deserve it."

And she didn't either. What about her own grief?

I saw it right here in my arms: someone so guarded, hurting all the time.

I mean, a wedding had made her sad.

Happiness had made her upset that night of December and Royal's union, in misery, and that was when I'd found her.

We had found each other in misery. Different reasons backed it, but we'd been in a similar place. I held heartbreak and the piss-poor decisions that resulted. She had a failed marriage, but the results the same. Different experiences, different events had broken us, and I now knew why she'd been in group therapy.

I now knew why she'd found me too.

It was like the universe knew we'd needed to be together that night, our worlds of chaos united.

My attention shifted when Brielle sat up, easing off my lap. She took a seat beside me, and I hated the distance.

"I left him because of it." She faced me then, frowning. "But you need to know what you're dealing with. You need to know I have no desire to have children. Something like that, what happened *changes* people, and I'm not going through that again."

I understood, nodding. "I get it." I did, but she might not always feel that way. I shook my head. "But with time, you never know how you may feel in the future or even years down the line."

Whatever she wanted to do, I'd wait. If that was where we were headed… of course, I would.

It blew my mind I was even having this conversation. Especially after the last year I'd had. Back at Brown, I'd unloaded a lot of crap into my life. Enough to make me leave. Enough to make me come here, but now, meeting her, it felt like a Godsend.

Like it'd all been worth it.

To go through that so I could come here, run into her and this *thing* we had. A relationship and one I could put my hands on and feel the realness of it.

And not the deceit beneath.

I hoped she felt that too, and I knew she did. I'd seen it in the shower. I'd seen it every day and every time we were together. She had feelings for me as real and tangible as I felt. She had love for me.

Like I had for her.

Her smile held no joy, no happiness. In fact, it shifted into nothing but sadness when she placed it in my direction.

"Because I have so long to try." She laughed, but again, no humor. She faced me. "I'm thirty-five years old, Ramses, and even if I did change my mind—which I won't—I don't have the time. I don't have those years."

"There are other ways to have children, Brielle," I said, this topic delicate, sensitive. I nodded. "Adoption. Surrogacy—"

"I said I won't change my mind!"

My head lifted, my mouth closing. I saw what she was doing here completely.

And I think she saw it too.

She was running without actually running from me, but the difference was, I knew how she operated now.

I knew her.

She pushed, and I pushed back. I'd always push back.

Since this was delicate, I decided to choose my words carefully. There were a lot of emotions in this conversation, and only some of them had to do with us, me and our relationship. This woman had a history, traumas that had nothing to do with me. But still, there was one thing she needed to know *about* me.

I placed my hands together. "I'm never going to be the reason you walk away," I said, surprising her. I shook my head. "I will never give you that, nor be your permission to step back. Make no mistake about that, Brielle."

And I wouldn't, I'd stand by her on this. The ball would always be in her court. At least, when it came to this.

She closed her eyes. "What if that's not what I want?"

My throat tightened. "I'd say you need to tell me, but when it comes to this?" My shoulders lift. "You don't get a choice. I'm here in this, and I won't be your reason."

I refused.

I wouldn't give her the easy way out, and this *wouldn't be* easy. It would be hard and something we'd both have to work at every day. She had her issues and I had mine, and we were in different places in our lives.

Call me a masochist, but that was what made this shit exciting, made it *real* and worth fighting for. We knew this worked because we fought for that shit. We didn't give up, problems be damned.

I guided her chin to look at me, but she only ended up pressing her head to my chest. Her arms ensnared my waist, and I held her, warmed her. I kissed her head. "I wish you'd just give up on this."

"What?"

My chin touched the top of her head. "Trying to run me off. Scare me away."

I didn't bend easy, and I made no exception when it came to her. If she wanted to end this, she'd have to do it herself.

Even if that possibility rattled me to hell.

CHAPTER
TWENTY-SIX

Ramses

A dumbbell clanked to the floor beside me, and at the sight of a familiar face, I shook my head. I curled my weight. "You know, you don't have to pretend you just happened to be here when I am." I smirked. "For December?"

Royal Prinze had a home gym. I knew because he rented from me. I'd obviously been over there, seen it, but in the past few days, I'd been doing nothing but seeing his mug here at the campus rec center with me.

The guy sent a familiar scowl in my direction, taking the weight bench beside mine. He extended two weights out of considerable size, possibly just to one up me. Today was weight day, but I'd tired myself the hell out in my runs lately.

I'd really been able to push them since they hadn't been with Brielle.

Heavy shit the other night, and she'd been avoiding talking about it since. Of course, I still saw her, texted her. But I didn't see her as much, and I think we both knew it had nothing to do with finals coming up for her and me and both our busy work schedules. She was doing her running, but just in a different way, and I hadn't pushed again.

I mean, look what had happened in the past.

It was best I gave her space, so I did that. As much as it sucked. In the present, it left me with lonely runs and only seeing her actual face a couple nights this week. One of those had been virtually, but that'd been okay. I was a patient man, but with my freed-up time, I had been working out a lot.

Hence, this whole thing with Royal Prinze now.

"Don't kid yourself, Mallick," he grunted between repetitions. After a labored set, he dropped the dumbbells, smirking. "I happen to like this gym."

"Sure." Absolutely zero percent these little run-ins had nothing to do with the fact I'd broken down and finally asked my female friend for advice about my girlfriend.

I hadn't given December many details about my conversation with Bri the other night. That was private, but I had said we'd had a talk, an emotional one that had left me unequipped to handle. I'd wanted a female perspective, I suppose.

Prinze's *visits* started happening shortly after that. He never said anything to me, of course, a chin tip here and there, but no way *in hell* this guy's expensive-ass gym wasn't being used in exchange to rub elbows with his fellow Pembroke collegiate. If anything, he'd be working out with Knight Reed at his frat. I'd heard Reed and his fraternity brothers had a pretty nice setup.

Prinze shook his head before picking up his dumbbells and starting another set, and I allowed him to play his little game of checking up on me. One he played up when he followed me to the chin up bars before back to the weight press benches. The dude even offered to spot me. At this point, I believed I had a stalker, and after he did his set (which he legit asked me to help him with—what the fuck), I asked him *yet again* what his deal was. If he was sick and dying, his wife should probably know about that. Because that was the only reason I could come up with that he'd ever actually chose to share time with me without his wife around.

He tossed me a towel as we chugged water, the guy sitting next to me in his cut off tee. "I suppose I just wanted to have a discussion with you."

"What about?" And subtlety was not this guy's strong suit. It took him several gym sessions and some stalking just to come out with it. I smirked. "And don't ask me how to help you with December if you fucked something up. I'm the wrong guy to go to."

I was the fucking *fuck-up* of fucked-up situations, and hell, if I knew how to fix them. If I did, there'd be no tension between my girlfriend and me right now and I'd know how to fix things.

Royal tossed his towel over his shoulder. "I don't need your help with Em, but I would like you to tone down some of your peoples' more than aggressive business tactics as of late." He frowned. "I've been told many of our clients at Prinze Financial are having to take out second and third mortgages just to deal with the recent Mallick Enterprises rent hikes on their businesses." He shook his head. "I get it. This is business. You're obviously trying to buy these people out for the land, but it's poor form and not the precedent you wanna set this early in the game. Not when you just started and barely warmed your daddy's seat."

"Wait. Wait. Back up." I was still messing with my seat belt and he'd already shot off in the car. I braced a knee. "You're saying Mallick is raising rents?"

"I know they are, and they're making Prinze's small business owners bankrupt. It's technically none of my business and it does make my company money, but it's just not classy, man. Knight and his people aren't even doing that kind of shit."

I still had no idea what he was talking about, and when he saw that, his eyebrows narrowed. "You didn't know?"

"No." In fact, had I known, I would have had some talks with some people. That wasn't cool, not at all.

I got out my phone, calling my secretary. Obviously, a meeting had to be had. My name was on this shit, but I had many people handling different facets of the business. Not everything went through me. It couldn't. Impossible.

Leann picked up, and I made sure to have her get me a meeting with Duncan Salsbury. Odds were, he did know about this. Maybe even directed the plans, but with a word, he'd stop them if I requested. He'd have to since he answered to me.

Prinze was right. That wasn't how I wanted to do business. Especially after meeting with LJ. He definitely opened my eyes to some stuff, how business should see people. Everyone was better because of it, and sometimes, it wasn't just about the money.

Royal stayed next to me while I made the call for the meeting, and after finalizing it, I hung up. "Thanks for alerting me. Good looking out. You're right. That's not how I want to do things and wouldn't, had I known."

"No problem." He tugged his towel off his shoulder, balling it. "And can I offer you some advice? For the future? I'm starting to take on some stuff too with my family business. Knight, too, with his, and I think we're all kind of going through some of the same stuff. I'm noticing a trend."

I shifted in his direction. "What kind?"

He frowned. "People thinking we're going to run our fathers', grandfathers', and their fathers' businesses. People used to doing things a certain way and believing we're going to continue their work. Like we ever would. Like we ever *could*."

He growled on the end there, and shit, I'd never felt words

so deep. We both knew who our families were. More specifically, who our *fathers* were.

They were in prison for the same crime.

They had both done the same deeds, held the same sins. And I could imagine the sobering reality of our pasts was even worse for Royal. He had to stare in the face the woman our fathers had hurt so deeply every day. December was my best friend.

But she was also his wife.

Sometimes I forgot that, my burden heavy but his probably heavier. He no doubt had to work through a lot of shit to even be with December, a lot of guilt that, though it had nothing to do with him, I was sure he felt. I sure had.

Our fathers were our blood, and despite their sins being their own, we continued to hold the weight of them.

Royal placed his hands together. "I'm not fully involved with my father's businesses yet. I'm just getting my feet wet since I'm in school, but even in the things I've taken on, people were trying to handle me. Get me to be a yes man to my father's agendas." He shook his head. "I called to hell with that. I let them know real quick I wasn't my dad. I wouldn't uphold that agenda, and hell if my future child would absorb that legacy I had as an example growing up."

I had to pause him for a second, putting my hand out.

He smiled at me, nodding. "Yeah, I'm going to be a dad."

"Jesus, man." Completely floored, jaw dropped. "December's the mother, right?"

Obviously, she was the mother. Obviously, I was giving him a hard time, and for about a second, I thought he'd knock me to the floor. He raised his fist and everything.

"Yeah, she's the fucking mother, asswipe." He gifted me with a rare chuckle. "We just found out. You didn't notice she wasn't drinking the other night?"

I'd been all over the place that evening, and that'd been

before Bri and I had an argument. I'd been trying to make sure she was okay, comfortable and everything.

I felt like a true asshole now for not noticing other things. Then again, my best friend hadn't told me either. I started to state that, and like Royal knew, he raised his hands.

"I think I ruined the surprise," he said. "She wants to tell you herself. Ask you to be godfather and all that."

Holy shit.

"He will have a grand total of four. Knight, LJ, and Jax included in that number."

"Or she." I crossed my leg at the knee, and he shot that lovely scowl.

"*He* will have four, and he won't see the legacy of my father. My dad beat the shit out of me most of my life. Blamed me for things that had nothing to do with me. It took a long while for me to see that, and when he does eventually make his way out of prison, old and fucking decrepit, he'll get to see the product of a good business. A *fair* business that his goddamn son built after destroying the money-grubbing clusterfuck his was. It will be a glorious day, and I can't fucking wait."

I leaned forward, the deepest conversation I'd ever had with this guy. I faced him. "You deserve that."

"And you do too." He nodded. "Don't let these people take advantage of you. Stand up. Stand firm. I love business. I love making money, but I don't have to do it my father's way. You can be the same."

I thought about that, enjoying business too. I did, but definitely not as much as other things.

"What if you don't love business?" I asked, shrugging. "What if I enjoy it, have a love for it, but have other passions too?"

That was a great way to put it. I always saw myself as a businessman, but there were things I enjoyed more *by far*.

Really, this was the deepest conversation Royal and I ever had. This guy and I didn't talk. Not about anything deep.

He tilted his head. "Then you either do what you want, step down, and let your people run shit the way *they want*." He shrugged. "Deposit the checks and go fulfill those passions…"

"Or?"

He grinned. "Maybe figure out a way to fuse the two. You're in charge either way." He nodded. "And that's also a goddamn glorious thing."

I laughed. Yeah, it was. We had the final say. We were it. Our fathers made us that way through pain and suffering, but that didn't have to continue. It could definitely start with us, change.

I put my hand out, and Prinze studied it for just a moment before taking it.

"Make 'em fucking *cringe*, Prinze," I said, nodding. "Your father?"

He squeezed my hand, smirking. "You, too, Mallick. You *will*, too."

I would.

We all would.

CHAPTER
TWENTY-SEVEN

Ramses

The decision to go see my father wasn't a hard one. It had been before.

It just wasn't now.

It almost felt easier after the meeting I'd had with my executive board today. A long time coming and I held nothing but confidence upon being escorted through the white collar prison. Governors and countless politicians had frequented the harsh brick halls.

Absolutely fitting.

Several guards guided me through, one after the other, an attentive assembly line. I was asked if I needed anything constantly. Doted over as if royalty. Nothing but the best for the affluent son of a rich killer. Dad may not have known about the murder of December's sister until after the fact, but his help with the cover-up basically put him in the same category as my uncle.

At least, in my eyes.

The man who raised me had contributed to no white

collar crime, yet here he was in the nicest prison in the state. Money sure did get one the best.

His quarters were no exception.

Private and away from the fray, two armed guards outside let me through. The sole heir of a self-imposed god didn't speak to his criminal-ass father from behind plate glass. He got the full view, all-star treatment. They took me right in to see my father.

"Mallick. You got a visitor."

At an old oak desk, actually writing like he had business to attend to. My father in an orange jump suit, his beard cut and trimmed, office ready.

The sight twitched a scowl.

That he could be arrogant enough to live his days this way, like he had the right for any type of comfort or luxury. His head lifted from his desk, and he was surrounded by the same, countless books on his shelves, a chess set in the corner.

His bed even had a comforter.

I smirked at this point, the luxuries of what money and status could buy. Sad thing was, my father's name alone could get him these things. He hadn't built this prison, conflict of interest, but he'd made money off one or two in the state. He'd had his hands dipped in everything, businesses all around.

I'd make it my mission to take him down a peg, starting now, and getting up from his desk, he didn't seem at all surprised to see me.

He even smiled.

He was arrogant enough to when he set his pen down and his guards arranged our meeting space. Dad was given a chair, myself the same. We could sit with each other, talk with the other, but he couldn't come within ten feet of me. This was something I'd requested.

At the present, I held more power than this man, unbuttoning my jacket and taking a seat. I'd come here straight from the office.

"Son," he said, blinking as if awed. He raised his head from his chair. "You've finally come."

Though, not for him, and not for any type of closure or *healing.* I really didn't need it from him.

I wet my lips. "I recently had a meeting with the board. I'm going in a new direction with Mallick."

Straight to the point, I had the guards hand him what I'd brought, then watched with great satisfaction as he read everything over from his chair. I owed my father absolutely nothing, but I did owe this to myself. I made decisions, took actions.

And I wanted him to know.

Like my arrival, no surprise twitched his eyes. Surprising, but I waited until he got to the end. This did jump his brows at this point, and with the amount of his company's assets I'd sold off, it probably should. Mallick was still operational in the real estate and development game. I wasn't fucking crazy. That was our money maker, *our business*, but I was diversifying and making an empire I could actually stomach running. Nothing based on greed or opportunity. A plan that put both people and myself in mind. This was the kind of company I could run, and he'd given me that power the moment he'd landed in here. I was the number one.

And he the two.

"Who's Lance Johnson?" he asked, and I nodded.

"A business partner." I'd given LJ exactly what he wanted, sold him Mallick properties and even went in with him on a few, making him a partner. This kind of collaboration I completely stood for, one that put the people in mind, and with him heading it, I could be completely hands off and place my attention toward things that called even more to me.

"You're working with him," Dad continued on. Taking out

his spectacles from his jumpsuit, he placed them on his nose. His lips parted. "And made money off the deal."

Because money could be made while still keeping your soul, and I watched as he scanned the documents to see where those funds went. I had plans for those too.

"Art galleries." He swung his gaze over to me. "Several?"

I nodded, investments I made in a string of them. I planned to hit all the major cities, but started with Chicago, Miami, and New York. I was working on a team to assist and build this new empire, a branch of Mallick focusing on the artistic sphere. "I'm taking Mallick into a new era. I'm collaborating with a network of national and international artists as well. Our pieces will be shown. Sold at these galleries."

"Our?"

My head bobbed once in acknowledgment, my legs crossing. "I'm an artist. An artist and a businessman. I want to live in a world in which I'm involved with the two, so I created one."

"It seems you have." Flipping the folder closed, Dad passed it off to the guard nearest him. They returned the documents to me. Dad sat back. "It seems you've done what you wanted."

"I have."

"And you're here because?"

"I wanted you to know." Point blank. I didn't owe him anything, but this wasn't about him. I wouldn't tiptoe around and follow my passions. I'd preach them from the rafters. He'd know who I was. He'd know how I ended up, how I fared and thrived despite him and his influence. I'd become my own man, and I'd done it without him.

I was done here, nothing else I needed to say. I handed the documents off to the guard. Dad could keep them, the copies a memento of my short time here.

Buttoning my jacket, I stood. "See you in a few years."

Because I would eventually. He hadn't murdered anyone

so his sentence was lighter, and he would be out of here eventually. I'd be ready when he did, and when he surfaced, it would be in his best interest to stay away.

The threat of that on my lips, my eyes narrowed. "Though, it'd behoove you to maybe reconsider that, seeing me?" I nodded. "Same goes for Mom. I know she's been coming to see you." I shook my head. "How about you not do that anymore."

Nothing more to say about that, I turned my back to him. I started to walk away before I heard him call my name.

"I'm proud of you, son," followed, and I closed my eyes. His sigh was deep. "I'm real proud of you. Proud that you're doing what you want to do. Proud that you're standing up to me. *Talking to me.* That was all I ever wanted for you."

I turned, angling a look. "And what would ever make you feel like I'd care about that?" I didn't. There'd been a time where I might have, but not now.

There had been a time, way back when anything this man touched I thought turned to gold. Where I simply wanted to breath his air, be him, despite who he was and what he'd done to me. He'd raised me with a firm hand, sent me to goddamn boarding school at one point for defiance, but even through all that, I'd wanted his acceptance. Like I needed it.

It had taken me all these years and countless mistakes to realize I didn't. I stood before him now a new person.

"I'm proud of that, too," he said, and the nerve of him to actually allow his throat to jump. To feel something about this moment, about me. He drew fingers down his beard. "I've made a lot of mistakes."

Oh, we weren't even going to go there. I tilted my head. "Don't you dare. A mistake is messing up your taxes. Not what you did and whose lives you've ruined."

He nodded. "I know. And back then, I blamed it on the protection of my family. Helping your uncle. Protecting you and your mom."

I laughed with no humor. "But now?"

He took a step forward, and the guards shifted, reaching for their batons. I lifted a hand, and they stopped. They answered to me here, not him.

My father saw that, his head shifting in their direction. He found me once again, the smile from before returning to his lips.

"It was selfishness," he said. "My image. I wanted to protect the image of my family. Protect me. It had nothing to do with anything else."

Shocked he was actually saying this, though I didn't let him see that. I wouldn't give him the satisfaction.

Dad took another step forward, and the guards watched me. I did nothing. He'd be bold to do something and he wouldn't here. Dad had no power in this situation with me.

"I held that knuckle-white, my image. My status." He shrugged. "Only to lose it. Only to give it to you."

"Funny what happens when you fuck up," I said. "And if we're done…"

"Almost." The guards allowed him to go back to his desk, and when he returned, he had a binder. He gave it to the guards, who gave it to me. "I've tracked all your accomplishments. All your wins over the years during my time here." He pocketed his hands. "I really am proud of you, and I just wanted you to know it's what's keeping me moving forward. To know that you're okay out there. You're very inspiring, son."

I scanned the pages, news articles mostly and internet pages. Awards I'd won, articles published at Brown. He even had a picture of me from the local paper back home, a ribbon cutting that I'd done recently.

They'd given my father resources all right to keep tabs on me, and once done, I gave the binder back to the guard.

"I'm glad to know you've been okay. That's why I wanted you to come here and why I asked your mom to ask you. I wanted you to know I'll always see you. I didn't before, and I consider that one of my greatest mistakes," he said. "I wronged you, son. Severely, and I know that now."

"So, what now?"

"Nothing now." He shook his head. "I'm in here. As I should be, but like you said, I won't always be." His head lowered. "I simply hope, one day, you'll give me the opportunity to see you again. And if not physically, *in person* in whatever way you can. I'd love to see where life takes you the rest of the way. Where you and, one day, your own family takes you."

My throat thickened, but he wouldn't see that either. I didn't care about what he hoped for, and this man wouldn't see my family. Not if I had something to do with it.

But I would have a family. It would take me some place, and that was what affected me. I could see that future as strongly as I felt it. I would have it.

I swallowed as I looked at him. "You probably won't get what you want."

His chin lifted, his expression as if my words didn't affect him. "That's the thing about hope, Ramses. Even if you don't get what you want, it pushes you on." He smiled. "It allows you to continue on with life. Live a good life even. I may be in here, but I'll never lose hope. I'll never stop trying."

He retreated back to his desk, picking up his pen as if he'd said nothing. He was always one to get the last word.

I gestured toward the guard, and they led me out, a place I never planned to see again. I'd finished my business here.

It was time I started living a life beyond hope.

CHAPTER
TWENTY-EIGHT

Bri

My thumb caressed the ruby red petals, bright and vibrant with life. Two dozen roses and not in a vase but bundled in thick paper and secured with a bow. I signed off for them, then plucked the card from between the stems.

Sorry.

I closed my eyes, my chest visibly concaving if it could. He had no reason to be sorry for anything. I'd been the distant one.

I hugged the pretty paper to my chest, burying my face in the smell. It took me about five seconds to remember I wasn't alone.

"Someone is either dating someone or has a secret admirer." Evie pressed the Diet Coke to her lips, her smile wide. "And must think quite the world of you for such a lovely gift. They're gorgeous, darling."

My heart hurt again as I eyed the roses, smelling them once more. Evie and I'd been surprised to have our lunch date interrupted by a flower delivery girl. She'd brought the roses.

They were gorgeous, *stunning* and completely unnecessary.

Oh, Ramses...

I hadn't done right by him lately. But then again, I definitely had a track record when it came to him.

I placed the roses on my desk, my sigh heavy. I rejoined my friend in the chairs reserved for my students. We ate lunch in here once or twice a week. Basically, whenever we could fit them in between our hectic schedules.

Crossing my legs, I popped a piece of apple in my mouth. "They are lovely." I nodded. "And he does think the world of me." He shouldn't, but he did. I folded my arms. "It's new."

Of course, I still hadn't told her. But not necessarily because Ramses and I were still waiting for graduation. I wasn't sure if we were even heading anywhere anymore.

You'd made sure of that.

I sure had, avoiding and when we were together, tense. I'd been distant, and he'd been letting me. My MO and his. He was going to let me pull the breaks but wouldn't let me use him as an out. He shouldn't. If things were going to end, I needed to end this.

I just didn't want to.

A smile to Evie's lips as she fingered a bloom. "I should have known you were seeing someone." She sat back. "You've seemed happier lately, Brielle. Brighter."

I had for a time. When Ramses and I had been in the thick of it. In the air of it. It'd been amazing, and I'd managed to botch it up.

I squeezed my arms. "Evie..."

I so wanted to tell her, tell her everything because she deserved to know. But the conversation moved on so quick, her talking about finals and everything. Her talking about our plans for the summer and things she'd heard.

"I hear you're stepping back a bit to do research this summer." She grinned. "To get an article published? That's so great, Bri. What inspired you?"

That'd been Ramses, one hundred percent. In our recent distance, I got to truly get a good hard look at myself.

And I didn't like the person I'd become.

I didn't like that I shelled into myself, that I pushed people away. I wanted to love life again, to take chances like him. I'd never forget how he showed me his dream. That night we made love in his art gallery, he'd been completely vulnerable with me. He told me he was taking chances. Showed me that more than once. He showed that with me, even when I'd given him every reason not to do so. Ramses was letting himself live life.

He was letting himself love.

Feeling the magnitude of that, I studied the gift on my desk, and in my silence, Evie lifted her chin.

"I see," she said, then squeezed my arm. "I'm so happy for you. You deserve this. With all you've experienced…" She shook her head. "You deserve it all."

Words for the truth tugged at my lips again, but before I could voice them Evelyn got a call. She lifted her finger, saying one second and I waved her to take it.

Crossing her legs with a smile, she turned into her call, and to give her space, I fingered the roses again. My phone buzzed in my lap, too, but I got a text message.

Ramses: How long are you going to make me wait before mentioning my gift? I'm sweating bullets here *sweating emoji*

I couldn't help it. I grinned and put so much power into it.

Me: I got it, but it wasn't necessary.

He sent me a smile in response, and his next message pinged quickly.

Ramses: Where are you right now?

I eyed Evie, still on her call. Whoever it was on the line seriously made her smile and I did too.

Me: Actually, with your mom. In my office. Why?

Ramses: Can you make up an excuse to leave?

Me: I could. Why?

He merely shot a smile emoji my way, asking me to come outside to my car. I felt bad about ditching Evelyn, but it turned out she'd wanted to take her call privately anyway.

"New beginnings to us both," she said, winking at me. She covered her phone. "Enjoy your day and your roses."

She disappeared after that, and I wondered about her new beginnings. I hoped they were good. I hoped they were everything, and though I shouldn't have hoped for my own, I did. I found them outside, his ankles crossed and leaning against my ride looking hotter than sin.

Ramses dressed for a spring run, shorts loose and displaying his powerful thighs, arms tight and hugged across his chest. His tee gave no room to bunch, butter smooth over his pecs and thick arms. Seeing me, he pushed off the tire. He never met me at school before but directed a hand to me like he had every day.

He brought me to him, until our hips touched, and he framed my face. He kissed me like it meant nothing.

When it meant everything.

When it felt like my world would end if he stopped, that my body would die without the taste. Soft, yet deliberate contact parted my lips, his finger curling beneath my chin when it ended too soon.

His boyish grin fluttered my insides, his hand cupping my cheek. "I was taking a chance you'd let me do that."

My lips buzzing, I felt like I'd let him do it again. But, putting hands on my hips, he placed distance between us. He extended a reach, and off the top of my car, he had the most curious thing.

"Pizza?" I questioned. He flipped the lid and the same pie from the night we met stared back at me.

Oh my gosh.

He nodded. "Goes with the rest of my gift. That is, if you're game?"

Since I was, I allowed him to tug me from the car. He opened the back and inside was a set of folded clothing. Like brand new, a bow around a box of tennis shoes and what appeared to be a pair of shorts, a tank top, and sports bra.

I'd question how he'd gotten these items into my car, but he did have the code. I'd sent him to my car multiple times to get things out of it when he stayed over on occasion.

"I figured pizza, then a hike," he said, his grin stretching. "What do you say, Jersey girl? Escape with me for the day?"

His thumb brushed beneath my chin.

As if I could ever tell this guy no.

———

Ramses took us to a nature reserve for the day, picking an afternoon I just happened to have an early day. My afternoon classes wrapped up early on Wednesdays.

Of course, he knew that.

We ate his pizza on the way. Though already having had lunch with his mom, I allowed him to devour the majority of it. Not that he minded that.

It was crazy thinking back on that night. We first met in an evening that, at the time, felt like absolute chaos. But since then, he'd somehow come to balance me, and I'd been able to be that calm for him. We just worked together.

We just worked.

I changed in the car for the hike while he waited outside, stretching while I exchanged pumps for Nikes and my blouse and pantsuit for sports clothing. Everything fit perfectly, which told me Ramses either guessed or cheated by being observant about the sizes in my closet.

Something told me the latter.

That was just Ramses. That was *always* Ramses, and as I joined him deep in the hills of nature, the woods cool with the changes of spring, I didn't want to be anywhere else. This, with him and being outside together, was pure harmony.

It was my heaven.

Ramses planned a break on an outlook, planned because he brought a blanket and waters. He was prepared. The view was scenic as we took that rest. The tops of trees were in a wide abyss before us, and he started to say something to me up here.

I never got to hear it.

I initiated that first kiss, his lips pinching between mine, and I had to say, I wasn't sure how I'd been able to fight it so long.

Something told me those thoughts were shared.

Our clothes stripped like it was second nature, for this man to make love to me up here and always. For him to hold me, passion-filled, and kiss me like we'd never been at odds. Like I hadn't been in my head *again* or attempted to push him away. Like we were destiny.

And this was it fulfilled.

Ramses entered me with a groan, his arm hooked around the back of my neck. His hips dropped deep. His taste was in the air, heat, sweat. He'd soaked through his shirt halfway through the hike, completely naked now as his hips rocked and he pulled my lips apart. Solid and beautiful male fucked me deep, my thighs hugging him close, my ankles knotted behind his muscular ass.

I rolled to mount him, naked, too, above abs stretched taut and tight, skin richly toasted with a honey tan. I worked my hips, and his head drilled back.

"Fuck," he gritted as he tugged my hips down to meet his

thrusts, my breasts bouncing, heavy and aching. He pinched a nipple, and I ground into the ecstasy, riding his cock in rapid rhythm. Believe it or not, I got on top to unravel him. But once again, he always turned the tides. He almost always had the upper hand when it came to us.

And somehow that was okay.

Somehow it was all right to give in, to give myself over to this and just be with him. Beyond the pressures. Beyond the thoughts and the labels in my head and strip everything down. To just be this man's girlfriend.

To just be his.

He came before I did, and my walls opened up, vibrating not far behind. I squeezed him inside me so tight I thought I'd die, and he kissed my breasts, sucking my nipples into his mouth while I came down from the high.

I held his head there, letting him caress me, care for me. I didn't want it to end.

I'd never been a crier during sex. Not that I didn't love sex. It'd just never made me emotional. But more than one time, he'd managed to make me do it. Today wasn't that day, but I'd be lying to say I wasn't compelled.

I'd be lying if I said I wasn't completely in love with him.

"I love you." Ramses breathed the words behind me, kissing my back, tasting my skin. He had his arms woven around me, his powerful body spooning me. His brow touched my head. "So much."

Trembles shook my very limbs, and reaching back, I ran my fingers over his short hair. I nudged him to kiss me, turning in his arms.

"I love you," he said again, to my face this time when he pulled my lips apart. "Fuck, how much I love you."

I loved him, sighing. "I love you too."

We stopped kissing for him to look at me, his fingers winding into my hair. He'd pulled it down, the pair of us so sweaty and messy. We both smelled like sex, all damp and heated skins.

His mouth dropped to mine. "You love me?"

Almost awe to his voice, but something told me it wasn't because he didn't know. I mean, he must have.

I folded a hand behind his neck. "I love you."

He needed to hear it. He needed me to admit it. His nose brushed against mine before he captured my lips in slow, rhythmic kisses. He grinned. "Of course, you do."

I laughed, the arrogant ass.

My arrogant ass.

He brought me beneath him, pressing his body on top of mine. I lost count how many more times we made love before he simply held me, the pair of us just lying in this moment. He drew lazy circles against the back of my neck, his soft breath in my ear.

"You know, I didn't bring you up here to fuck you." He touched his forehead to my hair, our fingers lacing. "But maybe I should play the lottery since I apparently have a lucky streak."

He'd normally get punched for less, but since he had my hands, I only got to hear his laugh. I smiled, and he hugged me, kissing my hair.

"I went to see my dad," he admitted. "But not for closure."

I turned around, looking at him. "What happened?"

As it turned out, a lot. He'd shifted the focus of his business, at least some of it. He'd decided to pursue the things he wanted while at the same time running his family's company in his own way.

"He said he was proud of me." He laughed, but it wasn't dry or sarcastic. Like he more so couldn't believe what had happened. He kissed my fingers before looping his arms around me. "That used to be all I ever wanted. He was really hard on me growing up. So, pleasing him used to mean so much. My entire world for so long."

"And now?"

His chin touched my shoulder. "Now, I'm living for me. For the future."

He did something next that had me watching his hands, our hands when he took that thick ring he always wore off his finger. The one with the gorilla. I'd never asked about it, figuring it was just a ring.

But now, he took my hand, placing it in my palm.

"I have friends... brothers," he corrected, shaking his head. "They give these to their girls, and I get it now."

"What is it?"

"It's our power," he said, nodding. "What we believed for so long to be our power. It seems so long ago now."

He folded my hand around it, kissing my fist.

"I am living for today," he continued. "For the future and *every day* with you that follows."

I opened my hand, looking at the ring. Smiling, I fingered it before looping my arms around his neck.

"I don't want you to give me your power." I touched his lips. "I want to share it. Share each other's."

He hugged me too, little space between us. Cupping the back of my head, he drew his body on top of me again. We lived in the moment. Those futures. It was the first time I'd ever forgotten about my past, and he did that.

And I had a feeling he would as long as I needed him to.

CHAPTER
TWENTY-NINE

Bri

Ramses had tickets for the Russian ballet on their tour in Chicago. The tickets he'd gotten from a colleague, and the night out had been a celebration for us both. It was the day before finals week, commencement at the end of the month. We were going to tell Evie soon about us and tonight, we just wanted to be a couple. I wasn't thinking about consequences or if someone would see us. I didn't care anymore. I just wanted an evening out with my boyfriend, and since I happened to love watching ballet in New York, that was what we'd decided to do.

Ramses passed the car off to the valet, and after we both checked in our coats, I escaped for a little potty break before the show. I came out to find him standing in front of the grand staircase leading up to the theater, hands in the pockets of his tailored trousers. He wore a tuxedo tonight, a handsome black with the crisp bow tie to match. The hems hit the hard curves of his solid frame, my man never looking so dashing, debonair. He was James Bond with Ryan Reynolds's boyish charm, sweeping around on his patent leather shoes to find me.

He pressed a hand to his heart, feigning death as if he hadn't seen me before, as if he hadn't escorted me inside himself.

I'd admit I cleaned up nice, the dark gown a smooth silk over my body. I also tended to be a fan of slits, and this one cut high.

Ramses wasted no time beneath the paintings of angels and gods donning the vaulted ceiling, one hand to smooth over my thigh while the other darted into my hair. He pressed just a light kiss to my temple, but a purposeful one, his thumb teasing the highest point of my slit. "Have I ever told you how *fucking* sexy you look in black?"

The growl in his voice held promise, his lips brushing my cheek before finding my eyes. He took my hand, kissing that.

I shook my head at him. "Only about twenty times since you picked me up."

And that was a guess, his smile a warm one as he laced our fingers. He leaned in. "Then it looks like I've got some making up to do. Not nearly enough."

He placed another kiss to my hand before extending his arm and hiking up my dress, I took it.

Ramses's tickets turned out to be for his family's box.

Because apparently, he had one of those.

His client's tickets hadn't been nearly as luxurious, but once I expressed interest in coming out, Ramses had decided to give them to his secretary for her birthday gift, I guess.

I suppose she was probably in the vicinity somewhere, and Ramses and I took two out of the six seats available to us exclusively. Once again, he wasted no time in placing his arm around me, and with the box's curtains drawn, he placed a hand on my thigh. We settled into the first act, and I had to say, I wasn't really watching all that much.

I played with Ramses's fingers mostly, the ones hanging

off my shoulder. The other time I spent looking at him, and he winked whenever he caught me. This was the first time we'd really been out together, no pressures or worrying about anyone catching us. Not that I really worried about that too much anymore. Times of the past just seemed so far away, and I leaned into him, just enjoying the show. It was lovely, of course, hypnotic. By the time the intermission came, I'd nearly drifted off between the calming nature of the show and Ramses's heat. Ramses shifted, and I sat right up.

He was checking his phone now that he could and excused himself to take a call since we had a few minutes. I guess he missed something important at work.

"Be right back," he said, kissing me before taking the call out of the box, and I decided to check my phone during the wait.

"Brielle?"

I angled a look back, and my eyes twitched wide, completely sitting up when Evelyn came in with a man I didn't know. He wore a tux, like Ramses, older, and Evie herself wore a lovely gown of a dark purple, shimmering crystals on it. She looked completely surprised to me, handbag clasped beneath her gloved fingers, and I had to have looked like a deer in headlights. She frowned. "Dear… What are you—"

"Mom?"

Stopped where he stood. Ramses exchanged a glance between his mom and whoever she'd arrived with before looking at me. His brow arched. "What are you doing here?"

I had no fucking idea what to even say at this point.

Oh, fuck.

Heart like someone reached in and squeezed it just to play around. Evie directed her eyes in her son's direction.

"Why I've come to see the show, of course," she said, her look curious. "In our family box. Though, we were late and missed the first half. Sweetheart, you know James from the country club."

This James extended a hand, which Ramses quickly took.

"Right. Yeah," Ramses returned, his expression also curious before twitching back to his mom.

His mom, who now had her attention directed at me. I stood, and her finger flicked my way.

"Have you two come together?" she asked, placing that out there. Ramses, in a quick step, crossed the distance over to me. I started to say something until he took the initiative.

"Actually, yes." He hovered a hand behind me, but I noticed not too terribly close. In actuality, he let it fall rather quickly before forcing a hand over the dark fade of his shaven head. "I had tickets. A date that fell through." He clasped his hands. "Anyway, I ran into Bri on campus. Mentioned them. She said she enjoyed the ballet so here we are. Tickets not wasted."

Here we were indeed.

He'd lied for me, completely, and I hated it as much as I failed to correct him.

Because in that next moment, I watched his mother and my friend's expression shift warm. No confusion, her smile quaint and full. This new scenario obviously made sense to her, and I was a coward. I was afraid for an alternative.

Whatever that may have been.

Evie's previous thoughts had obviously been her own, but this situation now appeared to be perfectly acceptable to her. She placed her hands together. "Oh, how nice, Ramses."

How nice. The dagger dug deeper. Like he was doing me a favor.

Just tell her.

The words itched, but cowardice was something else. It kept me locked in a box, tortured in the fear. I didn't want things to change, to lose this new awesome life I had. I wanted her in it, and I wanted Ramses too.

Like stated, selfish.

Ramses wet his lips in front of me, smiling without words. He partook in some back and forth with his mom and James before Evie hugged me, and we all took our seats. Ramses and I did sit next to each other, but with his mom and James in the seats beside us, we kept our distance reasonable and our touches nonexistent. We were two acquaintances again.

Like we'd always been a lie.

The second half to the ballet proved to be just as awkward as intermission. Ramses and I did keep to ourselves, and after, Evie talked to me while Ramses entertained James. It appeared James was Evie's date for the evening and the man she'd been talking to the day she'd left my office.

"I haven't told Ramses yet," she said, the men talking beneath the staircase after the show. Evie and I had left the theater in full banter, her talking and me just listening. My attention divided, I gauged it between chatting with her and trying not to look at Ramses.

Currently with James, he'd been doing the same thing, his hands in his pockets. He flicked a glance my way on occasion, and I hugged my arms, pretending not to notice. This was definitely not the precedent I wanted to set with his mom.

I mean, we were supposed to tell her soon.

Tonight's interception would just be the prelude to more lies. We were already going to have to lie, but now, we really *had* to lie.

I chewed my lip while Evie went on. She said she planned to tell Ramses about James soon, but it was new just like I hinted to her.

"I'm surprised you didn't just take Ramses's tickets and go with *your* new friend." She nudged me. "I'm sure Ramses would have sold them to you or even just given them to you, knowing him."

I was sure he would have, my nod firm. Eventually, we all made it outside and in front of the busy theater.

Evie had hooked my arm, and it was all I could do to fight her on after-show drinks. She and James planned to go to a place downtown, and she pushed both me *and* Ramses to join them.

"I would, Ma, but Brielle has to get back," he urged, kissing her cheek when she placed it out. "Long drive. You understand. And I have to be at the office first thing."

"You work too much, darling." She touched his cheek. "But I understand." She waved a hand at me. "Bri, I'll text you."

I nodded, giving her a hug before letting her go. In a stiff stance, Ramses offered to head with them to the valet. He said I could wait where I was so I wouldn't be in the rush of the traffic on the curb.

At this point, I just wanted to bury my face in my hands, and if I smoked, I would have done so then.

How had I fucked this up so bad?

Ramses appeared truly sick when he left me standing there, completely over all this, and I didn't blame him.

After all, he lied for me.

He'd always wanted to tell the truth, and I placed him in this predicament. Hugging my arms, I wandered outside the theater in thought. A cluster of photographers were around, snapping shots of the theater and the high class clientele. I'd heard a few celebrities had attended the show tonight.

I started to pass them when I was grabbed by one.

"Hey. That's Brielle Norrington!"

The flashes came first, bodies second as the majority of those photographers descended on me like locusts.

I was surrounded in a frenzy, people literally yelling at me in a fashion so familiar to my time in New York and Jersey, it churned my gut.

Flash.

"Brielle, what are you doing here?"

Another flash.

"Does Alec know? You're a long way from Jersey, New York?"

Flash. Flash. Flash.

"What do you have to say about the more recent speculations?"

I had no idea what that last pap meant, too busy framing my eyes and fighting the crowds. I elbowed for an out, trying to find Ramses. I started to call for him before a pap grabbed my arm, jerking me back so hard I about fell on my ass. Actually, if it hadn't been for all the paparazzi behind me, *I would* have fallen. They blocked the descent, and the pap whipped me around for a picture.

"Eh. Get your fucking hands off her!"

Ramses parted the crowd, a firm tower over a sea of heads. He got my arm too, but when that other pap tugged, he placed me behind him and shoved the guy. He bared teeth. "Back *off*."

The guy just wanted a picture. They always did, and where Alec and I had learned how to combat that over the years, Ramses hadn't. He engaged, and once he had, they did right back.

The pap's shove came from behind his camera, which Ramses grabbed and shot toward the ground. It exploded and the shutters around us followed, more flashes.

My heart sunk. "Ramses!"

The pap launched at him, roaring but Ramses grappled the guy's shoulders and slammed him into the pavement.

My breath stole.

Ramses loomed over the guy, wailing on him to keep him down. His fist knocked into him again and again, and my heart shot into my throat, the sweat cold and deadly on my brow. Shaking, I stumbled back which only landed me back into the sea of paparazzi.

"Is this your new boyfriend, Brielle?" They shoved. "The guy from the pictures?"

What... pictures?

I couldn't ask, too busy watching my boyfriend actually beat the crap out of a guy in front of me. The display froze me in my heels, a deep tremble in my legs. Thoughts from my past triggered, and I couldn't stop them.

Pain.

Alec's fists coming out of nowhere, the blind rage in his eyes as he turned into someone I'd never seen.

But that's not this. He's not him.

He wasn't, and I had to physically shake myself out of my head. The harsh severity of my past descended on me like storm clouds, and I grabbed my head, fighting the fear, and what my ex-husband had done. How he'd hurt me, hit me for something that wasn't my fault.

Wake up. Wake up. Wake up.

"Brielle."

I opened my eyes to find Ramses, Ramses easing me out of the fear, the pain. He lifted a hand toward me, but I could only see one thing.

His knuckles.

They'd split, an angry red. They bled from his work on the guy who was currently being dragged up by security. Security was pushing him away, all of them away. It seemed they'd seen what had happened and were controlling the situation.

A particularly large one in all back reached out to Ramses. "You okay, Mr. Mallick?"

I shouldn't be surprised they knew who he was, and thank god, he probably wouldn't see any repercussions from what he'd done. That should be what I was focusing on, that he was okay, and we were okay.

But all the blood.

His hand when he waved to the guy things were fine. He directed his attention toward me, speaking words I barely heard. I just kept seeing him hit that guy, over and over and...

"Brielle?"

I think he saw the fear in my eyes, how shaken I was. He called out for security assistance, and they kept the crowds back that had suddenly congregated on the sidewalk. It was a combination of more media and curious theater goers, all of which parted with the help of the theater's security staff. They gave us the room to get to our car, get out of there. Somehow my old life had found me again, and hugging my arms, I wasn't sure if I could get out of it this time.

I was still shaking after we got on the road.

CHAPTER
THIRTY

Bri

"What happened back there?" Ramses asked from the highway. He'd calmed down at this point. *I* had calmed down, but things were silent for a while. Quiet. His hand drew over his head. "Your ex is Alec Norrington? *NFL line-backer* Alec Norrington? That's what they were saying."

I was surprised he hadn't figured that out sooner. I mean, if he'd dug deep enough, he probably could have figured it out. Though, the internet knew me by my married name.

Even still, if he'd looked, he probably could have found out, and that was what had been so nice. At some point, it obviously hadn't mattered to him. My history. I swallowed. "I told you about the NDA."

The words had his jaw clenching.

"Yeah, I know." He swung a glance my way. "Are you okay?" he asked, but when he reached for me, I moved my hand away. It was just too soon.

He's not your ex. You know that.

He wasn't my ex but seeing him that way tonight certainly

hadn't felt good. I drew trembling fingers through my hair and Ramses noticed.

His eyes expanded. "You're shaking."

He reached for my hand again, and this time, I didn't withdraw. This time I let him, my hand physically spasming like I was coming down from something. My breathing escalated, and I dizzied, so much so that it took me a second to realize Ramses had pulled off the road.

He unstrapped, holding my hands. He advised me to place my head between my legs and I did.

"God, baby," he said, a worry in his voice I recognized. A fear I recognized, a fear for me.

I hated this, that we were going through this. But what's worse, I hated that it felt like I had to fight for this so hard, fight myself and everything around us just to make *us* happen. It seemed if it wasn't one thing it was another.

I closed my eyes. One thing I didn't hate was his hand on my back. His fingers pulling through my hair.

His rough touch on my skin.

The panic dulled with every stroke, the ache inflicted from a previous man dulling inside me. That pain, that trauma didn't come from this man who tended to me now. It never could.

I knew that so deep in my heart now it hurt. I felt the reality of that so hard. Ramses spent many moments bringing me back to him, and when I could breathe again, sitting up, he was here for me.

He brushed hair out of my face. "Tell me what you're feeling. All that scared you."

It had. I nodded.

"What can I do?"

I touched my forehead to his, breathing in everything about him. Shaking again, I placed my arms round him, and he buried his face into my neck.

"Tell me." He stroked my hair. "Please."

The ache in his voice I felt, like he was helpless and didn't know how to help me. It showed me even more about him.

Silent, my nose brushed his skin.

"Always make me feel safe," I whispered, my eyes closed tight. "I just need that. Always."

I heard my own ache, his, too, when he trembled around me.

"Did I scare you?" His voice thickened. "Back there?"

My answer had been a swallow in his ears, and he guided my face back.

He kissed my cheek before my mouth, holding me there.

"I promise I'll always do that for you. *Be that* for you," he said. Clasping my neck, he brought me into his. "I'm sorry. Sorry if I made you feel any different. I won't again, and I promise you that too. Never again, Brielle. You'll always feel safe with me. Always."

I believed him. I *loved* him.

My arms tight around his neck, I fell into the soft purr of his car. He would protect me always. I knew that, but we always seemed to have something happen outside of us. It was like the universe didn't want this to happen.

I held on tight as if to force it. I wanted to protect him too. *For him* to be and always feel safe. I didn't want to be the reason he'd ever have to fear losing that, but every day, day by day, that was what I felt. Like I'd be the one to break him. I didn't know how to stop it.

I didn't know if it could be.

CHAPTER
THIRTY-ONE

Bri

Evie entered my classroom on Monday as I was putting things away. She waved a hand from the door. "Can you come to my office after you're done?"

And then, she left. No time for me even to react. I hadn't seen or heard from her since yesterday, the ballet.

A slow dread formed. There had been paparazzi.

Even still, I refused to panic. She could just want to talk to me about something. I remained hopeful as I finished packing my bag but didn't drop it off in my office before heading straight to hers. I tapped a knock, and when she told me to enter, I did.

She wasn't alone.

Ramses sat in front of her desk, the back of his head angling back when I entered. Seeing me, his brow twitched up.

Evident surprise on his face, he either didn't know what this was about or simply hadn't anticipated seeing me.

Whatever the case, he sat while his mom stood off to the side. She waved me in. "Come. Sit."

Ramses's gaze followed me the whole way as I occupied the seat beside him. He started to say something until his mom took a seat behind her desk.

Completely unnerving.

Evelyn appeared nothing but the educator behind her desk, her features even schooled. I couldn't read her—at all.

And that scared the hell out of me.

My entire heart in my throat, I watched her open her hands.

"I'm just going to get right to it," she said, her first tell. An agitation in her throat, a wrinkle in her brow. Her lips pinched tight. "You two are together."

Not a question.

Not even an inkling of one.

Evelyn's hand touched her lips, and I didn't move.

I didn't dare.

Nor did I breathe. My friend swallowed before she wet her lips. "That's what TMZ is saying. You two are together. You two *are* together." She opened her hands. "As you both know there was a confrontation last night at the ballet. Considering your background with your celebrity husband Brielle, I'm not surprised about that. But what's alarming is the article was a follow-up to photos that surfaced apparently last week of you two."

I frowned.

Evelyn's jaw moved. "They had photos of you both at the store that were submitted by a student here on campus. A whole write-up on how she ran into you a while back, Brielle."

My mouth dried.

"She had a photo of you and her together," she paused, then placed a hand in front of Ramses and me. "And the pair of you holding hands at that same store."

I closed my eyes, not even able to get Ramses's reaction to the girl I'd obviously seen in the liquor department that day.

I didn't know she'd gotten pictures.

"Mom—"

"She submitted those photos to TMZ. And they must have come down here to follow up." Opening the laptop on her desk, she swung it around. "Because they caught the two of you again," she stated, her voice deadpan. "Kissing this time in the faculty parking lot."

My hand covered my mouth, that stolen kiss right before me, before us both. They snapped us right in the middle of it, my arm hooking around Ramses, and his hands on my hips. The evidence was there completely.

We were together.

This evidence caused Ramses's eyes to close, his hand folding over his face. "Mom."

"But I think what's worse," she paused, ignoring him again, "isn't that my son or even a colleague lied to me…"

Colleague.

I forced breath through my lungs. "Evie…"

She raised her hand, not finished. "Was that you," she directed a look at Ramses, "could actually let something like this happen again."

Again?

Ramses's jaw pierced his skin. He shot forward in his chair. "This situation isn't like—"

Her hands lifted once again, still not finished.

"You don't talk," she said before transferring her attention to me. She leveled me with a stare so hard I felt it from across the desk. Her teeth ran over her glossed lip. "I'm going to ask you a question, Brielle, and I need you to be perfectly honest with me. Your job depends on it."

My breath escaped.

Ramses growled. "Mother, you are *completely* out of line here."

"I said you don't talk!" Her face filled with color, beet red on normally fair skin. "You won't talk. Not until I hear from her."

From her...

Words like that and "colleague" didn't sit well, and if this conversation felt bad before, it really did now.

I faced Ramses, and at this point, he had his hands laced on his mom's desk. Fingers pressed to his lips. He knew something I didn't.

"Did you take advantage of my son, Brielle?"

I shot my gaze in her direction, completely serious with her question. My lips parted. "What?"

She nodded. "It was brought to my attention this morning by a fellow faculty member Ramses may have transferred out of your class. This faculty member saw your TMZ story and the potential circumstances in which you may have met my son worried him. He came to me. Ramses is currently a student in his class."

I folded a hand over my face.

Guy Donahue. It had to be him.

He was the only one who knew.

He was the only one I'd told, but before I could speak, Ramses angled in. His teeth bared. "Mom—"

"And my son confirmed with me just now you were his professor." Her manicured hand raised again. "I asked him that before you came in."

Ramses swung a glance in my direction, his hands opening. She'd obviously bombarded him with this, or he would have warned me.

I breathed into my hands, and in those moments, Evie leaned forward.

"So, I ask you again," she said. "Did you take advantage of my son?"

"That's *not* how we met," Ramses ground out. "And if you'd given me a second to speak when you asked me in here, I would have told you that." He shook his head. "Brielle and I met at December and Royal's wedding. She had no idea I was in her class. We both figured that out later."

"And lied to me about it." The breath eased from her lips. "Continued an affair as student and teacher."

"We didn't."

My voice arrived meeker than I wanted it to, and its presence had Ramses's hand moving in my direction.

He hesitated in the end, though. He didn't dare as he shouldn't. He nodded at me. "She's right. We didn't. Brielle cut everything off." He faced his mom. "We both did once we knew."

"Well, things obviously started up again."

"Yeah, once I wasn't her student." His eyes narrowed at Evie. "There isn't anything for you to look into here, Ma."

"Isn't there?" For the first time, emotion filled her words, no longer the educator and disciplinarian. This was a woman, a mom sitting in front of her son. Her jaw clenched at me. "Tell me, Brielle, did you know?" She leaned in. "Did you *care* if you did know? Or are you just another one of those women who takes advantage of a situation? Another professor taking advantage of her young students?"

The words popped the surface of an already heated and emotional conversation. I, personally, had been simply trying to keep up thus far.

But then she said this.

Ramses shot forward. "Mom, it is not like that, and you know it."

"He's gotten in trouble before with people like you," she claimed. "Older *women* like you who prey and like to take advantage of young men." She shook her head. "I know you've been through a lot of crap, Brielle. I feel for you. I *felt* for you. I got you this job." Her voice cracked at the end. "I trusted you."

I started to protest. I started to say something, anything,

but her words locked me in place. The accusatory nature of them, yes, but the fact that I was losing.

Losing her.

And losing him.

I stared at Ramses, at a loss for words beside me. He seemed to just be trying to keep up too, but I read between the lines here. She was accusing me of something that clearly had already happened before. Something that happened involving her son.

Oh, God.

Feeling sick to my stomach, I swallowed.

A soft plead touched Ramses's eyes, unsaid words parting his lips. I never gave them a chance to sound. Instead, I opted to face my friend. "Evie…"

"Please leave." She covered her face. "Please go. I can't…"

And I didn't make her. Because if what she said was true, I got it.

As much as I hated it.

Rather than deal with any of it either, I got up. I left, embarrassed and feeling like a complete idiot. I rushed from her chairs, out of her office, but Ramses hooked my arm before I even made it out of the building.

"Bri, it is not what she says," he urged right away. He wound me around to face him, a terror on his face I'd begun to connect with loss. The fear of losing something. Losing me. "What she said isn't what it sounds like."

"Am I fetish?"

"What?"

"Am I a *fetish*?" I backed out of his hands, his eyes twitching wide. "Is this a *thing* for you? Older women?" I had to ask the question.

I had to know.

Something told me this was the thing that happened to him at Brown. And though he hadn't lied to me about that. He hadn't told me about it either.

Would you have stayed if he had?

Probably not, enough odds stacked against us to not think I was also a fetish for him.

His brow launched up. "Of course not."

"Why of course not?"

"Because it's not true."

"How can I believe you?"

"Because it's me." His hands cage my face, his brown eyes scanning mine. "It's me. The man who is so fucking in love with you it fucking hurts. Who wouldn't hurt you. *I'd* hurt first."

My lips trembled, his firm hold guiding my gaze up to clash with his.

"What Mom said isn't true. Not the way she said it. She's just scared. She thinks what happened at Brown is happening again."

"What happened?" I asked, wanting so hard to give him the benefit of the doubt. Wanting to trust him.

"I'd hurt first."

I'd hurt first for him, too. Because I loved him, but I wasn't certain it'd be enough. The odds continued to be stacked against us and I was just so tired.

I wondered if he was tired, too. I mean, how much was just too much?

People started to pass us in the hall, and Ramses let go. But once the area was clear, he placed a hand on the wall and blocked both prying eyes and ears by putting his back to them. "For starters, she wasn't my professor. She was a mentor in my business program. An older mentor."

"How old?"

His eyes close before he faced me. "Why does that matter?"

It didn't. Probably not. I mean, what happened, happened.

His fingers drew down his mouth. "Forty. Forty-one?" He shook his head. "It doesn't matter."

It didn't, but I definitely couldn't stop my reaction to that.

I studied the wall and he adjusted, doing the same.

"We had no right getting involved," he said. "Especially because she was my mentor. I admit I rushed into it. Wanting it to happen..." He tapped the wall with his fist. "To feel something."

I braced my arms.

"I'd gotten tired of casually fucking," he stated. "I did a lot of that. Didn't want to get really involved after December and I didn't. I played the field and had fun, but I didn't want to do that anymore. I was about to graduate, and I guess I wanted something real."

"So why her? That woman?"

"I can't tell you." He frowned. "We had a connection. On the base level, but we had one. I shouldn't have gotten involved with my mentor, and there were signs it was a mistake besides the obvious. When I looked into those signs, I found out she was married."

My gaze jerked up.

His head bobbed twice. "Once I knew, I tried to end it. I did end it."

"What happened?"

His shoulders lift. "She didn't want it to end. Became obsessed and threatened to blackmail me if I did. She had influence over the department at Brown, over my grades and that's when I got my lawyers involved. My mom involved." He shook his head. "We were able to get it sorted, but not without a settlement. My mom was super adamant about keeping me out of any scandals. Got really crazy and protective. She paid the woman to let this thing go, stay away from me. Which she has. My lawyers advised transferring schools in addition due to the obvious."

I framed my face, visually cringing but not for myself or this situation we were in, but for him.

No wonder Evie hates me.

She thought this was happening again, an older woman taking advantage of her son and I didn't blame her. I'd probably hate me, too. I *would* hate me, too. I hadn't been pregnant for long, but in that short time I'd loved my unborn child as if they'd been with me every day. I'd want to destroy anyone who ever hurt them.

"Look at me, Bri."

I did. Though, he cupped my elbows anyway, directing me to look at him.

"This situation isn't like that." His palm cupped my head. "I know that, and you know that."

"But Evie doesn't."

"She will."

"And how could she?" I shrugged. "We've been lying to her. *I've* been lying to her. I have no credibility with her, and I shouldn't. Not after what happened to you. I'd feel the same way she does if it'd been the other way around."

His sigh fell heavy.

"I'm not saying it won't take time. Effort, but I'm imploring you to give my mother the benefit of the doubt. To not," his voice thickened, "to not default to your fallback. To not run. Not this time."

I cringed, unable to help it. I couldn't see how I looked from his eyes, but I knew how all this felt inside. I was being unraveled piece by piece.

He braced my head, his mouth to my ears. "I want you to fight for us. Fight through the grit and whatever comes next. Fight as hard as I will."

I touched my forehead to his chest, my fist balled when he worked his arms around me. I had no idea how long we stood there like that, and by the end, I felt drained. Like I'd physically died in his arms. I knew whatever I did next, we both did next, might affect our entire lives. For me, it would.

I couldn't see a life different from this moment now. My life had changed with him in it, and I wasn't sure if I could change back. That'd be like rewinding time. Impossible.

Impossible.

CHAPTER
THIRTY-TWO

Ramses

Weekly taco night occurred at my house this week. But that was because my mom bombarded me with it after I repeatedly ignored her phone calls and texts. One better, she showed up with the new man she was apparently dating.

"And then the guy says to me…" James chuckled, head actually thrown back like he couldn't contain himself before the rest of the joke even hit. He put his hands out. "Is that cheese on the table or an oil slick?"

Full blown laughter. Full *fucking* blown at the twenty-fifth dad joke I'd had to endure at my dining room table in under an hour. James was full of them, a man I knew from the country club. This wasn't a small city, but small enough for everyone in the city's elite to know each other. Yeah, I knew this guy. Average with above average funds. His family came from oil and migrated here.

Currently, I had to entertain the fact he took every opportunity he had to place his hand on my mother's, hers wrapped round his bicep as she simply *roared* at the dad-shit he said. I endured it behind a glass of Merlot, my attention only half there before James said my name.

"I think we've lost him, Evie." James chuckled once more, waving his hand. "I apologize. Once I get going, I run away with myself. I bore my own mother."

More vibrant laughter from my mother, my smile forced as hell, but I had a tendency to wear that shit on my sleeve…

When I was miserable.

The ache was still there. The distance felt. It'd been all I had to stay focused at work today.

Mom panned to me, noticing that. Her smile fell a little, but it returned upon her sudden attempt to engage me in conversation. She'd been trying to do that all night, the two of them having a completely coupled conversation. She'd been aware of my silence and once more, tried to fix the problem.

"Looks like the table could use more wine," I said, ducking out of the latest attempt. Pardon me, but I didn't feel up for it. I rose. "Be back."

I didn't come back. I stayed in the fucking kitchen with the chilled bottle in my hand. I was about two seconds from downing another glass right there when my mom did come in.

She looked fabulous as always, appearing only a fraction of her age in cigarette pants and a nice blouse. She'd put on makeup today. I assumed for *James*. Her arms folded. "Are you going to be miserable all night?"

"It depends." Pulling out a corkscrew, I got right into opening that bottle of wine. I popped the cork. "Is James going to tell dad jokes *all night*? Oh, and am I expected to call him Dad? You know, when you guys get married."

I was being a proper asshole. I'd blame it on being slightly intoxicated from the wine and the couple of tumblers of scotch I'd had before that. But, at the end of the day, I held my liquor pretty well. I was being an asshole *because* I was being an asshole in that moment, and Mom didn't give the reaction she normally would. She didn't hold me accountable or anything like that. She just stood there. She frowned there, and the expression pinched her lips tight.

Her manicured fingers danced along her arm. "You're the one who told me to date, Ramses." Her eyes lifted, her sigh full. "And now, you're upset."

We both knew how I was reacting tonight had nothing to do with that. Of course, I wanted her to date. I *always* wanted her to be happy.

Too bad she didn't want the same for me.

I'd left Bri after that bullshit in her office knowing full well I'd have no idea when I'd see my girlfriend again. I didn't call her or text her. It'd been nearly two fucking days, and I already felt on the brink of goddamn breaking.

That was the power Brielle had over me, the love I had for her. Because I loved her, I wasn't calling or texting her. We needed to sort out this shit with my mom first, and I didn't want to add anything more to her plate.

In the meantime, I had to pretend nothing was wrong, but I didn't have to stand around and endure any more of this shit.

Leaving the wine, I passed my mom, and she let me.

"Ramses."

Almost let me.

Her hand folded around my arm, shifting me and I made it easy because I respected her.

"I wish you wouldn't be so upset," she said, eyeing every surface of my kitchen but me. "I was just trying to protect you."

"Protect me." I panned her way, a nod as I propped a foot back to the wall. I shook my head. "You know, I told Brielle when we found out she was my professor and you were her friend—which neither of us knew either, by the way. Not at first."

Her lips moved over the other, her sight to the floor.

"I told her we should give you the benefit of the doubt." I eyed her. "I told her you'd be fine, and there was no reason to keep our relationship from you."

"Well, I guess we'll never know." Her head lifted, her frown deepening. "Because you did lie to me. She lied to me and had my son lie."

"Of course, that's all you heard." My hands tucked under my arms. "Of course, that's all you *see*. Because if you saw anything else, you'd notice, for the first fucking time in *years*, I can breathe again. I function again after all that shit with dad, everything with December and all that…"

Because she knew about that too, *aware*. Mom and I had never been totally open about it, but she'd known I had feelings for my friend. Ones I couldn't do anything about when we'd been in the thick of it. December had chosen someone else in the end.

My jaw moved. "I *feel* again, and I don't have to pretend I do." I nodded. "I actually do. For the first goddamn time in a long time, I do, and that's because of her. Because I love her. Because it's real with her."

Mom's throat worked, her expression shifting. She may have known all this if she'd given either of us a chance that day. If she'd trusted me. If she'd trusted her.

Rubbing my hand over my mouth, I pushed off the wall. "I get it. I'm your son. It's harder for you to listen when it comes to me because in your eyes, I'll always still be your kid."

Her head shook, tears blinking down. Real tears.

I hadn't seen my mother cry in years.

Not even through the divorce. She'd held them back. Stayed strong. Her fingers squeezed her arms. "I didn't protect you, Ramses. For years, I didn't. Not from your father." She covered her mouth. "I can't help but think what happened at Brown was my fault."

She would take on that responsibility. She would take on that pain, but she didn't have to.

I bought her in close. "You're the first one who told me Dad's mistakes are his, and mine are mine. I have fucked up. I'll probably fuck up a lot more." She laughed in my hands, and I smiled at her. "But you need to let me, and you have to trust her. She's your friend."

"You really love her?" she asked, and I nodded. Her lashes shifted away. "And she loves you?"

"She does."

And though that one was hard for her, Mom did look up at me. She braced the side of my face before her fingernails flicked my hair. "Did she make you cut your beautiful hair?"

Chuckling, I shook my head. She would focus on that. But that, I could take. That, she could judge. I'd take whatever she gave, as long as it left her open. As long as she *tried*.

I suppose it was harder for her when it came to me. I'd always be her kid. But Bri, she was her friend, and she should give her the benefit of the doubt. Bri was already hard enough on herself. Had already lost enough. I didn't want her to lose my mom, too.

I hugged her. "Give her a chance," I urged. "Trust her. Trust me."

She hugged me back. "Did you go see your father?"

Surprised by what she asked, I pulled back. "Yeah, why?"

"Because I'm on his do not see list." She touched my face but didn't seem mad. "Is finally being able to see him have to do with her, too?"

Maybe. At least these days, it all seemed to connect. When weren't the decisions in life affected by everything that snowballed from her? We were like organized chaos, all over the place but intentional at the same time. We might always be that way, and I'd certainly never be bored with her.

I made my mom promise me something that night in my kitchen, and she made me do the same. I promised to always be real with her, honest with her if she'd let each of us gain closure in our own ways. If she allowed us both to live our lives and experience both sins and victories. She did that, and I might entertain more of James's dad jokes. Hell, I'd even call him fucking father when it was time. I'd do whatever she wanted. And surprisingly?

She agreed with no hesitation.

CHAPTER
THIRTY-THREE

Bri

My soles hit concrete, my arms pumping. Anything I could do for my thoughts not to wander. The end of this terrible week saw me with another hard run, one I wrapped up the moment I turned the street corner on my block.

I slowed to a casual pace but tugged my earbud out at the sight of a familiar face.

Evie sat on the stoop leading up to my condo, her neck angled as if looking for something or someone.

She found me.

My arms fell to my side, my stride halted completely. She stood in my presence, still in her suit from her time at the office. I wondered if she'd come right from campus to here.

She pressed hands down her cream colored pants, adjusting her purse on her shoulder. "Could we talk?" She shook her head. "Just for a minute. I won't take a lot of your time. I waited when you didn't answer and one of your neighbors said you'd be back soon, that you just went for a run."

I tried to gauge her temperament with a racing heart. She didn't appear angry, but...

I brushed a restless hair out of my face. "Of course."

I was just happy she'd come, to see me. Of course, she could be delivering awful news. That I may be fired and couldn't return next year. Though, since Ramses and I hadn't done anything unethical in the technical sense, I wasn't quite sure that was legal.

But the Mallick family were very powerful people, and if she fought me for a place in this town, my job, I wouldn't fight her back. I'd betrayed her trust, lying to her, and that warranted both me leaving her school as well as her city. I'd leave if she wanted me to.

I cared about her.

Nodding, I had her follow me inside, into the elevator then into my condominium. I was completely aware of the awkwardness of this situation, and to keep myself busy, I immediately invited her into my kitchen.

"Can I make you something?" I questioned, placing my keys and earbuds on the kitchen island. I reached for the tea kettle. "Tea or I could even make coffee."

"Really, I won't take a lot of your time." Her hand raised in my direction, and she invited me for a seat in my own kitchen next to her.

I took it, swallowing hard. I placed my hand on the granite. "Evie, I'm so sorry."

"For what?"

My lashes fanned, my eyes twitched wide. I felt like I was being *Punk'd* for a second. I gazed around. "What?"

"Why are you apologizing?" Unbuttoning her jacket, she laced her hands on the island. "Because if it's for loving my son, changing him in more ways than I've ever seen..."

My mouth parted.

Hers lifted into a smile. "Why are you apologizing to me, Brielle?"

My throat thickened with heat, belly all coiled up, anxious. I chewed my lip. "I suppose for lying to you about it." I nodded. "For not being brave enough to tell you. You've done so much for me. I guess I didn't want to lose you. Your friendship."

It had meant so much, made me strong, brave. I'd taken the steps to start over here because of her, able to love again because of her. I'd done that because she'd brought me into her life and given me the means in which to take those chances. To come here and eventually, meet her son.

Who I was desperately in love with.

I planned to fight for Ramses, for us, but I also planned to give Evelyn time. I couldn't stay away from the man I loved and wouldn't. I did love Ramses, but I also loved her, too. I respected her enough to keep my distance, but it wouldn't have been forever.

She just happened to come to me first.

Taking my hands, Evie placed hers on top. "Over the years, I don't pride myself on how great of a mother I've been." Her smile fell sad. "My ex-husband, Ibrahim, was very abusive to Ramses. Not physically, but mentally. He was quite hard on him, held him to these impossible standards."

My stomach clenched, insides tight with heat. I nodded. "He mentioned."

His issues with his father contributed to a huge part of his anger, his decisions, as well as his insecurities. This wasn't unknown, and neither was his ability to overcome. He was putting all that anger and resentment for his father behind him. I knew because he'd mention the things he was doing with his life moving forward. He was doing the things he wanted in life without pressures or a need for acceptance. He was his own motivator now.

And he had the biggest cheerleader in me.

I'd make sure he'd always have support for the things he wanted to do, and as long as he allowed me in his life, I wouldn't go away. Not unless he wanted me to. I would fight for him.

"He's strong, Evie," I said to her. Because he was. "I bet that has a big part to do with you." I'd seen the things she'd done, the empire she had. I'd looked into it. The Pembroke history department hadn't had any female deans before her. She thrived in this world, commanded it.

She squeezed my hands. "I apologize to *you*, Bri. Because of all that with my husband, I'm very cautious when it comes to Ramses. Jump in when it's not even necessary. Especially after his issues at Brown."

And I got that, completely. I looked up at her. "I never should have lied to you. He didn't want to." I smiled. "He said we should give you the benefit of the doubt *always*, and I should have listened. I was just scared. I didn't want to lose you or our friendship."

Funny, this conversation we were having. Funny, because, before Ramses, I never would have had it. My default was to avoid.

But it seemed that wasn't the case now.

Evie put her hands on my face. "You will love him, won't you? Be good to him?"

I folded a hand on her wrist, nodding. "I was staying back to give you time. The only reason. I do love your son. I will be good to him." My smile widened. "I'm not going to step back again, but I respect you enough not to throw it in your face. I'm sure this is weird. *Will* be weird. Especially with the age thing. Our age difference."

I wouldn't lie and say that still didn't bother me or that we wouldn't have issues. People judging us or thinking things, but I was at the place now where I wouldn't be the one contributing to it. I'd be our biggest cheerleader in this too.

Her head tilted. "I suppose because he is my kid, yeah, that will be something I'll have to adjust to." She laughed a little. "But the age thing isn't an issue. I've got almost a decade on James."

"Seriously?"

She chuckled, tipping her chin. "And fuck anyone that has issue with that."

That had us both roaring at this point, which made me so happy. I really had feared losing her. I didn't want her to be a casualty to what I wanted.

Squeezing her hand, I brought her into a hug. "I love you, Evie."

"I love you too, honey," she returned. She squeezed harder. "And you take care of my son. I don't want to lose either of you."

I was completely with her there, and I would. So hard.

"He's intense," I said, pulling back. "Some days, I question if I'm strong enough for him."

"You are."

"How do you know?"

Her shoulders lifted, her eyes warm. "Because he chose you."

We ended our talk after tea in the end, a long talk in which she told me all about James. Things really seemed to be going well, and I was so very happy for her. She was starting to take back her life, too, a new beginning just like mine. I walked her to the door and offered to walk her down, but she told me she was all right.

We hugged one more time before I let her go, and I'd never felt so free. How I managed to get two pretty amazing people added into my life had me truly in awe. That life could be this good. I'd been so sad for so long, but I was more than ready to give in to the power of this healing. This town and these people, I had a feeling, were going to be good for me.

"You call me," she said at the door. "I'm sure you'll be busy with final grading, but don't lose touch."

I wouldn't, waving to her. I did have final grading now

that examinations were over, but the commencement that followed, I didn't anxiously anticipate anymore. As it turned out, Ramses and I didn't have to wait to tell the truth. And how nice that was.

I closed the door with nothing but a grin, my head touching the back.

I pushed off at the sound of a knock.

I opened the door without looking, thinking it was Evie. "Did you forget some—"

The words banded down in my throat, a set of male arms stretched heavy and wide in my door frame. They dropped down, and I stood back.

The man's head rose.

America's Most Sexiest Man Alive. He'd even made the Most Beautiful People list several times, but today, nothing but messy hair and a disheveled appearance radiated before me.

My mouth dampened. "You," I said, and he frowned.

His head lifted, growing another foot when he stood tall. "Me."

CHAPTER
THIRTY-FOUR

Bri

My ex-husband was drunk.

He stumbled on his way inside my condominium. I had no idea why I let him in. I'd been so shocked this was happening.

That he was here.

Alec Norrington sauntered the calculated steps of the inebriated into my home, still the size of a tank. Guys with his background, in those careers, tended to stay that size. Even when they spent more time at bars than at their homes during the final days of our marriage. My ex-husband had all but given up on life prior to our divorce, falling into himself, his misery, and I guess there had been signs where things were going. He'd gotten so depressed once we'd lost our child, and I had asked him to get help. Funny enough, he used to say he was going to his therapist on the nights he got wasted. He hadn't wanted help. He'd wanted to wallow.

And he'd wanted to hurt me in the process.

My hand ventured to my kitchen island, my gaze

studying my ex-husband as he entered the kitchen behind me. He shouldn't be here.

Alec eyed the room under his hair. It was way too long and not normal for him. "Someone here?"

His attention fell on the two teacups, the ones Evie and I had shared. I started to say no, but I wasn't sure if I should. Maybe he should know someone else was here.

"Why are you here?" I asked, keeping my voice level. I didn't want him to know this visit put me off, made me shake. He'd only hit me the one time, but that didn't mean he wouldn't again. I swallowed. "How did you find me?"

I hadn't gone out of my way to keep where I was from him. But I definitely hadn't told him where I was going. It was none of his business.

He smirked as his fingers drew down his mouth, but then, it was sad. He sat on one of my barstools, his hands lacing, and a flash of light in my periphery took my attention. My phone lay on the counter behind me, the countertop across from Alec near the range.

I edged a look down at it.

Ramses: Hey. Mom said she just left your place and passed someone on the elevator who looked like your ex-husband. You okay?

"Come here, babe."

My hand squeezed at my side, the thoughts barely surfaced to even think to grab my phone.

Alec faced my way, his hand out. "Come here."

I wasn't his babe. I wasn't his. I shook my head. "Why are you here?"

"Come here, and I'll tell you." His lips wet, mouth turned down. "Why do you have to make everything so difficult? I come all the way here. I send you flowers..."

What?

Ramses: I'm going to go ahead and come through. Just

need some peace of mine. Let me know otherwise, and I'll give you space.

Alec's hand continued to wave in my direction, my ex-husband clearly too wasted to notice I'd been eyeing my phone. He started to get up, to get me, and I didn't want to risk grabbing it.

I came *closer*, but I didn't take his hand.

"You sent those flowers?" I suppose it made sense. Besides the fact Ramses hadn't even done anything wrong that day I'd gotten them, he had technically gifted me with hiking clothes in my car.

Fuck.

The hike itself and the pizza had obviously been another gift, and the roses, though I wouldn't put it past Ramses, didn't seem like his style. He was very intentional in the things he did. Preferred spending time with me and not just words or little gifts. I mean, he did give me hiking gear, but he gave it in order to spend the day with me. Things like roses and chocolates, a secretary would send. They weren't personal.

Alec's personal assistant probably had sent them, and I wouldn't put it past him if she filled out the card, too. Alec had just never been good at getting out his emotions. He was a very physical person. He enjoyed tackling guys on the field and like most men, fucking any moment I'd granted him access to it.

Honestly, those narrowed traits were probably a big reason he had fallen into himself as hard as he had after we'd lost the baby. He really didn't know how to express those emotions and ended up blaming me.

My eyes flicked over to my phone, the screen dark. I didn't know what Alec would do if I tried to reach over and grab it. Or what I could do once I had.

He said he's coming.

"I want you back," my ex-husband said, basically laughable. He put his hands on his thighs. "The break up was dumb."

"And what do you call hitting me?"

"A mistake." He stood, and I backed up. He shook his head. "I won't hurt you, Bri."

I didn't know that.

And I didn't, backing up again. At this point, my cell phone was nearly across the room.

Alec placed his hands on the island. "Is this about that kid?"

"What kid?"

He shot me a look like I was an idiot, a snarl really when it curled his lip. "That *kid* the internet says your fucking." He nodded. "Yeah, I know about him. Looked him all up after the two of you went fucking viral over the weekend."

Oh my God.

I pushed a hand over my head. "That has nothing to do with you."

He swung around the island, and my butt touched the counter. My fists balled, and I started to turn around, reaching for something, anything to possibly arm myself with, but my ex-husband stopped.

His gaze circulated to the granite counter top.

"This other one his?" he asked, directing a finger toward the tea cups. He gazed around. "That little shit here?"

"He's not, and you need to go." I spoke braver than I felt in that moment, my swallow hard. "You need to get out of here. I don't know how you found me, or why you felt the need, but you *need* to go. We're divorced, Alec."

"A divorce you called over *one* mistake," he growled, completely trivializing that he had hit me, placed hands on me. He thrust a hand over his head. "And even though I didn't agree with it, I let you go. Figured you needed time."

I laughed, which only heated his gaze.

"I've known where you were for months. Some little bitch

tagged a photo of you and her at the store one day. Put me on it. Didn't take me long to figure out you'd gone back to teaching. Had my people make some calls and got your address. Wasn't hard."

I should have made it harder.

Forcing myself not to shake, I watched as he gave me back my space, retreating and taking a seat again. Maybe he saw he had rattled me.

"I figured with time you'd come back."

"Well, I'm not. I won't," I said, and like the universe knew I needed it, a knock filled my condo in the next moment. One that shot my ex-husband's gaze in the direction of the hall. It was so obviously Ramses. He'd said he was coming by.

"You expecting someone?" Alec asked, getting up, and I started to say yes and that he needed to get the fuck out again, but his waistband gave me pause. His shirt slid up as he kicked the barstool from underneath him.

The nine-millimeter on his hip had been old hat when we'd been together. The man hailed originally from Texas, something he'd always had, but in this situation...

"Alec."

He paused, facing my way. The knock on the door hit again, and I forced myself to ignore it. I swallowed. "You said you wanted to talk. Let's talk."

I waited with bated breath as this man righted and returned to his seat, so desperate for whatever he thought this meeting would result in that he did listen to me. He gripped his hands on the counter. "I do want to talk."

One more knock, only one until it stopped, and I closed my eyes.

I couldn't sink into the dread of my reality, Ramses leaving, *leaving me*, and this man in my kitchen. I couldn't because I needed to figure out what to do.

I had knives, but none easily accessible. I had a knife

drawer, but it was across the room and kept no guns like Alec.

I didn't know if, not hearing from me, Ramses would take the initiative and use his house key. I'd given him one for emergencies but wasn't sure if he'd just let himself in after the week we'd had. We were basically on a pause until I said something different.

The thought sobering, I eased forward, my ex-husband opening his hands. "Now, just hear me out, Bri."

His words were lost to the ether at the sight of movement behind him, a man lingering in the hall. A large man with broad shoulders and dark eyes.

Oh my gosh, Ramses.

I lost my breath in that moment, my stance rigid and straight. It was enough for Ramses to pass his gaze between Alec and me, the man still talking. And where Ramses may have introduced himself, he didn't. He stood there, watching on.

But then I mouthed: "Help."

Alec noticed, turning back, but arms looped around his neck, cutting off his words mid-sentence.

Alec choked, struggling against Ramses strong hold. He punched at Ramses's arms, and Ramses growled.

"Bri, get out of here. Call the cops!" Ramses roared, my ex standing, but even with his height, he fell just short of Ramses.

My boyfriend held on tight, but Alec had him in width. He was used to tackling guys twice Ramses's size and shot an elbow into my boyfriend from behind. Strengthening his hold, Ramses refused to let go, but then Alec backed him into the wall and I screamed.

"Ramses!"

I forgot completely about running. I forgot about calling the cops because the impact completely knocked Ramses's equilibrium off and he fell back.

He let go.

It was enough for Alec to reach back into his waistband, the action in slow motion. The man had death in his eyes, intention in his gaze. I knew he'd have no problem shooting Ramses right there in my kitchen. He'd have no problem killing him.

That was all I saw, my life and future flashing before my eyes.

It was enough for me to run.

It was enough for me to *act*, refusing to let this man take everything away from me. Ramses stood across the kitchen with his hands up, but while Alec moved that gun in the direction of my boyfriend, I found something to defend myself with.

I found something to end this.

The steak knife lodged into my ex-husband's back, coming out dripping, coated in red. Alec stiffened, ramrod straight, but he didn't drop the gun.

"Stop this!" I roared, tears streaming down my cheeks, and I stabbed again. "Stop!"

He merely stared back at me, rage in his eyes.

But then I stabbed again.

Again.

And again.

The rage slowly changed then, anger and fury twisting into something else. Something more deadly. That malice quickly transferred to fear, and it wasn't until he dropped the gun, falling to his knees, it turned into something else.

Vacancy.

His soul lost behind his gaze, his face hitting the floor, and I blinded completely at the sight before me. At *what happened* and didn't need to. My ex-husband didn't have to die. It didn't have to be this way.

"Brielle…"

It took me a second, a long second, to realize I was on the floor, sobbing and rocking with arms around me.

Ramses's arms, his strong body hugging me close. He held my bleeding hands, my arms shaking in his. "I know," he said. "I know."

Apparently, I'd been saying it out loud. That this didn't have to happen, over and over, I kept saying it, and each time Ramses kept saying he knew. He kept saying he understood. He told me it would be okay, and it took so long to believe him. That this nightmare would finally be over. That I could move on.

That I could heal.

I started to do that in his arms while we waited for the cops to arrive later that night. He'd taken the time to call them, but then, he was back with me. He was back to this, on the floor with me and holding me so tight.

I'd never felt so safe in my life.

CHAPTER
THIRTY-FIVE

Ramses

There was this thing my mom had told me a few years ago. After my dad's trial, then again once they'd finalized their divorce. She'd said, "After the ashes fall, things will be okay. After the ashes fall, we'll be all right, but only after the ashes fall, Ramses."

After the ashes fall.

Her words hit me in a new way that day Brielle's husband went after her. Because it wasn't my own trauma or even my family's this time. It was the woman I loved, her own rebirth as I stood by her. We had a sea of cops and noise we had to deal with that night. Her ex had died.

He was gone.

He'd succumbed to clearly his own insecurities and made Bri have to deal with those, too. I stood by Brielle during the thickness of it, and Mom came over too, doing the same. We were both there for her while this new reality manifested itself before her. Her own ashes were falling around her, and I found my mother's words surfacing again after the night concluded. I told Brielle these ashes would fall. They'd rest, and after, she'd be okay.

We'd be okay.

Back when my mom had shared the words, I honestly hadn't believed her, but going through everything with Bri, *meeting Bri*, told me what kind of place I was in, as well as what kind of man I'd become. I was living for the day and completely feeling it. I sunk into it with no life raft. I was alive for the good, but also for the bad. But one better, I was strong enough for both. I was brave enough to let in the good and not worry about it being taken away. But I also came equipped to handle whatever life decided to toss out along the way. That was how life was. One couldn't have one without the other. One couldn't truly appreciate love until they endured pain. I had endured pain. I had endured love, and Brielle had as well.

She later told me she'd been about to come see me, when her husband had intercepted her. That she'd planned to fight for us and ended up fighting for herself that night. What happened to her husband was truly horrible, but on the other side, she came out stronger. She was brave enough for the good and bad too. She was ready to live and take on whatever life gave her. We'd do that together.

After the ashes.

The next couple of weeks prior to commence were truly deplorable. Brielle had to deal with a lot of stuff she shouldn't have had to deal with. Press and the media alike surrounding her and her ex-husband's confrontation. He obviously hadn't left her condo alive that day, and once the media found out, they'd had a frenzy. The man was a beloved sports icon, there for his fans on the outside, but clearly, not for the woman who had probably trusted him most. I felt for the guy in the only way I could that didn't involve me punching a hole through a wall. He'd experienced trauma too, but in no way did that justify the way he'd treated Bri, then gone after her.

I gave Brielle everything she needed, of course, people to help her wrangle the sea of paparazzi that followed, and even Mom worked out things on campus. University staff were in the middle of final grading, but Mom made sure Brielle didn't have to worry about that. Mom even offered to let Brielle stay at her place while all this blew over.

Of course, Brielle couldn't stay at her own house or even my properties. People, the media, were well aware we were both together and that I'd been there the day of the confrontation. TMZ was after us both, had a field day, but we didn't split up. I set us up in a private place upstate, a place where we both took some time. We stayed there *together* until the day of the commencement ceremony.

I had no desire to even walk that day, didn't care, but Bri wanted that for me. In fact, it was the one normal thing she said we both should have. She wanted to be there for me that day, to support me, and she also didn't want me to miss the experience with my friends. Knight, Royal, and December were also graduating with me. We'd all passed our final classes, with flying colors even.

I did walk with the rest of my friends that day, did experience that time, but after, it was just Brielle and me again. It stayed that way until nearly a month later.

And that was only because my mother begged me to surface.

My graduation party couldn't very well happen without me. My mother's words, not mine. She'd waited to throw the whole thing until after Bri and I felt comfortable, and I made completely sure Bri was before telling my mom yes. I didn't push Brielle, but ironically enough, she'd been the one to push me. She said she wanted to party, party with me, and hell, if I'd turn down a moment to actually show her off to my world.

That was exactly what I did, my girlfriend not far from me that whole day in the manor I'd grown up in and around the people I cared about the most. Even my grandparents and some of my extended family had come out from Syria, and my mom's family too, who were normally sprinkled across the country. I introduced my girlfriend to everyone, *mine*, and even Brielle's parents showed up from Jersey. She said she'd invited them because she wanted them to meet me.

And how crazy was that?

How crazy our worlds were combining, a new future I could see happening right before me. If it were up to me, it'd be a lot sooner, but I did tread lightly when it came to my girlfriend. We were still very new, and even though I felt the way I did about her, I resisted defaulting to old habits and rushing things.

Even still, that didn't keep me from taking her father aside later that evening and having a little talk with him. I wanted to get a few things out in the open, and I felt better after I did. Ironically enough, after I shook her father's hand, I had a hard time finding Brielle. She'd said she was going to mingle and had spent the most time with my mother and even December today.

My best friend wasn't quite showing yet, and I did get on her for keeping that little detail from me. I'd confronted her via text not long after Prinze had spilled the beans, and she must have handed Prinze his ass immediately after.

I knew because he'd shot daggers at me most of the grad party.

It seemed our little coalition may have been short-lived because he scowled at me pretty much all damn afternoon. I mean, he always scowled but definitely more than normal. Even Knight, LJ, and Jax asked what his deal was. They'd come to the party too, brought their girls. Jax and LJ went to different colleges out of state, but it appeared they were already making plans to come back home following their own commencements.

We were all about to be permanent residents in Maywood

Heights. At least, for the foreseeable future, and some of us may have been surprised about that. This town had some crazy shit happen to all of us, yet we were all here. Coming back to our roots. We were all about to be in each other's lives again, and at the present, it seemed like for a very long time. I couldn't seem to get rid of these people.

And that might be okay.

LJ and I actually had a very healthy discussion regarding our future business endeavors. Well, as much as we could before Knight decided to bust it up. These boys really loved to one up the other, Jax and Royal coming in at one point too. Once that happened, of course, talks traveled to Royal and December, *their* baby. The couple had decided to make all us guys godfathers, and I think we all, at least me, were in awe of that. A new generation was coming and as it appeared, really soon. I even gave Prinze one of my father's best cigars, and I got that scowl of his to melt away for a little bit. We were going to be in each other's lives for a very long time, might as well start showing the world now we didn't completely hate each other.

I clasped Prinze's shoulder with a smile before leaving the group and heading off and finding Brielle.

She didn't leave my lap once I had.

In my mom's parlor, I kept a hand on her hip while the pair of us chatted with various guests, and it took me a second to realize Brielle kept filling up her wine glass during the conversations. Well, my mother's attendants were filling her glass. Mom had this event catered, and every time a server would come around to ask if we needed something, Bri would wave for a fill up.

Currently, she chugged it back while we watched Billie, Greer, and Cleo (LJ's, Knight's, and Jax's girlfriends) attempt to nudge details from December and Royal about their baby. It was too early to know the sex, but they wanted to know about the baby shower and all that, and they were inquisitive with the couple. Of course, this turn of topic had their guys about to fall asleep, but I was listening because I had a feeling I'd be the one to buy the pacifier cupcakes. It was a job I planned to volunteer for and wanted to. That kid would be terribly spoiled, by me and probably all his or her god-dads.

My hand on Bri's hip, I juggled my attention between my girlfriend and December, who spoke. The other couples were seated around us. This party was at my mom's manor, an open house. This room was about half full with party guests, but what wasn't was Brielle's glass. In fact, she snapped to have it filled again, and I nudged her.

"Everything okay?" I kissed her shoulder. My woman was sexy as fuck in all black once again. Her tight top exposed her shoulders, her pants cropped at the ankles. With her strappy heels, she basically looked like Olivia Newton-John at the end of *Grease*, which I'd fucking take. I frowned. "You're really laying into that wine."

"Am I?" she squeaked like she'd been caught, and Brielle Whitman-Quintero didn't squeak. She placed a hand on her chest. "Sorry, I'm just kind of all over the place."

Which worried me, about the need for it. She hadn't been this way all day, not even when I had her meeting the rest of my family. Of course, she expressed she'd been nervous prior but had handled it well.

My mom was a part of this powwow as well in the parlor, and curiously, I noticed her looking at us. She was with James, who she'd been dating for a couple of months now, and surprisingly, I'd been okay with that. I'd known the guy for a while. Our community was big, but also small. He was a divorcee himself, and after I'd probed him about his intentions (which I did, heavily), I deemed him suitable for my mother.

She deserved the best after all.

Anyway, I definitely noticed her *looking at* Brielle from across our conversation circle. She eyed her, her smile coy under James's arm. I even observed a little nudge of Mom's glass in our direction, and Brielle lifted a hand at her. At this point, something was going on, but before I could voice it, Brielle shifted on my lap.

She faced me, and I let her stand up. I was really curious now but crossed my legs.

Especially when she tapped her glass.

She did it with a flick of her nails, not a huge ordeal, but it did get the attention of the rest of the room, December, Royal, and the rest of the gang included. Brielle's face was beet red, and she smoothed her hands down her pants before speaking.

"I guess I just wanted to say something," she said, and I smiled. She put her glass out to me. "About Ramses. First off, I just wanted to wish him and all the rest of you graduates congratulations. Doing so is a huge accomplishment, so you all should be very proud."

She was aware my other friends had graduated too, and they raised their beverages to her, the rest of the room lightly clapping.

Brielle folded hands around her glass stem. "Ramses, what do I say about you?"

So that had the room laughing, me too when I waved a passive hand. I had no idea she'd be doing this, and though Brielle wasn't shy, being put on the spot at all wasn't one of her favorite pastimes. This speech was definitely putting her completely out of her comfort zone right now.

My Jersey girl.

She smiled at me. "An accomplished scholar and business-man. A wonderful son." She placed her glass out toward my mom before guiding it toward December. "And cherished friend."

Both Mom and December grinned, and that shit? Yeah, it kind of got some stuff caught in my throat a little bit. My girl-friend apparently loved placing me on the spot, too.

She faced me. "But also, an amazing man and fierce

protector." She paused, tucking a stand of hair behind her ear. "Many of you probably know this man saved my life. Whether you've read about it or heard directly from us. And though that's true, I'm sure most of you don't know it wasn't the first time."

I eyed her, surprised she was saying this.

I placed a hand out for hers, and she took it, lacing our fingers.

"Ramses, I'll never be able to thank you." Her voice thickened, and when she squeezed her eyes, that shit got me a little, too.

I fought it with a smile, keeping our hands laced and after she got herself together, she continued on.

She squeezed my hand. "And this is probably crazy. I've probably lost my entire mind, but I asked your mom for permission, and she's okay with it so..."

What the hell?

And then, legit, she got on her knees. Like really, on her knees before me.

She laughed in her heels, shaking her head. "I'm going to ask you a question. Because I know that's what you need. You need to know *I'm* okay with this, this question." She chuckled. "Because you are so good. You are and will fight your instincts because you need to know I'm okay with this before you'd ever ask. You'll always wait for me. Even if it goes against everything you feel."

I would do that, impulsive, but she was logical. She was, so I respected that.

I did tell her I'd wait for her. Even if that meant years down the line until she was ready. Until she wanted to commit to me.

"Ramses..."

I eased to the floor with her, guiding her to stand to her feet.

The room gasped.

Her father honestly thought I was crazy when I'd spoken to him today. I mean, Brielle and I'd been dating for like two seconds, but it didn't feel like that.

We only felt like forever.

I slid a black box from my pocket, and my mom literally squealed so loud that the whole room erupted in laughter.

I couldn't quite gauge Brielle's reaction. She had half her face covered with her wine glass and her hands, but I took that for a good thing.

"You really do know me," I said, popping the box open. Inside, was my great-grandmother's ring. I'd had it for what felt like forever. A diamond ring in the form of a lily, timeless, beautiful just like her. I took Bri's hand. "And I hope because you do, you're not surprised by this."

Her face gorgeously flushed, she shook her head. And when she removed that wine glass, she had tears in her eyes. She laughed. "Thank God, you saved me. I hoped you would." She palmed her face. "I'm like seriously mortified."

"I know." That had the whole room laughing, but once it faded, I stared up at her. "Brielle Whitman-Quintero, will you—"

"Yes."

I paused, eyeing her.

She covered her mouth. "Sorry."

More laughter, and I shook my head. "Brielle Whitman-Quintero, will you marry me?" I stated, then eyed the room. "Something you don't know about *her* is she always likes to take control."

"Yeah, she does!"

That came from the back of the room from, of all people, her parents. They were there too, her dad's glass in the air. He hugged Bri's mom's shoulders, the older woman basically in tears.

Bri's lips parted, facing me. "Did you tell my parents about this?"

"I even asked your dad," I said, winking. Of course, I had. I'd ask whoever I had to.

I held her hand, waiting there on my knees.

"Give him an answer, girl. You're killing us!" came from December, looking completely cheeky from Prinze's lap. He had his arms looped around her waist, shaking his head at her.

He kissed her. "Let them have their moment, princess."

This had December tsking, of course, but she waited with bated breath for Bri's answer. I think we all knew what she'd say. I mean, she had said yes already.

"We jump together," she said instead, and that was yes enough for me.

I placed the ring on her finger, and the room erupted in applause, my girl in my arms in the next second.

"Together," I returned against her mouth, spinning her around. We were both fucking crazy. We'd been together for definitely only a minute. But I liked this girl's crazy.

And she obviously loved mine.

EPILOGUE

Bri

"Everything here I'm seeing looks good, Brielle. Really good," Dr. Powell said, grinning at me. "Of course, we'll have to follow up. Overtime and as the years progress, but as it stands right now, I see no problems for the pair of you trying to conceive. In fact, I can imagine a really strong chance of success as long as what I'm seeing keeps up."

I could have gone behind Ramses's back with all this. Kept my appointment at the fertility clinic a secret. I still wasn't even sure if I'd ever change my mind about having children again.

I took his hand, in the chair beside me. He placed his on mine, and really, that was why I had. I didn't keep things from him. *We* didn't keep secrets. He'd always remain abreast of any decision I made when it came to my body or otherwise. We were each other's support systems, and that was what this had been about today. To give us *all* our options, to know if it was possible.

And now, we did.

The pair of us simply entered life this way now. We didn't close ourselves off to anything. I think life and the previous world I lived in made me lock myself up pretty tight, and not just when it came to my life. I didn't take chances, went at life with the smallest possible chance of failure. It made me feel secure and in control, but sometimes that wasn't what life was about. It was about climbing high dives and suggesting to get pizza with a guy over a decade younger than yourself. It was love, marriages, and second chances. Meeting Ramses Mallick had changed my life.

It had changed both our lives.

I would like to say after the pair of us left the fertility clinic that day, the news good and future hopeful, we did a little more talking about what was next. We had an entire drive over to December's baby shower, and though we had chatted in the parking lot, we didn't exactly *leave* the parking lot.

At least, not right away.

It was like a switch went off, and next thing I knew, I was in Ramses's lap in his Mercedes. Dr. Powell had given us the okay to move forward with conception...

And I guess we wanted some practice.

My hands hit the top of his car, my top unbuttoned as Ramses slammed into me from below. We typically liked to drive my car since it was an SUV. After he graduated, we'd moved in together into his Maywood Heights home and our cars had become interchangeable. We did like to drive my car since it was bigger and it gave us more room when, well, we got distracted with each other. I'd like to say parking lot fucks didn't happen a lot but...

"Fuck, Jersey girl. Fuck," he gritted, his powerful thighs slapping against mine. He'd gotten blackout windows so at least people didn't see us doing this crap, but still, it mortified me every time. That I literally couldn't keep my hands off this man for even a second longer to get home, or in this case, wait until after his friend's baby shower. December was only about fourteen weeks, but she'd already had a couple. The first, Ramses had actually helped her with, volunteering because he was just perfect and couldn't help himself. Something told me when he did finally become a dad, he'd run through fire and brimstone for our child. Especially if she was a girl.

Our child.

We obviously hadn't decided yet, but the possibility warmed my insides as much his mouth on my flushed skin. I did see myself having kids with him. I must have because we went to a fertility clinic. Ramses had me wanting to take chances again and explore new possibilities.

Smiling, I secured our lips, rocking my hips as his length tunneled deep. He hit me in places I didn't even know he could reach with the massive size of his cock, his hand slamming to the window as he gripped my hip. Digging in his heels, he used the traction to pretty much split me apart. He peppered my chest in hot kisses, tonging me between my breasts.

"We're going to be late," I gasped, gripping his shoulders. Even as I said the words, I closed my eyes.

His chuckle, gritted and aroused, escaped before he bit my chest. I'd already been on the cusp of an orgasm.

And then, he did that.

It ripped through me, a blaze to a dry desert. All explosion. All fury, passion, and complete heat.

"Fuck." On his heels, he did the same, his head rolling back and digging into the headrest. His fist punched to the ceiling on his way down from the high.

I laced my arms around him as my hips jutted, my inner walls spasming. His warmth burst into me, and I knew we'd have to do a quick clean up. We'd stopped using condoms a while back. Actually, not long after he'd proposed a few weeks ago. I'd always been on birth control and we both tested clean, but not wearing condoms was another sign of trust. One we both gave the other.

My hands smoothed across his jaw as I kissed him. I wore the diamond ring with ease on my left hand.

The same went for the band below.

This was a new development, the one on his left hand the same. We'd done something impulsive not long ago, something totally Ramses and *not* me. What could I say, Ramses Mallick had me taking more of those chances.

I'd take a million more.

His was gold on his left, the metal currently pressed into my waist. The decision to get married one shouldn't take lightly, and we hadn't. I mean, this was my second marriage and his first. It just felt right so we'd done it, and hell, if someone should disagree with that.

This was just another step toward the completion of us. A world of our own creation and rules. We wanted to get it done before he started really getting involved with his new businesses and I left for the summer. I was planning another dig overseas. I was going back to the basics for my research, and I'd probably see Ramses every few weeks as his schedule permitted. He was going to be increasingly busy in the upcoming months, and though I told him the dig would just be for the summer (I was coming back to teach in the fall), he made sure to write me into his schedule. Hell, he'd even agreed to put his life and plans on hold until I finished.

Of course, he had.

That was just him, but I was also me and I didn't let him. We could both get out of life the things we wanted and would. He couldn't get rid of me now that he'd placed this ring on my finger.

Once we got ourselves together (and I got out of his lap), we finally made it over to Royal and December's for her latest shower. I really couldn't remember who was throwing this one for her. She had so many people who loved and cared about her around her. It made me excited to be a part of this community. Ramses and I were settling here in Maywood Heights, building our lives and our futures, and it seemed we already had a fine support system to back us. Outside of Evie and her fiancé (yes, that had happened), Ramses had his friends from high school. I'd finally met them all at his graduation party, and we'd even all hung out together after.

I wouldn't lie. I had felt older than everyone else, but that came with the territory. Ramses had actually met some of my friends, too, when they came down from Jersey for his graduation party. Evelyn had basically invited everyone both Ramses and I knew. Especially when I'd told her I planned to propose to her son.

Was it weird my good friend and mentor was my mother-in-law now? Yes, but was I dealing with it?

More than well.

Ramses and I showed up only partially late to December's event, and of course, the mommy-to-be spotted him the moment we arrived. This shower was at Royal and December's house in Maywood Heights, a huge property in a gated cul de sac community. They basically lived in a castle like many of their friends. Knight and Greer didn't live in the same neighborhood, but their friends Jaxen and Cleo had moved in down the street. I'd heard their friend LJ and his girlfriend Billie were looking into the neighborhood as well.

"There you are!" December called, scurrying her way over in probably the cutest little top to show her baby bump off ever. She was still quite small, and from what I understood, the couple had been adamant about not knowing the sex of the baby at all prior to delivery. This, of course, drove the rest of us crazy, and already, I'd come to love this girl. She brought so much high-powered energy into Ramses's life and mine now as well. She hugged him tight upon getting to us. "Fashionably late."

"Well, uh, you know." Ramses passed off, chuckling. He brushed a kiss on her head before releasing her to me.

"Hmm," she said, eyeing him before taking me in the biggest hug. She loved hugs, and once done, she didn't let me go. She pointed at Ramses. "I'd be more hurt if everyone else didn't show up late, too."

She said this loud enough as she whipped around toward the others she'd previously been with. As per usual, their friends were coupled up. I spotted Knight, LJ, Jax, and their girlfriends all over by the food table. This particular shower was in the Prinzes' backyard with enough landscape design to place them well in the company of those featured in *Better Homes and Gardens*. I was talking hedges designed like animals and ponds with colorful fish. Completely fabulous, gorgeous.

Their friend Knight, the huge guy who ate pretty much everything us girls put in front of him whenever we all got together, shrugged. He pulled his girlfriend Greer over. "What?"

The other guys, Jax and LJ looked just as guilty, sipping on their beers and Royal, with them and their girlfriends, laughed. Royal lifted his beer. "You surprised, Em?"

"I guess not," December said, but did smile. She instructed us to go mingle, and I scanned the crowd, spotting Evelyn. This was a guys and girls shower, and she'd come with James.

Getting their attention, I lifted my hand to wave at them both.

December noticed.

Well, what she really noticed was the band I'd completely forgot to take off in the car.

Fuck.

"Oh my freaking God. What?!" She grabbed my hand, shooting a look at Ramses. "Arizona, did you guys get married?"

Did I mention the wedding had been an elopement? Completely off the cuff. Completely *crazy* just like my relationship with her best friend. We'd decided to do some traveling after the graduation party.

We'd hit up Vegas.

The plan had been to spill the beans after we got back, but I'd been supposed to leave my band in the car since today was about the baby shower.

I guess I got distracted.

I blamed Ramses, nudging him. He had taken off his ring, but I must not have noticed.

Scratching his neck, Ramses dropped an arm around my shoulders. "Eh, uh. We were going to tell you today."

"Really? When?" She tapped her foot, looking completely cute with her flushed cheeks and tiny belly. At this point, we'd gathered a crowd, her husband coming over and their friends.

Ramses chewed the inside of his cheek. "Was going to pull you aside. I swear, and before you ask, it was completely on a whim. We planned to throw a reception for everyone."

This didn't seem to make her feel any better. She groaned. "Does your mom even know?"

"Mom was there, so yes, she knew." Evelyn joined us with James, winking. Did I mention she came to Vegas with us, too? A family trip.

Ramses bent his long frame, kissing her cheek, before she hooked James's arm. Something told me they would have gotten married, too, had they been as crazy as us. She grinned at December. "And we took plenty of pictures for you, honey. For everyone."

Yeah, definitely didn't make her feel any better. At her side, Royal hugged her waist, then proceeded in reminding her that they kept the news of their baby under wraps for a little while. This did make her feel a little better and I found the two so sweet. They reminded me kind of Ramses and myself. He always kept me from the ledge. Talked me down. He'd been doing this from day one.

I looped arms around his waist, and he squeezed me. My husband. And no, I still couldn't believe that. We were two completely different people now. I was a different person.

And thank God for that.

December made us show her every picture we had between Evelyn's phone and mine. The small wedding in a chapel with tiny flowers and lovely garlands. I'd worn a white pantsuit I'd picked up at a local shop and Ramses had worn a suit he'd packed for our nicer dinners. It hadn't been the ridiculous side show that was my first wedding. Hell, *People Magazine* had even come out for that.

It'd been small. It'd been intimate. But most importantly, it'd been Ramses and me.

December and the other women in their friend circle squealed with glee and delight at every photo, but I had to say, none of their boyfriends shared their enthusiasm. I mean, this didn't surprise me. They were guys, but even Royal seemed to take a little interest in the captured moments. The other guys were downing their booze, looking borderline annoyed, before the really big one, Knight, put a hand in the circle.

And then, the craziest thing happened.

He got down on one knee, right there in front of everyone. The young man pulled a ring out of his jacket and popped it open in front of his tiny, blond girlfriend. They really were the cutest thing, completely mismatched, but then again, they weren't. Like all these guys, they just seemed to really go well with their other halves. Completely opposite like Ramses and me.

But then again, completely the same.

Greer stepped back upon being presented to, completely in awe at the man on his knees before her. She even had tears in her eyes as she pressed her small fist to her mouth, and I wondered if that was how I'd looked merely a few weeks ago, when my life had changed, and I'd gotten engaged.

That felt so far away now.

Ramses hugged me close. Like he knew my thoughts, he dropped a kiss down on the top of my head, and I squeezed his waist, watching what was clearly another proposal happening in front of us.

Knight almost looked shy in front of his girlfriend. His cheeks were flushed and everything. He frowned a little. "Believe it or not, I was going to ask you before all this. Tonight and a dinner… It was going to be awesome."

Everyone around laughed, but then gasped when another ring was pulled out.

LJ this time, the guy with the long blond hair Ramses was going into business with. Ramses had told me all about that and how excited he was for it.

Currently, his new business partner was on his knee too, taking his own ring out and popping the box open in front of *his* girlfriend. I'd only met his Billie a couple of times. She still had been trying to work out bringing everything over from their life in Indiana. Every time, I had seen her, she'd been a gem, though. A true darling with fiery red hair primed and placed, her smile gorgeous.

Her eyes shimmered in front of LJ. "What are you doing?"

LJ shrugged. "Well, Knight went rogue, so…"

"Yeah, he did."

Another ring and I couldn't make this up. Their friend Jaxen got on his knee as well. His girlfriend Cleo was super cute, super *tall*, and probably the nicest person I'd ever met. Honestly, within moments of meeting her, she was asking me about a charity event she was planning to put on for local animal shelters. Already wanting to get involved in town.

"Jax…" She squeaked, on her heels, and Jax took her hand.

He frowned. "It was supposed to be a combined proposal

tonight," he gritted, shooting Knight a look. But then, he snarled at Ramses. "Leave it to Mallick to show us up."

Ramses laughed, folding his hand on my hip. He set his chin on top of my head. "Don't let me cramp your style, boys."

Knight growled, but then faced Greer. "What do you say, dove? Marry me?"

LJ and Jax's proposals followed, and I could safely say, I hadn't seen anything like it. These guys hilariously trying to one up each other, yes, but all the love around. I barely knew these people. Really, I didn't know them well.

But as I watched all their guys put rings on their girls' fingers, December and Royal and Evie and James hugging close beside us, a feeling surfaced that hadn't been there even moments before arrival. Like these people were really about to mean something in my life. Like I had a place with them.

Like they were family.

I didn't know if that'd be true, but as I gripped Ramses's waist, his hold tight around me, I thought it.

Ramses kissed my temple, staying there. "I love you so much."

Smiling, I directed my brow to his lips, hugging him close and telling him the same. This man had somehow become my everything in so little time. He'd become *mine* as well as this little community. Old Brielle would have been scared by that, but new Brielle took chances. She had dreams. She loved and she lived, and she did so with her person, no fear.

There simply wasn't any room.

Acknowledgements

Wow, guys! We really made it. Eight books. EIGHT FREAKING BOOKS with these crazy characters, and I'm so happy to have had you along for the ride. I spent 2020 writing these books and writing/releasing them has changed my life. Literally, it changed my life. I'm now writing full time. A freaking dream and that's because of all of you folks. Thank you to all of you for reading my books and helping me live out a lifelong dream. I'm so happy December, Royal, and the gang have resonated with so many of you. Your constant messages of support have brought me to tears so many times. My husband (and dogs) think I'm crazy, bwhaha! I'm forever grateful to each and every one of you and I wanted to send a special shoutout to a few people.

Thanks to my husband and to Nikki (you know who you are ;D) for pushing me to publish these books! Oh, my gosh they almost didn't even happen. 2020 was friggin' insane, but they told me to keep going and I'm so glad they did. Thank you also to my PA, Jenny, who started working for me before I even published a book, omg! I still can't believe you reached out not even knowing anything about me. I just love you and thank you so much for being there on my team. Thanks to my cover artist and editors for the quick turnarounds and constantly being in my corner. Muah! Thank you also to my fellow authors friends! Love you guys so much! And HUGE thanks to my beta readers!!! You guys read books so fast. Seriously, how do you do it?? *kisses*

And extra special thanks for my readers, ARC reviewers, street team members, and anyone else who's ever reached out, read my books, or messaged me. You guys have seriously blown my mind with your love and support. Thank you to all my peeps in my Facebook group, "The Starlets." So many of you joined my group when I didn't even have a book out and I love you for that! You guys rock my socks. Seriously.

I've gotten so much love from both the reader and author community. I thank you all for allowing me to do what I love doing!

Lots of love,
Eden

P.S. - **The Court series isn't over!** You heard that right! Check out the details regarding the next generation of Court kids on the next page!

Check out the next generation of Court kids in...

Court Legacy!

Court legacy is a spin off series featuring the children of the original Court High and Court University kids! Ah! Purchase the first book in the series DIRTY WICKED PRINCE (which is about Royal and December's son) on Amazon today!

Did you know there's an entire website dedicated to Court University?

Simply join my newsletter for access to inspiration pics, teasers, and more! You'll also receive new release news from me =)

Gain access: https://bit.ly/3rf0wha.